ISLAM
AND THE
WEST

DR SHAHRAM AKBARZADEH is Senior Lecturer in Global Politics at Monash University. He is the author of *Uzbekistan and the United States: Authoritarianism, Islamism and Washington's Security Agenda* (London: Zed Books, 2004) and co-editor of *Muslim Communities in Australia* (Sydney: UNSW Press, 2001).

DR SAMINA YASMEEN is Senior Lecturer in Political Science and International Relations and Co-Chair of International Studies at the University of Western Australia. Her research areas include Islam's role in world politics, geo-strategic developments in South Asia and Muslims as citizens in non-Muslim societies.

ISLAM
AND THE
WEST

Reflections from Australia

Edited by
**Shahram Akbarzadeh and
Samina Yasmeen**

UNSW
PRESS

A UNSW Press book

Published by
University of New South Wales Press Ltd
University of New South Wales
Sydney NSW 2052
AUSTRALIA
www.unswpress.com.au

National Library of Australia
Cataloguing-in-Publication entry:

Islam and the West: reflections from Australia.

    Bibliography.
    Includes index.
    ISBN 0 86840 679 1.

    1. Islam and world politics. 2. Muslims – Political activity.
    3. September 11 Terrorist Attacks, 2001 Influence.
    4. Islamic countries – Politics and government.
    5. Western countries – Relations – Islamic countries.
    6. Islamic countries – Relations – Western countries.
    I. Akbarzadeh, Shahram. II. Yasmeen, Samina.

    305.6972

Cover design Di Quick, adapted from a photograph by Ian Phillips of Phillips & Father, University of Western Australia

CONTENTS

Preface   vii

Contributors   xi

Glossary   xv

1   Islam on the global stage   1
    Shahram Akbarzadeh

2   Islam and the West: containing the rage?   13
    Amin Saikal

3   In search of the Caliphate   26
    Kylie Baxter and Shahram Akbarzadeh

4   Islamic groups and Pakistan's foreign policy: 45
    Lashkar-e-Toiba and Jaish Mohammad
    Samina Yasmeen

5   Islamic religious education and the debate on its   63
    reform post–September 11
    Abdullah Saeed

6   The future of political Islam in Afghanistan   77
    William Maley

7   The 'war on terror' in Malaysia   93
    Osman Bakar

8   Jemaah Islamiyah terrorism and radical Islamism in Indonesia   114
    Greg Barton

9   Australian Islam, the new global terrorism   132
    and the limits of citizenship
    Michael Humphrey

10 Citizenship, identity and belonging in contemporary Australia   149
    Fethi Mansouri

11 Islam and the West: some reflections   165
    Samina Yasmeen

    Select Bibliography   173

    Index   183

PREFACE

Studying Islam and its role in the domestic and global arena is a growing field. The Iranian revolution of 1979 provided an impetus for studying Islam's relevance to domestic and world politics. Most of the literature, however, focused more on the domestic and less on the international. The situation dramatically changed with the terrorist attacks on the United States on 11 September 2001. Not only has Islam acquired a central place in analyses of the world situation, but effort is also focused on the causes and effects of Islamic militancy. Significant in this context has been the identification of Islam and the West as two distinct entities whose relationship needs to be investigated. The investigation has resulted in the emergence of two broad themes. For some analysts, the events of September 11 have reinforced the view that the relationship between Islam and the West is inherently antagonistic. Others emphasise the need to gain a deeper and more nuanced understanding of the dynamics governing Islam's place in the local and global arenas. These scholarly analyses coexist with folk mythologies in Muslim and non-Muslim states and societies. Some members of Muslim societies deny that Muslims played any role in the events of September 11 and subscribe to conspiracy theories aimed at undermining the Muslim world. In this context the West is presented as the enemy of Islam and Muslims. A similar but totally opposite view is prevalent among some non-Muslim societies, where individuals and groups are convinced of Islam's violent nature. Muslims are, therefore, viewed as essentially pitted against the liberal values enshrined in Western democracies.

In Australia discussions about Islam and Muslims have generally followed the global trends. Before the terrorist attacks in the United States, the arrival of asylum seekers in Australia by boat rekindled discussions about the place of Muslims in Australia. Most significant in this context was the Tampa crisis. The terrorist attacks provided an additional context for the discussion on how to deal with asylum seekers from the region around Australia. The Australian Government used the occasion to imply that a threat of terrorism was linked to such uncontrolled entry of asylum seekers. In doing so, it galvanised support for its re-election, but at the same time encouraged elements that viewed Islam and Muslims as distinct and possibly antithetical to Australian values. The Bali bombing and the attacks in Madrid, not to mention attacks in a number of other Muslim states, reinforced such imagery. The matter was made worse by evidence that international links with al-Qaeda may have reached Australian shores as well. For some in Australia, therefore, Islam poses a threat to Australian values. Others appear to make a distinction between Muslims and Islamic militants but tend to arrive at conclusions that reinforce the thesis of the relationship between the West and Muslims as inherently antagonistic. There is, however, a parallel view emerging in Australia that follows an approach taken elsewhere in the world. Those subscribing to this end of the spectrum favour the need to understand the multiplicity of Islamic views and their implications for local, regional and global scenarios. This group emphasises the need to ask questions about the nature of Islamic discourse and its meaning for today's world. Their focus remains on linking answers to these questions with developments at different levels.

Against the background of these parallel trends, Monash University and the University of Western Australia collaborated to organise a conference entitled 'Islam and the West' in August 2003. It was intentionally titled as such, rather than 'Islam versus the West'. The aim of the conference was to look at the developments and issues that have surfaced since the terrorist attacks, including the US invasion of Iraq. These include, for example, the nature of relations between Islam and the West (i.e. prospects of conflict and co-operation) and the future of Muslim communities in Western societies. The organisers felt that these questions, and other related issues, needed the systematic scrutiny and examination of scholars and practitioners to ensure that, first, we could arrive at a nuanced analysis that is informed by scholarly rigour and practical considerations and, second, we could make suitable recommendations to diffuse tensions.

The conference addressed three sub-themes. Firstly, it focused on Islam's relations with the West and an investigation into the nature of this relationship after September 11, the 'war on terror' and the US invasion of Iraq. It asked if these developments had validated the

Huntington thesis of the clash of civilisations. It also looked into the forces that work for dialogue between Islam and the West. Secondly, the participants focused on developments within Muslim states in the wake of the September 11 attacks. An attempt was made to establish the changes brought about by the recent manifestations of Islamic militancy and the manner in which Muslim states and societies have addressed them. Significantly, it looked at the role of Islamic militancy, the relative balance between the secularists and Islamic militants/orthodox groups in Muslim states, and suggestions for altering the balance. In this context, the role of Western states was also investigated. Finally, the conference looked at the reaction of Muslim communities in Australia to the negative interpretations of Islam and religiously motivated terrorism. It also dealt with how the 'host' societies are contributing to diversity in Islam.

The conference was opened with an address by Minister for Foreign Affairs and Trade, Alexander Downer. With the exception of chapters 3 and 4, all papers were presented and debated at the conference. All chapters in this volume have been subject to peer review. We hope that *Islam and the West* will provide an insight into how Australian academics view the relationship between Islam and the West locally, regionally and globally (see p.10). We also hope that it will contribute to and encourage serious, in-depth and balanced understanding of Islam and Muslims.

The editors would like to acknowledge the support of their home institutions and the generous sponsorship of the Australian Multicultural Foundation, the Asian Studies Association of Australia, and the Global Terrorism Research Unit at Monash University. We would also like to thank the referees who took the time to provide feedback and suggest changes. The responsibility for any omission, or mistakes, however, lies with the two of us.

SHAHRAM AKBARZADEH
SAMINA YASMEEN

CONTRIBUTORS

DR SHAHRAM AKBARZADEH is Senior Lecturer in Global Politics, School of Political and Social Inquiry, Monash University, Melbourne. He is researching the politics of Central Asia, the Middle East and political Islam and is currently exploring the interplay of religion and great power rivalry in Central Asia. His publications include *Uzbekistan and the United States: Authoritarianism, Islamism and Washington's Security Agenda* (London: Zed Books, 2004) and *Islam and Political Legitimacy,* edited with Abdullah Saeed (London: RoutledgeCurzon Press, 2003), as well as articles in international journals.

PROFESSOR OSMAN BAKAR is Malaysia Chair of Islam in Southeast Asia, School of Foreign Services, Georgetown University, Washington, DC. Formerly Professor of Philosophy of Science and Deputy Vice-Chancellor at the University of Malaya, Professor Bakar has published a dozen books and more than 100 articles on various aspects of Islamic thought and civilisation, including South-East Asian Islam. Some of his works have been translated into Arabic, Persian, Turkish, Urdu, Indonesian, Chinese and Spanish. Among his publications are *Classification of Knowledge in Islam* (Cambridge: Islamic Texts Society, 1998), *Islam and Civilisational Dialogue: Quest for a Truly Universal Civilization* (Kuala Lumpur: University of Malay Press, 1997).

DR GREG BARTON is Senior Lecturer in Politics and teaches Political Leadership, Global Islamic Politics, and Society and Culture in Contemporary Asia at Deakin University, Melbourne. His areas of research include the influence of Islamic and Islamist thought in Indonesia, their contribution to the development of civil society and politics, and the emergence of Jihadi terrorism. He has a general interest in religion and modernity, and in studying contemporary Islamic and Christian thought around the world. His most recent publications are *Indonesia's Struggle: Jemaah Islamiyah and the Soul of Islam* (Sydney: UNSW Press, 2004) and *Abdurrahman Wahid: Muslim Democrat, Indonesian President: a View from Inside* (Sydney: UNSW Press, 2002).

KYLIE BAXTER is conducting PhD research at the School of Political and Social Inquiry, Monash University, Melbourne. Her primary area of research is the development of Western Islamist organisations.

ASSOCIATE PROFESSOR MICHAEL HUMPHREY is Head of the School of Sociology. He has published widely on Lebanese Muslim immigrant culture and politics, Islamic movements, ethnic conflict, globalisation, human rights, political violence and terror, reconciliation and reconstruction. His major publications include *Islam, Multiculturalism and Transnationalism: from the Lebanese Diaspora* (London: IB Tauris, 1998), and *The Politics of Atrocity and Reconciliation: from Terror to Trauma* (London: Routledge Studies in Political and Social Thought, 2002).

PROFESSOR WILLIAM MALEY is Foundation Director of the Asia-Pacific College of Diplomacy, Australian National University, and has served as Visiting Professor at the Russian Diplomatic Academy (Moscow), Visiting Fellow at the Centre for the Study of Public Policy at the University of Strathclyde (Glasgow), and Visiting Research Fellow in the Refugee Studies Programme at Oxford University, UK. He is author of *The Afghanistan Wars* (New York: Palgrave Macmillan, 2002), edited *Fundamentalism Reborn? Afghanistan and the Taliban* (New York: New York University Press, 2001), and co-edited *From Civil Strife to Civil Society: Civil and Military Responsibilities in Disrupted States* (Tokyo: United Nations University Press, 2003).

DR FETHI MANSOURI is Senior Lecturer and Coordinator of Middle Eastern Studies, School of Social and International Studies, Deakin University, Melbourne. He is also Deputy Director of the Centre for Citizenship and Human Rights and founding member and convenor of the Refugee Studies Group. He has written numerous publications about Arab-Australians, asylum seekers and refugee policy, Middle Eastern affairs, and applied linguistics. He has recently co-authored *Lives in Limbo: Voices of Refugees under Temporary Protection* (Sydney: UNSW Press, 2004). Dr Mansouri currently holds a three-year Australian Research Council grant to investigate the long-term impact of the temporary protection visa regime on the welfare of asylum seekers and the organisational capacity of community organisations that work with them.

ABDULLAH SAEED is Sultan of Oman Professor of Arab and Islamic Studies and Head of Arabic and Islamic Studies, University of Melbourne. His research interests include Qur'anic hermeneutics,

Islam, pluralism and human rights as well as Islam in Australia. Among his recent publications are *Approaches to Qur'an in Contemporary Indonesia* (Oxford: Oxford University Press, 2004), *Muslim Australians* (editor; in press), *Freedom of Religion, Apostasy and Islam* (co-author; Burlington, VT: Ashgate, 2004), *Islam in Australia* (Sydney: Allen & Unwin, 2003), *Islam and Political Legitimacy* (co-editor with Shahram Akbarzadeh; London: RoutledgeCurzon, 2003), *Muslim Communities in Australia* (co-editor with Shahram Akbarzadeh; Sydney: UNSW Press, 2001), *Islamic Banking and Interest: a Study of the Prohibition of Riba and its Contemporary Interpretation* (New York: EJ Brill, 1996).

PROFESSOR AMIN SAIKAL is Director of the Centre for Arab and Islamic Studies (The Middle East and Central Asia), Australian National University, Canberra. He is the author of numerous works on the Middle East, Central Asia, and Russia, including *Islam and the West: Conflict or Cooperation?* (New York: Palgrave Macmillan, 2003), *Modern Afghanistan: a History of Struggle and Survival* (London: IB Tauris, 2004), and *The Rise and Fall of the Shah* (Princeton: Princeton University Press, 1980), as well as articles in international journals and major international newspapers.

DR SAMINA YASMEEN is Senior Lecturer in Political Science and International Relations, and Co-Chair of International Studies, University of Western Australia. Her areas of research include Islam's role in world politics, Muslim immigration in Australia and politico-strategic developments in South Asia. Her recent publications include 'Pakistan and India: the way forward', in Ramesh Thakur and Oddney Wiggen (eds), *South Asia in the World: Problem Solving Perspectives on Security, Sustainable Development, and Good Governance* (Tokyo: United Nations University Press, 2004), pp. 413–28; and 'China and Pakistan in a changing world', in K Santhanam and Srikanth Kondapalli (eds), *Asian Security and China 2000–2010* (New Delhi: Institute for Defence Studies and Analyses, Shipra Publications, 2004), pp. 309–19.

GLOSSARY

alim	scholar
al-Muhajiroun	The Migrants
Angkatan Belia Islam Malaysia (ABIM)	Muslim Youth Movement of Malaysia
Angkatan Bersenjata Republik Indonesia (ABRI)	Armed Forces of the Republic of Indonesia
Anjuman Sipah Sahabah Pakistan (ASSP)	Army of the Prophet's Companions in Pakistan
awqaf	religious endowments
Badan Koordinasia Intelijen Negara (BAKIN)	State Intelligence Coordination Agency
Barisan Alternatif	Alternative Front
Beit al-Ansar	House of Supporters
bid'at	innovation and departure from tradition
da'wah	the call to Islam
dar al-harb	land of war and anarchy; non-Muslim world
dar al-Islam	land of Islam and peace; Muslim world

fatwa	religious decree, edict, advice
fida-e-hamlay	suicide attacks
fiqh	jurisprudence/law
Hadith	Sayings of the Prophet

Harakat al-
    Muqawamah al-
    Islamiyyah (HAMAS)
	Islamic Resistance Movement

Harakat al-Tawhid al-Islami	Movement for Unity in Islam
Harakat-e Inqilab-e Islami Afghanistan	Movement for Islamic Revolution in Afghanistan
Harkatul-Jihad-ul-Islami (HJI)	Islamic Holy War Movement
Hezb-e Islami	Party of Islam
hijra	migration
Hizb al-Tahrir al-Islam	Islamic Liberation Party
Hizb-e Wahdat	Party of Unity
hudna	truce
hudud	limits (may include punishment for crimes)
ijtihad	interpretation
Ikhwan al-Muslimun	Muslim Brotherhood
Institut Agama Islam Negeri (IAIN)	State Institute of Islamic Studies
Ittehad-e Islami	Islamic Unity
izzat	honour
Jabha-i Milli-i Nijat-e Afghanistan	National Salvation Front of Afghanistan
Jaffar Umar Thalib Jaish Muhammad	Army of the [Prophet] Mohammad
jahiliyya	ignorance
Jamaat-ud-Dawa	Invitation to Islam Party
Jamiat-e Islami	Islamic Society
Jihad	struggle
jihad-e-kabira	Greater Jihad
jihad-e-saghira	Lesser Jihad

kalam	theology
Keadilan	Justice Party
Khuddam-ul-Islam	Servants of Islam
kuffar	unbelievers
kufr	disbelief
kuttab	traditional non-formal elementary schools
Lashkar-e-Toiba	Army of the Pure
madrasa	religious school
Mahaz-e Milli-i Islami Afghanistan	National Islamic Front of Afghanistan
mantiqi	geographical spheres of operation
mehfil	prayer centre
mujahideen	Islamic resistance fighters
pesantren	religious school
santri	observant Muslims
Sazman-e Jawanan-e Musulman-e Afghanistan	Afghan Muslim Youth Organisation
Sazman-e Nasr	Organisation for Victory
Sepah-i Pasdaran	The Guardian Army
Shari'a	Islamic law
Shura-i Ettefaq	Council of Unity
Sufi	Islamic mystic
Sufism	Islamic mysticism
Sunna	Prophetic traditions
tafsir	Qur'anic exegesis
takfir	disbelief
taqiyya	dissimulation of belief
tarikh	history
ulama	Islamic religious scholars
umma	Islamic community, community of believers
usroh	Islamic studies

1
ISLAM ON
THE GLOBAL STAGE

SHAHRAM AKBARZADEH

The September 11 attacks on the United States were unprecedented, with far-reaching consequences for international relations, especially for relations between the West and the Muslim world. The subsequent 'war on terror' and its extension to Iraq have brought to the fore a number of pertinent issues that deserve careful attention and analysis. These include, for example, the nature of relations between Islam and the West (i.e. prospects of conflict and co-operation). It may be a cliché to talk about the 'clash of civilisations',[1] and many scholars have argued that there are fundamental problems with the civilisational paradigm – especially with its treatment of 'culture' (whether Islamic or Christian) as homogenous and static, and its commensurate inability to take note of the history of cross-fertilisation between Islam and Christianity. However, warnings of an impending civilisational clash have been sounding ever louder in Muslim societies since September 11. The latest developments in Iraq have been portrayed in the Muslim world as a war of aggression by the world's sole superpower on a Muslim nation. Even in societies where Islam is not central to the political discourse, such as Morocco, the world is increasingly being viewed from a Huntingtonesque perspective.[2] It looks as though this paradigm has struck a cord in the Muslim world.

It is not an exaggeration to say that the idea of a civilisational clash has a certain appeal throughout the Muslim world, whether formulated by the former prime minister of Malaysia, Mahathir Muhammad, when he talked about the subjugation of Muslims by the Jews through the latter's domination of the West,[3] or expressed crudely by the stone-throwing youth in the Occupied Territories. There is an overwhelming sense that Muslims, because of their religion and cultures, are treated unfairly, that the international system is skewed against them and that little can be achieved through existing international mechanisms because they are ultimately controlled by Western powers, most importantly by the United States. This confrontational perspective is one way that many Muslims relate to the West and to international institutions. But there are at least two other approaches that could characterise this relationship: coexistence/tolerance and integration/harmony.

It is becoming more and more difficult to identify cases where Muslim actors view their relations with the West as harmonious. Turkey could be a rare example of this positive outlook. As a general rule, Ankara does not define its relations with the West as confrontational. If anything, it sees itself as partly Western – although its delayed membership of the European Union must have dampened Turkey's enthusiasm for integration in Western-dominated institutions. Turkey's refusal to allow access to US forces in the war on Iraq in 2003 and its reluctance to commit troops to the US occupation of its southern neighbour reflect popular sentiment and hint at a growing unease among Turkish leaders in identifying themselves too closely with Washington.[4] Historically, other examples of the integrationist paradigm exist: one might point to the pre-1979 Iran, which aligned itself firmly with the United States. The ruling monarchy saw no contradiction between pursuing a nationalist course and entering into security, economic and cultural frameworks that were dominated by Western powers. This approach, however, suffered a major setback in the wake of the Islamic revolution. In more recent times, the newly independent states of Central Asia have come to subscribe to the integrationist paradigm, although there is increasing evidence that public trust in the convergence of the interests of Muslim Central Asians and the West is being eroded as a result of US support for the corrupt and authoritarian practices of local rulers. On the whole, the integrationist paradigm is under severe strain. It is increasingly difficult to identify Muslim actors who see their future in harmonious terms with the West and who would place their faith in the unbiased workings of the international system.

Instead, a significant number of Muslim actors, especially ruling regimes, congregate in the middle of the conflict–harmony continuum. The paradigm of coexistence, with the obvious connotation of acknowledging and accommodating a divergence of interests and agendas, seems to define the prevalent attitude among Muslim leaders. The moderate leadership of Abdurahman Wahid in Indonesia (1999–2001), the militarist but moderate regime of General Pervez Musharraf in Pakistan, the pragmatic *ulama* (Islamic scholars) in Iran and even the conservative Saudi dynasty do not hide their differences with the United States, but maintain that it is possible to find equilibrium in their relations. The identifying feature of this relationship is mutual tolerance and coexistence. In contrast to the integrationist approach, proponents of coexistence entertain no illusions about the unity of purpose between Muslim and Western actors. Neither do they view unbridled integration in Western-dominated institutions as desirable or beneficial. Selective membership, which often favours economic ties but not political or cultural integration, is the defining characteristic of this middle path. The Saudi dynasty, for example, is keen to preserve and consolidate its economic ties with the global market, but is loath to subject itself to Western-originated values and highly reluctant to involve itself in institutions that promote them.

A number of fundamental points must be made explicit at the outset:

- There is no single Islamic perspective on international relations. All Muslim actors claim that their views conform to the essence, or the letter, of Islam. As a consequence there are as many Islamic positions as there are Muslim actors across Asia, the Middle East, North Africa and, increasingly, Europe.
- Muslim actors are spread across the conflict–integration continuum, with a significant concentration in the middle of that spectrum.
- The attitude of Muslim actors is not fixed and it is possible for them to shift along the continuum. Over recent decades, this movement has been towards the conflict end of the continuum.
- There are discernible differences between the attitude of political leaders and the masses, the so-called Muslim streets. Muslim governments and those close to political power tend to adopt the more pragmatic coexistence perspective while those distanced from power are inclined to confrontational interpretations of relations between the Muslim world and the Western-dominated international system.[5]

Muslim attitudes to the nature of conflict between the Muslim world and the West may be divided into two distinct categories:

1 Conflict is intrinsic to these relations. Coexistence is not possible between Islam and the West.
2 Conflict is a historical product. It is a condition that corresponds to the experience of European colonisation and American neo-colonisation of the Muslim world. By implication, this approach allows for the possibility of an end to conflict.

INTRINSIC CONFLICT

Candidates for the first category are exclusively non-government based and have a small, if highly active, following. Al-Qaeda may appear as the most prominent organisation that espouses a non-historical view of relations between the Muslim world and the West. It must be noted, however, that Osama bin Laden's repeated references to the plight of the Palestinians, the presence of *kuffar* (unbelievers) in Islam's holy land and the US support for the Saudi dynasty inject temporal aspects to this otherwise ideological clash. Other examples of such organisations are Hizb al-Tahrir al-Islam (Islamic Liberation Party) and its splinter group al-Muhajiroun (The Migrants), which have become very active since the 1990s. Such Islamic groups hold an apocalyptic vision for Islam in which the Muslim world will be revolutionised by purifying Muslim societies of corruption and un-Islamic practices, and by conquering the West. Relations between Islam and the West are accordingly, seen to be governed by zero-sum rules with no middle ground for mutually acceptable outcomes.[6] US-led operations in Afghanistan and Iraq and the continued occupation of Arab lands by Israel, a close US ally in the region, tend to reinforce the perspective that conflict between the two worlds is inevitable. In this world view, such incidents are seen as the occasional battlegrounds of the anticipated clash between Islam and the West.

Al-Muhajiroun rejects a middle ground between Muslims and non-Muslims in the international context. The idea of segregation is replicated in relation to the Muslim world (*dar al-Islam*) unified under the anticipated Caliphate and the rest of the world (*dar al-harb*). Al-Muhajiroun and Hizb al-Tahrir literature on this topic is sketchy but, based on their proclamations on Jihad, the clash of civilisations and the victory of Islam over *kufr* (disbelief), it is possible to make some considered speculations:

- The very first point is that *dar al-Islam* (land of Islam and peace) and *dar al-harb* (land of war and anarchy) are not compatible.
- This perspective rules out any notion of peace between the two camps, but it does not rule out the possibility of a temporary truce (*hudna*), which could theoretically last over an extended period.
- The Caliphate would override Muslim national entities and give rise to a multinational polity with uncertain prospects for existing international agencies and their relevance, most significantly for the United Nations. Hizb al-Tahrir and al-Muhajiroun do not articulate their vision beyond the generalities of favouring the consolidation of *umma* (the Islamic community) under the Caliphate. It is therefore not clear if they see a role for international organisations such as the United Nations in the dichotomous world of *dar al-Islam* and *dar al-harb*.
- Since the anticipated Caliphate is the rightful place of residence for Muslims, it may be inferred that the Muslim diaspora would be invited to return to *dar al-Islam*. But it is not clear how the Caliphate would relate to Muslims if they choose to stay in the West.

Crude as these speculative points are, they highlight the very ideological nature of the outlook adopted by Hizb al-Tahrir and al-Muhajiroun, which tend to distance themselves from the temporal trappings of historical events. At the same time, these groups cannot ignore history and current events, for fear of being seen as irrelevant by contemporary Muslims who face tangible challenges. Therefore, in relation to the United States and the United Kingdom, al-Muhajiroun presents a list of demands which, if fulfilled, would result in the cessation of hostilities. These are:

• Withdrawal of their forces from Iraq, Saudi Arabia, Qatar, Pakistan and Turkey
• Withdrawal of support for dictatorial leaders such as King Fahd, President Hosni Mubarak, President Bashar Assad and General Pervez Musharraf
• Withdrawal of support for Israel
• Termination of exploitative arrangements by US-controlled bodies such as the International Monetary Fund (IMF) and the World Bank
• Stopping anti-Islamic and anti-Muslim propaganda in the Western media, including the Hollywood.[7]

Fulfilling these demands, the al-Muhajiroun press release declares, 'would negate the urge for anyone to attack' the United States and the United Kingdom. This is an astounding declaration, because it says nothing about an ideologically based clash of Islam and *kufr*. Instead it is fully devoted to ideologically blind current issues. Fred Halliday, writing about Islamism in the 1990s, argued that many of the issues that galvanised Muslims, 'expressed as they may have been in Islamic terminology, were not specifically Muslim at all'.[8] This statement holds true for al-Muhajiroun's list of demands, at least the first four, which could have been raised by any group concerned with characteristically Third World issues of military subjugation, economic exploitation and national liberation.

This shift away from the realm of ideology to current affairs, with the obvious emphasis on tangible issues and grievances, offers an opportunity to move beyond rhetoric and address underlying problems that have caused tension between the Muslim world and the West. There can be no illusion that this is a tall order. Reforming US foreign policy in relation to the Muslim world and renegotiating the role of international monetary agencies would involve a fundamental change in international relations. The present movement for increased levels of global governance, with greater powers for the United Nations, and the reform of the Security Council to make it accountable to the General Assembly suggest that such a change is being contemplated.[9]

HISTORICAL CONFLICT

The above discussion of the shift towards a historical account of relations between the Muslim world and the West strengthens the position of those who point to the centrality of the experience of colonisation and neo-colonisation.[10] In this perspective, although relations between the two camps are marred by tension and at times outright conflict, such clashes are not inevitable. If a historical process has resulted in Muslim grievances, it is logical to assume that this process could be reversed. Other developments could remedy Muslim grievances and reduce tensions. This historical perspective does not have a fixed view of international relations. The concepts of *dar al-Islam* and *dar al-harb* are not central to this outlook. Instead, it sees conflict as conditional and potentially transitory, with the prospect of reaching a status of coexistence. The historical interpretation of conflict gradually edges towards the centre of the conflict–harmony continuum. A good number of Muslim statesmen and women subscribe to this interpretation, or variations of it. The views espoused by the Organisation of Islamic Conference (OIC) may be seen as the manifestation of this historically based perspective.

The OIC incorporates 57 Muslim states and purports to defend the interests of the *umma* globally. The founding session of the OIC was held in Morocco in September 1969, following an arson attack on the Al-Aqsa mosque in the previous month. The question of Palestine was clearly the catalyst for the coalescence of Muslim states, but beyond that the OIC has been a marginal player, unable to articulate an Islamic agenda or influence Western policies towards the Muslim world. Despite the centrality of the concept of *umma* in OIC documents and the obvious connotation of common destiny, the organisation has not acted in any way differently from other international bodies that bring together like-minded nation-states. As a result the OIC has been unable to present a unified position over and above the lowest common denominator that is acceptable to all member states. The list of OIC failures includes its inability to resolve the war between its two member states, Iran and Iraq (1980–88), its inaction in response to the Iraqi invasion of Kuwait and the subsequent war to eject Iraqi forces (1990–91), and – perhaps most important of all – its virtual irrelevance to various peace plans to resolve the ongoing Israel–Palestine dispute.

In 1992 the OIC seemed to have found its calling in the plight of the Bosnian Muslims – an urgent issue that was sufficiently high-profile to attract worldwide sympathy and yet remote enough not to have a bearing on the domestic politics of OIC member states. The OIC appealed to the United Nations to defend Bosnian Muslims and warned that UN inaction would precipitate 'collective measures' by the OIC to deal with the crisis. The OIC even issued a January 1993 deadline for the UN Security Council to take action. Faced with the Security Council's indifference, however, the OIC chose to quietly forget its own ultimatum when Muslim foreign ministers met in May 1993 in Karachi.[11]

Clearly, assessments of national interests have been too divergent, even among Muslim states, to allow effective collective action. This critical limitation was most evident in the OIC's failure to act in the recent Iraq crisis. The emergency Qatar meeting of the OIC, held on 5 March 2003 on the eve of the US attack, descended into a mud-slinging match between the foreign ministers of Iraq and Kuwait. The final declaration simply called on the UN to resolve the issue. The most explosive issue raised within the framework of the OIC was the potential for oil-producing Muslim states to use their leverage to deter the impending assault on Iraq. The former Malaysian prime minister Mahathir raised this possibility at the informal meeting of the OIC heads of state in Kuala Lumpur on 26 February 2003, but it was ignored by other Muslim leaders. The determination of the Gulf states not to use oil production as leverage in international relations was further demonstrated at a later meeting of the Gulf Co-operation Council, where Sheikh Hamad of Qatar expressed the prevailing attitude among oil-producing states: '[Oil] is an international material being used by the whole world. As we are civilised countries, we should not think about oil as a weapon. We should use it to improve the relationship between us and the others.' [12]

At the tenth session of the OIC in October 2003, under the chairmanship of the Malaysian prime minister, the organisation retained its moderate position in relation to US-occupied Iraq. The final communiqué welcomed the formation of the Governing Council as a first step towards restoring Iraqi sovereignty and appealed to the United Nations to take a greater role in the reconstruction of Iraq. Significantly there was no criticism of the United States, which prompted al-Muhajiroun to label the summit a betrayal of the *umma*.[13]

The Achilles' heel of the OIC is its fundamental principle of state sovereignty, which in practice excludes any effective move towards the consolidation of the multinational *umma*, despite its rhetoric. State interests are granted ultimate priority at all times over all other considerations, and this basic tenet both endorses the authority of ruling regimes to determine their respective national interests and allows Muslim rulers to present themselves as champions of the Islamic cause. To put it crudely, the involvement of political leaders in the OIC has more to do with domestic considerations of pacifying their Islamist critics and vying for prestige and authority within the Muslim world than with promoting an Islamic agenda on the international scene.

This feature of the OIC excludes it from taking an ideological position with regard to relations between Islam and the West. The organisation favours both coexistence between the Muslim world and the West and the resolution of tensions, because no Muslim ruler can conceive of surviving conflict with the West. The fate of Saddam Hussein is a vivid reminder of this glaring weakness. In this respect, the OIC is very pragmatic. However, Muslim rulers are also mindful of the public mood in the streets. They cannot afford to be seen to be too complacent or eager to settle differences with 'the great Satan', to borrow Ayatollah Khomeini's description of the United States. Regardless of their personal convictions, governing elite groups cannot afford to ignore, or to be seen to be ignoring, the grievances of their citizens against the perceived injustice of the international order. As a result, they cannot totally discard the paradigm of conflict, because doing so would be interpreted by their citizens and subjects as unconditional capitulation.

The OIC's commitment to the United Nations, through its permanent mission in New York and regular liaison with various UN agencies, is in response to the above constraints. By lobbying the UN to attend to tangible Muslim grievances, OIC member states hope to address growing public alienation and ease domestic pressures on their leadership.

TOWARDS A SOLUTION

The interpretation of relations between the Muslim world and the West as confrontational tends to imply a perpetual clash between two civilisations.[14] This approach has a certain appeal to many Muslims and to organisations such as Hizb al-Tahrir that deliberately emphasise the ideological and non-historical nature of this conflict. However, these organisations, as well as the state-based OIC, also identify tangible issues as being critical to easing tensions and even resolving conflicts. The Israeli occupation of Palestinian lands and the US support for Israeli policies are chief among Muslim grievances. This grounding of relations in definite temporal incidents is an important step towards a tenable solution.

Here the United Nations can play a central role in reversing Muslim alienation within the international system and encouraging confidence in the prospect of attaining an equitable outcome through existing (and reforming) international agencies. This is not a straightforward endeavour. The history of the United Nations and its role in the Middle East has caused unease and a degree of cynicism among Muslims. Amin Saikal has argued that the United Nations was blamed in the Middle East for sanctioning the creation of the state of Israel,[15] a move that was followed by five interstate wars and over five decades of regional instability. This negative image has been balanced over the years through the UN General Assembly's consistent support for the right of the Palestinians to national self-determination and the right of return for the Palestinian refugees. However, these resolutions adopted by the UN General Assembly remain unenforced. This is obviously a source of frustration for those who advocated their adoption and a greater source of mistrust among Muslims, who observe the ineffectiveness of the only truly multinational body in the face of the veto-wielding United States.

The failure of the United Nations to deliver justice for the Palestinians highlights the major Muslim grievance in relation to the international system. Justice has become a rallying cry for Muslims of diverse political persuasions, but it is the radical Islamists who are spearheading this challenge at the local and, increasingly, the international level. The perception of systemic injustice in the international system has galvanised Muslim opinion and has made the message of militancy, even Jihad, attractive for many Muslims. Never was Majid Khadduri's assertion, made in the 1980s, more relevant when he wrote that 'any public order devoid of justice tends to breed tensions and conflicts, and therefore would undermine and ultimately destroy the foundation on which peace is established'.[16] As the United States moves to reconstruct the Middle East in the wake of the regime change in Iraq, and the United Nations remains unable to bring a just resolution to the Israeli–Palestinian conflict, this warning remains pertinent.

Contrary to ideological proclamations made by the fringe Islamist groups, international justice need not be hostage to the ultimate supremacy of Islam over *kufr*. Justice does not have to wait for the spread of *dar al-Islam* to the whole world. There is a tacit acknowledgment by such groups that an equitable relationship between Muslim states and the West may be possible within a modified version of the existing system of nation states. Other Islamic actors are more emphatic in that respect. The OIC, for example, does not equate the search for international justice with moves to fundamentally overhaul the international system. From the moderate or radical perspective, however, the successful attainment of international justice would require an admission of guilt by Western powers for their perceived unjust behaviour towards the Muslim world as well as structural reforms of international agencies to protect the latter against any future violations. In many ways, foreign policy architects in the Islamic Republic of Iran have been searching for this kind of redress from the United States since the 1979 revolution. This yearning for equity is at the heart of the deeply felt sense of humiliation and anger that Muslims feel towards the United States for its blatant disregard of their interests.

Against this background, UN reforms acquire greater urgency and importance. Equity and justice, even when presented in Islamic garb, are universal and not essentially different from equivalent Western/Christian notions. There is nothing in these ideological demands that would make them fall beyond the purview of the United Nations. In fact the United Nations, in its General Assembly and various committees, has tried to deal with precisely the grievances that have caused alienation. Its numerous decisions on the equitable resolution of the Israeli–Palestinian conflict are evidence of the universality of the concept of justice, applicable to tangible problems. It is not utopian to argue that both the current trajectory of greater UN empowerment and the gathering international momentum for multilateralism to curb the hegemonist tendencies of the United States offer hopeful indicators for the future.

But until that day, in the aftermath of the September 11 attacks on the United States and the subsequent US operations in Afghanistan and Iraq, the present is fraught with uncertainties and challenges. Contributors to this volume deal with present issues on three levels. The first is the international context. Amin Saikal, Kylie Baxter and Shahram Akbarzadeh explore the broad implications of the growing tension between the Muslim world and the West. They set their analysis in the context of the US invasion of Iraq (2003) and reflect on the consequent heightened sense of alienation in the Muslim world, especially among Muslims on the political fringes.

The second level is a regional examination of South and South-East Asia. Samina Yasmeen, Abdullah Saeed, William Maley, Osman Bakar and Greg Barton examine the impact of the war on terrorism on the domestic and foreign policy-making of the region. The states involved are experiencing turbulent times, with fundamental ramifications for their future orientation. The obvious common feature explored by these authors is that the war on terror has become a tool for political manoeuvring, either for incumbent governments to gain greater leverage over society, or for opposition groups to enhance their standing and legitimacy. At the same time, it has also strengthened indigenous voices for the Islamic reform movement. This is most evident in Islamic education, as explored by Saeed.

The third level of examination is from the Australian national perspective. Michael Humphrey and Fethi Mansouri present well-considered analyses of the impact of the heightened sense of urgency in the war on terror on the celebrated notions of citizenship, tolerance and multiculturalism. The strain on these Australian ideals is palpable. Humphrey and Mansouri are justified in posing questions about the future of multicultural Australia.

As the US invasion of Iraq draws to a close, tension between the Muslim world and the West remains high. Emerging evidence of systematic torture by US forces in Iraq has dealt a major public relations blow to the carefully engineered message that Washington's operation was based on humanitarian considerations. The US image is tarnished. This setback would make it difficult for voices of moderation in the

Muslim world to argue the case of energised multilateralism as a remedy to Washington's intransigencies. Instead, the behaviour of US forces is likely to be seen by Muslims as further proof of the US hatred for and humiliation of Muslims, a belief that can hardly be conducive to bridging the gap between Islam and the West.

NOTES

1   Samuel Huntington, 'The Clash of Civilizations?', *Foreign Affairs*, Vol. 72, No. 3 (1993), pp. 22–49.
2   Hussain Haqqani, 'The American Mongols', *Foreign Policy*, No. 136 (2003), pp. 70–71.
3   Addressing the summit of the Organisation of Islamic Conference, the Malaysian prime minister said that 1.3 billion Muslims could not be 'defeated by a few million Jews ... This tiny [Jewish] community has become a world power. We cannot fight them through brawn alone. We must use our brains as well'. BBC News, 17 October 2003.
4   Agence France Presse, 2 March 2003.
5   For an insightful and up-to-date analysis, see Simon Murden, *Islam, the Middle East and the New Global Order* (Boulder, Col. & London: Lynne Rienner, 2002).
6   This is how Hizb al-Tahrir depicts relations between Islam and the West: 'the clash of civilisations is an inevitable matter. It existed in the past, exists now and will remain until the clash ends shortly before the Hour ... Do not be deceived, O Muslims, by the callers to the dialogue who place their heads in the sand and condone humiliation and defeat. Make the preparations required for the conflict, since the Capitalist Western civilisation has knocked you down militarily, politically and economically; however they will never defeat you intellectually. Your *'aqeedah* is hard to defeat; and it remains alive in the souls, except that some concepts of your civilisation ... have been afflicted with ... contamination ... So work to purify them ... by returning to the Book and *Sunnah*'. (From *The Inevitability of the Clash of Civilisation (Hatmiyyat sira'a ul-hadharat)*, al-Khilafah Publications, available online at <http://www.hizb-ut-tahrir.org/english/books/clashofcivilisation/clashofcivilisation.pdf>.
7   Al-Muhajiroun, 'The crusaders of the 21st century', press release, 24 March 2003, <http://www.almuhajiroun.com.pk/detail.asp?id=1353&id1=10>.
8   Fred Halliday, 'Transnational paranoia and international relations: the case of the "West versus Islam" ', in Stephanie Lawson, *The New Agenda for International Relations: from Polarization to Globalization in World Politics?* (London: Polity, 2002), p. 44.
9   See, for example, the collection in Eşref Aksu and Joseph Camilleri (eds), *Democratizing Global Governance* (London: Palgrave, 2003).
10 See, for example, Richard Falk, *Human Rights Horizons, the Pursuit of Justice in a Globalizing World* (New York, London: Routledge, 2000); Amin Saikal, 'Islam and the West?', in Greg Fry and Jacinta O'Hagan (eds), *Contending Images of World Politics* (Basingstoke and New York: Macmillan and St Martin, 2000); Amin Saikal, *Islam and the West, Conflict or Cooperation?* (New York: Palgrave Macmillan, 2003).
11 Cited in Dale F Eickelman and James Piscatori, *Muslim Politics* (Princeton: Princeton University Press, 1996), p. 140.
12 Agence France Presse, 3 March 2003.

13 Al-Muhajiroun, 'Conclusion of the OIC summit, lip service at the expense of the ummah', 18 October 2003, <http://www.almuhajiroun.com.pk/detail.asp?id= 1760&id1=10>.
14 Bernard Lewis, *The Crisis of Islam, Holy War and Unholy Terror* (London: Weidenfeld & Nicolson, 2003).
15 Amin Saikal, 'The United Nations and the Middle East', in Amin Saikal and Albrecht Schnabel (eds), *Democratization in the Middle East, Experiences, Struggles, Challenges* (Tokyo: United Nations University Press, 2003), p. 64.
16 Majid Khadduri, *The Islamic Conception of Justice* (Baltimore: Johns Hopkins University Press, 1984), p. 162.

2
ISLAM AND THE WEST: CONTAINING THE RAGE?

AMIN SAIKAL

Relations between the West (and more specifically the United States) and the world of Islam have grown very tense since the tragic events of 11 September 2001. The war in Iraq, the Bali bombing and a spate of other bomb blasts in South and South-East Asia, the Middle East, Africa and Europe targeting Western citizens and interests have added fuel to the flames. Many Muslims and their Western counterparts have grown profoundly wary of each other and fear what may eventuate. However, their apprehension has emanated from different bases. Unless they understand these bases, they are unlikely to build the necessary bridges of understanding to contain their anger towards one another and ensure the emergence after the war in Iraq of a stable order in world politics.

The United States was very careful from the start to portray its 'war on terror' as being directed against terrorism and barbarism, not against Islam and Muslims *per se*. Washington's main message was that Islam had been hijacked by a group of terrorists whose actions could find no justification in Islam. Shortly after the September 11 events, it even appeared that Washington and London had decided the time had come to remove a major anomaly in the US Middle East policy: the existence of one standard for its strategic partner, Israel, and another for Arabs and Muslims. They displayed an unprecedentedly firm commitment to securing a resolution of the Palestinian problem, based on the creation of a viable independent Palestinian state. In a rare recognition of moral equivalence between the plight of the Afghan and Palestinian peoples, British Prime Minister Tony Blair acknowledged Western mistakes in abandoning the Afghan people in the past, thus allowing their country to become a source of international terrorism, and in possibly not doing enough to resolve the Palestinian problem as a source of growing anti-American, and for that matter, anti-Western sentiment among Muslims in general, and Arabs in particular. In March 2002, US Secretary of State Colin Powell for the first time even endorsed the notion of an independent Palestinian state as part of a two-state solution, and this was backed by United Nations Security Council Resolution 1397 (12 March 2002).

VIEWS FROM THE WEST

None of these policy confessions and steps, however, could disguise the diversity of views that have concurrently emerged in the West about Islam and Muslims. The views emanating from the United States and its allies in general have on the whole been of three kinds.

The first view has been contained in official statements that have by and large emphasised the non-religious, non-ethnic and non-racist character of the campaign against terror, insisting that it is directed only against those who have abused Islam for their own misguided self-ish, messianic ends. The only significant slip in this respect came early on from US President George Bush, when he described the war as a 'crusade'. This term reminded Muslims of the medieval Christian cru-sades, which resulted in much brutality against the Muslim Arabs in Jerusalem, and immediately drew such widespread criticism that the White House was forced to withdraw the term.

The second view has been embodied in Italian Prime Minister Silvio Berlusconi's description of Western civilisation as superior to that of Islam. In late September 2001 he claimed that Western civilisation 'has guaranteed well-being, respect for human rights and – in contrast with Islamic countries – respect for religious and political rights'; he also voiced the hope that 'the West will continue to conquer [Muslim] peoples, like it conquered communism'.[1] Although he retracted this view under international pressure, he was not the only one to express it. Many other opinion-makers and commentators echoed such remarks in the Western media in one form or another.

The third view takes the form of a direct attack on Islam as a reli-gion that inspires terrorism and produces terrorists. Several US legis-lators – notably Tom Lantos – and prominent religious leaders, including Jerry Falwell and Pat Robertson, launched a campaign to vilify Islam and condemn it for promoting the kind of education, and justifying the type of activities, that produced al-Qaeda and the Taliban fighters. They have questioned the value of close ties with Saudi Arabia, based primarily on the principle of US provision of secu-rity to the theocratic Saudi regime in return for its guarantee of a ready supply of oil to the West.

The US and, to varying degrees, its allies have also commenced a series of tough policy and security measures, including singling out Muslims (particularly those from Arab backgrounds) for discriminatory investigation and treatment. While in some cases these measures have led to a number of al-Qaeda activists being tracked down in the United States and Europe, possibly preventing more terrorist attacks, in many other cases they have resulted in humiliation of innocent Muslims and in distressing human rights violations contrary to all the principles for which the liberal democracies publicly stand. As a result of the discordant voices of Western opinion leaders, and the harshness of these policies, Washington's official claim to respect the Islamic faith has won it little credit among Muslims.

The reactions of Muslims to these developments have naturally been diverse, reflecting the pluralism that exists in the domain of Islam. At official levels, all governments (except the fallen dictatorship of Saddam Hussein) have condemned terrorism and supported, or acquiesced in, the US moral claim to wage war against terror. Even the Iranian Islamic regime, which had all along opposed the Taliban but had equally been concerned about the growing US involvement around it, has done little to hinder the United States from pursuing its anti-terror goals. All governments in Muslim countries have denounced those misusing Islam to justify killing innocent people and have branded such acts as contrary to the teachings of Islam.

However, given the authoritarian nature of most regimes in Muslim countries, this masks the reality that public emotions below government level have been running high. In a Gallup Poll survey of public opinion carried out in the weeks following September 11 in nine key Muslim countries, a majority of respondents stressed that they did not think that 'the United States and the nations of the West have respect for Arabs or for Islamic culture or religion', with 53 per cent disapproving of Washington's policy behaviour.[2] This attitude seems to have hardened since the war in Iraq.

Citizens all over the Muslim world have found themselves squeezed to suffocation between domestic repression and exogenous vilification. They have felt anger over having to defend their religion and Islamic identity, and have despaired over the way the United States and its allies have claimed moral virtue, irrespective of their often contradictory and self-serving behaviour towards Muslims. Many cannot understand how the United States and its allies can avoid debating the main question: why did they do it? From their perspective, bin Laden and many of his operatives have not been uneducated lunatics, and they have acted not in a vacuum but in the context of historical and contemporary causes, motivating many Muslims to distrust the US Administration and some of its allies.

If they were pleased by earlier US and British pronouncements regarding the urgent need to resolve the Palestinian problem, they rapidly found their optimism misplaced. Once the United States and its allies had bin Laden, his al-Qaeda activists and their Taliban harbourers on the run, Washington's urgency about the Palestinian issue seemed to wane as quickly as it had waxed. President Bush's description of right-wing Israeli Prime Minister Ariel Sharon as 'a man of peace' shocked the Arab and Muslim worlds. Many Muslims believe that had it not been for President Bush's support of Sharon, the Israeli leader would not have been able, from early 2002, to exploit the legitimacy of the US war against terror to intensify Israel's suppression of Palestinian resistance, and to isolate and humiliate the elected Palestinian leader, Yasser Arafat – something which continues to the present day. They have seen nothing in Sharon's half century of public life to justify Bush's description of him. On the contrary, they regard Bush as little more than Sharon's puppet, proof positive for which they found in Bush's exchange of letters with Sharon in April 2004, which in their view marked a total capitulation to Sharon's extremist agenda.[3] By supporting not only Sharon's proposed unilateral withdrawal from Gaza without negotiating a final settlement to create an independent Palestinian state out of Gaza, the West Bank and East Jerusalem, but also his long-standing demand to retain Israel's large settlements in the West Bank, Bush struck a serious blow to the Palestinian cause and to US relations with Arab and Muslims. This support overturned the long-held US policy of upholding UN Security Council Resolution 242 and therefore opposing Israel's annexation of any Palestinian land that it occupied in the 1967 War.[4] In addition, the Bush Administration refused to criticise Sharon's policy of targeted assassination of militant Palestinian leaders – most importantly the assassinations of Sheikh Yassin, the spiritual head of HAMAS (Harakat al-Muqawamah al-Islamiyyah – Islamic Resistance Movement), and his successor, Dr Abdul Aziz al-Rantissi, in late March and late April 2004 respectively – and defended Israel's right to engage in what have been widely criticised around the world as acts of state terrorism. While Palestinian suicide bombings have wreaked cruel havoc amongst ordinary Israelis, for Muslims it has been the continued suffering of the Palestinians under a brutal Israeli occupation that has proved the most disturbing. They have become extremely distrustful of Washington and have had little reason to believe the Bush Administration's public claim that it is firmly committed to a settlement of the Israeli–Palestinian conflict on the basis of a two-state solution.

MUSLIM ATTITUDES

Conceding that the Muslim world is very diverse, four attitudes have emerged to play a central part in reactions and debate in the Muslim domain about September 11 and its aftermath.

MODERATE ISLAMISTS

The first attitude comes from moderate Islamists who uphold Islam as a dynamic ideology of political and social transformation, and a meaningful ideology of opposition to authoritarian regimes at home, but reject any form of violence as a means to achieving such objectives, unless their religion, life and liberty either at the individual or societal level are seriously threatened or invaded. Although they come in various forms, on the whole they subscribe to what has been termed 'Islamic liberalism' and adhere to the Islamic command that there is no compulsion in religion.[5] They operate mainly within loose organisations, informal small groups or at individual levels. Most Muslim intellectuals and informed Muslims fall into this category. They reject terrorism as unacceptable, and are appalled by those who have presumed to act in the name of Islam to take innocent lives, thereby placing Muslims everywhere under siege. They regard the September 11 events as providing a dangerous incentive to the United States and its allies to claim the higher moral ground to expand and deepen US dominance in the Muslim world, and to marginalise political Islam. They contend that al-Qaeda's actions have set back by decades the efforts of Muslims to achieve domestic reform, independence from foreign interference and a strong voice in the international arena.

The moderate Islamists are open to modernity, believe in the inevitability of progress, are well disposed to interfaith dialogue, and have no aversion to utilising Western knowledge and achievements to benefit their societies in a globalised world. Yet they are simultaneously critical of those US policy actions that either overlook the plight of the Palestinian people or give massive emphasis to the behaviour of some extremist Islamic groups when it is convenient to tarnish the image of Muslims in general. Their attitude towards the United States in particular, and the West in general, is one of love and dislike: they are keen to benefit from Western education, technology and institutions, and to secure access to Western countries as both migrants and visitors, but critical of Western policy behaviour towards the Muslim world and of arrogant claims of supremacy over Muslims. They are dedicated to renewal and reform as the best means of achieving salvation and prosperity.

RADICAL ISLAMISTS

The second attitude emanates from radical Islamists, who are again diverse in their ideological disposition and *modus operandi*. They share part of the platform of their moderate counterparts, especially in adherence to the fundamentals of Islam. However, they are far more puritanical and assertive in their political and social behaviour. They want Shari'a (Islamic law) to underpin the operation of the state, and regard political and social imposition and the use of violence, under certain circumstances, as legitimate means of creating the kind of polity they deem Islamic. They are not necessarily against modernity, but want to ensure that modernity is adopted in conformity with *their* religious values and practices. They are prone to act radically to redress perceived historical and contemporary injustices inflicted upon Muslims by outsiders, but do not necessarily extend this to cover similar injustices committed by Muslim against Muslim.

They hold the West, and the United States in particular, responsible for the political, social and economic plight and cultural decay of Muslims everywhere, and for the damage that European colonisation and post-1945 US domination of most of the Muslim domain inflicted upon Muslims. Many groups in the Muslim world are of this nature, ranging from some of the conservative followers of the leader of the Iranian revolution of 1978–79, Ayatollah Khomeini, to the Palestinian HAMAS and Lebanese Hizbollah. Notwithstanding their apocalyptic, extremist activities, al-Qaeda's leader Osama bin Laden and many of its leadership also fall into this category.

The radical Islamists regard the United States as their most dangerous enemy, not only for backing Israel's occupation of Palestinian lands, most importantly East Jerusalem, but also for propping up corrupt and dictatorial regimes in many Muslim countries. They cannot understand how the Bush Administration can support Israel's brutalities against the Palestinians, including the extrajudicial killing of Palestinian figures, as acts of self-defence, but condemn as terrorism the Palestinian resistance to Israel's occupation, irrespective of what form it takes. They share the widespread concern that what has become an international crisis since September 11 has been partly fuelled by a deliberate strategy of pro-Israeli neo-conservatives and 'reborn' Christians in the Bush Administration aimed at suppressing political Islam in pursuit of global domination.

NEO-FUNDAMENTALISTS

The third attitude comes from neo-fundamentalists, or those who adhere to a strict, literal interpretation of Islam, based on a particular school of thought emanating from particular Islamic scholars. What matters most to them is the text rather than the context. Without underestimating their diversity, on the whole they can be far more puritanical, sectarian, self-righteous, single-minded, discriminatory, xenophobic and coercive in their approach than the radical Islamists. Their understanding of religion is basic, and they are generally poorly educated but highly socialised in a particular religious setting. They are often popularly described as extremists or ultra-orthodox traditionalists. The Taliban militia and various Saudi-based Wahhabi and Pakistan-based Muslim Brotherhood and Deobandi groups are well-known examples of this category. Given the numerous overlaps between neo-fundamentalist and radical Islamist views, organic and organisational links have often developed between the two, with the latter using the former for human resources, protective purposes and outreach activities, including armed or terrorist operations. This was precisely the relationship between al-Qaeda and the Taliban, where al-Qaeda provided money and Arab fighters, and in return the Taliban harboured and helped al-Qaeda develop as a transnational force.

SOCIETAL ISLAM

The fourth attitude stems from the grassroots of Muslim society, whose knowledge of Islam is generally basic and forms part of a village-based way of life. Muslims at this level essentially follow Islam as a basic faith, and can be apolitical or political, depending on whether or not they feel their faith and way of life is threatened by hostile forces. Many of them are potential activists of Islam, vulnerable to manipulation by radical Islamists and neo-fundamentalists.[6] They constitute the bulk of ordinary Muslims, who if left alone could well remain preoccupied with their daily lives, especially in poor countries. However, they can easily be galvanised and mobilised by radical Islamists and neo-fundamentalists, whether they live in poor suburbs of cities or in the countryside of Egypt, Pakistan, Indonesia or elsewhere. The plight of Muslims at the hands of 'foreigners' can rouse them to action. The Taliban recruited many of their foot soldiers from among such people. Their views of what happened on September 11 and in its aftermath have been shaped by what they have been told by their local preachers and by radical and neo-fundamentalist Islamist activists. Those views can range from intense dislike of the United States to indifference towards it.

ROOTS OF TENSION

The September 11 events and their aftermath not only shook the United States and its allies, but also sent shock waves through the Muslim world, sharply escalating the tension. At the same time, the relations have remained both complex and multidimensional, containing elements of conflict and co-operation, perception and misperception, and cultural and social difference. However, the tension is rooted rather in political and politically motivated perceptual differences, with its intensity fluctuating according to the political utility of the issues that have occasioned the two sides to expose their differences. In this context, Western and Muslim entities are now more fearful and distrustful of one another than at any other time in contemporary history.

THE IRAQ CONFLICT

Against this backdrop, the war in Iraq has proved especially damaging. Indeed, Saddam Hussein's dictatorship enjoyed little popular support in Iraq and the Muslim world, given its brutal and in many ways un-Islamic nature. However, most Muslims have rejected Washington's approach to solving the problem as two-faced and irresponsible. They easily recall that it was the United States that left Saddam Hussein in place in 1991, knowing full well that he would continue to brutalise the Iraqi population. They realise that when he used weapons of mass destruction against his own people, the US Administration knew what was happening but did very little. They are suspicious of the reasons for which the United States and its two Anglo-Celtic allies took upon themselves – in defiance of the United Nations and international law – to secure the removal of that regime. Like most people in the rest of the world, they are appalled that a devastating war was imposed on the Iraqi people, at the cost of thousands of civilian casualties and infrastructural and historical destruction, for what they see as economic and geostrategic reasons. The failure of the occupying forces thus far to substantiate their original justification for war by proving that Saddam Hussein's regime possessed dangerous weapons of mass destruction,[7] or aided international terrorism, has reinforced their belief that this war and occupation have been part of a wider strategy to remake the Middle East in the image of the United States and its allies.

They are pained by the fact that in demolishing Saddam Hussein's regime, the United States and its coalition of the willing also destroyed the state in Iraq, with no appropriate plan for post-war management of Iraq. Although the United States has made much of its promise to bring democracy and human rights to Iraq, most Iraqis and their Muslim counterparts see this as nothing more than a gimmick. This impression was reinforced by the upsurge of violence and the use by the United States of heavy weapons against lightly armed resistance fighters in Fallujah in April 2004, at the cost of hundreds of civilian lives and massive destruction of property. This perception was further strengthened when it was disclosed in May that US and British soldiers have been engaged in widespread and systematic abuse and humiliation of Iraqi prisoners. Such was the extent of the vulgarity and inhumanity committed against the prisoners (as shown in photographs worldwide) that it not only caused a fury in the Arab/Muslim world and beyond, but also even humbled President Bush to say sorry to the prisoners and their families.[8]

The US Secretary of Defense, Donald Rumsfeld, has made it clear that whatever the nature of Iraqi 'democracy', it will have to be subordinated to US interests. He has rejected the idea of an Islamic government as a democratic outcome. To many Muslims this is a gratuitous provocation, almost as offensive as his early description of the chaos and insecurity that has followed the war as 'a little bit of untidiness' and of Israel's occupation of Palestinian lands as 'the so-called occupation'.[9] As the task of securing an effective interim Iraqi administration

has proved extremely difficult, the United States and its coalition partners have been forced to rely on the US-appointed Iraqi Governing
Council, many of whose members have come out of exile and which
has lacked popular legitimacy and proved to be disconnected from the
Iraqi people. The alternative has been a Shi'ite-led Islamic government,
which Washington has carefully sought to avoid, although it has been
conscious of the fact that alienating the Iraqi Shi'ite majority could easily confront the occupying forces with greater and more formidable
resistance.

The Iraqi resistance waged since the end of the war has not been
the work of Saddam Hussein loyalists alone; it has continued well
beyond the capture of Saddam and the killing of his sons. It is predominantly conducted by the Iraqi Sunnis, who are driven by their
diminishing status since the overthrow of Saddam Hussein's regime
and their close affiliation with the Arab world, and by many Jihadis
from both inside and outside Iraq, led by the al-Qaeda-linked Ansar al-
Islam. Today Iraq appears to have become a magnet for anti-US resistance for a good number of Jihadis from all over the Muslim world.
This is reminiscent of Afghanistan's transformation into a battleground
for Muslim Jihadis against the Soviet occupation in the 1980s. The
main difference between Iraq and Afghanistan is that in the case of the
latter the United States supported the Jihadis as Islamic resistance
fighters or mujahideen, but in the case of the former it has branded
them as terrorists.

It is also important to be reminded that the Iraqi resistance has not
reached its full potential yet. While opposed to the occupation, the
Iraqi Shi'ites, who have sectarian affiliation with Iran, have not been
very actively involved in the resistance. This appears to have been largely due to two main factors. One is the influence of the leading Shi'ite
cleric, Ayatollah Ali al-Sistani, who believes that, whatever the democratic arrangement the Americans may put in place, the Shi'ites' numer-
ical strength will ultimately have to prevail and therefore there is no
need for widespread violent Shi'ite resistance. Another is a resolve by
the Iranian Islamic regime not to encourage the Iraqi Shi'ites to pur-
sue anti-US action, lest it invite US retaliation against Iran. However,
if the Bush Administration fails to pass on full sovereignty to the Iraqis,
deprives the Shi'ites of their aspirations and opts to put pressure on the
Iranian regime as a member of its 'axis of evil', it will be hard to prevent the Iraqi Shi'ites from joining the resistance on a large scale and
Iran from providing at least covert support for them. The ill-judged
US move in April 2004 against the followers of Muqtadar al-Sadr – a
younger and far less credible religious figure than al-Sistani – and the
backlash it provoked provide a foretaste of what could be expected if
the Shi'ites were to turn against the United States in a big way.[10] The
general feeling among Iraqis and fellow Muslims around the world is

that the US policy approach to the management of post-war Iraq has been to maximise US and Israeli dominance rather than to enable the Iraqis to realise their aspirations. Many Arabs and Muslims have viewed the war as a gross exploitation of the post–September 11 global sympathy for the United States and as part of a strategy to enable a small group of neo-conservatives in the Bush Administration to achieve their 'power reality' goal of global domination.[11] The war in Iraq has reminded them of the long centuries of European colonisation of most of the Muslim world, and the US persistent globalist penetration of many Muslim countries since World War II, leading many of them to regard the war as imperialist and anti-Islamic. In addition, the war has not only played into the hands of the radical and neo-fundamentalist forces of political Islam but also galvanised many moderate Islamists – a development that Osama bin Laden and his operatives would celebrate. This would be a most unfortunate development because, if the West wants to build bridges of understanding, it needs to engage the moderates. In this case, Saddam Hussein, whom the United States once backed as an ally of sorts in the 1980s against Ayatollah Khomeini's Islamic regime in Iran, would have also achieved his objective – that is to make the US invasion of Iraq morally and politically indefensible.

If al-Qaeda was looking for an additional cause to galvanise support, the occupation of Iraq has certainly provided it. The Iraqi resistance has become a cause célèbre not only for al-Qaeda and its associated groups, but also for many Islamists and ordinary Muslims who have not supported al-Qaeda's extremism but have increasingly come to identify with al-Qaeda's causes. Despite the United States' upbeat predictions, the Iraqi resistance is likely to continue for the foreseeable future: it has support inside Iraq and popularity in the region, and is relatively cheap to maintain. While the methods by which it operates cannot be condoned, it has in many ways succeeded in defining the limits of US power. It has helped to invigorate all those forces in world politics that have opposed the US-led invasion, and enabled the UN to prove its relevance in the face of the Bush Administration's pre–Iraq war condemnation of the UN as irrelevant. The Iraqi resistance has struck a serious blow to the administration's unilateralist tendencies and its doctrine of pre-emption. It has strengthened the position of Iran not as a member of the 'axis of evil' but as a regional player, to the extent that some in Washington would now like to open direct dialogue with Iran to help bail itself out of its Iraqi predicament, despite the Bush Administration's public criticisms of Tehran's failure to make a full disclosure of its nuclear program.

Meanwhile, the ferocity of the Iraqi resistance has rendered remote the possibility of the United States using force against Syria and has left Israel in a position that is no better than when Saddam Hussein was in power. If the Bush Administration had banked on the possibility of using its occupation of Iraq to prompt Israel to reach a final settlement with the Palestinians and in return attract wider regional Arab support for its Iraq adventure, American uncritical support for Sharon has squandered that possibility. Israeli suppression of the Palestinian resistance and US operations to pacify the Iraq resistance have produced powerful parallel images of killings, destruction and humiliation that have led many Iraqis and their counterparts in the Arab and Muslim worlds to make no distinction between the Israelis and Americans as occupiers. This has reinforced their belief that the United States and Israel operate in the region in concert and in support of one another. More important than all this, the Iraqi resistance has badly discredited the agenda of the neo-conservatives in the Bush Administration to reshape the Middle East in the image of the United States and to marginalise the defiant forces of political Islam in world politics.

It is time that the United States and its allies focused on the root causes that have given rise to such forces as al-Qaeda and generated so much anger among the Muslims in general and Arabs in particular, and on a strategy to enable moderate Islamists to take the centre stage in dealing with the West. Changes will have to come from both sides, but as the most powerful actor in the world the United States bears a special responsibility to act prudently and to initiate the process of dialogue and trust-building with those forces of political Islam and ordinary Muslims who form the great majority in the Muslim world and are keen to have cooperative relations with the West. The United States is immensely powerful, but its military power too often undermines its capacity to act with subtlety and sophistication.

The United States could start the process of building a better world future by pursuing three major objectives. First and foremost is the need to secure a resolution of the Palestinian problem. Washington must recognise that Ariel Sharon's goal has always been to suppress the Palestinians, humiliate the Arabs, and ensure Israel's regional supremacy. His own rhetoric on returning from Washington in April 2004 made this clear. He never approved of the Oslo peace process and successfully killed it. To have any hope of bringing peace to the Middle East and as a prelude to creating a viable Palestinian state and to ensuring Israel's security, a future US administration must secure an immediate halt to Israeli settlement activities and to the construction of the intrusive 'apartheid wall' along the West Bank, and ensure a rapid Israeli troop pullout from the reoccupied Palestinian towns. Without this step, the US stands little chance of either generating the necessary basis for the creation of a viable Palestinian state by 2005, as promised under the 'road map', or gaining any regional support for its occupation of Iraq as a means to achieving wider stability in the Middle East. The second objective is to empower the Iraqi people to determine their own future under the supervision of the United Nations as the only international body with which the Iraqis could deal legitimately. This can be accomplished only if the United States re-embraces multilateralism rather than unilateralism as well as the principles of dialogue, cross-cultural understanding, and political co-operation and negotiation as the most potent instruments for resolving international problems. The third objective is to rebuild and secure Afghanistan as the frontline against terrorism and help reform neighbouring Pakistan. The Iraq conflict has become a major drain on resources and has diverted attention that should have been directed to addressing the Afghanistan situation and transforming Pakistan into a democracy, so that it would never again be able to generate regional conditions that could allow a network like al-Qaeda to flourish.

These objectives should be accompanied by US efforts to work together constructively with democratic forces, including moderate Islamists, in the Muslim countries to foster the necessary conditions for democratisation in compatibility with an *ijtihadi* interpretation of Islam. This would require the United States to abandon its support for and protection of authoritarian and concealed authoritarian regimes, which has been a very disturbing feature of US behaviour towards the Muslim domain for a long time, and act on the basis of multilateralist rather than unilateralist principles. Of course, this may entail short-term risks for US global interests, but in the long run it may help the United States to shape a world order which would be more conducive to and protective of its interests. A failure to move in this direction could entail a continuation of international terrorism, with further regrettable consequences for world peace and stability.

NOTES

1   *The Guardian*, 27 September 2001.
2   See Amin Saikal, *Islam and the West: Conflict or Cooperation?* (New York: Palgrave Macmillan, 2003), p. 17.
3   See Peter Slevin, 'Bush backs Israel on West Bank', *The Washington Post*, 15 April 2004.
4   For discussion, see Peretz Kidron, 'Sharon's initiative', *Middle East International*, 15 April 2004; Khalid Amayreh, 'Settlement fears', *Middle East Journal*, No. 723 (16 April 2004), pp. 14–17. On Resolution 242, see John McHugo, 'Resolution 242: a legal reappraisal of the right-wing Israeli interpretation of the withdrawal phase with reference to the conflict between Israel and the Palestinians', *International and Comparative Law Quarterly*, Vol. 51 (October 2002), pp. 851–82.
5   Surah al-Baqarah, 2: 256.
6   This has been a particular problem in Indonesia. See International Crisis Group, *Jemaah Islamiyah in South East Asia: Damaged but Still Dangerous* (Jakarta and Brussels: ICG Asia Report No 63, International Crisis Group, 26 August 2003).
7   See Joseph Cirincione, Jessica T Mathews and George Perkovich, *WMD in Iraq:*

Evidence and Implications (Washington, DC: Carnegie Endowment for International Peace, 2004).

8   For details, see *BBC News World Edition,* 6 May 2004.
9   United Press International, 28 August 2002.
10 On al-Sadr, see Juan Cole, 'The United States and Shi'ite religious factions in post-Ba'thist Iraq', *The Middle East Journal,* Vol. 57, No. 4 (Autumn 2003), pp. 543–66.
11 This is also a central argument in Richard A Clarke, *Against All Enemies: Inside America's War on Terror* (New York: Free Press, 2004).

3
IN SEARCH
OF THE CALIPHATE

KYLIE BAXTER AND SHAHRAM AKBARZADEH

What is radical Islamism? What inspires it? These are two basic questions that have gained urgency in the wake of the September 11 attacks on the United States. As an ideology, Islamism is not very different from other 20th century '-isms'. It shares with communism and fascism a fixation with conquering political power and totally restructuring society in line with what it holds to be pure and uncorrupted principles. Islamism extracts a political blueprint of action from the Qur'an and Hadith (Sayings of the Prophet). Islamism, or political Islam, is therefore a political ideology with its own perspective on the world. John Esposito and others have referred to political Islam as a response to the failure of ruling regimes in the Muslim world. The stark inability of these regimes to deliver prosperity and protect their cultural integrity has 'triggered self-criticism and a quest for identity and authenticity', giving weight to calls for the Islamisation of society.[1]

Political Islam opposes secular nationalism and rejects it as a foreign transplant in the Muslim world. Since its 'gestation phase' of the 1970s,[2] Islamism has been entirely focused on national affairs. While rejecting secular nationalism, it limited its vision within the arbitrary national boundaries of the Muslim world. These boundaries may have been inherited from colonial powers and have divided organic communities, but they have gained a certain degree of legitimacy, as evidenced by their acceptance even by Islamist groups.[3] The history of Islamism in the last three decades of the 20th century has been one of adaptation to the nationally defined political environment. The objective of establishing God's sovereignty has been conditioned by the existing parameters of nation-states. In places where Islamists have managed to capture state power and prod society towards their utopian vision, they have invariably been forced to accommodate the prerequisites of the state, eventually succumbing to its ultimate superiority. Not even the Islamic revolution in Iran, which inspired confidence and hope for Islamists, has been immune to this general trend. A decade after establishing the Islamic Republic of Iran, Ayatollah Khomeini acknowledged that 'the requirements of government supersede every tenet [of Islam], including even those of prayer, fasting and pilgrimage to Mecca'.[4] This failure to break away from the imperatives of state sovereignty has inspired the groundbreaking study by Olivier Roy, *The Failure of Political Islam*.[5]

The essence of Islamism, however, transcends territorial demarcations and national boundaries, and attempts by a number of groups to reclaim the supranational nature of Islam have been increasing. Two such groups are Hizb al-Tahrir (Liberation Party) and al-Muhajiroun (The Migrants), operating in Europe, the Middle East and South Asia. Both have an explicit commitment to Muslim unity and the restoration of the Caliphate. These are potent symbols. The Caliphate carries images of power and glory for Muslims and its invocation is a clear attempt to tap into the widespread sense of powerlessness in the face of Western encroachment into the Muslim world. The restoration of the Caliphate, it is argued by these groups, would establish the vicegerency of God on earth and empower the Muslim world to confront the West. This is an essential step in solving endemic problems in Muslim societies that have arisen as a result of deviation from the path of Islam and overriding the tenets of Islam by man-made/secular law.

The ideal of a Muslim Caliphate that would end all Muslim grievances may be an attractive banner, but it ignores the history of that institution. It overlooks political divisions within the Caliphate and competing claims to the title of Caliph by the Abbasids in Baghdad, the Fatimids in Egypt and Abd al-Rahman and his descendants in Spain (10th–12th centuries). Later the Ottomans and the Mughals claimed ownership over the Caliphate for two centuries, until the demise of the Mughal empire in the 18th century, leaving the Ottoman dynasty the uncontested Islamic power up to the abolition of the office of the Caliph by Turkish secularists in 1924. Subsequent efforts, including the May 1926 Caliphate congress in Cairo, failed to revive this institution.

In spite of this history, the Caliphate retains a nostalgic and emotive attraction for Hizb al-Tahrir and al-Muhajiroun, which have tried to free themselves from the conceptual constraints of the model of the nation-state. In this they have distinguished themselves from earlier Islamists, and they look to the international stage as their primary arena of activity. The recent terrorist attacks and the subsequent international 'war on terror' have injected into these groups significant energy and conviction as to the correctness of their worldview. This chapter traces the organisational and ideological history of these groups and explores the impact that the on-going Israeli–Palestinian dispute and the war in

Iraq has had on their political activity. The emphasis here is on al-Muhajiroun and its notion of the inevitable clash between Islam and *kufr* (disbelief).

HIZB AL-TAHRIR

Founded in Jordanian-controlled East Jerusalem in 1953, Hizb al-Tahrir (Liberation Party) is currently active in Europe and most of the Islamic world. Operating in secrecy, the party does not publicly identify its leaders. The seemingly global influence of Hizb al-Tahrir and its emergence in areas of increasing geostrategic importance, such as Central and South-East Asia, present a novel challenge to our conceptualisation of Islamic activism.

Hizb al-Tahrir is adept at utilising modern technology to propagate its views and provide guidance to its members globally. It maintains websites in a range of languages, with a sophisticated array of links to affiliated sites. This medium for transmission of the party doctrine appears to be quite effective, as it allows simultaneously for tight control over information and wide access to its members. The dispersed nature of the party's structure, however, makes it difficult to identify the actual number of members and the leadership hierarchy.

Hizb al-Tahrir identifies itself as a political party that has Islam as its driving ideology. This explicit commitment to Islam as a blueprint for political action and the rejection of man-made law is the overarching priority of Hizb al-Tahrir. It has set Hizb al-Tahrir on a collision course with ruling regimes in the Muslim world, which it rejects as illegitimate, and with the United States, which it rejects for its role in maintaining the power of such regimes. There appear to be some obvious parallels between the political world view of Hizb al-Tahrir and that of al-Qaeda. This has led some observers to paint them with the same broad brush. The Heritage Foundation (a conservative think-tank in Washington), for example, identifies the organisation as an Islamist group with an 'outlook and goals that are shared with al-Qaeda and other organisations of the global Jihadi movement'.[6]

The Hizb al-Tahrir doctrine centres on the writings of a Palestinian teacher, Taqi al-Din al-Nabhani (1909–77). Trained as a teacher of Islamic law, Nabhani found employment in the local legal system from 1938, and was appointed judge in 1945. During this time Nabhani became involved in politics and joined Ba'thist circles in the late 1940s. The establishment of the State of Israel was a major political event, and five years after his judicial appointment Nabhani resigned his post to commit himself to political activism. Nabhani's activism was influenced by the emergence of the Jewish state in Palestinian land, as well as by the pervasive sense of powerlessness in the face of Western encroachment into Muslim societies.[7]

In this period, Nabhani was committed to the ideal of Arab unity. In his writings, Nabhani explored the familiar Ba'thist concepts of pan-Arabism, the use of revolutionary vanguards and the structural shake-up of Arab societies. However, unlike the Ba'thist view of religion as only one facet of Arab identity,[8] Nabhani emphasised Islam as the fundamental component of identity and the core of the Arab nation. By 1952 Nabhani was disillusioned with the Ba'th party and was holding secret meetings with other like-minded individuals committed to the formation of a party that posited Islam as the only legitimate political system in the Muslim world. Replicating the experiences of other organisations formed under the tutelage of charismatic leaders, this group was originally referred to as Nabhaniyya. It adopted an overtly religious objective and identified itself unequivocally with the pan-Islamist movement that was emerging throughout the region. The new party's political platform included the rejection of man-made law and the assertion of the supremacy of Shari'a (Islamic law) throughout the Arab world, a doctrine that clearly echoed the political thinking of Sayyid Qutb (1906–66), who was propagating his message in Egypt at that time.

In January 1952, changes to the Jordanian legal code allowed for the registration of opposition parties, but Nabhani's attempts to secure legal registration for his new party failed twice, in November 1952 and January 1953.[9] The applications for registration were rejected on the basis that the party's platform was incompatible with the constitution. The ethos of Hizb al-Tahrir represented a fundamental challenge to the Hashemite dynastic rule and the Jordanian concept of the nation-state. Hizb al-Tahrir had a tortured relationship with the authorities in Jordan. State repression and persecution hampered its activities and in 1953 many of its leaders were imprisoned. Despite these setbacks, Nabhani's fledgling party was finally registered, along with five other new parties, by mid-June 1954.

Hizb al-Tahrir was not the only actor in Jordanian politics utilising Islam as a form of political expression. The Muslim Brotherhood, founded in Egypt in the 1920's, was also active in Jordan. The Brotherhood, like all opposition forces within Jordanian society, experienced a varied relationship with the authorities. Unlike Hizb al-Tahrir the Brotherhood – although advocating a return to the Shari'a – did not reject 'the Arab state system as it actually existed'.[10] Furthermore, the Brotherhood was successful in focusing attention on its social and educational agenda as opposed to its political objectives, thus creating a role for itself as a co-operative opposition group within the Jordanian political structure.

While initially confined to Palestinian areas such as Hebron, Jenin, Jericho and Nablus, by the mid-1950s Hizb al-Tahrir was building support in Amman and Beirut. It even ran candidates in Jordanian elections, but its preferred mode of operation was the development of grassroots support through secret meetings, study groups and leaflet drops. Hizb al-Tahrir's tendency to emphasise the importance of the 'revolutionary vanguard' and its clandestine activity has led some commentators to suggest it represented a synthesis of 'Islamist ideology and Leninist strategy and tactics'.[11] In the 1950s the Middle Eastern political context was dominated by the glorification of Nasser and the rhetoric of pan-Arabism. This was an adverse environment for a religious party such as Hizb al-Tahrir. Further exacerbating this situation was the presence of the Muslim Brotherhood, which was vying for the same potential support base. Hizb al-Tahrir thus found it difficult to distinguish itself from other political parties in the tumultuous political climate of Jordan at this time.

All Arab/Muslim organisations in this period rejected the establishment of the State of Israel and championed the cause of the Palestinians. Hizb al-Tahrir, however, was controversial in the way in which it formulated the Palestinian cause. While founded by a Palestinian and enjoying its greatest support amongst the displaced Palestinians, Hizb al-Tahrir denounced the concept of a national Palestinian state. Instead it called for the restoration of the Caliphate, which it believed would revitalise Muslim pride and pave the way for Muslim liberation from the illegitimate rule of the *kuffar* (unbelievers). It was hoped that this process would reverse the divisive experience of Arab nationalisms that had undermined Muslim unity and the ability of Muslims to resist European colonisers. From the Hizb al-Tahrir perspective, the Caliphate was the only appropriate response to the establishment of the State of Israel, the only power able to eject it from Muslim lands.

In terms of methodology, Hizb al-Tahrir called for the complete rejection of violence in 1954, and this position was held throughout the 1950s and 1960s.[12] However, Hizb al-Tahrir, or its members, was identified as active in a series of attempted coups in Jordan and southern Iraq throughout the late 1960s and early 1970s. Hizb al-Tahrir and other opposition groups were subjected to systematic government repression in this turbulent period. Although the focus had by this juncture moved from the personality of Nabhani to the platform of re-establishing the Caliphate, the death of the party's founder in 1977 was followed by a period of disorientation among party activists. The loss of the party's driving ideological force led to a period of political stagnation.

Hizb al-Tahrir received a new burst of energy as events in the Middle East and the Soviet Union signalled a fundamental shift in Muslim affairs. The 1979 revolution in Iran, which toppled the Pahlavi dynasty and founded an Islamic state, inspired Islamic activists throughout the region. For the first time in modern history, the power of the people appeared to have triumphed and had established the type of regime that had been idealised by Islamists for decades. The establishment of the Islamic republic in Iran had a ripple effect throughout the Middle East, with friends and enemies treating it as a catalyst for change throughout the region. The impact of the Iranian revolution on Hizb al-Tahrir, however, was somewhat subdued as a consequence of Shi'ite/Sunni sectarian differences.

While the Iranian revolution effected little change in the party's political fortunes, the subsequent collapse of the Soviet Union and the opening up of access to Muslim Central Asia offered Hizb al-Tahrir new opportunities for activism. Throughout the 1990s Central Asia as a whole – with Uzbekistan as the focal point – experienced a major expansion of Hizb al-Tahrir as a social and political force. In addition to the Central Asian region, the party has become visibly active throughout western Europe. The London branch of Hizb al-Tahrir was founded by Omar Muhammad Bakri from Syria, who subsequently split with the organisation in order to launch his own party – al-Muhajiroun (The Migrants).

In terms of political ideology, the two parties are virtually indistinguishable. The idealised goal of reviving the Caliphate is paramount for both. This Huntingtonesque approach to history sees the world divided between *dar al-Islam* and *dar al-harb*. It views the relationship between Islam and the West as one of unavoidable confrontation, and draws heavily on the Meccan phase of Islam, when the Prophet and his followers were forced to flee from persecution.[13] The ideas of migration from the abode of disbelief and the subsequent conquest of that realm by Jihad are especially appealing to Omar Muhammad Bakri, who chose to call his organisation The Migrants in the prophetic tradition.

AL-MUHAJIROUN

In 1983 Omar Muhammad Bakri founded al-Muhajiroun in Saudi Arabia. The name was clearly designed to invoke memories of the Prophet's *hijra* (migration) from Mecca to Medina and draw legitimacy from it. This historical memory of migration is a powerful inspiration to Muslims; the imagery of a group of exiled 'true believers' in an 'unbelieving' world resonates with Islamist groups. The organisation's name itself seeks to confer a sense of Islamic legitimacy.[14] The *hijra* model of political mobilisation has been explored elsewhere;[15] the idea of a vanguard of isolated pious believers preparing to return and 'conquer' *kufr* through their belief has been employed by many Islamist organisations.

Like many Islamist activists of his generation, the young Bakri was recruited by the Muslim Brotherhood in his native Syria. Expelled from Syria for his involvement in a revolt against the then President Hafez Assad, Bakri relocated to Beirut, where he joined the ranks of the Hizb al-Tahrir. Although the exact date is contested, Bakri moved in the early 1980s to Saudi Arabia, living under the alias of Omar Fustuk; al-Muhajiroun was established in the Saudi kingdom. Some sources suggest the founding of al-Muhajiroun was merely a front for the activities of Hizb al-Tahrir.[16] Given Bakri's active involvement in the latter at this point, this may well be the case. Bakri was subsequently expelled from Saudi Arabia in 1985 for political agitation against the royal family, a theme that has carried into the public rhetoric of his organisation. Settling in the United Kingdom, Bakri quickly gained a level of notoriety through his 1991 public call for the assassination of the then prime minister, John Major.[17] This did not prevent Bakri from becoming a legal resident of the United Kingdom, where he had launched al-Muhajiroun by 1996. The rationale behind Bakri's spilt with Hizb al-Tahrir and his subsequent launching of al-Muhajiroun is unclear. As an organisation committed to preserving the secrecy of its composition and leadership, Hizb al-Tahrir may simply not have offered Bakri the media profile he clearly desired. Since emerging as the leader of al-Muhajiroun, Bakri has become a media sensation, regularly interviewed and quoted. Despite its active Internet profile Hizb al-Tahrir shies away from such publicity, releasing statements anonymously and usually denying media approaches.

In addition to heading al-Muhajiroun, Bakri founded the al-Khilafah publishing house, serves on the UK Shari'a Court and teaches at the Shari'a College. The actual nature of the relationship between Hizb al-Tahrir and al-Muhajiroun is obscure, as the al-Khilafah publishing house releases many Hizb al-Tahrir publications. In the aftermath of September 11, Bakri has also presented himself as a spokesman for the international Islamist movement, repeatedly asserting his support for the ideology and methodology of Osama bin Laden. Al-Muhajiroun is known for its political rallies, the most infamous of these being the 2003 'Magnificent 19' conference, scheduled and publicised as an exploration of the causes of September 11.[18]

As well as the UK base of operations, al-Muhajiroun claims to operate branches in France, Lebanon, Syria, Kuwait, Bangladesh and South Africa. An organisation explicitly committed to proselytising, al-Muhajiroun's self-declared role is 'to invite the societies in which it functions to embrace Islam as a complete way of life'.[19]

As may be expected, al-Muhajiroun draws heavily on the political thoughts of Sayyid Qutb. Executed by the Egyptian state for treason, Qutb's most significant ideological legacy, and a major thematic attraction for al-Muhajiroun, is arguably the reworking of the concept of *jahiliyya* (ignorance). This concept has conventionally applied to the pre-Islam period in Arabia, where the population was 'ignorant' of God's wishes and lived in a state of barbarity and idolatry. Qutb, however, extended this concept to the contemporary period, and applied it to Muslim societies that refused to live by the Shari'a and violated the rights of others to uphold Islam. This extension had revolutionary repercussions for the legitimacy of the overwhelming majority of rulers in the Muslim world, and has been used by radical Islamists to justify their acts of political sedition, even violence. The implications of Qutb's ideas went beyond regime legitimacy and brought into question the very nature of state-building in the Middle East. For Qutb, legitimacy and power emanated only from God. Human intervention was justified only when it built on a divine foundation, and promoted the supremacy of the Shari'a, not when it contradicted it. To put it simply, sovereignty resided with God. This assertion was a fundamental rejection of the modern nation-states that were being constructed and consolidated throughout the Middle East by man-made laws and institutions.[20] The nation-state model, therefore, epitomised the heresy of man interfering with God's will and violating divine sovereignty.

Islamist groups have relied heavily on Qutb's political doctrine of *jahiliyya*. Al-Muhajiroun has employed it to reject Arab leaders from Palestinian leader Yasser Arafat to Pakistan's General Pervez Musharraf. It has also relied on Qutb's critique of the nation-state to dismiss the existing separation of the *umma* (Islamic community) into distinct nations, governed by man-made laws and to call for the restoration of a unified Islamic power: the Caliphate. From the perspective of al-Muhajiroun and that of other organisations like it, *da'wah* (the call to Islam) and the endeavour to revive the Caliphate are transnational and apply to all Muslims. This includes Muslims living in the West, an intriguing proposition that is beyond the scope of this chapter.

Al-Muhajiroun claims to have operational organisations in South Asia and Europe. However, in spite of its seeming transnational reach, al-Muhajiroun is essentially a UK-based organisation.[21] Within this national context it aims to function as a 'fifth column ... able to pressure ... the enemies of Islam'.[22] By mid-2003, al-Muhajiroun claimed a presence in around thirty UK cities. In a clear link to the organisation's Hizb al-Tahrir origins, al-Muhajiroun propagates its message through study circles, with seventy different groups meeting on a weekly basis. Furthermore, the Internet has become a primary tool for al-Muhajiroun. Affording both universality and anonymity, it allows al-Muhajiroun to reach a virtual audience that extends beyond its immediate followers. For an organisation that is banned in all UK universities, this medium provides a vital, and powerful, opportunity to publicise ideology and attract new members. In a confirmation of the central role the Internet plays in the dissemination of radical politics, the US authorities in late 2002 accused Bakri of conducting an ' "Internet Jihad" to destroy Western, US and Israeli sites'.[23]

However, since its inception al-Muhajiroun has been a marginal oppositional voice within the broader spectrum of British Muslims.

Without a strong political platform, and given its radical approach to politics, the organisation found itself struggling to attain relevance to the daily lives of the British Muslims it sought to influence. Following the attacks of September 11, the domestic political landscape of Western nations and the media attention on issues of Islam altered dramatically. Al-Muhajiroun clearly and unequivocally endorsed the terrorist attacks in the United States, and gained massive media attention as a result. The organisation's response to the subsequent US-led war on terror has been one of unwavering condemnation. The events of the 21st century, especially the invasions of Afghanistan and Iraq by Western coalitions, have generated a political platform for al-Muhajiroun that it appeared to lack in the pre-2001 era.

Despite its position as a fringe organisation, al-Muhajiroun attracts a significant amount of media attention. This has thrown Bakri into the public arena and provided him an open venue to air his opinions. Emerging in the media throughout the 2001–03 period, Bakri and other al-Muhajiroun leaders have issued a range of warnings with regard to terrorism, including both warnings of imminent attacks and of suicide missions by foreign Muslims. None of these attacks has eventuated. Mainstream Muslim associations in the United Kingdom have consistently expressed disappointment that the views and pronouncements of al-Muhajiroun gain currency in the media.[24]

Al-Muhajiroun's literature is full of references to Jihad, victory over *kufr*, and the restoration of God's sovereignty through the establishment of the Caliphate. This radical interpretation of Islam blames the West, and most importantly the United States, for humiliating Muslims and imposing un-Islamic rule on Muslim land. From al-Muhajiroun's perspective, this antagonism locks the United States and Islam in a perpetual conflict, which may be resolved only with the ultimate victory of one side. Al-Muhajiroun likens the US forces to crusaders and hints at a fundamental war between Islam and the West that is to be played out in more than one arena: 'The West realized since the WWI that there [sic] enemy is none other than Islam and the Muslims, they fear the Jihad which initiated from Afghanistan and Palestine and is now spreading to all parts of the world.' [25]

Such statements suggest that al-Muhajiroun not only identifies the current global political arena as a clash of civilisations between Islam and the West, it actually glorifies it. Bakri believes that history is vindicating the clash of civilisation theory, with the events of September 11 'a turning point that separated' Islam and the West.[26] The glorified conflict between the two protagonists is, in Bakri's world view, complemented by a long history of victimhood. In this heroic representation of Islam, it is now the victims who are rising to break the shackles of Western domination. Muslims are joining the battle, in Bakri's exaggerated view of history, to avenge the misdeeds of the West. Al-

Muhajiroun insists that 'what Muslims must understand is that America is at war with Muslims. Its only objective is to destroy the Muslim ideology and control the Muslim lands ... [America will have] no qualms in the genocide of the entire Muslim race which no doubt is next on the agenda.' [27]

Al-Muhajiroun is also concerned with the cultural elements of this clash. Consistently rejecting assimilation, it argues that the United States is attempting to exert hegemonic control through the 'disease of interfaith, multicultural society, ideas of Abrahamic religion, all human brotherhood, all religions being equal; [such ideas] are all mere lies and deceit and against the principles of Islam'.[28] From this platform, al-Muhajiroun seeks to discourage the integration of Muslims into Western societies. To facilitate this, Muslims are instructed to take guidance only from the Qur'an. The use of the Qur'an as a legitimising tool is a feature of the organisation, with most press releases citing verses to explain political positions.

Al-Muhajiroun's militant interpretation of Islam and its commitment to Jihad has led, not surprisingly, to its endorsement of the resistance campaigns in Iraq and Afghanistan. Bakri and Anjem Choudry, a lawyer by profession and a chief spokesperson for al-Muhajiroun, have defended the right of Muslims to travel to these theatres of war to engage in Jihad. In effect, al-Muhajiroun has been encouraging Muslims in the United Kingdom and elsewhere to fight British and US soldiers. This position has caused significant unease in the United Kingdom, and the media has run a plethora of alarming stories about the dangers posed by Islamist groups. The intense media attention and constant police surveillance appear to have taken their toll on al-Muhajiroun, which, while not abandoning its commitment to Jihad and the defeat of the US and British 'crusades', has refined its position in order to disallow Jihad on United Kingdom territory. According to al-Muhajiroun's concept of the 'security covenant', Muslims are forbidden to harm the community that has offered them protection. This legalistic interpretation of the covenant of security is restricted to the territorial confines of the host state, and does not extend to agents of that state beyond its borders.[29] British soldiers in Iraq and Afghanistan, for example, are considered legitimate targets for British Muslims who wish to perform their religious duty of Jihad.

Al-Muhajiroun's literature makes constant reference to Muslim grievances that epitomise the plight of Islam and justify violence against the West. The protracted Israeli–Palestinian conflict is the most prominent issue that has galvanised Muslims and continues to fuel Islamic radicalism. From the al-Muhajiroun perspective, the invasion of Iraq in March 2003 has become another example of Muslims' inability to withstand Western domination and the latter's determination to conquer Islam.

THE PLIGHT OF THE PALESTINIANS

Like many Islamist organisations, al-Muhajiroun devotes a significant proportion of its public statements to the Israeli–Palestinian dispute. The organisation's home page provides press releases and feature articles detailing both its ideological position and its interpretation of Muslim responsibility towards the Palestinian cause. Al-Muhajiroun websites provide a complete rejection of the legitimacy of the state of Israel.

In keeping with its historical world view, al-Muhajiroun presents the current situation in the Occupied Territories as symptomatic of the broader Western conspiracy to subdue Islam. The destruction of the Caliphate (Ottoman Empire) at the close of World War I is identified as the catalyst for social, moral and political degradation in the region. The political manoeuvrings of the Allies in the post–World War I period are presented as pivotal to this process. The Asia Minor Agreement of 1916, better known as the Sykes-Picot Agreement, negotiated to ensure Allied dominance over strategic areas, is condemned as a British plot to irreversibly 'disunite the Muslim land',[30] while the 1917 Balfour Declaration, with its stated support of a Jewish homeland, is understood as Western support for the establishment of a 'terrorist state on the Holy Land of Palestine'.[31]

These examples are critical to al-Muhajiroun's historical narrative and help to explain its current events and political agenda. Within this historical context, support for the Palestinian people is couched in religious, as opposed to nationalist, terms. Al-Muhajiroun's position on the Palestinian issue has radicalised over time, undoubtedly in response to the changing political context. In 1999 the organisation limited its press releases to statements of support for HAMAS and 'other Muslim groups ... continuing the struggle ... against the illegitimate state of Israel'.[32] Although the organisation rejected the peace process, the outbreak of the 2000 Al-Aqsa Intifada appears to have further intensified the organisation's public statements. By 2002 al-Muhajiroun's various sites specifically supported 'martyrdom operations' in Palestine.[33] The mujahideen (Islamic resistance fighters) were called upon by the organisation to 'eradicate this Cancer in the body of the Muslims ... once and for all ... [as] according to Islam, the land currently called Israel is occupied land and the Muslims must wage Jihad until the authority in that land is returned to the Muslims'.[34]

The methodology of Jihad to be employed in this context is not stipulated by al-Muhajiroun, a tactic that has allowed the organisation to claim on the UK website that it, in line with Hizb al-Tahrir, rejects violence while engaging in 'ideological and political interaction'.[35] However, 2003 saw an innovation in the Israeli–Palestinian conflict, with two British Muslims carrying out a suicide attack in Tel Aviv, signifying what the Israeli media identified as an internationalising of the conflict. The Tel Aviv bombers, Asif Muhammad Hanif and Omar Khan Sharif, were suspected of some degree of affiliation with al-Muhajiroun. Although any operational role in the Tel Aviv attack was quickly denied, Bakri and Choudry both issued public statements of support, with Bakri describing himself as a 'spiritual adviser' to both men.[36]

Intelligence agencies, both British and Israeli, tracked the movements of Hanif and Sharif to Syria in the months preceding the attack. The role that al-Muhajiroun leaders could have played in the operational development of the attack is questionable. Al-Muhajiroun may have provided the ideological context in which the two men developed their commitment to violence against Israel, and Bakri's public claims of al-Muhajiroun association with the two men may have been exaggerated for propaganda purposes. The Israeli response to the Tel Aviv attack was immediate, with strong pressure placed on the British Government to crack down on locally based Islamist organisations. Media coverage in Israel decried the United Kingdom as a haven for terrorists and, even more controversially, posited that a 'tacit understanding' exists between the United Kingdom and Islamists, that of non-interference in exchange for a ban of attacks on British soil.[37]

The involvement of individuals from the British Islamist community in international terror has been a matter of speculation and media coverage throughout 2003, with both Richard Reid (the unsuccessful shoe bomber) and Zacharias Moussaoui (the alleged twentieth September 11 hijacker) attending the Finsbury Park mosque in London.[38] Finsbury Park mosque has been a focal point of Islamism in the United Kingdom. At various stages the mosque has served as a base for both the radical Supporters of the Shari'a (SOS) and al-Muhajiroun. Nevertheless, al-Muhajiroun could not and would not claim direct operational involvement in the Tel Aviv bombing, for fear of a complete shutdown by the British authorities. While endorsing the 'martyrdom operation' of Hanif and Sharif, al-Muhajiroun issued a press release to reject claims that it was 'involved in the carrying of arms against anyone, let alone recruiting for Jihad'.[39] An opposing directive, however, can be found on the organisation's Pakistani site where, in early 2003, in the context of a looming conflict in Iraq, al-Muhajiroun exhorted followers to begin 'recruiting Muslims for Jihad'.[40] Furthermore, the organisation articulates clear support for those involved in Jihadi movements, with suicide operations in Palestine clearly supported throughout 2003. Al-Muhajiroun sites further insist that these acts 'must not be considered isolated incidents by extremists',[41] thus positing that such operations are a legitimate component of a mainstream Palestinian resistance.

While rejection of the status and legitimacy of the state of Israel has become a catch-cry of modern Islamist movements, al-Muhajiroun distinguishes itself through its position on the issue of Palestinian statehood. Given the organisation's clear objective of the restoration of a pan-Islamic state, a rejection of the nation-state system as it exists in the modern Middle East is not surprising. While central to the ideological legacy of Hizb al-Tahrir, this pan-Islamic objective does, however, complicate the organisation's determination to present a voice on the issue of Palestine, a conflict that in the modern context is usually (and popularly) understood in nationalist terms.

In keeping with its stated rejection of nationalism, echoing Islamist doctrine espoused by organisations such as the Muslim Brotherhood, HAMAS and Islamic Jihad and, finally, in a clear demonstration of the influence of Qutb's thought, al-Muhajiroun rejects the role of secular nationalist leaders in the Palestinian context. Nationalist regimes in the region are denounced as 'the eyes and ears of their colonial masters'.[42] Yasser Arafat, it claims, 'was portrayed as a symbol of Jihad ... until the façade was dropped and he was standing with America and Israel'.[43] Al-Muhajiroun seeks to undermine the resolution of Palestinian statehood through a rejection of the motivations and capabilities of nationalist leaders. Inherent in the determination to identify Arafat, the symbolic embodiment of Palestinian nationalism, with the United States is the belief that Islam alone can liberate Palestine.

Arguably, it is due to the prominence of the Palestinian issue within the broader spectrum of Islamist movements that al-Muhajiroun is vocal in its rejection of the state of Israel. It articulates a clear position in support of the Palestinian cause, in order to retain relevance within its cultural and political context. This is a vital political measure. The plight of the Palestinians, essentially a people locked in a localised, nationalist conflict, has become a metaphor for the perceived oppression of Muslims by the West.[44] The resolution of this conflict by the formation of a Palestinian state would both undermine and contradict the organisation's guiding ideology. A Palestinian state would be another blow to the ideal of the Caliphate. As a result, al-Muhajiroun insists that Palestinian aspirations for self-determination can be best served under the auspices of pan-Islamism and the supremacy of God's sovereignty. From this perspective, urgent though the Palestinian plight may be, its resolution is relegated to a distant point in the future that would follow the restoration of the Caliphate.

THE WAR IN IRAQ

The US-led invasion of Iraq in early 2003 placed al-Muhajiroun in a precarious ideological position. The United Kingdom, as the primary coalition partner of the United States, committed thousand of troops to the conflict. In the lead-up to the conflict, the Blair government played a critical role in the development of the weapons of mass destruction theory that triggered the invasion. The war on terror, even before the invasion of Iraq, was viewed by 70 per cent of British Muslims as a 'war on Islam',[45] and it was this sentiment that al-Muhajiroun sought to foster. Furthermore, it should be noted that although condemnation of the invasion of Iraq could be expected from groups such as al-Muhajiroun, this denouncement of the Blair Government's actions was shared by a range of moderate Islamic organisations, including the Muslim Council of Britain.[46] While a rejection of the UK Government's position is clear, the United States remained the primary target of al-Muhajiroun's criticism.

The US role in Iraq offered an opportunity for al-Muhajiroun to promote its pan-Islamist agenda. While articulating a clear position on the specific issue of Iraq, al-Muhajiroun used the situation as a vehicle to expound a world view that clearly transcends any specific location. This conflict is identified as one where Islam is pitted against an aggressive West, a conflict in which the United States is identified as the primary enemy. Al-Muhajiroun warns that 'this is not a war about Iraq rather it's a clash between the believers and the non-believers [which] will continue on every level, ideological, political, military and economic until there is a victor'.[47]

Similar to its approach to the question of Palestine, al-Muhajiroun places the contemporary issue of Iraq within a historical world view. This historical approach gives emotive meaning to contemporary events. The occupation of Baghdad (similar to that of Jerusalem, a city that has played a significant role in the historical development of Islam) is identified by the organisation as 'a grave violation to the very belief of every Muslim'.[48] In a further attempt to place current events within the context of Islamic history, the fall of the city was likened to the fall of Grenada in 1492.[49] Through the fusion of geography, history and faith, al-Muhajiroun attempts to articulate a pan-Islamic position that resonates with all Muslims. The United States, the traditional nemesis of Islamist organisations, is targeted by al-Muhajiroun as the primary aggressor in the context of Iraq, and is identified as a 'cursed and sadistic nation' [50] that seeks 'strategic control of the region'.[51]

Importantly, the press releases on Iraq do not reflect a unified position, leading to the conclusion that various individuals in the organisation may be responsible for authoring them. A survey of the press releases on this topic produces a range of possible motivations for invasion: regional hegemony, access to natural resources, revenge for the 2001 terrorist attack in the United States, and a manifestation of an impending 'clash of civilisations'. Al-Muhajiroun has asserted that 'the fundamentalist Christian crusade in Iraq is a continuation of the US policy and dream of total ideological, economic, military and political globalisation by their own version of man-made law'.[52]

Such press releases from the organisation provide vital insight into the world view that informs al-Muhajiroun and attracts young Muslims to its ranks. The rejection of man-made law is a cornerstone of al-Muhajiroun's ideology. This places the organisation firmly in the Islamist camp and presents the conflict as a clash between good and evil. Pitting divine laws against man-made laws in the context of the US invasion of Iraq not only justifies resistance to US occupation but contextualises it within the broader conflict between Islam and disbelief. The United States and its allies are depicted as the epitome of *kufr*, occupying Muslim lands and the seat of Islam's longest serving Caliphate. This is highly emotive rhetoric, and al-Muhajiroun has not shied away from using it to its advantage, attempting to posit it as the cause of Jihad against coalition troops, whom it labels *kuffar*: '[We] must have knowledge about our enemy, Allah (swt)[peace be upon him] has informed us about the intentions and mentality of the kuffar … [thus] we should raise out [sic] our voices and declare our support for the Jihad in Iraq'.[53] Qur'anic terminology is used not only to create greater resonance with the Muslim audience but also to present the issue of Iraq as symptomatic of underlying tensions that have existed for centuries.

Just as al-Muhajiroun rejected Arafat in the Palestinian context, it dismissed Iraq's Saddam Hussein, a secular dictator who opposed the restoration of the Caliphate. However, while Hussein's rule of Iraq was rejected, coalition military action to overthrow him was bitterly opposed because the effect of conflict on the greater Muslim community was seen to take precedence over the position of the Iraqi population. As the security situation in Iraq continues to deteriorate, al-Muhajiroun's condemnation of the coalition has increased dramatically. Al-Muhajiroun's world view and its concentration on Islamic solutions to issues facing the Muslim community are clearly identifiable in its assertion that Muslims should not join in 'stop the war movements … our only call at this time is Jihad to repel the invading armies'.[54]

The continuity of al-Muhajiroun's world view is apparent from the comparison of the focus on a broader Jihad in Iraq and its stated support of Jihadi actions to liberate Palestine. Indeed, within the rhetoric of the organisation, the two issues often merge into a single example of Western oppression and the need to resist it with armed action. Sheikh Abu Ivad, identified by al-Muhajiroun as the leader of the mujahideen resisting the occupation of Baghdad, asserts that there are 8000 fighters in Iraq from throughout the Muslim world.[55] The organisation's objective of linking Palestine and Iraq in the popular imagination can be seen in Sheikh Ivad's conclusion to his account of conditions in Baghdad: 'Allah grant me to be in the land of Palestine where I will be in the same situation and have the same opportunity to fight there.'[56] While it is impossible to verify the authenticity of such accounts, their inclusion on the official website of al-Muhajiroun suggests the organisation's endorsement of the views expressed.

Similar to its treatment of the Palestinian conflict, al-Muhajiroun presents the issue of Iraq as involving distinct, yet interrelated, roles for Muslims living inside the area of conflict and those living outside it. Those living in Iraq and the region are encouraged to take up arms to fight against the United States–led coalition, while other Muslims further afield are urged to provide material and moral support for the mujahideen. The allegations that al-Muhajiroun is involved in recruiting volunteers for Jihadi activities may be based on the organisation's endorsement of a pan-Islamic Jihad in Iraq. Muslims living in the West were encouraged by the organisation to confront the situation in Iraq 'by all means ... verbally, physically or financially ... or recruiting Muslims for Jihad'.[57]

The fundamental aim of al-Muhajiroun's public statements on the conflict in Iraq has been to encourage and foster a collective response from the international Muslim community. However, historical tensions within Islam have seriously hampered this cause. Al-Muhajiroun's views on the Shi'ite community, which constitutes a majority of the total population in Iraq, are deeply troubling. The Shi'ites are labelled collaborators with *kuffar* and accused of betraying Iraq and Islam. They are rejected for being 'trained by the United States' and for giving their 'allegiance to the coalition forces'.[58] As a result of this sectarian approach, al-Muhajiroun risks further isolating the very people it is attempting to influence. Western Muslims, enjoying the freedom of belief that is often denied in Muslim lands, have good reason to be wary of an organisation that, as well as endorsing violence, displays such intolerance of religious minorities. Given the example of Iraq within the version of a restored Caliphate idealised by al-Muhajiroun, the status of minorities appears far from secure.

CONCLUSION

Al-Muhajiroun and other Islamist organisations appear to have been given a new lease on life since the launch of the US-led war on terror. It may be ironic that US actions to eliminate al-Qaeda and its affiliated groups have fuelled the kind of resentment that has traditionally been the source of Islamist agitation and mobilisation.

Throughout the Muslim world each of the US military action's in Afghanistan and Iraq has been seen as a major humiliation at the hands of Western powers. For organisations such as al-Muhajiroun, such events provide a focal point in their anti-American and anti-Western rhetoric. The sense of powerlessness which al-Muhajiroun attempts to exploit is also sustained by the ongoing Israeli–Palestinian dispute.

The Muslim world feels powerless to redress the plight of the Palestinians and is forced to watch from the sidelines as Israel acts with impunity in the Occupied Territories. Appeals to the international community have not curbed Israel's transgressions. The failure of the international community to reach resolution in this conflict is a major source of disillusionment and anger in the Muslim world. Recent unilateral Israeli actions, such as the construction of the 'security fence' through West Bank and the Sharon plan to evacuate from Gaza but retain settlements in the West Bank, have only further intensified Muslim alienation. The unwillingness of the United States to challenge the government of Ariel Sharon has reinforced Muslim mistrust, providing fertile ground for Islamist recruitment.

These events are seen by al-Muhajiroun as undeniable evidence of the Western commitment to annihilating Islam and subjugating Muslims. The transnational nature of the Muslim community means that developments in Iraq and Palestine, while geographically distant, have resonance in parts of the Western Muslim communities. Al-Muhajiroun draws strength from the weakness of Muslim states to represent their case on the international stage and the recklessness of the United States in dealing with delicate issues of pride and self-worth among Muslims. Every blow to Muslim interests further entrenches the radical rhetoric of organisations such as al-Muhajiroun and its supporters in their vision of the impending apocalyptic clash between Islam and *kufr* – a vision that may be gaining attractiveness among some Muslims in the West.

NOTES

1 John L Esposito, 'Introduction', in John L Esposito (ed.), *Political Islam: Revolution, Radicalism, or Reform?* (Boulder, Col: Lynne Rienner, 1997), p. 2.
2 Gilles Kepel, 'Islamism reconsidered', *Harvard International Review*, Vol. 22, No. 2, p. 23.
3 Shahram Akbarzadeh, 'State legitimacy', in Shahram Akbarzadeh and Abdullah Saeed (eds), *Islam and Political Legitimacy* (London: RoutledgeCurzon, 2003), p. 170.
4 Cited in Robert Woltering, 'The roots of Islamist popularity', *Third World Quarterly*, Vol. 23, No. 6, p. 1134.
5 Olivier Roy, *The Failure of Political Islam* (Cambridge, MA: Harvard University Press, 1994).
6 Ariel Cohen, 'Hizb ut-Tahrir: an emerging threat to U.S interests in Central Asia', 30 May 2003, *The Heritage Foundation, Policy Research and Analysis*, available online at <http://www.heritage.org/Research/RussaiandEurasoa/BG1656.cfm>.
7 Suha Taji-Farouki, *A Fundamental Quest. Hizb al-Tahrir and the Search for the Islamic Caliphate* (Grey Seal: London, 1996), p. x.
8 For discussion of the primacy of issues such as language and history to Ba'thist ideology see: Saleh Omar, 'Philosophical origins of the Arab Ba'th Party: The work of Zaki al-Arsuzi', *Arab Studies Quarterly*, Vol. 18, No. 2 (1996), pp. 23–38; Ulrike Freitag, 'In search of "historical correctness": the Ba'th party in Syria', *Middle Eastern Studies*, Vol. 35, No. 1 (1999), pp. 1–16.
9 Suha Taji-Farouki, *A Fundamental Quest*, p. 7.

10 Kamal Salibi, *The Modern History of Jordan* (IB Tauris & Co: London, 1993), p. 175.
11 Ariel Cohen, 'Hizb ut-Tahrir: an emerging threat'.
12 Uriel Dann, 'The Hashmite monarch 1948–88: the constant and the changing – an integration', in Joseph Nevo and Ilan Pappe (eds), *Jordan in the Middle East. The Making of a Pivotal State 1948–88* (Frank Cass: Essex, 1994), p. 23.
13 Suha Taji-Farouki, 'Islamists and the threat of Jihad. Hizb al-Tahrir and al-Muhajiroun on Israel and the Jews', *Middle Eastern Studies,* Vol. 36, No. 4 (2000), pp. 21–47.
14 R Scott Appleby, 'History in the fundamentalist imagination', *The Journal of American History,* Vol. 89, No. 2 (2002), p. 498.
15 Michael Doran, 'The pragmatic fanaticism of al Qaeda: an anatomy of extremism in Middle Eastern politics', *Political Science Quarterly,* Vol. 117, No. 2 (2002), pp. 177–91.
16 'Sheikh Omar Bakri Muhammad', *Jewish Virtual Library*, available online at <http://www.us-israel.org/jsource/biography/Bakri_Muhammad.html>.
17 'Stay away from public buildings', *The Yorkshire Post,* 11 February 2003.
18 Eleventh-hour intervention by the British authorities resulted in all four venues cancelling the conference.
19 Al-Muhajiroun, 'The truth about Omar , Asif and al-Muhajiroun', 3 May 2003, available online at <http://www.muhajiorun.com>.
20 Roxanne Euben, 'Premodern, antimodern, or postmodern? Islamic and Western critiques of modernity', *The Review of Politics,* Vol. 59, No. 3 (1997), pp. 429–60.
21 In March 2004 the Pakistani branch of al-Muhajiroun split with the main UK-based organisation. The impact of this development on the structure of the organisation and its presence in South Asia is, as yet, unclear.
22 Al-Muhajiroun, 'The policy of al-Muhajiroun in the West', available online at <http://www.muhajiroun.com>.
23 'UK-based Islamist warns of al-Qa'idah attacks on US, Britain if Iraq is attacked', *al-Sharq al-Awsat,* 23 November 2002.
24 Ori Golan, 'One day the black flag of Islam will be flying over 10 Downing Street'. *Jerusalem Post,* 27 June 2003.
25 Al-Muhajiroun, 'The crusaders of the 21st century', 24 March 2003, available online at <http://www.almuhajiroun.com.pk/detail.asp?id=1352&idl=14>.
26 B Alloni, 'Interview: Sheik Omar Bakri Mohammad', *United Press International,* 13 September 2003.
27 Al-Muhajiroun, 'The flowing of blood in Iraq', 20 January 2003, available online at <http://www.almuhajiroun.com.pk/detail.asp?id=1317&dl=14>.
28 ——, 'Haram to imitate the disbelievers', 26 December 2002, available online at <http://www.almuhajiroun.com.pk/details.asp?id=1250&idl=14>.
29 ——, 'Aqd Al Amaan: the covenant of security', available online at <http://www.almuk.com/obm/Islamic_Topics/jihad/covenant.htm>, p. 7.
30 Al-Muhajiroun, 'The crusaders of the 21st century'.
31 ——, 'The crusaders of the 21st century'.
32 ——, press release, 7 November 1999, available online at <http://www.almuhajiroun.com>.
33 ——, 'Saudi regime kill ulema to please Bush', 30 May 2003, available online at <http://www.al-muhajiroun.com.pk/detail.asp?id=1501&dl=14>.
34 ——, 'Muslims to call for the destruction of the Jewish state', 17 May 2002, available online at <http://www.muhajiroun.com>.

35 ——, 'The truth about Omar, Asif and al-Muhajiroun'.
36 Nick Fielding, 'Passport to terror', *The Sunday Times*, 4 May 2003.
37 Ori Golan, 'One day the black flag of Islam will be flying over 10 Downing Street'.
38 'Seven still held after police mosque raid', *Press Association*, 21 January 2003.
39 'Seven still held after police mosque raid'.
40 Al-Muhajiroun, 'Iraq: the international crusade against Islam and Muslim countries continues', available online at <http://www.almuhajiroun.com.pk/details.asp?id =1301&id1=14>.
41 ——, 'Fascist Jewish state will never see peace', 20 April 2003, available online at <http://www.almuhajiroun.com>.
42 ——, 'Muslim rulers: agents of the West', 20 December 2002, available online at <http://www.almuhajiroun.com.pk/details.asp?id=1229&id1=14>.
43 ——, 'Muslim rulers: agents of the West'.
44 Michael Doran, 'The pragmatic fanaticism of al Qaeda: an anatomy of extremism in Middle Eastern politics', p. 124.
45 ICM poll for the BBC results in Andrew Grice, 'Most British Muslims see war on terror as war on Islam', *The Independent*, 24 December 2002, p. 2.
46 See Iqbal Sacranie, Secretary General of the Muslim Council of Britain, in Ingrid Bazinet, 'Muslims in Britain denounce Black Day, warn of revenge strikes', *Agence France Presse*, 20 March 2003.
47 Al-Muhajiroun, 'The crusaders of the 21st century'.
48 ——, 'The occupation of Baghdad', 17 April 2003, available online at <http://www.almuhajiroun.com.pk/detail.asp?id=1415&id1=14>.
49 M. al-Shafi'i, 'Islamists cited on US-Iraqi-Syrian "deal", suicide elements in Iraq', *The Financial Times*, 13 April 2003.
50 Al-Muhajiroun, 'The flowing of blood in Iraq'.
51 ——, 'The American military presence in the Gulf', 27 January 2003, available online at <http://www.almuhajiroun.com.pk/details.asp?id=1230&id1=14>.
52 ——, 'The crusaders of the 21st century', available online at <http://www.almuhajiroun.com.pk/detail.asp?id=1353&id1=10>.
53 ——, 'The occupation of Baghdad'.
54 ——, 'The crusaders of the 21st century'.
55 ——, 'Press release from Iraq: translation of the 1st press release given by Sheikh Abu Iyad, the Amir of the Mujahideen in Baghdad', 14 March 2003, available online at <http://www.almuhajiroun.com>.
56 ——, 'Press release from Iraq: translation of the 1st press release given by sheikh Abu Iyad the Amir of the Mujahideen in Baghdad'.
57 ——, 'Iraq: the international crusade against Islam and Muslim countries continues'.
58 ——, 'The occupation of Baghdad'; 'Press release from Iraq: translation of the 1st press release given by Sheikh Abu Iyad, the Amir of the Mujahideen in Baghdad'.

4

ISLAMIC GROUPS AND PAKISTAN'S FOREIGN POLICY: LASHKAR-E-TOIBA AND JAISH MUHAMMAD

SAMINA YASMEEN

The discipline of international politics has traditionally ignored the role played by religion. The explanation resides in the primacy since the end of World War II of the geostrategic/realist paradigm, which approached relations between states and political entities from the standpoint of national interest. Acceptance of the notion of maximisation of national interest, and the regulation of this behaviour through the 'balance of power', have been used to understand, explain and predict developments at global, regional and state levels. Religion and culture were the unintended victims of such an approach to world politics. The neo-liberal ideas that emerged at the beginning of the 1970s did not alter the situation. While acknowledging the role of transnationalism and links between states and societies, as well as re-emphasising the idea of harmony of interest within the international community, neo-liberalists also denied religion a place in the study of world politics.

The Islamic revolution in Iran (1979) posed a challenge to these approaches but was not taken up by the discipline of international politics. It was only after the end of the Cold War and the Gulf War of 1991 that the role of religion, especially Islam, was acknowledged. Samuel Huntington's identification of fault lines between civilisations and the possibility of a clash between them reflected this acknowledgment of the role played by different cultures and religions in world politics. However, the extreme nature of claims made by Huntington paradoxically reinforced the tendency to locate religion's role within national/state boundaries. Political Islam was studied largely in terms of Islamic movements within states and, with a few exceptions, the linkage between Islam and foreign policy continued to be ignored. Such a limited approach contributed to either ignoring or marginalising transnational links among Islamic groups. The omission was significant, given the emphasis accorded to non-state actors within the context of global social movements dealing with, for example, environmental, AIDS, landmines, globalisation and human rights issues.

The terrorist attacks on the United States in September 2001, the Bali bombing in October 2002 and the Madrid bombing in March 2004 have forced a reassessment of approaches adopted for the study of international politics: not only is the role of Islam being increasingly acknowledged, but also hitherto unknown transnational Islamic movements are being accorded attention. There is, however, a dearth of studies exploring the links between the world views of these movements and their role in the foreign policies of their respective states, as well as their impact upon regional and global developments. Are these movements one of the instruments of the concerned states' foreign policies or are the states hostage to these movements?

This chapter attempts to answer these questions with reference to the role of Lashkar-e-Toiba (Army of the Pure) and Jaish Muhammad (Army of the Prophet) in Pakistan's foreign policy. To this end, it is divided into three parts: first, the context in which Islamic militant groups emerged in Pakistan; second, an outline of the origin and world view of the two groups; and, third, an assessment of their place in Pakistan's foreign policy before and after 11 September 2001. It argues that having emerged in the context of state-sponsored Islamisation in Pakistan and the weakness of the state in the 1990s, Lashkar-e-Toiba and Jaish Muhammad were used as instruments of Pakistan's foreign policy. However, in the post-September 11 phase, these groups have emerged as relatively autonomous units. Their revised world view suggests that they are not totally under Islamabad's control. This new situation complicates policy choices for Pakistan. While participating in the war on terrorism, Islamabad may now need to target some of its own former allies.

THE CONTEXT FOR MILITANCY

The role of Islamic groups in Pakistan can be understood in terms of a distinction between societal and state-sponsored Islam. Societal Islam refers to the process in which a series of independent or interlinked economic, political, military, social and cultural factors cause groups in society to identify more closely with Islam than was the case previously. This identification takes the form of increased references to the primacy of Islam in the society, but it also extends to ideas for organising the state along Islamic lines. State-sponsored Islam, on the other hand, refers to the process whereby the state or the government introduces piecemeal ideas about Islamisation for the purposes of seeking political legitimacy. At one level it indicates the significance attached by members of the society to their Islamic identity, but at another level it also sets in motion processes whereby the society is encouraged to internalise Islamic ideas and identity by means of the media, educational institutions and formal legislation. The state patronises institutions that communicate the notions of Islam supported by the authorities and alters cultural practices either slowly or more drastically.

It is important to mention that the nature of Islam introduced and the ability and willingness of the state or society to Islamise are closely linked to the power equation between those subscribing to alternative views of Islam. In other words, the relative balance between those subscribing to liberal or orthodox Islamic values in decision-making circles and/or society determines the directions taken by the process of Islamisation. Also, the relationship between societal and state-sponsored Islam is often cyclical and not linear in nature: the state may introduce policies that create new ideas of Islamic culture and cause the societal groups to make demands on the government by using the language of Islam. In a similar vein, the societal groups may gain control of state institutions and introduce their own notions of Islam in a manner not prevalent before this control. The Iranian revolution of 1979, the emergence of a theocratic regime in Tehran and subsequent use by Iranian women of Islam to secure more rights provide a vivid example of such a cyclical relationship between state-sponsored and societal Islam. Equally importantly, the effects of such a relationship are not always clearly identifiable and cannot necessarily be controlled by those initiating the Islamisation process. Both state-sponsored and societal Islam can result in unintended consequences by unleashing forces and ideas that may not follow the lines favoured by the state or the dominant societal groups.

Pakistan has experienced the cyclical relationship between state-sponsored and societal Islam along with its unintended consequences for more than twenty years. Although Pakistan was created in the name of Islam, the balance of forces had remained in favour of liberal Islamic groups for nearly two decades. They portrayed Pakistan's identity as a state for Muslims where followers of other religions could also live as equal citizens. Those subscribing to the idea of Pakistan as an Islamic state were kept at bay, with limited influence on the construction of the state's identity and the implementation of its policies. The situation changed as some liberal Muslims began to use Islam for political purposes after the 1965 Indo-Pakistan war. Zulfiqar Ali Bhutto introduced the idea of Islamic socialism as a means of seeking support from the masses against the Ayub Government. The same policy was adopted by the military regime led by General Yahya: it used Islamic language to secure support from some Islamic groups in the society. The Indo-Pakistan war of 1971 opened up additional space for the Orthodox Islamic groups to voice their opinions about the place of Islam in the

Pakistani state and society. However, it was only after General Zia ul-Haq took over power in July 1977 that the balance tilted in favour of those subscribing to Orthodox interpretations of Islam. Motivated by a desire to seek political legitimacy for his regime, General Zia established a de facto alliance with Jamaat-I-Islami and launched a number of policies aimed at 'Islamising' Pakistan. The Hudood Ordinance of 1984, for instance, incorporated elements of Islamic codes (Shari'a) into Pakistani law for crimes such as drinking and adultery committed by Muslims. The state also used the media and the educational system to create a new emphasis on Islam and Orthodoxy. The process had an impact on the cultural understandings and expressions of Islam in society. It also strengthened the Orthodox Islamic groups, which became the beneficiaries of the state's policy of Islamisation.

The Soviet invasion of Afghanistan in December 1979 and the subsequent alliance between Pakistan and the United States further strengthened the relative position of the Orthodox Islamic groups in Pakistan. As a front-line state against the Soviet occupation, Pakistan provided the base for waging Jihad against the Marxist regime in Kabul. Aided by the US Government and other regional and European states, a number of *madrasa*s (religious schools) in Pakistan were encouraged to prepare mujahideen for rolling the Soviets back. The Inter-Services Intelligence (ISI) played a pivotal role in the process: in addition to facilitating the use of a language of Jihad among those enrolled in *madrasa*s, it also acted as a conduit of weapons for the mujahideen. The experience gained was also used by the Zia regime for keeping domestic opposition under control. For instance, it implicitly supported the creation of Anjuman Sipah Sahabah Pakistan (ASSP – Army of the Prophet's Companions in Pakistan) in September 1984 as a counterweight to a renowned politician, Abida Hussain in Jhang.[1] At the same time, a number of other Islamic groups were also allowed to operate freely and publish their own information on what it means to be a Muslim. Consequently, by the time of Zia's death in August 1988, Islamic groups had become a significant part of Pakistani society.[2]

The democratic era (1988–99) did not alter the balance between liberal and Orthodox Islamic ideas. The constitutional amendments passed during General Zia's era had created a troika in which the balance of power remained with the president and/or the chief of army staff (COAS). Given the precarious position both Benazir Bhutto and Nawaz Sharif found themselves in as prime ministers, neither of them was able or willing to stem the tide of Islamic Orthodoxy. On the contrary, like their predecessor they also used Islam for political legitimacy: they avoided voicing criticism of Orthodox Islamic groups and refrained from questioning the legislative changes introduced by General Zia. This perpetuated a multiplicity of views on the place of Islam in Pakistan: liberal Islamic ideas, Sufi (mystic) traditions and

Orthodoxy coexisted, with implications for the society and culture. Pakistan's integration into the globalised world was parallelled by the re-emergence of a traditional Islamic dress code among some sections of the society. More importantly, a preference for Orthodoxy led some groups to opt for radical militant ideas as well.[3] Coupled with the proliferation of small arms in the country in the wake of the Jihad against Soviet occupation, the militancy resulted in increasing sectarian violence. At the same time, intelligence agencies, especially the ISI, acquired more strength. Building upon its experience during the 1980s, the ISI emerged as the dominant determining force for selecting and funding various Islamic groups. Lashkar-e-Toiba and Jaish Muhammad owe their existence to this interplay between social, political and cultural forces in the 1980s and the 1990s.

LASHKAR-E-TOIBA AND JAISH MUHAMMAD

ORIGINS

Lashkar-e-Toiba grew out of the shared experiences of the struggle against the Soviet occupation of Afghanistan, in which a number of Pakistanis, Afghans and Arabs participated. During these years, a group of Pakistani lecturers in Islamic Studies at the Engineering University (Lahore) were influenced by their Saudi Arabian counterparts. Convinced of the value of Jihad against the Soviets, they had established an instructional centre, Markaz-ud-Dawa-wal-Irshad (MDI), in 1986 under the leadership of Professor Hafiz Mohammad Saeed.[4] They also established military training camps in Kunnar, Afghanistan, where mujahideen for Afghanistan were trained. Once it became obvious that the Soviets were preparing to pull out of Afghanistan after the Geneva Accord of 1988, the attention of this group shifted towards Kashmir. The shift was made possible as a result of the emerging disillusionment in the Indian part of Kashmir with the manner in which the Indian Government was dealing with a series of social, economic and political problems in the Muslim majority state. The uprising in the Indian part of Kashmir started at the end of 1989 and provided the starting point for this redirection of Jihad away from Afghanistan and towards liberating Kashmir. Lashkar-e-Toiba was formally established on 22 February 1990 by Hafiz Mohammad Saeed to wage a Jihad in the Indian part of Kashmir.

The militant group with MDI as its parent organisation succeeded in establishing a significant presence in Pakistan during the 1990s. Its headquarters was in Muridke, a town near Lahore, from which administrative, educational, propaganda and Jihadi activities were coordinated. In addition to providing social welfare services, it also included an academy called Al-Mahdal-Aala-ud-Dawa-tal-Islamia, where religious training was given to both boys and girls.[5] Lashkar also extended its operations across the four provinces of Pakistan and Azad Kashmir (Pakistani part of Kashmir). Until 2001, it was reportedly operating 1150 offices at the provincial, district and *tehsil* (below district) levels.[6] It was operating military training camps in Pakistan and in Azad Kashmir. By 1995, Lashkar had also established a sister organisation in the Indian part of Kashsmir.[7] Lashkar drew support from a number of sources: while the exact membership is difficult to assess, available information suggests that within Pakistan it managed to establish a strong presence in southern Punjab, northern Sindh and parts of Baluchistan. It also drew support from Kashmiris, Afghans and foreign Muslims who were willing to participate in the Jihad in Kashmir. By 2001, Lashkar claimed that 14369 Jihadis had been martyred in the struggle against Indian occupation in Kashmir.[8] Of these, 172 were identified as martyrs of Arab, Afghan, European and other nationalities.[9] The military activities of Lashkar-e-Toiba were parallelled by an active information/publication set up. Darul-Andulus became the major publishing house for the group. Apart from publishing books on the rights and duties of Muslims and on Jihad, it also published a monthly magazine, *Mujalla-tud-Dawa*.

Jaish Muhammad was created nearly ten years after the formation of Lashkar-e-Toiba. Maulana Masood Azhar, another veteran of the Afghan war, founded the group in January 2002. He had been a member of the Harkatul Mujahideen (HM), a group that was initially engaged in Jihad in Afghanistan but afterwards redirected its efforts towards the Indian occupation of Kashmir. In the early 1990s, he was also instrumental in bringing HM and another Islamic movement, Harkatul-Jihad-ul-Islami (HJI), together under the banner of Harkatul-Ansar (HA). However, in 1994 he was arrested during a secret visit to India and was imprisoned. His release was made possible on 31 December 1999 when a group of militants hijacked an Indian Airlines aircraft and demanded the release of Maulana Masood Azhar and others.

Within a month of being released, on 31 January 2000, Masood Azhar formally announced the formation of Jaish Muhammad. It drew support from former members of the HM, HJI and HA. This support was used as a reason for Jaish Muhammad to occupy offices of the HM, which created conflict between the two groups. The issue was resolved through the active mediation of Osama bin Laden, who had been known to Masood Azhar since his participation in the Afghan Jihad. Thereafter, Jaish Muhammad was able to establish a strong presence in Pakistan. Its presence was strongest in Karachi (Sindh), Multan and Bahawalpur (Punjab), but it also recruited members from Waziristan, Malakand, Kohat, Bannu and Dera Ismail Khan in the North-West Frontier Province and Panjgor in Baluchistan.[10] Like Lashkar-e-Toiba, it attracted support from Afghans, Arabs, and some Europeans and other nationalities, but non-Pakistanis appeared to be relatively fewer in number than those who joined Lashkar.[11]

By 2002, Jaish Muhammad was operating through 78 district and 390 *tehsil* offices in Pakistan. It had also established a major presence in Muzaffarabad, Azad Kashmir, where a military training camp was set up, and had established similar camps in other areas, including Balakot, Hajeera and Manshera. At the same time, it established organisational structures to take care of the families of the martyrs and of those who were imprisoned by Indian authorities. Equal emphasis was placed on a strong publication unit to disseminate the message of Jaish to ordinary Pakistanis and others.[12] In addition to publishing a number of books on Masood Azhar's ideas, the unit published a fortnightly magazine *Jaish Muhammad* and one specifically for women, *Binat-e-Aisha*.

WORLD VIEWS

Lashkar-e-Toiba and Jaish Muhammad represented two different religious traditions: while the former identified itself as representing Ahle Hadith ideology, Jaish Muhammad placed itself strongly within the Deobandi tradition. Despite their theological differences on the nature of an Islamic state, the two groups appear to have subscribed to a somewhat similar world view. This view approaches developments in world politics in terms of global, regional and local scenarios. The notion of civilisational clash, which has received criticism elsewhere, underpins this multilayered level of analysis. Both these groups start from the assumption that the world is divided between the Muslim *umma* (community of believers) and the non-Muslim world, and that the latter aims to subjugate and oppress the former. At the global level, this animosity and negativity is seen as being led by the most powerful state, the United States.[13] At the regional level, the two groups identify states that have their own anti-Muslim agenda that qualifies them for an alliance with the United States. The identity and policies of these regional states may vary but they are all guided, to varying degrees, by animosity towards Muslims. The local level refers to the situation in Muslim states and the dominant views in these states, which may or may not qualify them for becoming a part of the larger American agenda of subverting Muslims and Islam. The view essentially resembles the neo-Marxist world view: the fundamental contradiction in the world is seen as being that between the *core* and *periphery*. It conceives of global relationships in terms of collusion, co-operation and exploitation, where the core states use those at the periphery to perpetuate their control.

In somewhat similar vein to the neo-Marxists who accept the need to fight against this perceived exploitation, Lashkar-e-Toiba and Jaish Muhammad also emphasise the need for struggle. Jihad forms an essential element of this struggle. Members of the Lashkar-e-Toiba approach the idea of Jihad with a strong commitment. They argue that the Qur'an has instructed all Muslims 'to strive against [the unbe-lievers] with the utmost endeavour'.[14] For them, Jihad is a soul puri-fier that enables Muslims to realise their true potential, but they question the distinction between *Jihad-e-saghira* (the Lesser Jihad) and *Jihad-e-kabira* (Greater Jihad). In their view, Islam orders its fol-lowers to engage in armed struggle so that they can ultimately earn God's blessings, defeat the *kuffar* (unbelievers) and establish an Islamic system.[15] The struggle, in their view, justifies *fida-e-hamlay* (suicide attacks), but they do not identify these as suicide. Instead, attacking the enemy with life and belongings is presented as the high-est form of struggle and sacrifice.[16]

For members of Jaish Muhammmad, the Qur'an's main concern is Jihad. In the words of its founder, Masood Azhar, the Qur'an enjoins Jihad upon all Muslims as long as *kuffar* remain powerful. The strug-gle is seen as creating conditions in which non-Muslims would be pun-ished for their wrong-doings and lose their cultural appeal: no-one would wish to follow their example. Muslims would benefit from this process: they would be able to vent their anger against the *kuffar* and develop co-operative relationships with fellow Muslims. They would also receive God's love in return. Failure to wage Jihad, on the other hand, is presented as earning the wrath of God, who would replace the misguided Muslims with those prepared to perform their primary duty of Jihad.[17] The followers of Jaish Muhammad, however, emphasise that Jihad needs to be waged under a religious leadership.

Lashkar-e-Toiba and Jaish Muhammad, however, differ on the role of women in Islamic society and this difference has implications for their idea of Jihad. For members of Lashkar, women are expected to stay at home and perform the role of nurturers. They are to accept the limits imposed by their husbands on their involvement in the public sphere. At the same time, they are encouraged to take pride in their role as indirect participants in Jihad. They are to provide their men with a supportive environment that will enable them to participate in Jihad. Women are also encouraged to accept the martyrdom of their men graciously and as a sign of God's blessing on their entire family.[18] Jaish Muhammad, on the other hand, views women as both nurturers as well as active participants in Jihad, if necessary.[19]

Before September 11, the two groups also differed on the relative attention given to the global, regional and local scenarios. Despite the fact that leaders of both groups had contacts with Osama bin Laden, and had maintained training camps in Afghanistan during the Taliban era, Jaish Muhammad *did not always* portray the United States as an enemy of the Muslim world. It made occasional references to US poli-cies, but criticism of Washington was couched in the broader termi-nology of the *kuffar*. The discussion of regional scenarios also lacked a detailed discussion of states outside South Asia that posed a threat to Muslims. This was despite the fact that Masood Azhar had reportedly visited Zambia, United Kingdom, Kenya, Sudan, Somalia and Uzbekistan in the early 1990s. His lectures on Jihad, for instance, only infrequently referred to the situation in Bosnia. A similar situation existed with reference to local scenarios: apart from indirect references to the 'little danger felt by the *kuffar* from local leadership', Jaish Muhammad's publications and Masood Azhar mostly remained content with alluding to the links between the three levels of their world view.[20]

In contrast, Lashkar-e-Toiba accorded greater attention to the links between global, regional and local scenarios. The United States was characterised more often in Lashkar's publications as posing a threat to the Muslim nation. These publications also focused more on developments around the globe, including the situation in Bosnia marked by ethnic cleansing, Somalia, Palestine, South Korea and Indonesia. They also voiced explicit opinions about the networks established between the United States and local agents in Muslim states. In early 2001, for instance, the monthly publication of Lashkar-e-Toiba analysed the emphasis placed on the economy by Pakistan's President Pervez Musharraf in terms of the influence of Western ideas. The conflict in Kalimantan in February 2001 was also explained with reference to links between Christians in Indonesia who were being instigated by 'outsiders'. An article in *Mujalla-tud-Dawa*, for instance, stated that 'neighbouring states, Australia and Poland provide weapons [to Christians in Indonesia] and American assistance is also at the forefront'.[21]

Both Lashkar-e-Toiba and Jaish Muhammad, however, shared a view of India as the main regional enemy of Muslims in South Asia. Indian history was presented as centuries of Hindu proclivity to treachery as a means of perpetuating their political rule. Kautilya's Arthashastra was used as evidence to support this claim. The Bharata Janata Party (BJP), with its links to the Rashtriya Swami Sevak (RSS), was identified as the modern-day embodiment of Hindu hatred against Muslims, while former Indian prime minister, Atal Bihari Vajpayee, was credited with implementing the Hindu agenda in India and South Asia. Kashmir occupied a central place in this characterisation of India: it was seen as evidence of Indian attempts to subjugate and oppress Muslims. In line with the general preference for Jihad, therefore, they argued that Muslims were obligated to struggle against Indian oppression. Interestingly, the idea of Jihad was also justified in terms of the subcontinental notions of *izzat* (honour). Members of both Lashkar-e-Toiba and Jaish Muhammad equated Kashmir with home and the oppression of Kashmiris in India as 'rape of sisters and mothers'.[22] Such a situation, they argued, necessitated a resolute response, with a view to winning freedom for Kashmiri Muslims.

INFLUENCE ON PAKISTAN'S FOREIGN POLICY

BEFORE SEPTEMBER 11: A REGIONAL FOCUS

Before September 11, the commitment by Lashkar-e-Toiba and Jaish Muhammad to confront the Indian presence in Kashmir was used as an instrument of Pakistan's foreign policy by some sections of the deci-sion-making circles. This, in turn, was made possible by the multiplic-ity of views within the Pakistan Government on the nature of Indian hostility and the appropriate responses. These views could be broadly categorised as moderate, Orthodox and Islamist in nature. Those sub-scribing to the moderate view considered Indian hostility to be condi-tional: in their opinion, a combination of sufficient defensive capability and engagement carried the possibility of containing Indian hostility towards Pakistan. The Orthodox and Islamist groups, on the other hand, considered Indian hostility to be unconditional. Convinced that only resolute action could neutralise a perceived Indian threat in a post–Cold War era of growing amity between Washington and New Delhi, they suggested a series of strategies. One suggestion was to build close links with Afghanistan in the post-Soviet era, with a view to acquiring strategic depth. Another suggestion focused on exploiting the altered geostrategic situation to undermine Indian security, with a special emphasis on Kashmir: the uprising in the Indian part of Kashmir in 1989 was perceived as such an option. By supporting the opponents of the Indian Government in Kashmir, those subscribing to the Orthodox view argued, Pakistan could pay India back for its role in the creation of Bangladesh in 1971. It could also 'bleed' India. For Islamists, supporting the Kashmiris in India was not just part of paying the Indians back but also a duty for Pakistani Muslims. They had an obligation to stand by other Muslims, especially those in Kashmir, which should have really been part of Pakistan. Such commonality of views guided the Islamists and the Orthodox groups to opt for 'non-conventional' means of responding to the situation in the Indian part of Kashmir. Simply translated, this meant creating, promoting, and supporting groups within and outside the Indian part of Kashmir, with a view to undermining New Delhi's control over the princely state.

Lashkar-e-Toiba and Jaish Muhammad, while established at differ-ent times, occupied a special place in this strategy favoured by the Islamists and the Orthodox groups. Although concrete evidence is unavailable, it is common knowledge that these groups were created and patronised by the ISI. The similarity of views on India held by the militant groups and sections of the Pakistan Government supports the suggestions and claims that they were created as part of the Pakistani strategy vis-à-vis India. The ease with which these groups were allowed to operate and raise funds in Pakistan and Azad Kashmir lends further credence to this view. In line with a policy adopted by the ISI in the early 1990s, Lashkar-e-Toiba was permitted to raise funds independently. Its members placed collection boxes in a number of shopping centres, mosques and other areas where people could donate money for 'Jihad in Kashmir'. Lashkar, along with other militant Islamic groups, was allowed to raise funds by collecting hides of slaughtered animals during the days of the Eid-ul-Adha celebration. According to some reports, it also used criminal networks to render 'services' to those willing to contract them for settling issues with others. Jaish Muhammad had access to similar fund-raising options. The funds thus raised were used for a series of educational, administrative and military purposes.

Both Lashkar-e-Toiba and Jaish Muhammad were allowed freely to recruit members for their respective organisations. The process was not limited to *madrasa*s but was extended to civil society as well. According to some reports, Jaish Muhammad adopted a policy of turning up at schools in Azad Kashmir without any prior arrangement and urging students to join in the Jihad in Kashmir. Lashkar adopted a similar attitude, but was able to attract support through other more open channels as well. Those subscribing to the Orthodox ideas of Islam, although sometimes having limited educational qualifications, were also recruited from Punjab, Sindh and Azad Kashmir. Equally importantly, the two militant groups were able to establish and maintain camps where recruits were trained for different periods: some for only three weeks, but others for longer in preparation for combat in Kashmir.

That sections of the Pakistan Government used these militant groups as an instrument of foreign policy is further vindicated by the ease with which the groups could cross the cease-fire line in Kashmir. Although both these organisations took the credit for these crossings and campaigns in the Indian part of Kashmir, some sources suggest that it would not have been possible without either the direct assistance or implied support from the Pakistan forces assigned to the cease-fire line.[23] These infiltrations enabled Lashkar and Jaish Muhammad to engage in a number of campaigns, predominantly in Kashmir but also in other parts of India. The first infiltration by members of Lashkar-e-Toiba took place in August 1992. Thereafter it continued military campaigns and claimed to have killed more than 1200 Indian army officers and soldiers by early 2001. Lashkar also introduced the idea of *fida-e-hamlay* (suicide attacks). Its attack on the Red Fort in Delhi in December 2000 was a major example of such a campaign against Indian authorities. Jaish Muhammad, on the other hand, reportedly engaged in 89 *fida-e-hamlay* during 2000–01 and killed more than 1400 Indian soldiers and officers.[24]

The Indian Government reacted to the use of militant groups as an instrument of Pakistan's foreign policy. Throughout the 1990s, it accused Pakistan of training and sending insurgents into the Indian part of Kashmir. Pakistan consistently denied the accusation and portrayed activities of Lashkar-e-Toiba, Jaish Muhammad and other groups as part of the Kashmiri freedom struggle. It maintained that it was providing only moral support to the Kashmiris that was justified in light of the UN resolutions, and that the freedom fighters were relying on their own efforts to acquire weapons and training.

AFTER SEPTEMBER 11: A MORE GLOBALISED WORLD VIEW

The terrorist attacks on the United States on September 11 changed the context in which Pakistan could use the militants as an instrument of its foreign policy. As Islamabad was forced to revise its policy towards the Taliban in Afghanistan and join the US-led coalition for its 'war on terror', it was obvious that it could not continue to support and use Lashkar-e-Toiba and Jaish Muhammad against Indian control of Kashmir. That New Delhi rearticulated its opposition to Pakistan's policy in terms of combating terrorism made it even more difficult for Islamabad to avoid a reappraisal of its policy in Kashmir. However, Islamabad was slow in undertaking and implementing this change of policy. It was only after the terrorist attacks on the Indian Parliament on 13 December 2001 that Islamabad began demonstrating an interest in controlling the Islamic militant groups.

As the United States froze the financial assets of both Lashkar-e-Toiba and Jaish Muhammad and declared them terrorist organisations, the Pakistan Government also began to restrict the movements of the leaders of the two groups. Meanwhile, it adopted 'creative' solutions to perpetuating its support for the militants, while remaining part of the US-led coalition against terrorism. For example, Jaish Muhammad's leader, Masood Azhar, was placed under house arrest as a sign of this shift in Pakistani policy. At the same time, Lashka-e-Toiba was allowed to reincarnate itself as Jamaat-ud-Dawa (Invitation to Islam Party). Its leader, Hafiz Saeed, announced the group's decision to shift the operations of Lashkar-e-Toiba to Azad Kashmir under the declared leadership of Maulana Abdul Wahid of Poonchh. Lashkar was to continue its struggle against India, but Jamaat-ud-Dawa was to carry out 'a political, religious and reform programme in Pakistan'.[25] Such an approach suggests that the Islamist and Orthodox groups in Pakistani decision-making circles were not prepared to totally abandon the militant organisations operative in Kashmir. The Indian Government's decision to mobilise troops along the international border and demand that Pakistan cease support for terrorism demonstrated the limits of such a policy. The likelihood of a conflict, with the attendant possibility of its escalation into a nuclear exchange between India and Pakistan, prompted the US Government to take a stronger stand vis-à-vis Islamabad. Faced with the US pressure, President Musharraf announced a ban on Lashkar-e-Toiba and Jaish Muhammad on 12

January 2002. Major offices of the two groups were sealed and a number of their workers and leaders were arrested.

The Pakistan Government's approach to these groups in the first few months of 2002 indicated that, despite the ban, Islamabad was using the two militant groups as indirect instruments of foreign policy. It expected New Delhi to withdraw its troops from the international border as a quid pro quo for banning the groups. As the Indian Government delayed the withdrawal, however, these groups were allowed to resume their activities. Their leaders were released and they were able to raise funds nationally. However, the terrorist attacks in Kaluchak in May 2002 and the declaration by the Indian prime minister of the need for a 'decisive battle with Pakistan' forced a further modification in Pakistan's policy. US pressure prompted the moderates in Pakistan to entertain the idea of further restricting the activities of the militant groups. By mid-2003, Pakistan's President Musharraf was giving categorical assurances that militant training camps would not operate on Pakistani soil.

Despite Islamabad's categorical assurances, however, Lashkar-e-Toiba and Jaish Muhammad have not ceased to be a factor in Pakistan's foreign policy. This continued relevance is linked partly to the persistence of Islamist and Orthodox ideas among those making decisions about Pakistan's foreign policy. President Musharraf had taken steps to weaken the hold of these groups over the ISI in the wake of the US attacks on the Taliban. While less powerful than before, Lashkar-e-Toiba and Jaish Muhammad still retain some control. Fear of Indian hostility and ideas about Pakistan's Islamic identity and related obligations to help other Muslims still persist among them. They are reluctant to give up their support for those fighting in Kashmir after the Pakistan Government's 'U-turn' on Taliban. Hence, while not openly opposing the attempts to rein in the militants, some Pakistan Government agencies have turned a blind eye, especially to the activities of Lashkar-e-Toiba. In its reincarnated form of Jamaat-ud-Dawa, Lashkar continues to raise funds by placing collection boxes around the country, including in elite areas in major cities. Their publications and propaganda are not targeted and they circulate with little restriction.

The relative autonomy acquired by the two militant groups also explains their continued role in Pakistan's foreign policy. Having been created and supported by intelligence agencies, both Lashkar and Jaish Muhammad are emerging as rather autonomous actors within Pakistan. This autonomy was apparent soon after the terrorist attacks on the United States in September 2001.

As the Pakistan Government shelved its Afghan policy of the 1990s and joined the US coalition against terrorism, Jaish Muhammad increased its references to the United States as the main enemy of the Muslims. The frequency of these references further increased after

Washington declared Jaish Muhammad to be a terrorist organisation. Commenting on the decision in an editorial, Maulana Masood Azhar maintained that Jaish's designation as a terrorist organisation by Washington was 'a medal' for the group. It was proof that Allah's enemies were worried by Jaish's activities, and that Indian authorities had sought US help to confront an organisation that had been in operation for only eighteen months. Identifying links between the American global strategy and developments within Pakistan, he said: 'It is possible that Pakistan's brave and honourable leaders would claim to be helpless, or would take tough measures [against Jaish Muhammad]. We are not worried. If they [the Pakistan Government] harass mujahideen, they will not be spared by mujahideen's Allah.' The editorial ended with a warning for Islamabad: 'We hope that our leaders would not stop this holy task [of Jihad] and would not incur the wrath of Allah. Jaish's message and mission is absolutely clear. But if Jaish is harassed, it would take a stand and fully resist [the Pakistan Government].' [26] That Jaish was able to implement these threats became apparent after President Musharraf formally banned the group on 12 January 2002. Within a few months, it recreated itself under a new name, Khuddam-ul-Islam (Servants of Islam). By late 2003, one of its members claimed: 'We are still doing our work'.[27] The group was once again targeted by the Pakistan Government in November–December 2003 as part of its efforts to rein in militants.[28]

Lashkar-e-Toiba was equally vehement in its criticism of the United States and its war on Afghanistan. It maintained that the Taliban regime was being unfairly accused of harbouring terrorists, and that Osama bin Laden was not a terrorist. An Ulama Convention held at Muridke on 31 October 2001 declared that the US attacks on Afghanistan were tantamount to US attacks on Islam, and equated 'American aggression with the crusade of a new century'. The convention categorically rejected the Pakistan Government's policy of cooperating with the United States and identified it as against the 'religious and national interests'.[29] As in the case of Jaish, Lashkar-e-Toiba members also began to warn the Pakistan Government of the consequences of siding with the United States. They were, however, careful to use more moderate language than Jaish Muhammad: President Musharraf's regime was portrayed as misguided and one that failed to appreciate that Pakistan was the 'real target' of American policies in the region. Instead of threatening this regime with 'retaliation', Lashkar-e-Toiba limited itself to suggesting that 'those co-operating with non-Muslims to subjugate Muslims in Afghanistan, Chechnya, Palestine, and Indonesia need to reflect upon their actions and decide if they want to face the fires of hell or earn a place in the heaven'.[30] More importantly, as President Musharraf was assuring Washington of his regime's commitment to rein in the militants,

Lashkar-e-Toiba continued to publish a list of its campaigns in the Indian part of Kashmir as evidence of its independence.[31] The reluctance to compromise on the question of Jihad in Kashmir persisted, even as the Pakistan Government provided assurances to Washington that Lashkar-e-Toiba and related groups would not be allowed to infiltrate into India and initiated a dialogue with New Delhi on issues affecting Indo-Pakistan relations.

The US invasion of Iraq in March 2003 and subsequent events have further reinforced the view among the two groups that they need to continue their struggle against the United States. Lashkar-e-Toiba, while operating as Jamaat-ud-Dawa in Pakistan, has engaged in a process of rereading history in its bid to emphasise the need for struggle against Washington. Within a few months of the US attack on Iraq, for instance, it published a book that presented Saddam Hussein as a Muslim leader who had played a significant role in promoting Islam. The US portrayal of Saddam as a threat was shown as indicative of anti-Muslim global strategy. Faced with such a perceived threat, members of Lashkar-e-Toiba have articulated their commitment to continuing the struggle against the United States and its regional allies. Jaish Muhammad has expressed similar views. However, just as in the immediate aftermath of the US attack on Afghanistan, it has adopted a more critical attitude towards not just the US Government but also its local allies. In an editorial for *Binat-e-Aisha* in November 2003, for instance, Masood Azhar drew parallels between Qadianis (a group declared non-Muslim by the Pakistani Government in the 1980s) and the policies of the present Pakistani regime. He suggested that Islamabad's decision to provide the US with bases against the Taliban, and its apparent willingness to send troops to Iraq instead of condemning US policies were reminiscent of the ideas propagated by the founder of the Ahmadi sect, Mirza Ahmed. Implied in this criticism was the suggestion that by joining hands with Washington, the Pakistani regime had exited the fold of Islam as well.

These articulations of the US threat and public attacks/comments on the policies of the Pakistan Government suggest that the two groups created by sections of Pakistan's decision-making circles are no longer *totally* under the control of the government. They have emerged as autonomous actors with a capability to question and adopt their own policies on issues they consider important. The Pakistan Government, therefore, is facing a situation where, while participating in a coalition against terrorism, it cannot guarantee that groups created by it will not participate in terrorist activities.

PAKISTAN AND MILITANCY

What implications does the autonomy acquired by the two militant groups have for Pakistan's foreign policy?

The answer to this question is less than promising. At the global level, their relative autonomy undermines Pakistan's participation in the war on terrorism. Given their sympathies and shared experience with members of al-Qaeda, members of these groups can be safely expected to adopt a policy not necessarily favoured by Islamabad. The increased emphasis accorded by these groups to the links between global, regional and local scenarios lends credence to such an assessment. In fact, Jaish Muhammad is believed by Pakistan authorities to have been involved in the bombings in Karachi in 2002.[32]

At the regional level, their operations during 2002 and 2003 suggest that they can continue to limit Pakistan's ability to improve links with India. While Islamabad is engaged in improving people-to-people relations and has agreed to negotiate with New Delhi on a host of issues, including Kashmir, members of these groups may undermine the process by engaging in terrorist activities in India.

An equally significant threat exists at the local level. Given their views on the links between the global and the local, these groups (particularly Jaish Muhammad) have been promoting their Jihadi ideology inside Pakistan as well. Jaish has been implicated in the attack on President Musharraf in December 2003.[33] In the long term, it can be argued, the relationship between the Islamic militants and the Pakistan Government may come to resemble the relationship between Washington and the Afghan mujahideen of the 1980s. The erstwhile supporters may become the targets of an ideology of Jihad by those they once supported.

ACKNOWLEDGMENTS: I wish to acknowledge and thank my dear mother, Begum Sarfraz Iqbal, for her help with research on this topic. She provided her assistance with a smile and without showing strains of the heart condition that took her life before the work was finished. May her soul rest in peace. Thanks are also due to my husband James Trevelyan and his family for their support, and to Wendy Chew for her assistance in finalising the chapter.

NOTES

1   For basic information on ASSP, see Musa Khan Jalalzai, *Sectarianism and Ethnic Violence in Pakistan* (Lahore: Izharsons, 1996), pp. 221–24.

2   For details of a number of other groups created during the Zia period and in the early 1990s, see Musa Khan Jalalzai, *Sectarianism and Ethnic Violence in Pakistan.*

3   Samina Yasmeen, 'Pakistan and the struggle for "real" Islam', in Shahram Akbarzadeh and Abdullah Saeed (eds), *Islam and Political Legitimacy* (Routledge, New York, 2003), pp. 70–87.

4   *Patterns of Global Terrorism – 2001*, United States Department of State, May 2002, p. 99; Mohammad Aamir Raana, *Jihad Aur Jihadi: Pakistan Aur Kashmir key Aham Jihadi Rahnamaoon ka Ta'arif [Jihad and Jihadis: Introduction to Significant Jihadi Leaders of Pakistan and Kashmir]* (Lahore: Mashal, 2003), p. 21.

5   Abu Musa, 'Al-Mahdal-Aala-ud-Dawa-tal-Islamia: Ta'arif, Sargarmian, Nizam-e-

Ta'lim au Tarbiyat' [Al-Mahdal-Aala-ud-Dawa-tal-Islamia: introduction, educational and training programs], *Mujalla-tud-Dawa*, January 2001, pp. 59–62.

6 Mohammad Aamir Raana, *Jihad-e-Kashmir Au Afghanistan [Jihad in Kashmir and Afghanistan]* (Lahore: Mashal, 2002), p. 237.

7 Dr Manzoor Ahmad, 'Mujahedeen-e-Lashkar-e-Toiba: Mah au Saal key Aaenay Mein' [Mujahedeen of Lashkar-e-Toiba: through months and years], *Mujalla-tud-Dawa*, February 2001), p. 20.

8 ——, 'Mujahedeen-e-Lashkar-e-Toiba: Mah au Saal key Aaenay Mein', p. 19

9 Mohammad Aamir Raana, *Jihad-e-Kashmir Au Afghanistan*, p. 32.

10 ——, *Jihad-e-Kashmir Au Afghanistan*, pp. 153–54.

11 ——, *Jihad-e-Kashmir Au Afghanistan*, p. 32. According to this information, until 2001 only 41 martyrs were of non-Pakistani and Kashmiri origin.

12 The information in this paragraph is based upon the information in Mohammad Aamir Raana, *Jihad-e-Kashmir Au Afghanistan*, pp. 140–60.

13 See, for example, Maulana Mohammad Masood Azhar, *Khutbat-e-Jihad [Lectures on Jihad]*, Vol. 2 (Karachi: Maktaba Hassan, 2001), p. 70.

14 Sura 25: 52.

15 See, for example, Abu Saad Ehsan Allah Shahbaz, 'Jahedum bey Jihada Kabira ka maani au mafhum' [The meaning of Jihad and Greater Jihad]', *Mujalla-tud-Dawa*, January 2001, pp. 18–19.

16 See, for example, Hafiz Abdur Rahman Maki, 'Fidai Hamlay Qaroon-e-Aula sey Tasalsil key saath Sabit hein' [Fidai attacks have continued since early days], *Mujalla-tud-Dawa*, May 2001, pp. 9–16.

17 Maulana Mohammad Masood Azhar, *Khutbat-e-Jihad*, Vol. 2, pp. 38–59.

18 See, for example, Umm Hammad, *Hum Maein Lashkar-e-Toiba Ki [We the Mothers of Lashkar-e-Toiba]*, Vol. 2 (Lahore: Darul-Andulus, 2003).

19 See, for instance, the portrayal of Prophet Mohammad's Aunt Safia bint Abdul Mutlab, which identifies her as the first Muslim woman to kill a non-believer. Bint Syed Fayyaz Hussain, 'Syeda Safia bint Abdul Mutlab', *Binat-e-Aisha*, December 2003, pp. 11–13.

20 See, for example, Maulana Masood Azhar, *Khutbat-e-Jihad [Lectures on Jihad]*, Vol.1 (Karachi: Maktaba Hassan, 2001), pp. 19–45.

21 Abu Ahmed, 'Indonesia: Aik Hazar Muslamanoon ka Isa'I Zalmon key Haathon Qatal-e-Aam' [Indonesia: open massacre of one thousand Muslims by Christians], *Mujalla-tud-Dawa*, March 2001, p. 27.

22 From personal interviews in Pakistan.

23 Based on personal interviews with officials and analysts in India and the United States in January and March 2003.

24 Mohammad Aamir Raana, *Jihad-e-Kashmir Au Afghanistan*, pp. 156, 254.

25 'Lashkar moves offices to valley', *Dawn*, 25 December 2001.

26 Mohammad Masood Azhar, 'Jaish key le'ay Tamgha' [A medal for the Jaish], *Jaish Muhammad*, Vol. 2, No. 15 (November 2001), pp. 5–7.

27 'The blackmailer vs the terrorist', *Daily Mail*, Internet Edition, 7 October 2003, <http://dailymailnews.com/200310/07/column.html>.

28 'Offices of banned outfits sealed', *The News*, Internet Edition, 5 December 2003, <http://www.jang.com.pk/thenews/dec2003-daily/05-12-2003/main/main9.htm>.

29 'Ulama Karam Masajid se Jihadi Qafelay Rawana karein' [Ulama should send Jihadi caravans from mosques], *Mujalla-tud-Dawa*, November 2001, p. 27.

30 'Jis ney ham [Muslamoon] per hathiyar utha'ya who hum mein sey nahein' [The

one who used weapons against [other Muslims] is not one of us], *Mujalla-tud-Dawa*, Vol. 13, No. 8 (August 2002), inside front cover.

31 See, for example, Dr Manzoor, 'Mujahedeen Kashmir ney 141 dehshat gard Bharati Faujion ko paar kar deya' [Mujahideen of Kashmir killed 141 Indian terrorist soldiers], *Mujalla-tud-Dawa*, August 2002, pp. 5–8.

32 Tim McGirk, 'The monster within', *Time*, 26 January 2004, available online at <http://www.hvk.org/articles/0104/123.html>.

33 ——, 'The monster within'.

5

ISLAMIC RELIGIOUS EDUCATION AND THE DEBATE ON ITS REFORM POST–SEPTEMBER 11

ABDULLAH SAEED

A significant problem with the current debate on the reform of Islamic religious education is that it gives no clear definition of Islamic religious education. Indeed, the long history and the number of models of Islamic religious education make definition virtually impossible. Despite this complexity, many commentators, particularly Western, discuss Islamic religious education using simplistic assertions and negative generalisations. Furthermore, in the eyes of many Western commentators, all Islamic religious educational systems and institutions seem to be virtually identical. Post–September 11, these commentators argue that reform of Islamic religious education has become imperative, as it is perhaps the most important source of anti-Western attitudes among Muslims and is a breeding ground for terrorism and violence. This chapter opposes this simplistic notion of Islamic religious education and provides an overview of Islamic religious education and an outline of its growth and decline in the pre-modern period. This chapter also addresses the debate on reform in the modern period as well as the impact of September 11 upon that debate.

EDUCATION IN THE EARLY ISLAMIC PERIOD

In the early Islamic period, broadly speaking, there were three different strands of Islamic education. These were the juridical-theological, the philosophical-scientific, and the mystical-spiritual.[1] Of these, the earliest and most important was the juridical-theological, which began when the Qur'an was revealed to the Prophet Muhammad in the early 7th century CE. Throughout the 7th and 8th centuries, several sub-disciplines developed within this strand, including the Hadith (Sayings of the Prophet), *tafsir* (Qur'anic exegesis), *tarikh* (history), *fiqh* (law), *kalam* (theology) and related disciplines such as Arabic linguistics. During the 8th and 9th centuries CE, the translation of (mainly) Greek scientific and philosophical works into Arabic led to the burgeoning of the philosophical-scientific disciplines. Key works on mysticism began to emerge somewhat later. Major centres of learning were found in Damascus, Mecca, Medina, Cairo, Baghdad and Cordoba. In these cities, rulers and *ulama* (Islamic religious scholars) supported teaching, research and the dissemination of knowledge. Libraries were also established throughout the Muslim world and rulers competed with each other to attract great scholars to their domains. Thus, over this period Islamic civilisation contributed greatly to all aspects of knowledge.[2] This contribution ranged from the Islamic disciplines to philosophy and the natural sciences, and to literature and the arts. Between the 8th and 11th centuries CE, this great range of disciplines was included in the category of Islamic education. On the whole, it was expected that scholars would be accomplished in a broad range of disciplines, with as much emphasis being placed on breadth as on depth.

The juridical-theological disciplines, however, remained dominant in Islamic religious education up to the modern period. Even philosopher-scientists and mystical-spiritual orders could not ignore this field. In the caliphates or emirates, Islamic law was the law of the land. Practitioners of Islamic law, therefore, needed knowledge of the law, while the state required a supply of competent and well-trained judges and administrators of justice. Even within Islamic law, over time, the educational system opted for specialisation in one school of law. This was largely because, in different regions, different schools of law predominated: Hanafi in the Ottoman Empire; Maliki in areas such as North Africa and Spain; Shafi'i in Egypt and South-East Asia; Hanbali in parts of Arabia; Ja'fari in Iran.

As far as mystical-spiritual education is concerned, from the 8th and 9th centuries CE a strong current of mysticism (Sufism) emerged in the Muslim world. Later, from the 11th, 12th and 13th centuries, a number of mystical orders developed, such as Qadiriya and Naqshabandiya. The mystical orders concentrated on one specific area of education, the mystical, which varied from order to order but was essentially concerned with the training of the novice through various stages until the desired ultimate objective of 'reaching God' and spiritual purification was achieved. In the mystical system, there was little emphasis on philosophical-scientific or juridical-theological education.

The early Islamic age of great intellectual achievement began to wane in the 12th century, with an increasing tendency to give priority to 'religious' disciplines over 'non-religious' disciplines. Even before that, distinctions were made between religious and non-religious disciplines, and voices could be heard warning against the dangers of the non-religious disciplines. The formal separation of religious and non-religious disciplines, however, owes much to the famous theologian Abu Hamid al-Ghazali's (d. 1111) discussion on Islamic disciplines and how Islamic education should be structured. In Sunni Islam, Ghazali's ideas came to dominate Islamic education and its institutions, right up to the modern period. Ghazali believed that the purpose of knowledge was primarily connected to happiness in the hereafter. Because religious sciences served this purpose best, they were at the top of his hierarchy of knowledge. In Ghazali's view, the non-religious disciplines included areas of knowledge that were 'useful' and 'relevant' and others that were highly dangerous, such as metaphysics, which he saw as a threat to religion. Ghazali's systematic attack on philosophy in his well-known work *Tahafut al-Falasifa* (*The Incoherence of Philosophers*) provided the foundation for the denigration of the study of philosophy in much of the Muslim world, in particular the Muslim East. From then on, the philosophical-scientific disciplines gradually became marginal within the domain of Islamic education.[3] The fate of the philosophical-scientific disciplines can be gleaned from Ibn Khaldun's (d. 1406) comment on how such disciplines were flourishing in Christian lands in Europe: 'We learn by report that in the lands of the Franks on the north shores of the sea philosophical sciences are much in demand, their principles are being revived, the circles for teaching them are numerous, and the number of students seeking to learn them is increasing.' [4] By contrast, at the same time, Muslims on the whole, particularly in Sunni Islam, were being discouraged from studying the philosophical disciplines.

FROM INDIVIDUALS TO INSTITUTIONS

Before the establishment of foundations and formal state-supported educational institutions in the 10th and 11th centuries, the practice was for students to move from one scholar (*alim*) to another, or from one town to another, in search of education. Private teachers (not necessarily scholars) gave lessons to individual students or small groups of students at home or at mosques. These teachers played a significant role in teaching basic literacy, numeracy and the fundamentals of religion, particularly to children. Beyond that, no formal educational institutions of higher learning existed. Aspiring students had to study with an *alim* in their own town or had to travel to another town where the *alim* lived. Students would study under *ulama* who had different areas of specialist knowledge; for example, an *alim* might be well-known for his expertise in a particular book on the Hadith, or in *tafsir* or theology. This style of education continued until the establishment of educational institutions such as al-Azhar in Cairo (originally a Shi'ite-Ismaili institution established in the 10th century) and Nizamiya in Baghdad (a Sunni institution established in competition with al-Azhar).[5] These institutions were established largely to train judges, administrators of justice and other state bureaucrats. At Nizamiya, the curriculum covered areas such as *tafsir,* the Hadith and *fiqh* (the religious disciplines), as well as philosophy, logic, linguistics, medicine, mathematics and astronomy (the rational disciplines).[6]

The establishment of these two institutions saw a gradual increase in the growth and expansion of similar institutions across the Muslim world, supported by specific endowments. Students were at times encouraged with subsidies or stipends so that they were supported throughout their period of study. Without such endowments, it would have been financially impossible for many students to seek education in a foreign town. From the 13th century onwards there was a significant increase in educational institutions in the Muslim world. However, by that time, these concentrated mainly on juridical-theological education and less on philosophical-scientific areas.

The increase in the number of institutions in the educational arena was not matched by an increase in creativity and innovation in education. The juridical-theological system by then did not seem to have the capacity for innovation, creativity or original research that had existed from the 8th to the 11th centuries. Creativity gave way to mediocrity, preservation of the 'heritage', and blind imitation. This emphasis on imitation and preservation meant that scholars keen to put forward new ideas were often discouraged or ostracised. Associated with this was the adoption of uncritical rote learning, memorisation and unquestioning acceptance of authorities. The system gave a prominent place to earlier scholarship and increasingly led to suspicion of original and creative thinking. Except in rare cases, authors writing about Islamic law and theology were interested only in compiling commentary upon commentary and in summarising those commentaries in a vicious circle of doing and redoing that was devoid of any originality.[7]

Related to this was the decline in philosophical-scientific learning. The philosophical-scientific disciplines came to be viewed as not sufficiently religious for the educational institutions of Cairo, Baghdad, Damascus and other major centres of Islamic learning. In fact, fatwas were issued by several leading jurists prohibiting the teaching of philosophy because, in their view, it might lead to the corruption of faith and the questioning of the fundamentals of religion.[8] Some philosophical works were burnt, and in some cases philosophers had to flee for their lives. By the early 19th century, Islamic religious education in key centres of learning, whether Cairo, Mecca, Medina, Baghdad or Damascus, had certain characteristics in common, such as the restriction of the curriculum to religious disciplines, and reliance on memorisation and rote-learning. These institutions and their curricula remained unaffected by developments in Europe.

REFORM DEBATE IN THE MODERN PERIOD

Muslim thinkers debated educational reform from the mid-19th century. Among the first to advocate reform in the modern period was Sir Sayyid Ahmad Khan (d. 1898) in the Indian subcontinent. He saw the Islamic religious education offered in seminaries in India as backward, anti-modern and too legalistic. He wanted the institutions and seminaries to renew their curricula, pedagogy and structures in keeping with modernity. He advocated adopting Western methods of education, including secular subjects in the curriculum, learning foreign languages such as English and discarding superstitions. Ahmad Khan, like many modernists, took a positive view of Western civilisation and intellectual practices, in contrast to many other Muslims of his period, who viewed the West and Western civilisation with hostility. Modernist reformers recognised that Muslim societies were lagging behind the West in terms of intellectual, social, political and economic development. To rectify this, they asserted that there existed a great need for Muslims to learn from the West. In Egypt, Muhammad Abduh (d. 1905) also advocated the reform of Islamic religious education, with particular emphasis on the al-Azhar seminary, but he was opposed by the *ulama* of al-Azhar. Despite pressure to reform its curricula and teaching, al-Azhar resisted significant reform well into the 1960s.[9]

The debate on reform continued in the 20th century in almost all key Muslim communities. Naturally, the intensity of the debate, and the support for reform expressed by intellectuals, administrators of Islamic religious educational institutions, *ulama* and state education authorities varied from country to country, and, even within one country, from region to region and from institution to institution. The reformers saw Islamic religious educational institutions as an important part of Muslim life, at both the individual and collective levels. Graduates of these institutions played or were expected to play a significant role in society, as *ulama*, muftis, teachers of religion, imams at mosques, and community leaders. Their roles required that they be aware of and knowledgeable about the reality of the modern environment. The reformers believed that in order to achieve this objective, the religious educational institutions had to undergo significant reform in two areas: curricula and teaching methods.

In relation to the curricula, many reformers argued that the distinction between religious and non-religious disciplines should be rethought, particularly as the two had existed side by side in early Islam. Knowledge – be it religious or non-religious – was important and useful, and Muslims, it was argued, were under an obligation to acquire it (including knowledge that in the post-Ghazali period was frowned upon). Islamic educational institutions, it was further argued, should broaden their curricula with modern disciplines from the social and natural sciences as well as foreign languages. In the religious disciplines, several reformers proposed that students should study Islamic writings from all areas of Muslim intellectual output, be it law, literature, philosophy, mysticism or theology. Several reformers also believed that one of the most effective ways to open the minds of students was to expose them to critical methods of inquiry and to encourage them to understand Islam within its social, political, cultural and historical contexts. It was believed that such a course of action was bound to expose issues of permanence and change, immutability and mutability, the universal and the particular, the absolute and the relative in Islamic law, ethics, morality, institutions and world view.[10]

From the reformers' point of view, designing a curriculum to incorporate Islamic and other areas of knowledge would not itself lead to the desired change. The key strategy for improvement was a radical shift in the purpose of teaching and an overhaul of the key pillars of what was considered valid practice in teaching. Teaching was no longer to be concerned solely with the transmission of knowledge or the exposition of difficult texts, as had often been the case in the pre-modern period. The teacher was to be a facilitator of critical discussion, of the exploration of the link between an issue and its context, not seeking one correct answer but freely exploring all possible aspects of a problem.[11]

In the 20th century the debate on reform of education in general, and of Islamic religious education in particular, led to the establishment of (a) a number of 'modern' Islamic institutions of higher learning and (b) state-funded schools, in which Islamic religious education was taught alongside secular subjects.

INSTITUTIONS OF HIGHER LEARNING

One of the important developments in the wake of the debate on reform of Islamic education has been the establishment of a number of Islamic universities and the reform of existing seminaries. Some of these institutions concentrate entirely on Islamic studies; others combine Islamic studies with other disciplines; others have faculties of Islamic studies alongside secular faculties such as medicine, engineering and law.

The Islamic University of Saudi Arabia is an example of the first. It is a relatively recently established university (1961) and its focus is entirely on Islamic studies. It has five Islamic faculties: law, theology, the Qur'an, the Hadith and Arabic. This type of Islamic university adopts a classical model of Islamic studies in a modern university setting. It has a formal curriculum and modern infrastructure, and uses modern methods of teaching and assessment. A shortcoming in teaching, however, is the lack of training in critical thinking. Teaching and learning exist within an authoritative framework in which the teacher is dominant. The research process often consists merely of collecting segments of information and putting them together in an ordered but uncritical form. Students exercise caution in the selection of research topics, as anything sensitive or controversial is likely to be rejected by potential supervisors. Finally, the whole curriculum is driven largely towards producing graduates who, to a large extent, rely on memorised knowledge, with no critical evaluation of that knowledge.

The International Islamic University of Malaysia is an example of an institution that was intended to remedy the problems associated with more traditional Islamic universities. It comprises not only Islamic disciplines but also others such as medicine, engineering, science, architecture and information technology. However, there is a strong Islamic ethos in all of its faculties, and ideas related to Islamic knowledge and culture are taught throughout the university. The curricula of Islamic disciplines are considered modern, and are offered in a modern setting by staff who are expected to have both modern and traditional education and who may have spent time in universities in the West or in other Islamic countries. The traditional method of focusing on specific texts (books) has been supplanted by a focus on issues, themes and problems. The university stresses the importance of writing as a means of communication and expression. Foreign languages are taught for both research and communicative purposes. Both English and Arabic are used for instruction, even in the teaching of Islamic disciplines.[12] This university is modern in terms of its physical and academic infrastructure, curricula, teaching methods, course objectives, and its interest in relating what students study to the modern context. In a sense, the International Islamic University of Malaysia represents one of the most progressive institutions in contemporary Islamic education. However, even there – particularly in the faculty that is primarily concerned with what is called 'revealed knowledge' (Islamic studies) – teaching and learning continue to take place to some extent in an ethos of traditionalism, albeit with a degree of flexibility, freedom and creativity absent in many traditionalist Islamic universities.

A third model is represented by the reform of existing traditionalist institutions of Islamic higher learning. In Indonesia in the 1950s and 1960s, a number of institutes called Institut Agama Islam Negeri (IAIN – State Institute of Islamic Studies) were established, initially in Yogyakarta and Jakarta. In the 1960s, the IAIN system was transformed in an attempt to bring secular and religious education under one roof, with a more modern form of religious education. The purpose was to foster the development of a cohort of Muslims who had a more modern understanding of Islam and its role in a modern society and were predisposed to view modern institutions and modernisation itself in a positive light.[13]

The reform of the IAINs was guided by a particular philosophy that stressed that Islam was not incompatible with modernity, that it could provide a vision of a prosperous future, and that it fostered tolerance and religious pluralism. On the basis of this philosophy, Mukti Ali, the first minister of religious affairs entrusted with their reform, aimed to change the IAINs to modern institutions of Islamic learning whose graduates would be open-minded agents of modernisation, able to contribute towards changing the traditional outlook of many Indonesian Muslims. This entailed exposing IAIN students to various trends in Islamic thought, both classical and modern as well as orthodox and heterodox. Students and lecturers were given considerable freedom to explore and discuss ideas, even when such ideas were in conflict with traditionally accepted dogma. The less orthodox views of Ibn Arabi, the excesses of Sufism, and the theology of the rationalist thinkers of Islam, for example, were studied, lectured on, discussed and openly portrayed as acceptable. There was no censorship of this discourse and students were not criticised for expressing views that appeared to be unorthodox compared to those current in many other Islamic universities.[14]

PUBLIC SCHOOLS

In the Muslim world, private elementary schooling that focused on reading and writing, recitation of the Qur'an, and some basic skills in the local language was provided by what is known as *kuttab* (traditional non-formal elementary schools).[15] In the 20th century, Muslim states replaced these with schools with more broadly based curricula. While there are differences in the management of school education across the Muslim world, a common characteristic is the provision of a broad-based secular education, with the allocation of some periods in the week to Islamic religious education, the time allocated and content varying from country to country. Usually, the number of periods allocated to Islamic religious education is between two and four per week, but Saudi Arabia tends to give much more time to religion-related areas in its school curriculum. An important characteristic of this religious education is that it tends to emphasise a few, relatively safe, basic principles of Islam. Topics covered include: (a) how to perform the basic rituals such as the daily prayers, fasting and pilgrimage, and the formal prayers that are recited in these rituals; (b) some of the norms and values of Islam, such as the importance of honesty, truthfulness and respect for elders and parents; (c) recitation of the Qur'an and the rules associated therewith; (d) rudimentary information about the life of the Prophet; (e) and, in some countries perhaps, a little about the history of Islam and how Islam was introduced into that country. These religious education curricula omit or minimise important aspects of Islamic history, such as the conflicts that occurred among Muslims from time to time, or the notion of Jihad. Not only are the topics innocuous, but also some of the material presented appears to be irrelevant and too abstract for school students. After ten to twelve years of such instruction in the school system, perhaps the most students can expect is to memorise prayers for the daily rituals and learn some basics of Islam and some Islamic values and norms.

THE SEMINARY AS A CHALLENGE TO REFORM

While most of these developments are encouraging, the future of many Islamic seminaries where reform has not occurred remains a key concern for Muslim thinkers. These seminaries (often called *madrasa*s) vary enormously in their curricula, coverage of disciplines, methods of teaching, and attitudes to issues such as modernity and reform of Islamic law and theology. Such seminaries exist in most Muslim communities. In Pakistan, there are nearly 10 000 such schools; their number is probably close to 30 000 in both India and Indonesia (where they are called *pesantren*).[16] Some are very small with a few students, and others may have several thousand students, such as the well-known Deobandi seminary in India.[17] Some also have boarding facilities. Some teach only traditional Islamic subjects, while others combine these subjects with so-called secular subjects. Some rely on rote learning and memorisation; others encourage exploration and creativity. Some are ultra-conservative, while others are modern, progressive and liberal. By and large, most would fall into the traditionalist-conservative category. A few, in Pakistan and Indonesia, have been accused of teaching students to engage in violence.

An example of a typical seminary in Pakistan is Jamia Salafiya, in Faisalabad, an Ahle Hadith seminary. Its students enrol after finishing primary school, at around twelve years of age. Younger students join its Qur'an memorisation classes. After a minimum of eight years of study, successful students receive a certificate (equivalent to a BA in Pakistan), which allows them to become imams or religious education teachers at school level or at similar seminaries. The seminary's curriculum is traditional and is centred on some of the Islamic disciplines. During the first two years, students are introduced to the Arabic language, primarily basic grammar. Arabic is taught not necessarily for communicative purposes but to prepare students to read classical Islamic texts. Students are introduced to classical disciplines such as the Hadith, *tafsir* and theology. Some of the texts may be in Urdu, and texts in Arabic are often translated by the teachers into Urdu so that students can understand them. The focus is on mastering the set texts rather than a particular discipline. Examinations are used to test the memorisation and understanding of texts. Also ignored in this model is the link between knowledge, for example the Hadith, and its context, such as the development of the Hadith and the debates surrounding it. The curriculum is highly authoritarian, and the teacher's function is to transmit knowledge, to explain, and to convey to the students what is to be learnt and how it is to be learnt. Students are not encouraged to critically explore the issues raised in texts or in the class; their role is often limited to memorising or studying the prescribed texts.

While the Salafiya seminary introduced some reforms in the 1980s, 1990s and beyond, it is still traditional in its approach to education. However, there are far more traditionalist seminaries in Pakistan and elsewhere in the Muslim world.[18] It was primarily these seminaries that Western commentators were targeting for criticism in the post–September 11 period.

REFORM DEBATE POST–SEPTEMBER 11

Since September 11, many Western commentators have argued that traditional Islamic religious education provides Muslim militant extremists with the ideological basis for activities that are anti-Western and terrorist. The educational institutions referred to are Islamic seminaries, *madrasa*s and universities. Pakistan was singled out largely because of its diplomatic connection with the Taliban and because the Taliban harboured al-Qaeda members. Saudi Arabia's system of Islamic education was seen as subversive to a certain extent, because fifteen of the nineteen September 11 hijackers were Saudis. In the case of Saudi Arabia, the *Asia Times* wrote:

> Education has also been a lightning rod of controversy lately. Many Saudis worry that the nation's religious-based schooling inadequately prepares the young for careers in a globalised and technologically advanced world. America has also attacked the Saudi school system, accusing it of indoctrinating pupils with Islamic fundamentalism.[19]

Thomas Friedman of the *New York Times* stated more succinctly:

> Bin Laden's challenge was an attempt by the extreme Islamists to break out of their island and seize control of the secular state island. The states responded by crushing or expelling the Islamists, but without ever trying to reform the Islamic schools – called *madrasas* – or the political conditions that keep producing angry Islamist waves. So the deadly circle that produced bin Ladenism – poverty, dictatorship and religious anti-modernism, each reinforcing the other – just gets perpetuated.[20]

This view of Islamic educational institutions as sources of potential terrorists was also evident before September 11. For example, after his visit to Haqqania *madrasa* in Pakistan (which was seen to be strongly connected with the Taliban), Jeffrey Goldberg of the *New York Times* wrote: 'The Haqqania *madrasa* is, in fact, a Jihad factory. This does not make it unique in Pakistan. There are one million students studying in the country's 10000 or so *madrasa*s, and militant Islam is at the core of most of these schools.'[21]

In the aftermath of September 11, governments in both Muslim and non-Muslim countries sought to use the so-called war on terror to discredit Islamic religious educational institutions. Even in a number of Muslim majority countries, authoritarian governments sought to close a number of *madrasa*s and gain control of the *madrasa* system, an area that has traditionally remained largely beyond official reach. The opportunity provided by the war on terror to bring such *madrasa*s under the control of the state was therefore attractive. Pakistan announced sweeping reforms of its *madrasa* system and Bangladesh is exploring ways of following suit. China has utilised the opportunity to closely monitor Islamic education curricula in the troubled province of Xinjiang. In India in April 2002, the Parliamentary Standing Committee on Home Affairs sought 'strict action against religious fundamentalist institutions which have come up in the country, particularly along the India–Nepal border, with the help of Pakistan ISI for indoctrinating young minds to wage holy war against India'.[22] However, according to the Indian *Milli Gazette* editorial, 'No *madrasa* has been ever [sic] named or taken to court, no terrorist has been ever [sic] found in their premises, no texts have been found which teach terrorism'.[23]

Despite this rhetoric, there is little evidence given for a strong connection between terrorist acts by certain Muslims and Islamic religious education in general. Islamic religious education has existed for the past 1400 years in many societies and across the continents, yet on the whole its institutions do not have a record of producing terrorists. None of the Muslim extremist groups or their well-known leaders, as named by the American FBI, are graduates of Islamic religious educational institutions. This applies even to bin Laden and to Ayman al-Zawahiri of the Egyptian Jihad. The nineteen hijackers (and the twentieth, currently in prison in the US) named by the FBI as responsible for the September 11 attacks were not graduates of Islamic religious education. This is not to deny that exceptions exist. In South-East Asia, Jemaah Islamiyah, with which Abu Bakr Bashir and others accused of terrorism are associated, is closely connected with Islamic religious education. Jemaah Islamiyah runs a *madrasa* in Indonesia, but it is only one of several thousand *madrasa*s and seminaries in Indonesia, the vast majority of which have no connection to terrorism or terrorists. More importantly, there are fifty-six Muslim majority countries, all of which have Islamic religious educational institutions. Such institutions exist also in Muslim minority contexts. If Islamic religious education as such is responsible for terrorism and anti-Westernism, then we should be witnessing terrorism and anti-Westernism on a global scale. A final point is that Islamic religious educational institutions (particularly in Sunni Islam) have tended to support the status quo and not oppose political authorities, even when such authorities are autocratic, authoritarian and unjust. This is in part to do with the Sunni theological position that one should avoid creating havoc in the community.[24] Finally, most Islamic religious educational institutions provide a service by offering some form of education to the marginalised and disadvantaged in their communities. In Pakistan, for example, thousands of often marginalised students enrol in these institutions, without which they would not have access to any form of education.

In the post–September 11 environment, the debate on the reform of Islamic religious education, which began in the 19th century, has changed. For many Western commentators, reform primarily appears to mean changing the system of Islamic religious education in order to produce a generation of more West-friendly Muslims. In this view, references to violence, Jihad and intolerance towards non-Muslims and the West are to be removed from the religious education curricula, where such references exist. Presumably this is to be achieved through the coercive power of the state to force a set curriculum on the religious educational institutions. This may also mean that the state will monitor these institutions and keep them under strict control. The model appears to be authoritarian, coercive and top-down.

Predictably, this brand of reform has been severely criticised by a wide range of Muslims. Several important discussions on these developments have taken place, including on the al-Jazeera television network, which has a global audience of close to 100 million. While many of the prominent academics and scholars invited to take part in these debates had long argued for the reform of Islamic religious education, they refused to accept that the West in general and the United States in particular should or could impose on Muslims a particular brand of reform, especially in such a sensitive area as Islamic religious education. As one of the scholars who participated stated, the brand of Islam that is promoted is an Americanised Islam or a 'CIA Islam', devoid of any ability to withstand and resist injustice, oppression, persecution, neo-colonialism and neo-imperialism. The idea that a non-Muslim government or its institutions could dictate to Muslims what Islam is and what Islamic religious education should be was, in their view, tantamount to compromising Islam's independence.

While the reform of Islamic religious education is an important issue for many Muslims, they reject perceived US attempts to impose such reform upon Muslim societies. In fact, attempts by external actors to do so may in fact thwart the internal project of reform that has been developing over the last century and a half. The war on terror may well be the biggest stumbling block to the reform of Islamic religious education, as it is creating a strong feeling of vulnerability in many parts of the Muslim world. Even in the West, where Muslims have a high degree of freedom to experiment with and explore the interpretation of key Islamic texts and doctrines, it is becoming increasingly difficult for the more liberal-minded among them to advocate their views because of a defensive, conservative backlash. A sense of frustration is emerging among many progressive Muslims, which could retard any drive towards major reform of this important area. In the current climate, intellectuals, thinkers and scholars who argue for reform may also be labelled traitors, apostates or heretics by others in their communities. The voices of reform in Muslim majority countries, and in the West, could also be silenced by future geopolitical developments. Within the Muslim world there exists a sense of being targeted by the Western world, particularly given that to many Muslims the war on terror does not seem to differentiate between militant and non-militant Muslims (and the latter may include traditionalists, so-called fundamentalists, Islamists and liberal Muslims). In the current sensitive climate, even many reform-minded Muslims believe that internal attempts at reform must not be seen as the result of external pressure.

Throughout Islamic history, reform and change have been associated with a number of factors. One factor has been the degree of confidence on the part of the community, or *umma*. In times of prosperity, security, freedom, and lack of external threat, Muslims have embraced new values, institutions and ideas, as happened in the 8th, 9th and 10th centuries. In periods characterised by external threats, such as the Mongol invasion and the sacking of Baghdad in the 13th century, that confidence dissipated, as did intellectual freedom, creativity and acceptance of the 'Other' to a certain extent. Within communities struggling for survival, any talk of reform or change could be seen as too destabilising to be entertained. Even in the 20th century, the discussion of reform among Muslims often succeeded in places where there was confidence, prosperity, security and freedom. In adverse conditions, such as the current climate, societies are more likely to cling to the status quo, including in matters of religious education. If reform of Islamic religious education is to occur, and I believe it should, it must come from inside Muslim communities.

NOTES

1   For a detailed discussion of these three areas, see Francis Robinson, 'Knowledge, its transmission, and the making of Muslim societies', in Francis Robinson (ed.), *Cambridge Illustrated History: Islamic World* (Cambridge: Cambridge University Press, 1998), pp. 208–19.
2   Francis Robinson, 'Knowledge, its transmission, and the making of Muslim societies', pp. 208–49.
3   Al Tibawi, *Islamic Education: Its Traditions and Modernization into the Arab National Systems* (London: Luzac & Company Ltd, 1979), p. 44.
4   Cited in Al Tibawi, *Islamic Education*, p. 44.
5   For a discussion on how teaching took place in these institutions, see Francis Robinson, 'Knowledge, its transmission', pp. 221–22.
6   Yoginder Sikand, 'Reforming the Indian madrasas: contemporary Muslim voices', available online at <http://www.islaminterfaith.org/oct2002/article.html>.

7 Fazlur Rahman, *Islam and Modernity: Transformation of an Intellectual Tradition* (Chicago: Chicago University Press, 1982), pp. 37–39.
8 For Ghazali's views on this, see Abu Hamid al-Ghazali, *Tahafut al-Falasifah* (Beirut: Dar al-Fikr al-Lubnani, 1993).
9 In the early 20th century, it had to include subjects such as geography, sciences, and history, but these were mainly taught at the lower levels of the Azhar system (primary and secondary). In the 1960s, the Egyptian Government imposed a series of reforms on the institution, including the establishment of faculties of engineering and medicine and the introduction of law into the Faculty of Shari'a. Despite these changes, the curricula and teaching in the religious disciplines remained traditional to a large extent.
10 Abdullah Saeed, 'Towards religious tolerance through reform in Islamic education: the case of the State Institute of Islamic Studies of Indonesia', *Indonesia and the Malay World*, Vol. 27, No. 79 (1999), pp. 177–91.
11 ——, 'Towards religious tolerance through reform in Islamic education'.
12 For information about the International Islamic University, see its homepage at <http://www.iiu.edu.my/>.
13 Abdullah Saeed, 'Towards religious tolerance through reform in Islamic education'.
14 ——, 'Towards religious tolerance through reform in Islamic education'.
15 AL Tibawi, Islamic Education, p. 26.
16 Manzoor Ahmad, in his study of Indian Muslim education, estimated their number at around 30 000: see Manzoor Ahmad, *Islamic Education: Redefinitions of Aims and Methodology* (New Delhi: Genuine Publications, 2002), p. 32, cited in Yoginder Sikand, 'Reforming the Indian madrasas: contemporary Muslim voices', available online at <http://www.islaminterfaith.org/oct2002/article.html>.
17 For a history of the Deoband seminary, see Barbara D Metcalf, *Islamic Revival in British India: Deoband 1860–1900* (Princeton: Princeton University Press, 1982).
18 For a history of the syllabus and methods of teaching of the Indian *madrasa*s, see Muhammad Sharif Khan, *Education, Religion and the Modern Age* (New Delhi: Asish Publishing House, 1999), pp. 84–102. Cited in Yoginder Sikand, 'Reforming the Indian madrasas'.
19 Ian Urbina, 'Middle East rumblings in Riyadh', 8 February 2003, available online at <http://www.atimes.com/atimes/Middle_East/EB08Ak03.html>.
20 Thomas Friedman, 'Breaking the circle', *New York Times*, 16 November 2001, p. 25.
21 Jeffrey Goldberg, 'Inside Jihad U: the education of a holy warrior', *New York Times*, 25 June 2000.
22 *Kashmir Times*, 25 April 2002, cited in an editorial 'Crusade against madrasahs in India', *The Milli Gazette*, New Delhi, 23 June 2002, available online at <http://www.muslimnews.co.uk/news.php?sub=158>.
23 'Crusade against madrasahs in India'.
24 Abdullah Saeed, 'The official ulema and the religious legitimacy of the modern nation state', in Shahram Akbarzadeh and Abdullah Saeed (eds), *Islam and Political Legitimacy* (London: RoutledgeCurzon, 2003), pp. 19–20.

6
THE FUTURE
OF POLITICAL ISLAM
IN AFGHANISTAN

WILLIAM MALEY

The mixing of religion and politics carries considerable perils, and in recent times few countries have demonstrated this as powerfully as Afghanistan. The despotic and anti-modernist rule of the Taliban movement stands as a warning of where this path can lead. However, as Afghanistan is a country overwhelmingly populated by sincere Muslim believers, it would be pointless to suggest that the route to political salvation lies in an immediate embrace of secular values and institutions, which neither resonate culturally with the attitudes of the mass population, nor provide a secure basis for legitimating new political institutions. The question of what the future holds for political Islam in Afghanistan is therefore an immediate and practical one. This chapter argues that, while the experience of practical political leadership has exposed significant gaps in the political philosophies of Afghan Islamic groups, extremist Islam – although alien to the vast majority of Afghans – nonetheless has the potential to be used to draw together opponents of a more Westernised approach to politics, in much the same way as it served as an ideology of countersystemic mobilisation during the Soviet occupation of Afghanistan in the 1980s.[1] It is therefore important that moderate forces expropriate the legitimating potential of liberal Islam, before extremist Islam can be turned against them by their opponents.

This chapter is divided into four sections. The first examines the historical roles of Islam in Afghanistan, and traces some of the influences that have given Islam in Afghanistan its distinctive character. The second section examines the way in which Islam came to be politicised, in Kabul in the pre-communist era, and more generally after the Soviet invasion. It sets out some lessons from the conflict between different

Islamic groups after 1992, and highlights the transnational character of the forces that took shape or were created in the course of these events. The third section maps the key forces of political Islam that remain on the scene and identifies the factors shaping their prospects. It argues that, even though political Islam has substantially deradicalised in recent years, in order to marginalise extremist forces it is necessary to create space for those moderate Islamist forces that look to Islam as a source of moral inspiration and guidance. The fourth section offers some brief conclusions.

ISLAM IN AFGHANISTAN

Islam in Afghanistan reflects a confluence of diverse values and interests, which derive in large measure from Afghanistan's colourful history. It is by now a banal proposition that Afghanistan lies at the crossroads of historical conquest empires that have left their marks on contemporary Afghan society. The first Islamic intrusions into what is now Afghan territory came in the first century of Islam's existence, when Arab raiders made their way into the Kandahar region; the presence of a small Arab minority in Afghanistan testifies to the effects of this experience.[2] Throughout Afghanistan's history, Islam as practised on its soil has involved an arresting mixture of nostrums derived from the Qur'an and the Hadith, with local values, traditions and interests on the one hand and transnational sources of inspiration on the other. These influences have given Islam in Afghanistan a kaleidoscopic character, the sheer diversity of which can often baffle the casual observer. Pragmatic moderation can sit alongside occasional manifestations of alarming extremism.

The population of modern Afghanistan is overwhelmingly Muslim, but within it can be found much of the sectarian and ritual diversity found elsewhere in the Muslim world. The majority of the population is comprised of Sunni Muslims who follow the Hanafi School of jurisprudence. Sufi brotherhoods have significant influence in different parts of the country, with the Naqshabandiya and the Qadiriya the most important. There is also a substantial Shi'ite minority, although there are no reliable ways of estimating the exact proportion of Shi'ites in the overall population. The Shi'ites are largely drawn from two particular social groups, the Hazara and the Qizilbash, although there are Pushtun Shi'ites as well, members of the Turi tribe. The Hazaras, who have a distinctively Central Asian phenotype, have long experienced significant discrimination on ethnic and sectarian grounds,[3] and on occasion have engaged in the Shi'ite practice of *taqiya* (dissimulation of belief) in order to protect themselves from a threatened onslaught.

The sophistication of Islamic doctrine and practice in Afghanistan varies markedly across different strata of society. At the top,

Afghanistan has been exposed to some of the most potent tendencies in the wider Muslim world. The arguments of famous reformers such as Sayyid Jamaluddin Afghani (1839–97) and Muhammad Abduh (1849–1905)[4] had an impact on Afghan circles in the early years of the 20th century, not least through the influence of the Afghan journalist and intellectual Mahmoud Tarzi, some of whose followers came to be known as the Young Afghans. These circles were also inspired by the modernisation programs of secularists such as Mustafa Kemal Ataturk. In more recent times, the attitudes of Egyptian Muslim Brotherhood writers such as Hassan al-Banna (1906–49) and Sayyid Qutb (1906–66), as well as the Pakistani Maulana Maududi (1903–79) proved influential in shaping fundamental critiques of the character and functioning of the Afghan state, both before and after the communist coup of April 1978. At the base of society, in the villages where the bulk of the Afghan population live, the ideas of these figures had scarcely any impact. There, village Islam predominated – an interesting mix of conservative social values and startling pragmatism, with great emphasis on ritual but little on theology. The rhythm of village Islam is well captured by a comment made by an elder and recorded by Willem Vogelsang: 'One half of the Koran is fine, the other half we write ourselves'.[5]

While Islam does not have a clergy in the strict sense of the term, in Afghanistan there has always been a collectivity of religious notables whose socialisation and training merit some attention. Here, one of the most important influences was the famous Dar al-Ulum *madrasa* at Deoband in British India,[6] whose vice-chancellor visited Kabul in 1933 to congratulate the new King Zahir Shah on his ascent to the throne, and which produced over a hundred Afghan graduates.[7] Deobandi doctrine is conservative, and while open to mystical Sufi traditions, forthrightly opposes innovation (*bid'at*) in matters of religion. The influence of Deoband was not just felt directly by those who travelled to India to study; it was also manifested in the attitudes of the Afghan *ulama* who fell under the sway of Deobandi ideas, although the *ulama* of modern Deoband would hardly recognise what has been done by some of their followers.[8] The mechanism for transmission of these ideas was typically the private *madrasa*. In the state-funded sector, especially following the establishment of the Faculty of Shari'a at Kabul University in 1952, different influences were felt. The Faculty of Shari'a enjoyed support from al-Azhar University in Cairo, and the consequence was 'a shift in spiritual inspiration from the Subcontinent to the Arab world'.[9]

This was to set the scene for religious mobilisation two decades later, but, to put this in context, it is important to note that from time to time religion had played a major role in political mobilisation in Afghanistan's past. Notable examples were the Roshani movement amongst the Pushtuns in the 1500s, led by Bayezid Ansari, and the mujahideen movement of Sayed Ahmad Barelvi in the early 19th century; in each of these cases, a charismatic leader used religious symbols to mobilise the masses. Religious leaders could be a potent force. This is one reason why Amir Abdul Rahman Khan, who ruled from 1880 to 1901, moved to constrain what could loosely be called the religious establishment. Fearing contamination from abroad, he mounted a systematic campaign against the ideas of the ultra-conservative Sheikh Muhammad ibn Abdul Wahhab and his followers.[10] He also moved to weaken the economic base of religious notables by nationalising religious endowments (*awqaf*), which had provided a substantial foundation for the *ulama* to function as an autonomous force.[11] This proved sufficient for his purposes, but it did not undermine the religious establishment completely, and in 1928 it mobilised to procure the ouster of his grandson Amanullah, whose tenure as a reforming monarch (1919–29) was terminated by a revolt supported by religious forces.[12] The *ulama* still had muscles to flex when they chose.

THE POLITICISATION OF ISLAM IN AFGHANISTAN

Discussing the politicisation of Islam in Afghanistan leads one down the tricky path of defining political Islam. This is a much more challenging exercise than one might first think. It was in Afghanistan, with the mobilisation of Muslim groups against the Soviet occupiers following the Soviet invasion of Afghanistan in December 1979, that this issue first came into sharp focus, and here the lead was taken by the French scholar Olivier Roy, who used the term *islamiste*, rendered into English as Islamist, to describe a particular ideological or philosophical agenda of a particular group. 'The Islamists', he argued, 'are intellectuals, the product of modernist enclaves within traditional society'. Islamist thought 'has developed from contact with the great Western ideologies, which they see as holding the key to the West's technical development. For them, the problem is to develop a modern political ideology based on Islam, which they see as the only way to come to terms with the modern world and the best means of confronting foreign imperialism'.[13] Given this context, it is not surprising that Islamist scholars have confronted, from an Islamic perspective, some of the same issues that have preoccupied Western political theory, such as the appropriate roles of the state, and the means by which political power can be legitimated. If Islamism as a concept runs into difficulty, it is because of its breadth. In a recent study, Graham Fuller defines an Islamist as someone who believes 'that Islam as a body of faith has something important to say about how politics and society should be ordered in the contemporary Muslim world and who seeks to implement this idea in some fashion'.[14] Unfortunately, this blurs a crucial distinction between the *different* 'fashions' in which ideas can be implemented. Some Islamists do not see any limits to what can legitimately be done to bring about their model of a good society; others do. This distinction mirrors the one drawn by Robert Nozick between different forms of utopianism,[15] and is vital if one is not to tar different individuals with the same brush.

This is not just a matter of academic interest, but can have troubling practical consequences. In 1995, the columnist and pamphleteer Daniel Pipes wrote an article in the widely read journal, *The National Interest*, in which he identified pre-Taliban Afghanistan as one of a number of 'fundamentalist regimes', and called on the West to 'pressure fundamentalist states', of which he bizarrely identified Afghanistan as one, 'to reduce their aggressiveness'.[16] This indiscriminate criticism of the forces led by Ahmad Shah Massoud, which for years has been under assault from extremists, spoke very poorly of his understanding of the Afghanistan situation. It could only have comforted the Taliban movement and their Pakistani backers, who were eagerly seeking US support. Indeed, many young Americans might have lost their lives in late 2001 if those attacked by Pipes as 'fundamentalists' had not been on hand to join the US in Operation 'Enduring Freedom'. Pipes's error was to conclude that all political Islam in Afghanistan was fundamentalist and therefore to be opposed. This approach had much in common with the cruder variants of Marxist theory, which claimed to offer decisive 'scientific' insights into social realities, obviating the need for any serious fieldwork.

None of this is to suggest that there are not dangerous men in the realm of political Islam. It is all too obvious that there are.[17] Islamists can be as uncompromising as extremists from any tradition. Islamic groups can exhibit the absolute truth claims, blind obedience, sense of ideal time, conviction that the end justifies the means, and commitment to holy war that Charles Kimball plausibly argues mark the point when religion becomes evil.[18] Nevertheless, between these groups (Islamist extremists) on the one hand, and those Muslims who effectively accept the separation of religion and state (Muslim secularists) on the other hand, can be found figures who wish to see Islamic values and traditions shape the state and politics, but recognise that that there are limits to what can legitimately be done to bring this about (Islamist moderates). Within each of these categories, of course, more complex sub-categories can also be found.

These different tendencies could be observed in the Islamic movement in Afghanistan in the 1960s and 1970s. On the one hand, it was a movement of intellectuals, with Roy dating the establishment of the movement to 1958.[19] Key figures were Ghulam Muhammad Niazi, Sayed Musa Tawana, Burhanuddin Rabbani and the journalist Minhajuddin Gahez. On the other hand, students became heavily involved: Kabul University and the Kabul Polytechnic Institute were hotbeds of political debate and ferment in the late 1960s. The organisational manifestation was the Afghan Muslim Youth Organisation (Sazman-e Jawanan-e Musulman-e Afghanistan), which involved such figures as Ahmad Shah Massoud, Gulbuddin Hekmatyar, and Engineer Muhammad Eshaq. Overall leadership fell to Niazi (until 1972) and Rabbani thereafter. Following the successful coup mounted in July 1973 by former prime minister Muhammad Daoud against his cousin Zahir Shah, the bulk of the Islamists fled the country, rightly fearing the influence of the communist *Parcham* faction within the new regime. An attempt to stage an uprising against the regime in 1975 proved an abject failure, and the Islamist movement split shortly thereafter,[20] with Rabbani heading a more moderate wing known as the Islamic Society (Jamiat-e Islami) and Hekmatyar a radical group, the Party of Islam (Hizb-e Islami). Rabbani's approach was more inclusive and gradualist. Hekmatyar's approach had much in common with that defended by Lenin in his notorious essay *Chto delat'?* ('What is to be done?'), in that he embraced the anathematisation of opponents as 'unbelievers' (*kuffar*), and demanded unswerving loyalty from his followers.[21] There was also an ethnic dimension to this, although neither grouping sought to highlight it. Hekmatyar was a Khurrati Pushtun from Baghlan, whereas Rabbani was a Badakhshi Tajik, whose views and strategy were congenial not only to fellow Badakhshis, but also to key Panjsheri Tajiks such as Massoud.

The communist coup of April 1978 and the Soviet invasion of Afghanistan in 1979 provided an opening for some of these figures to play crucial roles in the politics of their country. Islam provided a natural ideological foundation for the mobilisation of opposition to communist power,[22] and figures such as Rabbani, Massoud and Hekmatyar came to play prominent roles. The Afghan resistance, known collectively by the title mujahideen, was a complex phenomenon, linking grassroots fighters, local communities and political activists, some of whom were in exile in Pakistan.[23] Key Sunni parties included the Jamiat and the Hizb; an offshoot of the Hizb that took the same name but was led by Mawlawi Muhammad Younos Khalis; a small Saudi-backed party, the Ittehad-e Islami (Islamic Unity) led by Abdul Rab al-Rasoul Sayyaf; and three parties that came to be labelled 'traditionalist' and that were largely drawn from the Pushtun ethnic group – the Mahaz-e Milli-i Islami Afghanistan (National Islamic Front of Afghanistan), led by Pir Sayid Ahmad Gailani, a prominent Sufi; the Jabha-i Milli-i Nijat-e Afghanistan (National Salvation Front of Afghanistan), headed by Sebghatullah Mojadiddi, another very prominent Sufi; and the Harakat-e Inqilab-e Islami Afghanistan (Movement for Islamic Revolution in Afghanistan), led by Mawlawi Muhammad Nabi Muhammadi, who drew support from Deobandi *ulama* trained in private *madrasa*s. The Shi'ites were not attracted to these parties, and gravitated towards other bodies. These included, amongst Hazaras, the Shura-i Ettefaq (Council of Unity) of Ayatullah Beheshti, the Sazman-e Nasr (Organisation for Victory) of Abdul Ali Mazari, and Sheikh Muhammad Akbari's Sepah-i Pasdaran (The Guardian Army); and amongst Qizilbash the Harakat-e Islami of Asif Mohseni.[24] The Shi'ite parties were quite heavily influenced by Iran,[25] which in 1990 succeeded in drawing them into the Hizb-e Wahdat (Party of Unity), although Sheikh Mohseni's party soon reasserted its independence. Just as Iran influenced these parties, Pakistan, as host to Sunni parties and millions of Afghan refugees, sought also to choose favourites, and the party that won the bulk of its backing was Hekmatyar's Hizb , which had long had integral ties to Pakistan's Inter-Services Intelligence (ISI) directorate. Hekmatyar also worked closely with Arab volunteers who drifted towards Afghanistan with the tacit approval of their own governments, who were often glad to see the back of them.[26] One of these was Osama bin Laden, who ran a guesthouse for Arab supporters called the Beit al-Ansar (House of Volunteers) and formed close ties with Hekmatyar and Sayyaf.[27]

The mujahideen were never a united force, and some of the divisions amongst them were severe. The worst schism was that between Ahmad Shah Massoud and Hekmatyar. When the communist regime collapsed in 1992, Hekmatyar's official spokesman candidly remarked that 'Hekmatyar can't agree to anything that includes Ahmed Shah Massoud'.[28] This schism was partly grounded in personality differences. Both men were charismatic figures, but while Massoud was an energetic figure who prided himself on remaining in the field with his troops and the communities who supported him, Hekmatyar was a cold and controlled leader who based himself in Peshawar in Pakistan, invariably surrounded by circles of bodyguards. The schism also reflected their different ethnic origins, but fundamentally it was a result of the gulf between their visions for a future Islamic Afghanistan. Hekmatyar's approach was essentially totalitarian, with the Hizb under Hekmatyar aiming to occupy the commanding heights of the political system. He was also viscerally anti-Western. Massoud was committed to a more consultative and participatory system, and did not share Hekmatyar's hostility to the West.

Not that Massoud had much opportunity to show his colours. The collapse of the communist regime in 1992 did not simply involve the collapse of a government; it exposed the collapse of the state as well. Thus, when Massoud occupied Kabul, at the request of the new head of state, Sebghatullah Mojadiddi, he took over the symbols of state power but not functioning state mechanisms; the same applied to Rabbani when he became president of the Islamic State of Afghanistan in June 1992, a position he was formally to occupy (in and out of

Kabul) until December 2001. Almost immediately, Kabul came under vicious rocket attack from the Hizb-e Islami, and nothing approaching 'normal' government, let alone distinctively Islamic government, was to feature in the years that followed.[29] Rather, more moderate Islamists found themselves metaphorically stabbed in the back by Islamist extremism.

Hekmatyar was strongly backed by Pakistan in his spoiling endeavours, but proved spectacularly incapable of securing mass popular support or holding and retaining significant tracts of territory. This was the context of the move, orchestrated by Pakistan's interior minister at the time, Major-General Nasseerullah Babar, to promote a new militia, the Taliban, as a device for furthering Pakistan's interests. In time, this amounted to a 'creeping invasion' of Afghanistan.[30] It also came to pose a significant danger for Pakistan,[31] as became clear on 11 September 2001. The Taliban were not a natural outgrowth of Afghan society, but a pathogenic force, in which a distorted version of Deobandi doctrine was propagated by socially disturbed combatants whose credentials as Islamic thinkers were virtually non-existent.[32] They succeeded in seizing Kandahar in 1994, Herat in 1995 and Kabul in 1996, but outside the Pushtun ethnic group their support was wafer-thin, and given their antediluvian social policies, especially towards women, they proved incapable of securing international recognition.[33] As time passed, their unsophisticated leadership, headed by Mullah Muhammad Omar, increasingly fell under the influence of Osama bin Laden – ironically himself a kind of modernist[34] – and his al-Qaeda associates, who were credibly implicated in the bombing of US embassies in Kenya and Tanzania in August 1998, and whose presence in Afghanistan made the Taliban regime even more distasteful to the wider world. The influence of foreign extremists seems to have played a significant role in driving the Taliban's own acts of extremism, such as the massacre of the Shi'ites in Mazar-e Sharif in August 1998 and destruction of the great Buddhas of Bamiyan in March 2001. Millions of Afghan Muslims breathed a sigh of relief in late 2001 when the Taliban regime was smashed into fragments.

ISLAMIC FORCES
IN CONTEMPORARY AFGHANISTAN

Political Islam in Afghanistan has been substantially deradicalised in recent years. In the light of the bitter struggles of 1992–96 and the experience of Taliban rule, there is very little evidence that ordinary Afghans believe that political Islam offers a key to solving Afghanistan's complex problems. There are several good reasons why this disillusionment was to be expected. First, the political theories of the Islamists were in a fundamental sense underdeveloped, since they provided a circular explanation of how an Islamic state would arise. As Olivier Roy has written, 'for the Islamists, Islamic society exists only through politics, but the political institutions function only as a result of the virtue of those who run them, a virtue that can become widespread only if the society is Islamic beforehand. It is a vicious circle'.[35] Second, in practice the motivations of Islamist political actors could be crudely opportunistic rather than high-minded,[36] although it would be unfair to paint all Islamists in so unwholesome a light. Talk of building an Islamic *state* is not a particularly salient feature of mainstream Afghan political rhetoric, and while the Afghan constitution-drafting process culminated in the adoption in January 2004 of a new constitution which provided, in article 3, that 'no law can be contrary to the beliefs and provisions of the sacred religion of Islam',[37] it drew for the most part on Western rather than Islamic analogues for its specific details.

Islam is thus not lodged at the heart of the politics of transition in Afghanistan. The basic framework for the post-Taliban political transition was provided by the 5 December 2001 Bonn Agreement, negotiated in Germany by non-Taliban Afghan forces under the auspices of the UN Secretary-General's Special Representative for Afghanistan, Lakhdar Brahimi. The text of the Bonn Agreement was hardly infused with religious references. It did, however, express appreciation to 'the Afghan mujahidin who, over the years, have defended the independence, territorial integrity and national unity of the country and have played a major role in the struggle against terrorism and oppression, and whose sacrifice has now made them both heroes of Jihad and champions of peace, stability and reconstruction of their beloved homeland, Afghanistan', and to 'His Excellency Professor Burhanuddin Rabbani for his readiness to transfer power to an interim authority which is to be established pursuant to this agreement'.[38]

The dominant figures in the interim and transitional administrations established pursuant to the Bonn Agreement were all Muslims, but of very different stripes. Hamed Karzai, the compromise candidate who emerged as president, was a Muslim moderate, formerly the spokesman for Sebghatullah Mojadiddi, whose selection owed more to his status as a Durrani Pushtun than to his religious attachments. The key economic policy makers, Finance Minister Dr Ashraf Ghani and Central Bank Governor Dr Anwar-ul-haq Ahady, were Western-educated technocrats who owed their positions to their expertise. Defence Minister Muhammad Qasim Fahim and his key associates, while marked by long-standing connections to Rabbani's Jamiat, were widely perceived as intent upon defending political interests – namely the claim of former mujahideen opponents of the Soviets and the Taliban to exercise a dominant position in the political system – rather than religious doctrine. Pushtun critics of Fahim painted this agenda as an ethnic one, aimed at marginalising Pushtuns because of their past toleration of the Pushtun Taliban,[39] but rarely offered any religious interpretation of these differences, since Fahim, like most Pushtuns, was a Sunni Muslim.

The forces that more strongly merited the label Islamist were formally outside the Afghan Transitional Administration. (They were virtually all Sunni Muslims, for Shi'ite political mobilisation suffered significant setbacks in the 1990s.) The most prominent of those not directly opposed to the transitional administration was former president Rabbani, who relinquished office in a statesmanlike fashion in 2001. He remains a prominent political figure, sometimes mentioned as a future candidate for elected leadership, and would have a good chance of winning some kind of parliamentary seat. Rabbani was and is more of a scholar than a political organiser. As a young man, he studied at al-Azhar University in Cairo, and wrote a thesis criticising the rationalism of the Murtazalite sect; he also translated into Persian some of the key writings of Sayyid Qutb. Despite affiliations to the Muslim Brotherhood, however, Rabbani supported the US troop deployment in Saudi Arabia following Iraq's invasion of Kuwait in August of 1990, and that set him firmly apart from Hekmatyar and bin Laden. His following is largely personal: he distanced himself from the Jamiat bureaucracy upon becoming president, and is now a notable figure rather than party leader. Some of his followers have recently been accused of thuggish efforts to intimidate political opponents,[40] but there is no evidence linking him directly to their actions. His main weakness is occasional acute lack of political judgment: in 1992, he accurately described Hekmatyar as 'a dangerous terrorist who should be expelled from Afghanistan',[41] but in 1993 gave in to Pakistani pressure and signed a power-sharing agreement with him.[42] This came to naught because Hekmatyar preferred to retain the role of spoiler, but in 1996 Rabbani erred again by offering him the prime ministership, and Hekmatyar's acceptance of the offer seriously undermined Rabbani's legitimacy.[43]

A different kind of Islamist, and one much more extremist in orientation, is Abdul Rab al-Rasoul Sayyaf. A junior colleague of Rabbani's in the Shari'a Faculty at Kabul University – Rabbani held the rank of *pohand* (professor), whereas Sayyaf was a *pohanmal* (associate professor) – he had studied in Saudi Arabia and spoke excellent Arabic. A relative of the communist dictator Hafizullah Amin who was overthrown by the Soviets in 1979, he enjoyed very little support in Afghanistan during the 1980s but was sustained by Saudi financial backing. He was also accepted by some of Rabbani's associates not simply as an Islamist former colleague, but as an ethnic Pushtun; his attachment to Rabbani from 1992 was sometimes cited by those who wished to challenge the claim that Rabbani headed a Tajik administration. However, his ideological orientation (which many observers characterised as Wahhabi) was manifested in hostility to both Sufism and to Afghanistan's Shi'ites. His Ittehad-e Islami militia was credibly implicated in hideous atrocities against Hazaras in Kabul, most notably the Afshar massacre in February 1993,[44] and it is no wonder that many Shi'ites were filled with horror when they saw Sayyaf sitting in the front row of participants at the Emergency Loya Jirga in Kabul in June 2002, and playing a prominent role at the Constitutional Loya Jirga in December 2003–January 2004. Reports in 2003 point to Sayyaf's militia resuming the kind of intimidation of the Shi'ites for which it earlier had become notorious, especially near Paghman.[45] Given the scale and regularity of these abuses, it is hard to see how Sayyaf himself could escape all responsibility. The kind of extremism that Sayyaf represents is inconsistent with any kind of pluralistic politics or social life based on tolerance of diverse opinions.

In this respect, Sayyaf is not *ideologically* remote from some of those who have firmly positioned themselves to oppose the transitional process – notably Gulbuddin Hekmatyar, who after being expelled from Iran in 2002 resumed a career of spoiling, and fragments of the Taliban who continue to undertake military operations against US forces, the International Security Assistance Force (ISAF) and Western aid workers, using the borderlands of Pakistan as an operating base, quite possibly with ISI approval. These forces could be dangerous in the long run. Their objectives are to harass Westerners in the hope of inducing Western powers to exit Afghanistan before the Western-backed Afghan forces are strong enough to survive a concerted campaign to undermine them; and to strike if possible at key regime figures (such as Hamed Karzai, who narrowly survived an assassination attempt in Kandahar in September 2002). Using religious rhetoric to justify attacks on Western forces is part of their strategy, and an issue that supporters of the transition process need to address.

The future prospects of extremists such as Hekmatyar and the Taliban will crucially depend upon the cohesion of the transitional political elite, the degree of success in crafting new institutions for Afghanistan, the durability of international support for Afghanistan's transition, and the scale of meddling by Pakistan. In other words, the capacity of Islamic extremists to play a role in Afghanistan's future will depend upon the willingness of the wider world to sustain a process that will establish the extremists' irrelevance. Successfully sustaining the process involves the achievement of three interconnected objectives: the provision of security for ordinary Afghans, the mobilisation of resources to reconstruct the country, and the winning of generalised normative support for the new central state – that is, ensuring its legitimation. Decisions crucial to realising these objectives need to be made in Washington, London, Berlin and Paris rather than in Kabul. Politics in Afghanistan is haunted not just by the collapse of the state, but also by the breakdown of trust, which is an insidious feature of disrupted states.[46] Reconstituting trust involves creating arenas in which political actors with sufficient shared objectives can work together. It is doubtful whether elections will foster such co-operation, since their effect is to incite competition between moderate Islamists and Muslim secularists.[47] Rather, Afghanistan requires concerted efforts to facilitate basic co-operation between all moderate forces, secularist *and* Islamist, to block the efforts of those who are truly opposed to seeing Afghanistan move ahead.

CONCLUSIONS

Afghanistan, and South-West Asia, are far from stable or secure,48 and to some the mere suggestion that moderate Islamists could have a role to play in Afghanistan's future might consequently seem misplaced. In the West, individual freedom and democratic practices flourished after the effective separation of church and state was accomplished and in some countries accorded constitutional force. Afghanistan, however, is not simply a *tabula rasa* on which creative actors can sketch a new future. It took several hundred years for the political systems of key Western countries to take shape, and the bloodshed that accompanied that process should not be forgotten: the American Civil War, World War I, and World War II featured, as key belligerents, states in which the experiences of the Enlightenment weighed heavily, and yet this did not prevent a dreadful slide into barbarism. In Afghanistan, Islam remains a potent force with which to legitimate political power, but, more seriously, it also retains its potential to delegitimate the exercise of power. For this reason, it is important that as wide a range of Islamic forces as possible be co-opted to support the transition that the Bonn Agreement commenced, in order to weaken the risk that Islam will be mobilised as an oppositional ideology.

Texts, including religious texts, do not have voices of their own. 'Any text', writes Khaled Abou El Fadl, 'including those that are Islamic, provides possibilities for meaning, not inevitabilities. And those possibilities are exploited, developed and ultimately determined by the reader's efforts – good faith efforts, we hope – at making sense of the text's complexities. Consequently, the meaning of the text is often only as moral as its reader. If the reader is intolerant, hateful, or oppressive, so will be the interpretation of the text'.[49] This applies in the political realm as much as any other. An authoritarian reader of Islamic texts will be able to conjure up an interpretation to support an authoritarian political order. A moderate will find and highlight messages of moderation, starting with the proposition in the Qur'an (*Sura al-Baqarah* 2: 256) that there shall be no compulsion in religion. A notion that political Islam is *inherently* totalitarian simply flies in the face of this logic, and is a barrier to understanding the realities of the world in which we live.

Ultimately, the political voices of *moderate* Islamists are not something to fear. Of course, this is not to say that moderate Islamists are all pure and perfect human beings. As much as any other Afghan political actors, they are cut from the crooked timber of humanity, and have suffered the brutalising effects of decades of disruption in their homeland. Nevertheless, it is worth recalling that the Taliban targeted mainly moderate Islamists (rather than Muslim secularists) between the movement's appearance in 1994 and its seizure of Kabul in 1996. It was moderate Islamists (rather than Muslim secularists) who remained staunchest in their opposition to the Taliban between 1996 and 2001. It was a moderate Islamist, Ahmad Shah Massoud, whom al-Qaeda agents assassinated on the eve of the September 11 attacks, and moderate Islamists (rather than Muslim secularists) who partnered the United States in the attack on the Taliban and al-Qaeda thereafter. Moderate Islamists, in other words, have been among the most determined *enemies* of Islamist extremism in Afghanistan. To lose sight of this is to lose sight of one of the most important realities of contemporary Afghan politics.

NOTES

1   See William Maley, *The Afghanistan Wars* (London: Palgrave Macmillan, 2002), pp. 58–60. On Islam as a way of life in Afghanistan, see Thomas J Barfield, 'Radical political Islam in an Afghan context', in *Political Transition in Afghanistan: the State, Islam and Civil Society* (Washington, DC: Asia Program Special Report No. 122, Woodrow Wilson International Center for Scholars, June 2004), pp. 15–17.

2   See Thomas J Barfield, *The Central Asian Arabs of Afghanistan* (Austin: University of Texas Press, 1981).

3   See Sayed Askar Mousavi, *The Hazaras of Afghanistan: an Historical, Cultural, Economic and Political Study* (New York: St. Martin's Press, 1997).

4   See Elie Kedourie, *Afghani and Abduh: an Essay on Religious Unbelief and Political Activism in Modern Islam* (London: Frank Cass, 1966).

5   Willem Vogelsang, *The Afghans* (Oxford: Blackwell, 2002), p. ix.

6   See Barbara D Metcalf, *Islamic Revival in British India: Deoband, 1860–1900* (Princeton: Princeton University Press, 1982); Muhammad Qasim Zaman, *The Ulama in Contemporary Islam: Custodians of Change* (Princeton: Princeton University Press, 2002).

7   Asta Olesen, *Islam and Politics in Afghanistan* (Richmond: Curzon Press, 1995), pp. 188, 198.

8   Kenneth J Cooper, 'Afghanistan's Taliban: going beyond its Islamic upbringing', *The Washington Post*, 9 March 1998.

9   Asta Olesen, *Islam and Politics in Afghanistan*, p. 189.

10 See Christine Noelle, 'The anti-Wahhabi reaction in nineteenth-century Afghanistan', *The Muslim World*, Vol. 85, Nos. 1–2 (1995), pp. 23–48.

11 See Ashraf Ghani, 'Islam and state-building in a tribal society: Afghanistan

1880–1901', *Modern Asian Studies*, Vol. 12, No. 2 (1978), pp. 269–84; R D McChesney, *Waqf in Central Asia: Four Hundred Years in the History of a Muslim Shrine, 1480–1889* (Princeton University Press, 1991).

12 See Asta Olesen, *Islam and Politics in Afghanistan*, pp. 144–66; Leon B Poullada, *Reform and Rebellion in Afghanistan, 1919–1929: King Amanullah's Failure to Modernize a Tribal Society* (Ithaca: Cornell University Press, 1973); Senzil K Nawid, *Religious Response to Social Change in Afghanistan 1919–1929: King Aman-Allah and the Afghan Ulama* (Costa Mesa: Mazda Publishers, 1999).

13 Olivier Roy, *Islam and Resistance in Afghanistan* (Cambridge: Cambridge University Press, 1990), p. 69.

14 Graham E Fuller, *The Future of Political Islam* (New York: Palgrave Macmillan, 2003), p. xi.

15 Robert Nozick, *Anarchy, State and Utopia* (Oxford: Basil Blackwell, 1974), pp. 319–20.

16 Daniel Pipes, 'There are no moderates: dealing with fundamentalist Islam', *The National Interest*, No. 41 (1995), p. 57. Pipes's preoccupation with political Islam had earlier led him to endorse support for Saddam Hussein's regime in Iraq: see Daniel Pipes and Laurie Mylroie, 'Back Iraq', *The New Republic*, Vol. 196, No. 17 (1987), pp 14–15.

17 See Emmanuel Sivan, *Radical Islam: Medieval Theology and Modern Politics* (New Haven: Yale University Press, 1985).

18 See Charles Kimball, *When Religion Becomes Evil* (New York: HarperCollins, 2002).

19 Olivier Roy, *Islam and Resistance in Afghanistan*, p. 69.

20 David B Edwards, *Before Taliban: Genealogies of the Afghan Jihad* (Berkeley and Los Angeles: University of California Press, 2002), pp. 239–41.

21 See David B Edwards, 'Summoning Muslims: print, politics, and religious ideology in Afghanistan', *Journal of Asian Studies*, Vol. 52, No. 3 (1993), pp. 609–28.

22 See Eden Naby, 'The changing role of Islam as a unifying force in Afghanistan', in Ali Banuazizi and Myron Weiner (eds), *The State, Religion, and Ethnic Politics: Afghanistan, Iran, and Pakistan* (Syracuse: Syracuse University Press, 1986), pp. 124–54; Eden Naby, 'The concept of Jihad in opposition to communist rule: Turkestan and Afghanistan', *Studies in Comparative Communism*, Vol. 19, Nos. 3–4 (1986), pp. 287–300; Eden Naby, 'Islam within the Afghan resistance', *Third World Quarterly*, Vol. 10, No. 2 (1988), pp. 787–805; Graham E Fuller, *Islamic Fundamentalism in Afghanistan: Its Character and Prospects* (Santa Monica: RAND R-3970-USDP, 1991).

23 See William Maley, *The Afghanistan Wars*, pp. 57–84; Barnett R Rubin, *The Fragmentation of Afghanistan: State Formation and Collapse in the International System* (New Haven: Yale University Press, 2002), pp. 184–246.

24 See Sayed Askar Mousavi, *The Hazaras of Afghanistan*; David B Edwards, 'The evolution of Shi'i political dissent in Afghanistan', in Juan RI Cole and Nikki R Keddie (eds), *Shi'ism and Social Protest* (New Haven: Yale University Press, 1986), pp. 201–29; Kristian Berg Harpviken, *Political Mobilization among the Hazaras of Afghanistan: 1978–1992* (Oslo: Report No. 9, Department of Sociology, University of Oslo, 1996).

25 See Hafizullah Emadi, 'Exporting Iran's revolution: the radicalization of the Shiite movement in Afghanistan', *Middle Eastern Studies*, Vol. 31, No. 1 (1995), pp. 1–12; Hafizullah Emadi, 'The Hazaras and their role in the process of political transformation in Afghanistan', *Central Asian Survey*, Vol. 16, No. 3 (1997), pp. 363–87.

26 See Anthony Hyman, 'Arab involvement in the Afghan war', *The Beirut Review*, No. 7 (1994), pp. 73–89; Barnett R Rubin, 'Arab Islamists in Afghanistan', in John L Esposito (ed.), *Political Islam: Revolution, Radicalism, or Reform?* (Boulder: Lynne Rienner, 1997), pp. 179–206.

27 Peter L Bergen, *Holy War, Inc.: Inside the Secret World of Osama Bin Laden* (New York: The Free Press, 2001), p. 54.

28 *International Herald Tribune*, 22 April 1992.

29 See William Maley, *The Afghanistan Wars*, pp. 194–217; Amin Saikal, 'The Rabbani Government, 1992–1996', in William Maley (ed.), *Fundamentalism Reborn? Afghanistan and the Taliban* (London: Hurst & Co., 1998), pp. 29–42. In a letter published in *The National Interest*, No. 42 (1995), p. 114, Daniel Pipes defended his description of the Rabbani Government as 'fundamentalist' on account of 'its efforts to implement the sacred law of Islam'. This flight of fancy betrayed a serious ignorance of what life was actually like in Afghanistan at this time.

30 William Maley, 'Confronting creeping invasions: Afghanistan, the UN and the world community', in K Warikoo (ed.), *The Afghanistan Crisis: Issues and Perspectives* (New Delhi: Bhavana Books, 2002), pp. 256–74.

31 See William Maley, 'Talibanisation and Pakistan', in Denise Groves (ed.), *Talibanisation: Extremism and Regional Instability in South and Central Asia* (Berlin: Conflict Prevention Network: Stiftung Wissenschaft und Politik, 2001), pp. 53–74; Tim Judah, 'The Taliban papers', *Survival*, Vol. 44, No. 1 (2002), pp. 68–80.

32 For varying interpretations of the Taliban phenomenon, see William Maley, 'Introduction: interpreting the Taliban', in William Maley (ed.), *Fundamentalism Reborn? Afghanistan and the Taliban* (London: Hurst & Co., 1998), pp. 1–28; Ahmed Rashid, *Taliban: Militant Islam, Oil and Fundamentalism in Central Asia* (New Haven: Yale University Press, 2000); Barnett R Rubin, Ashraf Ghani, William Maley, Ahmed Rashid and Olivier Roy, *Afghanistan: Reconstruction and Peacebuilding in a Regional Framework* (Bern: KOFF Peacebuilding Reports 1/2001, Swiss Peace Foundation, 2001); Neamatollah Nojumi, *The Rise of the Taliban in Afghanistan: Civil War, Mass Mobilization, and the Future of the Region* (New York: Palgrave Macmillan, 2002).

33 See William Maley, *The Foreign Policy of the Taliban* (New York: Council on Foreign Relations, 2000).

34 See John Gray, *Al Qaeda and What it Means to be Modern* (London: Faber & Faber, 2003).

35 Olivier Roy, *The Failure of Political Islam* (Cambridge: Harvard University Press, 1994), p. 60.

36 David B Edwards, *Before Taliban*, p. 289.

37 See *Qanun-e Asasi-i Afghanistan* (Kabul: Transitional Islamic State of Afghanistan, 1382 AH).

38 Quoted in William Maley, *The Afghanistan Wars*, p. 270.

39 See International Crisis Group, *Afghanistan: the Problem of Pashtun Alienation* (Kabul and Brussels: International Crisis Group, 2003); Conrad Schetter, *Ethnizität und ethnische Konflikte in Afghanistan* (Berlin: Dietrich Reimer Verlag, 2003), p. 585.

40 See Human Rights Watch, *'Killing you is a very easy thing for us': Human Rights Abuses in Southeast Afghanistan* (New York: Human Rights Watch, 2003).

41 BBC *Summary of World Broadcasts* FE/1461/B/1, 17 August 1992.

42 William Maley, 'The future of Islamic Afghanistan', *Security Dialogue*, Vol. 24, No. 4 (1993), pp. 383–96.

43 ——, *The Afghanistan Wars*, pp. 215–16.

44 ——, *The Afghanistan Wars*, p. 205

45 Human Rights Watch, *'Killing you is a very easy thing for us'*, pp. 30–37.

46 William Maley, 'Institutional design and the rebuilding of trust', in William Maley, Charles Sampford and Ramesh Thakur (eds), *From Civil Strife to Civil Society: Civil and Military Responsibilities in Disrupted States* (New York and Tokyo: United Nations University Press, 2003), pp. 163–79.

47 See Jack Snyder, *From Voting to Violence: Democratization and Nationalist Conflict* (New York: WW Norton, 2000).

48 William Maley, 'Security and stability in Southwest Asia', in David W Lovell (ed.), *Asia-Pacific Security: Policy Challenges* (Singapore: ISEAS, 2003), pp. 141–53.

49 Khaled Abou El Fadl, *The Place of Tolerance in Islam* (Boston: Beacon Press, 2002), pp. 22–23.

7

THE 'WAR ON TERROR' IN MALAYSIA

OSMAN BAKAR

If the tragic September 11 terrorist attacks on the heart of the United States could be compared to an earthquake, then its tremors may be said to have been felt as far east as Malaysia and Indonesia, the heartland of Islam in South-East Asia. More consequential, these tremors in turn have caused the eruption of new regional 'earthquakes', the biggest being in the world-famed tropical resort of Bali, a holiday paradise for Western tourists. Smaller tremors have also been felt in various Philippine and Indonesian islands, but these have been largely unnoticed or ignored by the outside world. Warnings that other South-East Asian nations, especially Malaysia and Singapore, would be hit by such earthquakes were frequently made, usually by Western governments based on their own intelligence sources and much to the annoyance of regional leaders like Mahathir Muhammad,[1] the recently retired Malaysian prime minister. Thus far these nations have been spared the catastrophe that has befallen the Philippines and Indonesia, the two worst hit in the region.

What is really the nature of these man-made earthquakes? It is quite clear these are political earthquakes, since all the explosions that have rocked the region in the last few years appear to be politically motivated acts of terrorism. Although this terrorist wrath is possibly directed at the ruling establishment in each country concerned, its primary underlying motive is evidently anti-Americanism.[2] The extension of the US war on terrorism to South-East Asia is supposed to combat al-Qaeda, contain its threat and ultimately destroy its global network, thus ensuring the protection of American interests in the region. However, the Bush Administration's decision to declare South-East Asia the United States' second front in the war on terrorism has increased both anti-American sentiment and the threat of terrorism against Western interests in the region.

The Philippines, America's former colony, was chosen to be the front-line state in the South-East Asian war on terrorism. The new front was officially opened in Zamboanga in the southern part of the country on 31 January 2002 with the launching of the joint Philippines–US military exercises called Balikatan. These exercises were to be followed by ground operations on the island of Basilan against the so-called militant Muslim separatist group, the Abu Sayyaf. Many in the country, and the region, have criticised the opening of this front as unjustified, a view also echoed within the United States itself. Critics contend that the US military presence to create the front is 'disproportionate to the evidence of terrorism in South-East Asia', thus suggesting some form of 'ulterior motive'.[3] So heated has the ensuing debate on the wisdom of the front become and so sensitive is the issue for many Filipinos that the Philippines President, Gloria Macapagal-Arroyo reportedly appealed to US Secretary of State Colin Powell to stop referring to the Philippines as the 'second front' in the war on terrorism.[4]

In the aftermath of the Bali bombing on 12 October 2002, regional perspectives on terrorism altered. While many acknowledge the existence of the terrorism threat to the region, the wisdom of extending the US military presence in South-East Asia is still questioned. Rather than an extension of armed conflict, regional voices call for a non-military approach to fighting terrorism.

Even before the official launching of the 'war front-line' in the Philippines, Malaysia and Singapore were already engaged in their own 'little wars' on suspected Muslim militants. Malaysia's first so-called 'pre-emptive strike' against the militants pre-dated the attacks in America on September 11. However, the momentum of Malaysia's war on militants increased significantly after 2001 as the country came under strong pressure from the US to investigate the extent of local involvement in international terrorism.[5] In January 2002 the Singaporean Government, a strong supporter of US military presence in the region, announced the arrest of fifteen suspected terrorists in December 2001 under the *Internal Security Act*. With these arrests, the government claimed to have broken up a network of militants targeting Western and Israeli embassies, as well as their business interests and military installations. Of those arrested, thirteen were said to be members of a secretive organisation, the Jemaah Islamiyah (JI), an organisation suspected of links to al-Qaeda.[6] The arrest of Ibrahim Maidin, JI's top leader in the city-state, helped to reveal the extensive and well-coordinated nature of the organisation's regional network,[7] and with this intelligence breakthrough the regional war on terrorism entered a new phase. As ASEAN has increased the coordination of counterterror measures against the JI and other militant groups, the war on terrorism has extended to the whole region. The 'internationalisation and militarisation'[8] of the war on terrorism through the deployment of US troops in the Philippines has also had a significant impact on the attitudes of South-East Asians, especially Muslims. In addition, the close links between the Abu Sayyaf, the main target of the Filipino and US troops in Mindanao, and the JI, hunted by the intelligence and security apparatus in neighbouring states dictate that security efforts be co-ordinated and executed at the regional level.

The events of September 11 and its aftermath had a significant impact on South-East Asian Islam, and the range of responses to it have both immediate and long-term implications for relations between the Muslim world and the West. Malaysia, as an important case study of this regional experience, is the focus of this chapter. Clearly, Malaysia is active in the regional war on terrorism, a fact that the United States and its allies have duly recognised and appreciated. However, while committed to fighting terrorism nationally and globally,[9] Mahathir was also critical of the current US vision and conduct. Quite obviously, as a high-profile Muslim political leader with a constituency of admirers spanning the whole Muslim world, Mahathir sought to publicly distance himself from the United States.

There is considerable evidence of Mahathir's desire to be seen as politically independent. For example, the Malaysian Government blocked attempts by the Bush Administration to have Yazid Sufaat, a Malaysian citizen suspected of being an al-Qaeda operative, extradited to the United States for questioning over the September 11 attacks.[10] Mahathir frequently criticised the United States and its Western allies for handling the war on terror poorly and for failing to address the underlying factors that cause 'ordinary people with families, sufficient income and (who enjoy) a comfortable life ... to die a horrendous death'.[11] According to Mahathir, the US mismanagement of the underlying causes of terrorism has also had a negative impact on global economic conditions and security. Finally, Mahathir has indicated his belief that the US-led war on terror has succeeded in turning Huntington's idea of a 'clash of civilisations' into reality.[12] The situation is only exacerbated by the anti-Islam outbursts of certain prominent right-wing Christian leaders who are closely identified with the power base of US President George Bush.[13] Mahathir's sentiments on US conduct may be dismissed as misconceived in the West but they are widely shared by Muslims in the region, including his domestic opponents.

Within Malaysia, the Mahathir government was accused of exploiting the war on terrorism. In aid of 'national security', the Mahathir Government sought to weaken the opposition by curtailing its democratic freedom and arresting its political activists under the country's *Internal Security Act*. A pertinent point to consider is the extent to which Malaysia's active participation in the regional war on terrorism has had an impact upon democracy in the national context. To many observers of regional politics, the continuing democratisation of South-East Asian Muslim nations is a necessary, although admittedly insufficient, precondition for a permanent regional victory against terrorism. Three post–September 11 events stand out as having particular influence on political Islam in South-East Asia: the war on the Taliban in Afghanistan, the war against the Abu Sayyaf, and the war in Iraq to overthrow Saddam Hussein. All three involved the US and a Muslim group or nation. Such events have helped to energise Malaysian political Islam to new levels and to intensify the domestic contest between the country's major political groups for identification and popularity as the defenders of Islam against the West. However, far from moving in the direction of a single, united response and adopting a legitimate 'Malaysian position' on such international issues, the two largest Malay-Muslim opposing political parties – United Malays National Organisation (UMNO) and the Islamic Party (PAS) – have been exploiting them to score points against each other and bolster their political fortunes at the national level.

IMPACT OF SEPTEMBER 11 ON MALAYSIAN ISLAM

The impact of September 11 and its aftermath on both the United States and the Muslim world has been far-reaching. Many innocent lives have been lost and property has been destroyed or damaged on both sides. Civil liberties have been curtailed and a sense of insecurity prevails, with ordinary citizens worrying when the next terrorist strike might hit New York, Riyadh or Jakarta. Many more people have encountered physical pain and humiliation. Many Muslims would argue, however, that Muslim countries have suffered far worse horrors than the United States and its Western allies from the consequences of September 11 and face the possibility of even more terrorist and political violence exploding in their midst. Clearly relations between the Islamic world and the West have worsened to the point where many now believe the cultural and political divide between the two is about to rupture completely to create the foretold 'clash of civilisations'.

Many Muslims poignantly question whether the three wars the US has launched in the post–September 11 period have actually helped to swell the human reservoirs of disgruntled and angry young Muslims. The war on terror does not appear to have stemmed the tide of fresh recruits to the cause of Jihad against the West. Claims by the perpetrators that the Bali bombing was in retaliation to the US war in Afghanistan seem to support the above assertion. The war on terrorism appears to have defeated its own purpose. Instead of combating terrorism, the US policy has contributed to its escalation. What then might be a better alternative?

Malaysia is both an active member of the Organisation of Islamic Conference (OIC), which is supposed to represent the interests of the 1.4 billion-strong global *umma* (Islamic community), and a close neighbour of the Philippines. Malaysia hosted the sixth Muslim Heads of State meeting in its new administrative capital, Putra Jaya, on 16 October 2002 and is currently serving a three-year term as chair of the OIC's secretariat. With the blessings of both President Arroyo and the OIC, Malaysia is also currently leading the peace negotiations between Manila and the Moro Islamic Liberation Front (MILF), the country's largest Muslim separatist group, with membership links to JI and al-Qaeda. The two roles – by no means unrelated – have provided Malaysia with a rare opportunity to help the OIC form new perspectives on terrorism and methods of combating it that are sensitive to the legitimate interests and concerns of both the Islamic world and the West.

The OIC has long taken an interest in the peaceful resolution of conflict in the Mindanao region. However, its brokered peace agreements have failed to produce lasting results. In the light of the regional determination to win the war on terrorism and the emergence of a new, more pragmatic, leadership of the MILF, Malaysia's present mandated attempt to help secure peace in Mindanao may well have a better chance of succeeding than earlier attempts. How Malaysia responds at both the national and international levels to the larger issues of religious extremism and the impact of the war on terrorism is therefore now of importance to South-East Asia and the OIC, as well as to relations between the Islamic world and the West.

CONFLICTING PERCEPTIONS OF THE WAR ON TERROR

The September 11 attacks evoked widespread sympathy for the US in South-East Asia. Muslims throughout the region were horrified by the senseless barbarity of an attack that was carried out in the name of their religion. In Malaysia, Mahathir – well known for his frequent angry outbursts against the West – paid an unexpected visit to the US embassy to sign the book of condolences. The embassy received a huge number of messages of sympathy from a broad cross-section of the Malaysian public, including leaders of the opposition political parties such as PAS, traditionally a vocal critic of US foreign policies in the Islamic world. The late Fadzil Noor, then president of PAS, and Abdul Hadi Awang, its current leader, were among the prominent *ulama* in the Islamic world who issued a press statement expressing condolences to the families of the victims. The statement also expressed deep sympathy for the United States. It was unfortunate that this statement, issued at such a crucial time, was hardly mentioned in the Western mainstream media.

However, Malaysian sympathies evaporated quickly when the US counterattacked in the declared war against terrorism by sending its troops into Afghanistan, Mindanao and Iraq. Various global surveys[14] conducted in the two years since the 'liberation of Afghanistan from the al Qaeda-backed Taliban' have shown that the once widespread Muslim sympathy for the United States has been replaced by an increasing resentment for the way that the superpower is prosecuting the war on terrorism. The 2003 global survey conducted after the Iraq invasion by the Washington-based Pew Research Center for the People and Press showed that hostility toward the United States in Muslim countries such as Indonesia, Turkey, Jordan, and Pakistan had intensified when compared to its level in 2002 after the invasion of Afghanistan.[15]

Malaysia was not included in the 2003 survey. Nevertheless, if the opinions of Muslim political and religious leaders and the leaders of non-governmental organisations across the spectrum are taken into consideration, it may be concluded that the majority of Malaysian Muslims have become more critical of the United States since the wars in Afghanistan and Iraq were launched. Importantly, according to a survey by the *New Straits Times*, most respondents 'were opposed to the policies of the Bush administration, rather than the U.S. or its citizens per se'.[16] The survey reveals three major issues that have caused sympathy for the United States to diminish and hostility towards it to worsen. These are the US backing of Israel in the latter's continued occupation of Palestine, its invasion of Afghanistan, and its invasion of Iraq. The general perception Malaysian Muslims have of the post–September 11 United States is that, despite the Bush Administration's pronouncement in support of the creation of the Palestinian state, its support for Israel is becoming excessively unjust. Also, despite repeated assurances to the contrary, the US global war on terrorism continues 'to be seen as a war against Islam and Muslims'.[17]

There was widespread hostility in Malaysia to the wars in Afghanistan and Iraq, cutting across the traditional political divide and including the non-Muslim political parties. In a closed-door meeting with President Bush during the Asia-Pacific Economic Cooperation (APEC) summit in Shanghai, held two weeks after the aerial bombing of Afghanistan, Mahathir voiced his strong opposition to the war and 'the anger and frustration of the Muslim world' at the bombings.[18] Mahathir's main justification for his stand was his fear of massive civilian casualties, a fear that turned out to be not totally unfounded,[19] and his belief that 'attacking Afghanistan was not the solution to the problem' of terrorism. On the first day of the bombing, he told the Malaysian Parliament that although Malaysia supported the war on terrorism, it was opposed to the military strikes on Afghanistan, which it considered to be counterproductive.[20] He emphasised Malaysia's right to adopt a different approach to fighting terrorism, a stand that Mahathir claimed Bush had understood.

As Afghan civilian casualties mounted, Mahathir became more critical of the war, as is seen in a speech he delivered when he hosted an international conference on terrorism in Kuala Lumpur, less than a month after meeting Bush in China. In an obvious reference to the Bush Administration's rationale and conduct of the war, he argued that attacking Afghanistan was unbecoming of civilised people, since it was as unprincipled as the attacks of September 11.[21] He asserted that the operation in Afghanistan would not result in the killing or capture of all the terrorists but could 'actually result in the spawning of more terrorists', who would be 'willing to die to avenge what is to them a gross injustice and cruelty'.[22]

The above considerations apart, domestic politics was without doubt an important factor in influencing Mahathir's decision to oppose the US military operations. No Malay-Muslim leader wishing to have political support from his community could afford to be seen taking even a 'neutral' stand in the conflict. Mahathir was concerned about possible militant reactions from Muslims in his country and the sectarian exploitation of the issue by opposition parties, particularly PAS, that could adversely affect Muslim support for his own party. Clearly PAS took a far stronger position on the issue, with some of its leaders accusing the United States of being a 'terrorist state'. The late Fadzil Noor had rejected September 11 as a 'heinous crime', yet as the war on terror was launched he became so incensed by the US operation in Afghanistan that he openly called for a Jihad against the United States.

In Fadzil Noor's view, a Jihad on behalf of Afghanistan was justified since the country was attacked without any strong proof of its involvement with terrorism. From this perspective, the war in Afghanistan was formulated as being not simply against the Taliban but rather against all Muslims.[23] Controversially, Noor also gave the green light to party members who volunteered to go to Afghanistan to fight on the Taliban side. Although he claimed that his call for Jihad was not in defence of the Taliban regime, but rather in defence of Afghanistan as 'an Islamic nation being attacked by an enemy of Islam',[24] many in the country failed to see the distinction and perceived PAS to be sympathetic to the version of Islam advocated by the Taliban, and even to al-Qaeda. This view was reinforced when, within days of the US air strikes against Afghanistan, the party held a demonstration led by Fadzil Noor in front of the US embassy in Kuala Lumpur, with many in the crowd 'brandishing Osama bin Laden T-shirts and pictures' and calling the United States 'the mother of all terrorists'.[25] Several other anti-US rallies and demonstrations were held not only in the capital city but also in more distant, smaller towns, such as Alor Star in Kedah in the north, Mahathir's home state.[26]

However, reactions to the US attacks from partners of PAS in the Barisan Alternatif (Alternative Front) were less fiery. Keadilan (Justice

Party), the predominantly Chinese Democratic Action Party (DAP) and the Malaysian People's Socialist Party (PRSM) all opposed the attacks on several grounds,[27] but none of them issued calls that could be construed as inflaming the already volatile situation in Afghanistan and dragging the Muslim world into a larger confrontation with the West. Their more or less similar position on the Afghanistan issue was perceived as much closer to Mahathir's than to that of PAS. They all agreed that seeking 'an end to terrorism' and bringing 'to justice the perpetrators of the September 11', should be achieved not by waging war but 'through the international legal system'. These three parties have no liking for al-Qaeda and the Taliban regime.[28] Their main consideration, like that of Mahathir, in opposing the attacks was that they would lead to heavy civilian casualties. As the US aerial bombardments and military operations continued, many notable Malaysian critics of the war, including the DAP leader Lim Kit Siang, a Chinese non-Muslim who is the country's most senior opposition leader, contended that the United States' war on terrorism had degenerated into a 'war of terror' against innocent Afghan civilians.[29]

In Malaysia's domestic arena, questions of the legality of the US action and its implications united political leaders from both the ruling and opposition parties.[30] However, this unification did not conceal the differences of political opinion. The uncompromising call to Jihad by PAS was rejected by other political parties. Most non-governmental Muslim organisations, including the large and influential Angkatan Belia Islam Malaysia (ABIM – Muslim Youth Movement of Malaysia), also dissociated themselves from PAS and its call for Jihad. For PAS, the legitimacy of the call to Jihad was not negotiable. PAS might have seen the US military campaign in Afghanistan as an opportunity to bolster its image as the 'defender of Islam', but subsequent developments in Malaysian politics suggest this was ill-conceived. The ruling UMNO seized on the PAS call to Jihad to portray the opposition party as 'Malaysia's Taliban'. The general public concern about terrorism in the wake of September 11 negatively affected the political fortunes of PAS. Even its efforts to gain political mileage from humanitarian initiatives in Afghanistan seemed to be ineffective, as it had to compete with the better organised and publicised humanitarian works of the UMNO-dominated government.[31]

The invasion of Iraq further hardened the low opinion of the US among Malaysian Muslims. To many Malaysians the invasion of Iraq came as no surprise, only tending to confirm their earlier view of US foreign policy under President Bush. To express their anger at the United States, Muslim organisations, political or otherwise, went through the same rituals as they did after the Afghanistan bombings: Jihad declarations, anti-US rallies and demonstrations, critical media statements and promises of humanitarian aid to war victims.

ANWAR IBRAHIM'S CRITIQUE

With two Muslim countries as current scenes of the war on terrorism, criticism of the US has been widespread in the Muslim world. What is clearly lacking is self-criticism, an attempt at a self-reflection or self-understanding of the internal problems of the Muslim world that have contributed to the 'Muslim catastrophes' in Afghanistan and Iraq. In this context, Anwar Ibrahim's critique of Muslim responses to September 11 and the Bush Administration constitutes something both rare and significant. In an article in *Asia Time* under the arresting title, 'Who hijacked Islam?', he went beyond expressing deep sympathy for the United States and delivered a strong condemnation of the September 11 terrorist attacks. He also criticised Mahathir's government for its 'hypocritical' stand on the tragedy.[32] Anwar wanted the Muslim response to the attack to go beyond simply issuing press statements of sympathy for the victims and for the United States. In his view, Muslims should condemn the attack and 'the condemnation must be without reservation', because that would be in conformity with the teachings of their own religion. He introduced the article with a quotation from the Qur'an: 'Let not your hatred of others cause you to act unjustly against them.' According to Anwar, this verse provides a scriptural basis for condemning September 11 and rejecting violence as means of achieving political goals, irrespective of how legitimate those goals may be.

Anwar argued that Muslims have 'legitimate grievances against the US' but that responses such as those of Muhammad Atta and his fellow terrorists and sponsors were categorically wrong and harmful. Furthermore, Anwar asserted that terrorism has inflicted injustice on Islam on two counts: it has taken innocent lives in the name of Islam and it has caused a backlash against Muslims. This position was distinct from the common Muslim response to the September 11 attacks, which expressed sympathy for the victims but was uncompromising in placing the blame on the United States. It is not surprising that Anwar's position found little echo in the national media. Anwar's harshest criticism was reserved for the Mahathir Administration, which he accused of employing the state-controlled media 'to stir up anti-American sentiments, while employing a much more accommodating language for international diplomacy'.[33]

Anwar's article was significant in several respects. First, of fundamental importance was the fact that this article constitutes the first widely known critique of Muslim responses to September 11 by a prominent Muslim leader. Many Westerners have been critical of Muslim responses to the attacks worldwide, because of their apparent vacillation between condemnation and understanding, but Anwar's critique is particularly important, since it presents an 'internal' perspective that comes from within the Muslim community. Given the magnitude of the backlash against Muslims and Islam, the events of September 11 were eventually bound to generate a Muslim self-examination that would lead either to a healthy internal debate or to deep sectarian conflicts within the community. Anwar's article is precisely such a piece of self-criticism, which has helped to set in motion, at least in the Malaysian context, a national debate on how Muslims should respond to the aftermath of September 11.

Second, in giving his article the title 'Who hijacked Islam?', Anwar obviously sought to convey the message that mainstream Islam believes in and practices moderation as the core teaching of the religion but has been 'hijacked' by the extremists. He argues that, because of both internal and external factors in the post–September 11 Muslim world, there is likely to be a long battle for the soul of Islam between the moderate mainstream *umma* and the extremist fringe groups. The adoption by extremist groups of the concept of 'goals justify any means', is something utterly misleading from the Islamic point of view. As a guiding principle of political action, it is undoubtedly one root cause of political violence and terrorism in many Muslim countries. If the fight against religious and political extremism in Muslim countries is going to be lengthy, it is because the roots of extremism are many and complex.

Finally, Anwar makes important comments on the roots of Muslim terrorism. He presents a self-examination or self-criticism and distances himself from the tendency among Muslims to blame others for the predicament of the Muslim world. He emphasises the internal, rather than the external, causes of Muslim terrorism, citing three major causes: lack of political and social freedom, lack of Muslim participation in the global processes at the non-governmental levels and the failure of the Muslim world to address major international issues of the *umma*. He contends that the last two factors are largely responsible for nurturing among Muslims widespread feelings of alienation, bitterness and anger against the global order and the remaining superpower. Reflecting popular Muslim views, he considers the tragic suffering of the Afghani people, which led to the Taliban rule, that of the Iraqis under and after Saddam's repressive regime (especially the impact of international sanctions) and, of course, the Palestinian–Israeli conflict as the most explosive political issues in the Muslim world.

That a chaotic and violent Afghanistan torn apart by ethnic and religious strife has proved to be a fertile breeding ground for international terrorism has been clearly visible to the international community. The fate that has befallen modern Afghanistan is basically a problem of the Muslim world, but, since the Soviet invasion in late 1979, it has also been a problem for the international community. Iraq could yet emerge as a far worse breeding ground for international terrorism than Afghanistan if current trends in sectarian conflicts and violence continue and the overall security situation deteriorates further. South-East Asia in general and Malaysia in particular have already experienced the bitter impact of Afghanistan-bred terrorism on the region. Malaysia has to deal with the threat of terrorism posed by its own citizens, such as the Malaysian Mujahidin Group (KMM) who received their training in the Afghani Jihad against the Soviets.

Anwar fears that 'necessity will prompt the United States to seek the collaboration of the governments of Muslim countries' in the fight against terrorism, a collaboration that could occur at the expense of 'democracy and the protection of human rights'. He shares the perception that ruling 'autocrats of all types will seize the opportunity to prop up their regimes and deal a severe blow to democratic movements' as they 'terrorize their critics and dissenters'.[34] If that were to happen, Anwar contends, the new democratic movements in the Muslim world 'will regress for a few decades'.

Ironically, the suppression of democracy, political participation and civil society by Muslim governments tolerated by the United States is likely to undermine the very ability of the United States to win the war on terrorism. Anwar is convinced that 'democracy, political participation and civil society' are the essential factors that will provide the final answer to terrorism. His own country, Malaysia, may be far more democratic than many other Muslim countries, but the same pattern still prevails. Anwar is critical of Mahathir for exploiting the terror war to discredit and stifle his Islamic opposition, particularly in resorting to detention without trials.[35]

Anwar and Mahathir represent two different Malaysian responses to September 11 and the US-led war on terror. Both have condemned Muslim terrorism in the strongest possible terms, and they have done so with the expressed view of defending and protecting the 'true' Islam. They have also rejected the identification of Muslims and Islam with terrorism. Both Anwar and Mahathir fully support the war on terrorism, and both agree that the most effective way of fighting terrorism is to remove its causes. But the two differ in their assessment of these root causes, a factor that is reflected in their attitudes towards the United States. For Mahathir, the principle cause is the unresolved issue of Palestine. He argues that the Muslim world is angry with the West - particularly the United States – because as it is unable to help the Palestinians, it expects the West to find a just and peaceful solution to the Israeli–Palestinian conflict. However, as the Muslim world sees it, the West is unwilling to stop 'the Israeli terror' against the Palestinians, let alone trying to find a long-term solution. This, Mahathir has argued, reinforces the view that the West is anti-Palestine, anti-Arab, and anti-Muslim. Mahathir sees September 11 as a consequence of that Muslim anger, not – as many US commentators have claimed – as a manifestation of Muslim jealousy for the good life and the freedom enjoyed in the United States. While most Muslims could contain their anger, a few 'resort[ed] to terror tactics'. So convinced is Mahathir of the cause–effect relationship between the Palestinian problem and Arab–Muslim terrorism that he has no hesitancy in claiming 'there would not be those who would be willing to kill themselves in that horrible fashion on September 11' had there been no Palestine issue.[36]

For Anwar, as earlier discussed, the principal cause of Muslim terrorism is the suppression of 'democracy, political participation, and civil society' in Muslim countries. This is a critical internal factor that goes beyond feelings of helplessness and despondency over the fate of the Palestinians. Anwar does not reject the significance of the Palestinian issue, but asks a more fundamental question: what accounts for Muslim helplessness over the Palestinian fate? Anwar's answer to the question is that Muslim leaders have failed to resolve the Palestinian issue and the main reason for that failure is their denial of freedom to the Muslim masses to participate in the real decision-making processes at both national and global levels. The Muslims directed their frustration and anger first at their rulers for their failures and only later at the West, after it became clear that it would not abandon authoritarian regimes in the Muslim world and would not impose a just solution to the Palestinian–Israeli conflict.

In Anwar's view, the deeper source of Muslim discontent is not the dissatisfaction with the West but rather dissatisfaction with Muslim rulers. In light of this view, the Palestinian issue – insofar as it is a Muslim problem – is seen as just one of many manifestations of this internal problem. He cites the pre–September 11 Afghanistan civil war as another example of the same problem that may equally be presented as an important cause of terrorism. What this means is that if Mahathir could confidently assert 'there would have been no September 11 if there has been no Palestinian issue', Anwar with equal confidence could say 'September 11 would not have occurred if there had been no Afghanistan civil war that helped to produce al-Qaeda'.

Anwar's approach combines promotion of democracy, political participation and civil society with firmness and justice in dealing with extremists and terrorists. He is critical of Mahathir's conduct of the terror war, which he sees as lopsided, since it projects firmness at the expense of justice and democracy. From Anwar's point of view, Mahathir did the right thing by forcefully condemning Muslim terrorism and he also did well in containing the terrorist and extremist threat in Malaysia, but he failed to guarantee legal justice to suspected terrorists, an integral part of any long-term resolution. In Anwar's view, Mahathir also exploited the fear of terrorism for his personal and political gains by portraying the main opposition party, PAS, as sympathetic to suspected terrorist groups. On both counts, Anwar sees Mahathir as a failure in defending the true Islam. From Anwar's point of view, to conform to the true Islam, Muslim 'intellectuals and politicians must have the courage to condemn fanaticism in all its forms', but in the same breath they must also 'condemn the oppressive regimes that dash every hope of peaceful change'.[37]

Anwar's position on terrorism and its causes serves two important objectives critical to his political future. His emphasis on the internal causes of Muslim terrorism shifts the blame away from the United States. This is a significant move, because it makes him a moderate, in contrast to the fiery anti-Western rhetoric of Mahathir. Anwar needs the support of Western agencies to sustain his 'politics behind bars'; in keeping with this objective, his moderate position would assure a positive response from the West. Anwar's position has important implications for his role in the Muslim world. His emphasis on self-criticism and the implied need for a return to the essence of Islam combine to make Anwar a leading Muslim voice for Islamic regeneration and reformation.

WINNERS AND LOSERS

Many observers of Malaysian politics have claimed that the biggest winner in Malaysia from the political climate created by September 11 and the war on terror is none other than Mahathir himself. Professor Jomo Kwame Sundaran of the Faculty of Economics and Administration, University of Malaya, has described September 11 as one of several 'God-sent' episodes for Mahathir.[38] Other 'divine gifts' to Mahathir mentioned by Jomo were the nation's strong financial recovery in 1999 and 2000, the rise of Islamic militancy such as the al-Ma'unah, and the internal squabbles within the Alternative Front. All these episodes helped to reverse his declining political fortunes following the 1997 Asian financial crisis, the 1998 sacking of Anwar from the government and UMNO, and the UMNO's poor performance in the 1999 general elections. The decline of Mahathir's position prevented him from leaving office because it would have marred his legacy. He did not wish to be remembered as a weak leader. The September 11 episode helped reverse the decline: Mahathir was able to use these turbulent events to his advantage and bolster his political standing in Malaysia and the rest of the Muslim world. Once this was achieved he was able to leave office from a position of strength.

The threat of Islamic militancy in Malaysia predates September 11. In July 2000, Malaysia's largest arms heist involved the al-Ma'unah. A year later, eight people were arrested, members of the KMM, a secretive organisation with alleged links to international terrorism. The government characterised both groups as militant, with the ultimate objective of applying their own interpretation of an Islamic state through violence. It also claimed that they maintained links with the

PAS: among the arrested KMM members was Nik Adli, a PAS youth leader and son of Nik Aziz, the spiritual leader of PAS. PAS rejected these allegations and confirmed its commitment to the establishment of an Islamic state through democratic and peaceful means.[39]

There was a widespread perception that the arrests were part of Mahathir's orchestrated political plot to stem the growing opposition that followed the strong showing of PAS at the national polls only months earlier. Eager to dispel that perception, some of Mahathir's non-Malay allies in the ruling coalition joined the opposition in calling for an open trial of those arrested and for convincing proof of the existence of KMM.[40] The al-Ma'unah case ultimately was presented in court but not that of the KMM. Following police investigations, detained KMM members have either been released or held under the *Internal Security Act*, strengthening the critics' suspicion that the arrests were politically motivated. The KMM case met with public scepticism because Malaysians mistrusted Mahathir, who was at his lowest ebb of popularity at the time. Amid disputes over allegations of religious militancy came the events of September 11, which changed the global political climate and thus the course of Mahathir's political fortunes.

In the climate of heightened anxiety about possible extremist and terrorist networks in Malaysia, many Malaysians were prepared to give Mahathir the benefit of the doubt and support his strong stance against alleged terrorists. It seems that many voters were also prepared to tolerate his authoritarian rule for the sake of security. The first visible sign of a change in the people's attitude to Mahathir's National Front was the victory of its candidate in a by-election held only a few months after September 11, with a much greater majority than in the 1999 general elections. Mahathir himself attached much significance to the result by describing it as 'the regaining of the Barisan National's honor'.[41]

Ironically, it was Mahathir's opposition to the war in Afghanistan that helped his political comeback. He exploited to the full the 'strategic errors' of PAS in supporting the Taliban, and the information that linked PAS members to an international terrorist network. He portrayed his political enemies as extremists and himself as a moderate. Analysts and critics acknowledged his success in 're-engineering Malaysian politics' to his advantage after September 11 but warned that he could not continue to reap political benefits from terrorism and security issues for long.[42] Mahathir seemed to take heed of this warning. Apparently satisfied he had regained enough credibility and honour as leader to make an exit from power, he unexpectedly announced his resignation from the UMNO presidency on 22 June 2002, less than a year after September 11, in an emotional closing speech at UMNO's general assembly. He was persuaded by party leaders to continue as president until October 2003, when Malaysia was scheduled to host the OIC Heads of State summit meeting. This offered Mahathir an honourable and respectable exit from the national leadership. His OIC opening speech was widely appreciated in the Muslim world for its frank assessment and treatment of the global Muslim malaise but was strongly criticised in the West. His summit declaration, 'Jews rule the world by proxy', guaranteed his grand and well-publicised departure from the political scene.

Mahathir's reversal of political fortune following September 11 was at the expense of PAS. The ruling UMNO and PAS both attempted to exploit the war on terrorism, particularly the attack on Afghanistan. However, the declaration of Jihad by PAS to defend the Taliban against the United States and its allies made it vulnerable to a massive propaganda attack through the state-controlled media. UMNO accused PAS of being 'Malaysian Taliban' and PAS found it difficult to refute this accusation, especially given its open commitment to the implementation of Islamic law. For example, in the Kelantan and Trengganu provinces, where PAS dominates local government, it has pushed for the supremacy of Islamic law. These political blunders have been exploited by UMNO in a concerted propaganda campaign against PAS, which has been extremely damaging to PAS. The few by-elections that have been held after September 11 have clearly pointed to a significant drift of voters back to the ruling party. With the new prime minister, Abdullah Badawi, distancing himself from Mahathir and playing his 'moderate Islam' card well, PAS suffered its worst electoral defeat since 1955 when it lost Trengganu and barely retained Kelantan in the March 2004 elections.

In a sense, Anwar is another big loser in the war on terrorism. Imprisoned in 1999 for 15 years, Anwar could lose simply by being forgotten. His political enemies and Mahathir's hard-core supporters would have preferred him to become completely irrelevant and disappear from the political scene. They almost got their wish when Keadilan was totally wiped out in the recent elections, except for the parliamentary seat of Permatang Pauh, which it barely retained through Anwar's wife. For Anwar's supporters, it is critical to keep the 'Anwar issue' alive. In Malaysia and in many other countries, especially the West, Anwar has not yet been forgotten. However, the war on terrorism has, to a certain extent, eclipsed the Anwar issue. It is against this backdrop that Anwar's contribution may be seen. His essay 'Who hijacked Islam?' presented a perspective that was distinct from the perspectives of both Mahathir and PAS. This was an opportunity to maintain his relevance to the debate on the war and its conduct in South-East Asia.

Interestingly, a major consequence of the war on terrorism is the move towards experimentation with democracy in Afghanistan and Iraq. As the world debates the future of both democracy and terrorism in the two countries, Anwar's political belief that democracy will be the key to fighting extremism and terrorism in the Muslim world makes him not less but more relevant to contemporary Muslim politics.

In a negative and controversial way, Anwar also reappeared in the limelight by being linked to terrorism. There had been attempts to link Anwar and the Free Anwar Campaign (FAC) to terrorism through his associations with international Muslim organisations that have been subjected to US investigation of their alleged funding of the terrorists. The most recent, and also the most widely reported, attempt was an allegation by the executive director of the Washington-based Search for International Terrorist Entities (SITE) during an interview with Australia's Special Broadcasting Service (SBS).[43] Anwar has dismissed SITE as 'a minor research outfit, which is known to be anti-Islam and has condemned just about every Islamic organization in the US as being involved with terrorism'.[44]

Apparently, Anwar's alleged link to terrorism has been inferred largely from his association with the Virginia-based International Institute of Islamic Thought (IIIT), of which he was one of the directors. The IIIT, an intellectually oriented organisation with close links to Muslim leaders such as Mahathir and former president Habibie of Indonesia, and best known in the Muslim world for its 'Islamisation of knowledge' programs,[45] has been investigated and cleared of links with terrorist groups. Accusations of a link between Anwar and international terrorism remain unsubstantiated, but they have the potential to damage his political position. Anwar has been actively denying such claims and has tried to chart an independent political course for himself that is not tainted by violence. His article in *Asia Time* was a significant step in that direction, but the long-term implications of the war on terror will depend, to some degree, on how Badawi handles the Mahathir legacy.

DEMOCRACY AND TERRORISM

Anwar may be the most well known advocate of Muslim reforms and greater democratisation in Malaysia, but he is not the only one. Among prominent leaders of non-governmental organisations who support democracy and human rights, albeit in an Islamic context, are individuals such as Chandra Muzaffar, the president of Just and the leaders of Anwar's former ally Keadilan. Sharing the same pro-democracy sentiments are the Muslim youth organisation, ABIM, and the small but highly visible women's group, Sisters in Islam. Among political leaders, there are many voices from within the ranks of both the opposition and ruling coalition who believe that Malaysia needs more democratisation. There is no doubt that many Malaysians hope for improvement in political conditions in the post–September 11 period.

Prime Minister Abdullah Badawi offered some hope for a more

enlightened democracy in post–Mahathir Malaysia in his maiden speech in parliament.[46] According to Abdullah, 'democracy is the best system of governance', and Malaysians must work for a more open society 'to ensure that a culture of democracy thrives'. However, he also spoke of the need to be firm in dealing with 'extremism, terrorism, and militancy'. He seemed to be confident that the pursuit of democracy can be reconciled with a strong stance on terrorism, although he did not explain how the two goals can be realised. Unlike Anwar, Abdullah did not explicitly say democracy was the key to winning the war against extremism and terrorism, although the spirit of his speech suggested a similar conviction. He called for a comprehensive study into the formation of militant groups and why they commit terrorist acts,[47] thus committing himself to a long-term and less politicised approach to fighting terrorism.

Many welcomed Abdullah's parliamentary speech as encouraging and were further delighted to see the release of nineteen alleged Muslim militants from detention under the *Internal Security Act (ISA)*. These included four students from a religious boarding school in Pakistan suspected of having links with JI.[48] Even Anwar acknowledged that Abdullah is on the right track, although he also detected conflicting messages, such as Abdullah's assurance that he would not change Mahathir's policies and practices. Many Malaysians believe Abdullah will eventually depart from his predecessor's policies and practices, but very few expect him to do this so soon after becoming prime minister. As in all smooth transfers of power, Abdullah's assurance of continuity is to be expected.

However, dictated by his political interests, Anwar had been exerting pressure on Abdullah to 'expand the democratic space' and discard the country's oppressive laws like the *International Security Act* and the *Printing Presses and Publications Act*.[49] In Anwar's view, the country needs meaningful democratic reforms, starting with the removal of oppressive laws. This becomes especially important when the general decline of democratic standards in recent years is taken into consideration. When Anwar was denied bail while awaiting the outcome of an appeal against his conviction for sodomy, he became more critical of Abdullah. He accused Abdullah of hypocrisy in his pledges to combat corruption and foster transparency, since the denial of bail clearly showed Abdullah was still unable 'to free himself from Mahathir's grip' and guarantee the independence of the judiciary.[50] Abdullah, however, rejected Anwar's accusation, maintaining that he had met the judiciary to tell them of his respect for their independence.[51]

Notwithstanding this growing feud between two long-time political rivals, there is a real possibility that, for the first time in the history of modern Malaysia, its citizens will live in a more liberal and democratic environment and experience a more enlightened democratic pluralism. Although both Abdullah and Anwar appear to be committed to democracy and fighting extremism, an important factor in itself, it remains to be seen whether democracy in Malaysia will be given a real chance to prove it can function as the key to fighting extremism and terrorism. Until Malaysians are given that chance, Abdullah's task is to expand the democratic space as Anwar has insisted and to ensure the flourishing of a democratic culture as he promised in his maiden parliamentary speech. Until his release, Anwar is expected to continue to play the role of Abdullah's critic from behind bars. However, he may yet benefit from Abdullah's commitment to democracy. Many will measure the progress of democracy in Malaysia, on which Abdullah's credibility depends, against the resolution of the highly politicised issue of Anwar's imprisonment.

If democracy is to be presented as the key to winning the war on religious extremism and terrorism, a position on which Abdullah and Anwar seem to converge, then there is a need to address the issue of the ideological dimension of terrorism and to demonstrate how democracy is most suited to combat fanaticism. However, in order to address that issue a suitable environment should be made available for a free and enlightened discourse on Islam, democracy and terrorism. Democratic reform in Malaysia – a predominantly Muslim country – presupposes the compatibility of Islam and democracy. It might even put forward Islam as a pillar of political pluralism – a proposition with far-reaching international relevance. If Malaysia can move forward in that direction, September 11 will be best remembered not as a political shock that landed the United States in a deeper entanglement with the Muslim world, but as an event that helped change the course of political Islam in many Muslim countries.

NOTES

1   Mahathir was deeply angered by frequent US post-Bali travel alerts regarding the possibility of terrorist action against Westerners in South-East Asia. To Mahathir, this was 'beyond understanding', since from his perspective the United States and its allies, such as Australia, are no safer from terrorists than the South-East Asian nations. In fact, concerned about the impact of such travel warnings upon regional tourism and foreign investment, Mahathir and his ASEAN counterparts issued a statement calling on the US to 'refrain from issuing warnings against traveling in Southeast Asia' at their 2002 annual summit. This call was rejected by the United States, which felt it had a 'responsibility to warn US citizens about potential dangers they may face while abroad'. See *Agence France-Presse,* 5 November 2002, and Patrick Chambers, 'Malaysia dismisses US warning, sees paranoia', *Washington Post,* 21 November 2002.

2   Although the Bali bombings claimed seven Americans, and eighty-eight Australians, the perpetrators have claimed that Americans were their main target in response to the bombing of Afghanistan.

3   See Nicholas D Kristof, 'The wrong war', *New York Times,* 19 February 2002. For

South-East Asian criticisms, see 'Wrong target', *Far Eastern Asian Review*, 18 April 2002.

4   Larry Chin, 'The United States in the Philippines: post 9/11 imperatives', Center for Research on Globalization, 17 July 2002, available online at <http://www.globalresearch.ca/articles/CH01207A.html>.

5   'Government says JI terror threat under control', 21 March 2003, available online at <http://www.malaysiakini.com/>

6   The Singapore government made arrests in December 2000. However, these were only announced on 5 January 2002. For details see, for example, Seth Mydans, 'Singapore accuses Islamists of bomb plan', *New York Times*, 6 January 2002. The number of accused militants detained without trial is now thirty-seven, most of them alleged members of JI. The government claims that with these arrests the local chapter of JI has been eliminated. See 'Singapore winning battle against JI but critics lash out at detention laws', 15 January 2002, available online at <http://www.afp.com>

7   On JI's regional network, see the International Crisis Group's publication, *Indonesia Backgrounder: How the Jemaah Islamiyah Terrorist Network Operates*, Asia Report No. 43 (11 December 2002), available online at <http://www.crisisweb.org>; Rohan Gunaratna, *Inside al-Qaeda: Global Network of Terror* (New York: Columbia University Press, 2002), pp. 174–203; Zachary Abuza, *Militant Islam in Southeast Asia* (Boulder, Col: Lynne Rienner, 2003).

8   The Philippines Constitution bars foreign troops from operating in the country unless under a treaty. With critics pointing to the unconstitutionality of the US presence, the government was forced to formulate terms of agreement for the deployment of US troops. See the full text of the *Terms of Reference for the Republic of the Philippines-US Exercise BALIKATAN 02-1*, signed on 7 February 2002.

9   On Mahathir's ideological position on global terrorism, see his *Terrorism and the Real Issues* (Subang Jaya: Pelanduk Publications, 2003).

10 Brendan Pereira, 'Detained Malaysian denies paying for Sept 11 attacks', *Straits Times Interactive*, 1 February 2002.

11 Mahathir has taken up the theme of the US mishandling of the war on terrorism and its global impact in his addresses at various international forums. See Mahathir Mohamed, *Terrorism and the Real Issues*, particularly chapter 10 which contains the text of his speech delivered at the World Economic Forum in Davos, Switzerland on 24 January 2003.

12 Lawrence Barlett, 'Clash of civilizations looms between Islam and the West: Mahathir', 20 July 2003, available online at <http://www.malaysiakini.com>; see Mahathir, *Terrorism and the Real Issues*, p. 108, where he asserts that 'about 1.3 billion Muslims were identified as the potential enemy' who had to be 'harassed, restrained and detained indiscriminately'.

13 In Malaysia's view, 'these anti-Islam extremists pose just as much threat to global security as any terrorist group'. See *New Straits Times*, 16 November 2002.

14 See, for example, *What the World Thinks in 2002* and *Views of a Changing World* (2003) released by The Pew Research Centre of the People and the Press, Washington, DC; also Gallup Poll Editors, *2002 Gallup Poll of the Islamic World* (Gallup Press, 2002).

15 A commentary on the report states: 'In 2002, in a survey of 38 000 people in 44 countries, the Pew Research Center found that US global image had slipped. But when we went back this spring after the war in Iraq – conducting another 16 000 interviews in 20 countries – it was clear that favorable opinions of the US had

plummeted'. See Andrew Kohut, *Anti-Americanism: Causes and Characteristics*, The Pew Research Centre (10 December 2003).

16 See Sheridan Mahavera, 'Comment: love–hate relationship with America', *New Straits Times*, 14 June 2003, based on discussions with Malaysian Muslim leaders.

17 Sheridan Mahavera, 'Comment: love–hate relationship with America'.

18 See 'Bush tells Asian leaders: save the civilized world', *Associated Press*, 21 October 2001.

19 Marc Herold, a US economics professor at the University of New Hampshire, claimed that 'between 7 October and 6 December, US aerial attacks on Afghanistan had killed an average of 62 innocent civilians a day'. See his 'An average day in Afghanistan', 29 December 2001, available online at <http://www.pubpages.unh.edu/~mwherold>. See also Marc Herold, *Blown Away: the Myth and Reality of Precision Bombing in Afghanistan* (Monroe, Maine: Common Courage Press, 2004).

20 See 'Bush more rational now, says Mahathir', *Bernama*, 8 October 2001.

21 The 16 November 2001 speech has been published in Mahathir, *Terrorism and the Real Issues*, chapter 2. On Mahathir equating the US 'retaliation' against the Taliban with the events of September 11, see p. 32.

22 '[T]he killing of the Afghans and the destruction of the country is likely to anger a lot of Muslims. Their governments may not, though it is very likely that they too could be angered by wanton acts against a brother Muslim country. But certainly the vast majority of Muslims in whichever country are going to get very angry. And of the many millions of angry Muslims there would be quite a few who would join the ranks of the terrorists and be willing to die to avenge what to them is a gross injustice and cruelty.' Mahathir, *Terrorism and the Real Issues*, p. 34.

23 See the party's online paper <http://www.harakadaily.net>, 8 October 2001; 'Mahfuz wants government to provide military aid to Taliban', 11 October 2001, available online at <http://www.malaysiakini.com>

24 'Malaysia battles anti-US protest, Mahathir says stop bombing Afghans', 12 October 2001, available online at <http://www.islam-online.net>.

25 'Anti-US protests worldwide', *The Guardian*, 13 October 2001.

26 Ismail Hashim, 'Demonstrati Anti Amerika: 5 Ditahan di Kedah', 9 October 2001, available online at <http://harakadaily.com>.

27 See media statement of DAP's leader Lim Kit Siang, 'US – cease air strikes in Afghanistan!', 9 October 2001, available online at <http://www.dap-malaysia.org>. As the aerial bombings dragged on claiming more 'collateral damage', Kit Siang issued more media statements critical of the United States. For these, see the website cited above.

28 This attitude may be best illustrated by Keadilan's congratulatory message to Hamid Karzai on his appointment as the head of the interim government of Afghanistan. See Keadilan's media release on the 26 December 2001, available online at <http://pemuda-keadilan.org>.

29 See Lim Kit Siang, 'US airstrikes in Afghanistan – shame on parliament', 2 November 2001, available online at <http://dapmalaysia.org>.

30 Lim Lit Siang, 'US airstrikes in Afghanistan – illegal war against international law?', 30 October 2001, available online at <http://www.dapmalaysia.org>.

31 On the various Malaysian humanitarian missions to Afghanistan, especially the government-sponsored ones, see <http://www.mercy.org.my>.

32 Anwar Ibrahim, 'Who hijacked Islam?' *Asia Time*, Vol. 158, No. 15, 15 October 2001, reproduced in *New Perspective Quarterly*, Vol. 19, No. 1 (2002). Anwar

wrote this article in his prison cell in Sungei Buluh near Kuala Lumpur, where he is serving a total of fifteen years sentence for his 1999 conviction on charges of corruption and sodomy. Anwar has claimed Mahathir fabricated these charges.

33 Anwar Ibrahim, 'Who hijacked Islam?'.
34 This point is particularly significant considering Anwar's status as a former government leader and an identity in the Muslim world. See, for example, commentary by Ziauddin Sardar, 'Islam has become its own worst enemy: Muslims in denial', 21 October 2001, available online at <http://www.observer.co.uk/comment/story/0.6903.577787.00.html>.
35 See Michael Richardson, 'Mahathir boosted by terrorism stance', 31 October 2001, available online at <http://www.cnn.com/2001/WORLD/asiapcf/southeast/10/31/malaysia.mahathir>.
36 Mahathir, *Terrorism and the Real Issues*, p. 37.
37 Anwar Ibrahim, 'Who hijacked Islam?'
38 Susan Loone, 'God-sent episodes strengthened Dr Mahathir's position', 1 August 2002, available online at <http://www.malaysiakini.com>.
39 ——, 'We reject taking up arms: Nik Aziz', 8 March 2001, available online at <http://www.malaysiakini.com>.
40 Tong Yee Siong, 'Charge KMM detainees in court: Gerakan Leader', 20 August 2001, available online at <http://www.malaysiakini.com>.
41 See 'BN retains Indera Kayangan, larger majority', 19 January 2001, available online at <http://www.malaysiakini.com>.
42 See 'Mahathir more firmly in control after Sept 11: Singapore analyst', 20 August 2002, available online at <http://www.malaysiakini.com>.
43 SBS *Dateline* report that contained allegations of Anwar's link to terrorism, including an interview with SITE's director Rita Katz was aired on 22 October 2003. See 'Aussie report is slanderous, says Wan Azizah' and also 'Free Anwar campaign refutes terror link alleged in SBS report', 25 October 2003, available online at <http://www.malaysiakini.com>.
44 See Yoon Szu-Mae, 'Anwar looking on legal action against media over accusations', 27 October 2003, available online at <http://www.malaysiakini.com>.
45 Leif Stenberg, *The Islamization of Science: Four Muslim Positions, Developing an Islamic Modernity* (Lund: Almqvist & Wiksell International, 1996).
46 See 'Pak Lah pledges democracy in maiden parliamentary speech', 3 November 2003, available online at <http://www.malaysiakini.com>.
47 See 'Pak Lah orders study on terrorists', 6 November 2003, available online at <http://www.malaysiakini.com>.
48 See Yap Mun Ching, '10 alleged militants released from ISA detention', 25 November 2003, available online at <http://www.malaysiakini.com>.
49 Anwar Ibrahim, 'No need for Pak Lah to wait 1000 days', 5 November 2003, available online at <http://www.malaysiakini.com>. See also Arfa'eza Aziz, 'Anwar tells Pak Lah to expand democratic space for all', 6 November 2003, available online at <http://www.malaysiakini.com>.
50 See M Jegathesan, 'Drama in court following judgment', 21 January 2004, available online at <http://www.malaysiakini.com>.
51 See 'PM defends judiciary after Anwar outburst', 27 January 2004, available online at <http://www.malaysiakini.com>.

8
JEMAAH ISLAMIYAH TERRORISM AND RADICAL ISLAMISM IN INDONESIA

GREG BARTON

The shock waves sent around the world by the September 11 terrorist strikes were felt strongly in Indonesia, as in other Muslim countries, but it was the bombing in Bali on 12 October 2002 that really shook the world's largest Muslim country. In this generally pro-Western nation, both attacks were met with waves of sympathy and concern for the victims and their loved ones; but whereas the September 11 attacks, awful though they were, seemed a long way off and completely without connection to Indonesia, the Bali bombing confronted Indonesia with the horrible reality that global terrorism was its problem too and that Indonesia now had to deal with it at home.

The Bali bombing challenged our understanding of Indonesian Islam. The conventional wisdom for decades has been that Islam in the 'Malay world' of South-East Asia generally, and in Indonesia especially, is quintessentially different from the Islam of Pakistan and the Arab world, where extremist understandings of Islam intimidate otherwise secular governments into supporting their demands and abrogating to them the final say in how Islam is interpreted. This view holds that radical Islamism will never represent a serious political force in Indonesia and that Islamist extremists make up such a small proportion of Indonesia's 200 million Muslims that they represent no significant threat. The bombing in Bali and the subsequent discovery that it was the work of local extremists linked to Jemaah Islamiyah, itself apparently linked to al-Qaeda, has challenged this view but it remains resilient nevertheless.

In support of a sanguine reading of Islamic politics and social movements in Indonesia is the fact that traditional Islam in Indonesia is highly Sufistic and richly imbued with the tolerant syncretism of folk Islam. Moreover, the fact that the majority of *santri* (observant

Muslims), who represent approximately 50 per cent of Indonesian Muslims, are affiliated with either the 40-million-strong traditionalist organisation Nahdlatul Ulama (NU) or with the 30-million-strong modernist organisation Muhammadiyah – both moderate in their political outlook – is seen as a further reason for believing that radical Islamism will never be more than a peripheral phenomenon in Indonesia. Since the fall of Soeharto in May 1998, however, radical Islamism has been centre stage. In the run-up to general elections in April 2004, and direct presidential elections in July and September of the same year, radical Islam enjoyed considerable immunity from public censorship and criticism. Several factors can be identified to explain why this should be so. Firstly, Islamism, in all its various forms, has arguably always had stronger support in Indonesia than is generally acknowledged. Secondly, in his final decade in power, Soeharto himself recognised this and actively courted Islamist support, in the process allowing the radical Islamists he had previously persecuted to 'come in from the cold' and entrench themselves within the establishment.

Ironically, this contributed to the growth of support for radical Islamism in the senior ranks of the military. The Asian economic crisis struck Soeharto's already weakened regime in late 1997 with surprising ferocity, precipitating its final collapse in May 1998. A now familiar pattern of action emerged, in which radical Islamist militia linked to factions within the military exacerbated intercommunal tensions in communities that had been stretched to breaking point by catastrophic economic collapse.

The tragic consequences of this were all too apparent during the brief reformist presidency of liberal Islamic intellectual, and long-time leader of NU, Abdurrahman Wahid, when thousands died in intercommunal conflict in Ambon and its hinterland, and in North Maluku and Central Sulawesi. Wahid provoked the ire of the Islamists with his progressive policies. They quickly came to regret their part in his election and led the push to replace this bellicose reformer with the quiescent Megawati Sukarnoputri.

While Indonesian Islam continues to be generally tolerant, it also now seems clear that radical Islamism is a rising force in Indonesian politics. Indonesia can no longer be said to be immune to the globalising influences of neo-Wahhabi radicalism and Jihadi extremism.

A MULTIDIMENSIONAL APPROACH

Some important questions, unpalatable though they may be, now need to be asked. Is radical Islamism ratcheting up its influence in post-Soeharto Indonesia? Are elements within the military continuing to opportunistically support radical Islamist militia, as they have done in recent years? Are elements of the political elite showing signs of exploiting the appeal of radical Islamist ideas as a way of leveraging their political power? Are moderate Islamic intellectuals facing increasing opposition?

The big question is what this means for the future. Although a definitive answer is impossible, we do need to ask whether a small radical Islamist minority, aided and abetted by opportunistic elements in the civil and military elite, and by deteriorating economic and social conditions, could come to disturb the religious and political freedoms of a moderate majority, particularly in outlying provinces.

Too much of the commentary in the media about Islamist terrorism, both with respect to Indonesia and the wider Muslim world, has been simplistic and superficial in its analysis. The truth is seldom neat and simple, and if we are to apprehend it, we need to move beyond reading things at face value. Effective engagement with this subject, especially if the intention is to anticipate and influence future developments, requires a multidimensional approach that gives careful attention to three distinct elements: the seminal ideas, the pattern of history and the contemporary context.

READING ISLAM

Judging by appearances is seldom a good idea in any area of life. When it comes to religion, it is a particularly inept strategy – we are likely either to equate difference with danger and become prejudicial, or to be blinded by the exotic and become naive and uncritical. To interpret, for example, the traditional Islamic dress and manner of the Acehnese as indicative of religious extremism would be a foolish error. To then link this, as some in the international media have done, with the Acehnese struggle for self-determination and paint it as religious conflict is an even graver error, one that blinds us to the real issues and the underlying problems of injustice, human rights abuses and military brutality. On the other hand, it is equally foolish to dismiss the 'Ngruki network', associated with the Central Java *pesantren* (religious schools) of Abu Bakar Bashir, or the outwardly ordinary *pesantren* of Laskar Jihad's Jaffar Umar Thalib, as representing nothing more than religious conservativism simply because their ramshackle *pesantren* in Central Java look much like the thousands of traditionalist *pesantren* run by the moderate NU.[1]

It is important that we look beyond appearances and pay attention to ideas, behaviour and the changing specifics of the social and political context. This, however, is precisely where we run into trouble. Traditionally, the study of ideas has been left to orientalists, or text-oriented experts, whose careful scholarly approach has not generally extended to a consideration of social and political engagement and the real-world application of the documents that they are studying. At the same time, comparatively few political scientists and commentators have a deep knowledge of the religious thought associated with the groups they are observing, and frequently all political parties or groups with an Islamic connection tend to get lumped in together. In addition, if it is rare to find an effort to understand both the mindsets and the political activism of these groups, it is even rarer to find this knowledge linked to an awareness of the changing political and social context in which the groups operate.

ISLAM AND ISLAMISM

There are many ways in which we could choose to begin to analyse and categorise Islamic movements and political parties, but it is hard to see any better point of departure than belief itself and the ideas and ideologies by which these groups define themselves.

One of the most helpful and precise terms to emerge in recent years is that of 'Islamism'. Islamists, or those who hold to Islamism, believe that Islam can and should form the basis of political ideology. If handled with sensitivity, the term 'Islamism' is one that both 'insiders' and 'outsiders' can relate to with a reasonable degree of common understanding. That is considerably more than can be said of terms like 'fundamentalism' and 'radicalism', both of which tend to be profoundly ambiguous.

If Islamists find in Islam something of a blueprint for political engagement, non-Islamist Muslims find nothing more specific than values and principles. A significant minority, however, find in these core values of Islam a counterargument to Islamism. They argue that not only should Islam be first and foremost a personal faith, but it should also accept and respect differences of opinion, commitment and practice. They embrace terms such as 'liberal' and 'progressive', fully aware of the connotations of these terms in post-enlightenment Western thought. Where Islamists tend, to varying degrees, to see the relationship between Islam and Western conceptions of modernity as problematic, liberal Islamic intellectuals find an essential congruity between Western Judeo-Christian thought and Islam.

Liberals are comfortable with articulating their political vision in terms of Western concepts such as democracy, human rights, modernisation and the separation of 'church' and state. Islamists, on the other hand, tend to draw more selectively on such ideas and instead argue that society will overcome the problems of modern life only when it becomes truly Islamic. To this end, Islamists tend to place great stock in legislative reforms that commit the state to taking an interest in the Islamisation of society and, in particular, most see the implementation of the Shari'a (Islamic law) as a panacea for society's ills. In its most extreme forms, Islamism is radical, revolutionary and utopian.

Some might question whether it is even appropriate to talk of radical Islamism representing a threat. After all, what moral basis is there for normatively judging and singling out radical Islamists as a threat? Certainly terrorism is a threat, but only a small minority of radical Islamists are terrorists, so what justification is there for tarring all radical Islamists with the same brush? It is important to avoid the implicit suggestion that religious conservatism – sometimes erroneously called fundamentalism – is inherently bad or problematic. There are plenty of conservative, sometimes very conservative, religious traditions around the world that, for all their lack of appeal to us as outsiders, cannot fairly be said to be doing any harm. In fact, it could well be argued that the world is a richer place for their presence. The Amish of North America, for example, represent an extremely conservative approach to Christianity, but their conservatism does no harm to any outside their community. They are legalistic and have strong religious convictions but they are not concerned with changing broader society outside their own communities to conform to their convictions. There are many conservative Muslim communities that display similar characteristics and, like the Amish, they might sometimes be referred to as fundamentalist (even if, like the Amish, they could more accurately be described as hyperconservative traditionalists).[2] Islamism, however, means something quite different from this sort of fundamentalism. Islamism represents a particular response to modernity that has transformed the religion of Islam into a political ideology. Islamism is therefore pre-eminently concerned with changing society by political means in order to bring both the state and society into conformity with a particular understanding of Islam. This involves, among other things, formalising the state's constitutional and legislative recognition of Islam and, for radical Islamists, the introduction of the Shari'a. It is important to recognise that many who voted for Islamist parties in Indonesia such as the United Development Party (PPP) do not hold radical Islamist views.

The problem with radical Islamism is that it seeks to impose a 'tyranny of a minority over a majority' and is unconcerned with trespassing on the rights of others. In practice, aggressive legalism and the application of a narrow understanding of the Shari'a can lead to serious erosion of human rights, especially those of women and of the poor and the weak.[3] Radical Islamists would take issue with this objective, preferring instead to argue that they are simply working out the will and purpose of God on earth. Islam is, after all, by definition a path by which one submits to God ('Islam' shares the same tri-consonant root – slm – with salam, and its cognate, shalom; a Muslim is literally one who submits to, and finds peace with, God). What makes radical Islamism such an energetic and confronting political and social force is its certain conviction that it knows the mind of God. In their narrow epistemology, involving a literalistic and reductionistic approach to the Qur'an and the Hadith (Sayings of the Prophet), and to thirteen centuries of Islamic thought that has been shaped by a complex, multivalent reaction to, and borrowing from, modernity, radical Islamists exchange ambiguity, ambivalence and irony for certainty, decisiveness and freedom from doubt. Unfortunately, in unwaveringly embracing a world view that sharply divides true believers from 'others', they also diminish their capacity for empathy, compassion and tolerance.

Radical Islamism is ultimately anti-liberal in spirit and often anti-democratic, although it is not necessarily adverse to using democratic means where they offer an advantage. Nevertheless, it is important to make a distinction between radical Islamism and terrorism. Strictly speaking, terrorism is not an ideology but a means, an instrument to achieve particular ideologically determined ends. Many who could be described as being radical Islamists on account of their ideological position would nevertheless argue earnestly and sincerely that the 'means' of terrorism do not justify the 'ends' of their ideology. Adopting a radical Islamist position by no means determines support for the use of violence and terrorism. This distinction is extremely important because there exists a very real danger that initiatives to root out terrorist networks will have unintended consequences, including the transformation of non-violent Islamists into militant Islamists. At the very least, harsh repression can, and often has, played into the hands of Islamist terrorists by perversely boosting their personal charisma and the perceived legitimacy of their cause as they seek to seduce disillusioned youth. Already in Indonesia there is great anxiety among moderate leaders about the possibility of radicalisation as a direct consequence of what is perceived to be the indiscriminate demonising of Islam and of Muslims.

Another term that is often used in this area is 'Jihadist'. Using Jihadist to denote militant radical Islamists is more appropriate because it differentiates militant from political radical Islamists. Militant and political Islamists frequently appear very similar, not least because that is their deliberate intention, but they differ in very important ways.

Political Islamists, such as Hamzah Haz, seek to appeal to Islamist sentiments to win electoral support. Some hold to a deeply radical ideology and, although prepared to use democratic means, could not be said to be liberal democrats. Their long-term ambition is to bring about a radical restructuring of society through (and this is where both their ideological epistemology and their strategic policy intentions become very vague) the application of the Shari'a as a universal panacea, and associated constitutional reform. For these radical Islamists, the Iranian revolution of 1979 stands out as an inspirational example of what can be achieved by a determined minority with 'God on their side' – even if they reject the revolutionary path.

There is another, larger, group of political Islamists who are not arguing for radical change and are, in their convictions, essentially conservative. They too may talk of the application of the Shari'a but, when they are more closely interrogated, it is clear that the changes that they have in mind are modest and essentially symbolic, rather than radical and profound. For these moderate political Islamists, the transformation of the Indonesian state into an Islamic state along the lines of Malaysia is a much more attractive ideal than something approaching post-revolutionary Iran. Typically, supporters of PPP tend to incline to the Malaysian model, while supporters of the Justice and Welfare Party (PKS) and the Crescent Moon and Star Party (PBB) are inclined to the Iranian model. It is not at all clear where Hamzah Haz himself stands, although he appears to represent the 'right', or radical Islamist, wing of his party, PPP.

Jihadi Islamists, such as Abu Bakar Bashir, belong in an entirely different category. They share the views of radical political Islamists but see them as not going far enough. For them the world is divided – according to their narrow, literal, reading of the Qur'an – between the realm of war and the realm of Islam, which is the realm of peace. Theirs is a Manichean struggle between good and evil, in which they justify pre-emptive acts of violence against those (non-Muslims or Muslims) who are said to be opposing – collectively or individually – Islam's true cause. Traditionally Jihad, which literally means 'struggle', is understood in two ways:

1   as a struggle to do good and especially to reform oneself, spiritually and personally – this is said to be the Greater Jihad and is much written about in the Sufi tradition;
2   as an exercise in physical self-defence along the lines of Just War theory – this is the Lesser Jihad.

For Jihadi Islamists, Jihad is externalised and universalised as an essential component in a radical, romantically utopian, revolutionary ideology. Contemporary Jihadi Islamists tend to draw heavily on the narrowly reformist teachings of Wahhabi Islam that underlie official state Islam in Saudi Arabia. Ironically, however, they are also critical of the Saudi regime, charging it with interfering with the consistent application of Wahhabi teaching. For this reason, they are sometimes described as being neo-Wahhabi, because their narrow and austere understanding of Islam, in strictness and zeal, exceeds even the conservatism of official Saudi Wahhabism. Nevertheless, the successful promulgation of neo-Wahhabi thought around the world, often – but not always – with a Jihadi Islamist emphasis, owes a great deal to the generous financial backing of powerful elements within the Saudi state.[4]

It also needs to be noted that, for several decades in Indonesia and Malaysia, many individuals and groups influenced by Wahhabism have remained essentially quiescent in their expression of Islam. That is to say that, like the Amish, they have been fundamentalist in their narrow, scriptural interpretation of religion, but their activism has focused on personal spiritual development rather than radical politics, and as individuals and communities they have turned inwards in their attempts to find a sanctified space for piety and have not attempted to recreate the state in their image.[5]

The other reason for the confusion in the use of terminology is related to the way the Wahhabi movement has emerged on the international scene and onto our TV screens. Wahhabism, in its 18th century roots, is very much a pre-modern movement. What makes it a force in the 21st century is its cross-pollenisation with a very modern, very 20th century movement. The result is the Jihadi Islamist movement that burst explosively into our consciousness on 11 September 2001. The Jihadi Islamism that drives al-Qaeda is the result of a union between Saudi Arabia's Wahhabi movement and Egypt's Muslim Brotherhood.

The Wahhabi movement gained focus, intellectual profundity and a modern revolutionary ideology when it took in sacred trust the Jihadi vision of Sayyid Qutb's Muslim Brotherhood. It did not give birth to the Jihadi Islamist terrorism of al-Qaeda, however, until the Soviet invasion of Afghanistan. When young Afghan and Pakistani mujahideen were joined by fighters from Saudi Arabia and all across the Muslim world, including from South-East Asia, in their struggle against the Soviets in the mid-to-late 1980s, Jihadi Islamism entered a critical new phase.

A vitally important area to watch in Indonesia in the coming years is the synergistic relationship between Jihadi and political Islamism and the degree to which Jihadi Islamism exerts influence over, and is supported by, political Islamism. Also important to watch is the transformation of previously quiescent Islamic fundamentalists into active Islamist radicals no longer merely content to cast their vote for the Islamist parties but rather feeling compelled to enter into the struggle to change society directly.

AL-QAEDA AND SOUTH-EAST ASIA

Before the Bali bombing the most comprehensive scholarly report to tackle the question of Islamist radicalism in Indonesia, and possible links with international terrorism, was a report released in early August 2002 by the Brussels-based International Crisis Group (ICG), entitled *Al-Qaeda in Southeast Asia: the Case of the 'Ngruki Network' in Indonesia*.[6] Two months after the attack in Bali, ICG's representative in Jakarta, Sidney Jones, released a second report, entitled *Indonesia Backgrounder: How the Jemaah Islamiyah Terrorist Network Operates*.[7]

Careful to avoid casual speculation and, especially in the case of the second report, oriented towards assembling data rather than attempting broad-ranging analysis, the reports are rich in detail and provide an unprecedented insight into militant Islamism in Indonesia.[8] Towards the end of 2002, two other scholarly studies emerged to round out our understanding of radical Islamism in Indonesia: Robert Hefner's 'Civic pluralism denied? The new media and Jihadi violence in Indonesia', which deals specifically with Laskar Jihad; and Martin van Bruinessen's article, 'Genealogies of Islamic Radicalism in Post-Suharto Indonesia', which is more global in scope and valuable in mapping the influence of Wahhabi and radical Islamist schools of thought, but nevertheless weakest in its treatment of JI.[9] On the 26 August 2003, two weeks after the Marriott bombing in Jakarta, ICG published a third comprehensive report on Jemaah Islamiyah, entitled *Jemaah Islamiyah in Southeast Asia: Damaged but Still Dangerous.*[10] This report makes extensive use of interrogation depositions by JI members detained following the Bali bombing to construct a detailed picture of how al-Qaeda-linked terrorist training camps functioned in Pakistan and the Philippines and how JI developed out of cohorts of South-East Asian mujahideen who studied and taught in these camps after fighting in Afghanistan in the late 1980s. The present discussion draws extensively on these three ICG reports, before moving on to attempt an analysis of what impact these developments might have on broader social and political developments.

The first ICG report represents an exhaustive review of reliable, public-domain data about Jemaah Islamiyah links in Indonesia before the post-Bali bombing investigations. It focuses on the loose network of radical Islamists associated with the Pondok Ngruki *pesantren*, led by the outspoken preacher Abu Bakar Bashir and situated in the village of Ngruki near Solo in Central Java. Abu Bakar Bashir, who is also commander of the Majelis Mujahidin Indonesia (MMI – the Indonesian Mujahideen Council), the radical organisation founded in Yogyakarta in 2000 and to which many Pondok Ngruki graduates belong, draws inspiration from the Darul Islam (Abode of Islam) rebellion led by Sekarmadji Maridjan Kartosuwirjo in West Java in the 1950s.

After the collapse of the West Java and South Sulawesi rebellions, relatively little was heard about Darul Islam style radical Islamism in Indonesia until the late 1970s. In mid-1977, the Soeharto regime arrested 185 people, many with Darul Islam connections, and accused them of belonging to an organisation it referred to as Komando Jihad. It is not clear whether this fresh crackdown on radical Islamism was precipitated by a genuine, grassroots resurgence of interest in Darul Islam radicalism, or whether the Indonesian military – known at this time as ABRI (Angkatan Bersenjata Republik Indonesia – the Armed Forces of the Republic of Indonesia) – was simply attempting to flush out and make an example of radical Islamists ahead of the 1977 general elections.

The other key leader of the so-called Komando Jihad/Jemaah Islamiyah being monitored by Indonesian intelligence, and subsequently arrested together with Abu Bakar Bashir in November 1978, was Abdullah Sungkar from Brebes, Central Java. Abu Bakar Bashir and Abdullah Sungkar were finally tried in 1982 and both were initially sentenced to nine years in prison. These sentences were overturned on appeal, however, and the pair were released with their sentences reduced to the three years and ten months that they had already served before their trial. Returning to Pondok Ngruki, they worked hard to build up a network of supporters. If the alleged Jemaah Islamiyah network of the 1970s was substantially a fiction created by BAKIN,[11] during the mid-1980s it was made a reality by Bashir and Sungkar and their followers, newly radicalised by the experience of military repression. Bashir and Sungkar encouraged their followers to return to their villages and establish *usroh* (Islamic studies) cells of around a dozen members to live communally and to avoid all non-Islamic institutions. As well as in Solo, Islamist discussion groups and cells emerged in nearby Yogyakarta. In this city of universities and colleges, many students who were angry with the increasingly corrupt and repressive Soeharto regime, and disillusioned with the West that supported it, found inspiration in the 1979 Islamic revolution in Iran. They translated and published, and read and discussed, the writings of Islamist intellectuals such as Ali Shariati and Murtaza Mutahhari of Iran, Hassan al-Banna, and Sayyid Qutb of Egypt's Muslim Brotherhood and Maulana Maududi of Pakistan's Jamaat-i-Islami.

While in self-imposed exile in Malaysia, Bashir and Sungkar continued to maintain active links with associates in Indonesia, not just in Central Java but also in Jakarta, in West Java, North Sumatra and South Sulawesi, where they were able to recruit small numbers of volunteer mujahideen fighters for the struggle against the Soviets in Afghanistan. In the mid-1990s, Bashir and Sungkar appear to have undergone a significant shift in their position, following contact with Usama Rushdi of Gama Islami, the radical breakaway faction of Egypt's Muslim Brotherhood. Gama Islami (or al-Gama'at al-Islamiyah, to give it its full name) is closely linked to al-Qaeda and was led by Sheikh Umar Abdul Rahman, the Islamist teacher convicted in the United States for his part in the 1993 World Trade Center bombing. The Gama Islami connection saw Bashir and Sungkar move beyond the old Darul Islam vision of establishing an Islamic state within Indonesia, or at least making the Indonesian state more Islamic, to the more radical, pan-Islamic position of calling for the re-establishment of an international Islamic Caliphate. This shift was initially the cause of some dispute within the Ngruki exile community but in time it came to be accepted by the network as a whole.[12]

Following the resignation of President Soeharto in May 1998, Bashir and Sungkar returned to Java. Sungkar died soon after returning from exile but Abu Bakar Bashir was able to re-establish himself in Pondok Ngruki and spearhead a push to unite all groups wishing to implement the Shari'a in Indonesia. In August 2000, at a time when President Abdurrahman Wahid was facing overt challenges from radical Islamist groups (including the Laskar Jihad militia that had been established earlier that year and which had sent thousands of fighters to Maluku despite his orders to block them), Bashir was able to organise a three-day Mujahideen Congress in Yogyakarta. This remarkable gathering drew delegates from across the archipelago, representing virtually every Islamist group in the country. The main achievement of the congress, apart from its success as a show of strength, was the establishment of MMI, an organisation ostensibly dedicated to preparing the way for the establishment of a new pan-Islamic Caliphate. Significantly, Hizb al-Tahrir, the Jordan-based militant Islamist organisation calling for the reestablishment of the Caliphate sent a number of observers to the congress in Yogyakarta, an indication of its growing influence in Indonesia. Abu Bakar Bashir was declared amir ul-mujahidin, or commander, of MMI's governing council and Abdul Qadir Baraja was appointed head of its fatwa (decree) section. Other people closely linked with the Ngruki network, including a number who had fought in Afghanistan and studied in Pakistan, made up much of the leadership of MMI.[13]

The reason why the ICG focused on the Pondok Ngruki network in its August 2002 report is that at the time all the known al-Qaeda links with Indonesia were produced by this one network. The four main Indonesians alleged to have close links with al-Qaeda are all involved with Pondok Ngruki: Fathur Rahman al-Ghozi, 'Hambali' (Riduan Isamuddin) Abu Jibril and Agus Dwikarna.

The December 2002 ICG report also details how Hambali, the suspected mastermind of the Bali bombing, planned the West Java Christmas Eve bombings and recruited footsoldiers for such operations. It also explores JI and MMI operations on the islands of Lombok and Sumbawa, east of Bali and in Kalimantan and Sulawesi. Much of that specific information has now been overtaken by developments, but it is significant that the findings of investigations in 2003 have confirmed the correctness of the general line of analysis in the ICG reports of 2002.

The third ICG report dealing with JI, published on the 26 August 2003, is significant for the way in which it fills out in great detail a picture of the training of JI operatives in Pakistan and Mindanao. This report draws together a variety of primary-source information, including ICG interviews, but is primarily dependent upon detailed analysis of the interrogation depositions of JI members arrested after the Bali bombing. The August 2003 ICG reports draws the conclusion that:

> If some early accounts painted JI as an al-Qaeda affiliate, tightly integrated with the bin Laden network, the reality is more complex. JI has elements in common with al-Qaeda, particularly its jihadist ideology and a long period of shared experience in Afghanistan. Its leaders revere bin Laden and seek to emulate him, and they have almost certainly received direct financial support from al-Qaeda. But JI is not operating simply as an al-Qaeda subordinate. Virtually all of its decision-making and much of its fund-raising has been conducted locally, and its focus, for all the claims about its wanting to establish a South East Asia caliphate, continues to be on establishing an Islamic state in Indonesia.
>
> ... JI also maintains alliance with a loose network of like-minded regional organizations all committed in different ways to jihad. The Makassar bombings of 5 December 2002 were not the work of JI, for example, but they were carried out by men who had been trained by JI in Mindanao and who had the motivation, manpower, and skills to undertake a JI-like attack. JI had also made very pragmatic use of thugs (preman) as necessary, particularly in Ambon.[14]

The report clearly establishes that the members of JI's senior leadership fought and trained in Afghanistan and Pakistan between 1985 and 1995, as did many of its key operatives, including those later involved in carrying out bomb attacks in Indonesia and the Philippines. For these JI leaders, the Afghanistan/Pakistan experience was clearly a formative, radicalising one. For some younger members, fighting as mujahideen in Maluku and Sulawesi and training in Mindanao appear to have provided a similarly formative, radicalising experience. Even now it is not at all clear how many Indonesians went to Afghanistan and Pakistan, although it is possible that many hundreds were involved.

Key JI operatives such as Fathur Rahman al-Ghozi (a graduate of Bashir's *pesantren* in Ngruki) and Imam Samudra (who on 10 September 2003 was sentenced to death by judges in Denpasar for his part in masterminding the Bali bombing) trained at Camp Saddah, Pakistan. Beginning in 1991, recruits from Indonesia, Malaysia and Singapore commenced a formal three-year course of training at Camp Saddah.[15]

At around the same time, Abdullah Sungkar and other senior 'Afghan alumni' formalised the structure of JI and set it forth in a small book entitled *General Guidelines for the Jemaah Islamiyah Struggle (Pedoman Umum Perjuangan al-Jamaah al-Islamiyah)*. According to this book, at the head of JI's command structure was an *amir*, Abdullah Sungkar (and after his death in 1999, Abu Bakar Bashir), who appointed and directed a governing council, the central command of which oversaw the four *mantiqi* (geographical spheres of operation) – *mantiqi* I, Malaysia-Singapore; *mantiqi* II, Western Indonesia; *mantiqi* III, Mindanao, Sabah, and Sulawesi; and *mantiqi* IV, Papua and

Australia; which in turn were divided into *wakalah* (districts), a religious council and a disciplinary council.

Although the senior leadership of JI are all Afghan alumni, many of its footsoldiers are simple *pesantren* graduates. It needs to be reiterated, however, that the vast majority of Indonesia's 14 000 plus *pesantren* teach a moderate rather than a radical understanding of Islam. Only five *pesantren* are closely linked to JI and teach a Jihadi interpretation of Islam: Pesantren al-Mukmin in Ngruki, Pesantren Sukohardjo in Solo, Pesantren Al-Muttaqien in Jepara (Central Java), Pesantren Dar us-Syahadah in Boyolali (Central Java) and Pesantren al-Islam in Lamongan (East Java). To this short list could also be added Lukmanul Hakiem, in Johore (Malaysia), but this *madrasa* was closed by the Malaysian authorities in 2001. Outside of this small 'blue-ribbon' or 'Ivy League' group of *pesantren,* the ICG report also identifies a slightly larger group of Jihadi *pesantren* located in Java, Kalimantan and Sulawesi.[16] Fortunately, unlike the situation in Pakistan where a much larger proportion of *madrasa*s actively support Jihadi extremism, these *pesantren* represent but a small fraction of all *pesantren* in Indonesia.

Clearly the alumni network of *pesantren* graduates is an important element within the JI structure, but of great importance also are the bonds formed through marriage alliances across South-East Asia, particularly between Malaysian and Indonesian members of JI.[17]

REGIME CHANGE AND REFORM

Indonesia is still in the initial stages of regime change, as the young nation attempts to break with three or four decades of military-backed authoritarianism and establish full democracy. Such transitions are not always successful (consider Pakistan), and even when they are, they can take fifteen years or more (think of the Philippines). It is the fraught nature of the circumstances in which Indonesia finds itself today – midway on a journey from military-backed authoritarianism to liberal democracy – that affords opportunities for Indonesia's radical Islamists to influence society and politics to an extent out of all proportion to their small numbers.

Significant elements of the Soeharto regime, in the form of both institutions (few of which have changed significantly) and individuals (most of whom continue to exercise power), remain in power. Corruption ranks amongst the worst in the world (in a comprehensive 102-nation report by Transparency International released in August 2002 Indonesia is perceived to be the seventh most corrupt nation in the world).[18] Not only has little, if any, overall progress been made in fighting corruption since the fall of Soeharto more than five years ago, there are also strong indications that, in certain areas, corruption has become even worse. Moves to decentralise government, although begun with good intentions under BJ Habibie's' interim presidency, were ill-conceived and the transition was poorly managed, further exacerbating rentier capitalism and endemic corruption in the regions, where the orderly and centralised corruption of the Soeharto era has been replaced by a chaotic free-for-all. At the same time members of parliament, who now wield real power, and senior bureaucrats, have become increasingly rapacious, having grown accustomed to a dramatic inflation of the payments required to lubricate the wheels of progress.

Enduring endemic corruption is both a product of a weak legal system and an obstacle to serious judicial reform. Consequently, rule of law is incomplete at best, and non-existent at worst. International observers watching the trials of the Bali bombers in Denpasar might find hope in witnessing a display of rare professionalism and transparency. Many may not realise, however, just how rare and unusual are the sorts of trials currently being conducted in Bali. As Indonesia's war on terrorism rolls on into its second year, there is a real danger that subsequent trials will not prove so satisfactory. One factor making this very likely is the possibility that investigations into JI and other militant Islamist groups will uncover matters that elements of the military would rather not have brought into the light of day. At this point there is no evidence of Indonesian Armed Forces (TNI) involvement with JI, nor is there any reason to imagine that extensive and substantial links exist. Unlike Laskar Jihad, JI is opposed to all forms of secular government and is therefore ideologically opposed to working with the Indonesian military. This is not to say, however, that some groups and individuals currently associated with JI do not have past dealings with the TNI. Indeed it would be very unlikely that no secondary links exist. Given the way in which the military is able to completely distort and direct legal proceedings where its interests are at stake – as the disappointing lack of prosecutions resulting from the military-related violence in East Timor in 1999 makes abundantly clear – there are strong grounds for being concerned about future proceedings.

Despite its commitment to withdraw from the parliament in 2004, the military remains outside of full civil control. Elements of the military continue to abuse human rights, and the institution as a whole, for reasons over which it does not have full control, remains deeply enmeshed in organised criminality. This means that many of the basic incentives and pressures that drove the military to exploit radical Islamist militia in recent years continue. It now seems likely that this might also occur in Aceh, as it has in Maluku and Sulawesi.

COUNTERING RADICAL ISLAMISM

What should we say about the threat of radical Islamism in Indonesia? What policy responses are appropriate, desirable or possible? Because radical Islamism, in its roots, is a religious movement even more than it is a political movement, one of the most effective ways to counter the threats posed by both political Islamism and Jihadi Islamism is to win the support and confidence of the moderate Muslim mainstream and strengthen the hand of Islamic liberals. As noted earlier, there are worrying signs that the tide of public opinion in Indonesia may once again be turning. The moderate majority in Indonesia, who only in 2003 began to be persuaded that Jihadi Islamism in the form of Jemaah Islamiyah represented a genuine, home-grown threat, are now beginning to have second thoughts.

Also stymieing Indonesia's efforts to deal with JI and related militants is the fact that radical Islamists enjoy strong party-political and military connections and support. In part this has to do with their usefulness to elite power-brokers during this period of regime change and transition. This affords them a considerable degree of freedom to act and consequently amplifies their capacity to intimidate their opponents.

Finally, while both the radical Islamists and Islamic liberals enjoy a catalytic effect in influencing Muslim society, the related 'ratchet effect' of such influence tends to work much more strongly in favour of the radicals. In other words, gains made by radical Islamists are very difficult to reverse, and over time the cumulative effect of a series of small gains can be considerable, whereas gains made by liberals are much more easily lost. The crucial thing to watch now is the manner and extent to which Jihadi Islamism and political Islamism influence each other; and the critical challenge is to disengage these two very different Islamisms from each other and limit their ability to seduce and persuade moderate Muslims who are feeling confused, anxious and fatigued to the point of depression about Indonesia's crisis-ridden state, the failure of reform and the criticism of the international community.

CONCLUSION

To begin to understand the challenges facing Indonesia today, it is essential to have a sound grasp of three distinct but interrelated aspects of the issues involved: the seminal ideas, the pattern of history and the contemporary context.

When considered from the perspective of seminal ideas, it is clear that Indonesian Islam has been globalised to an extent and in a way not previously recognised. Jihadi Islamism, born of the union of the totalism of Sayyid Qutb and proselytising exclusivism of Wahhabism, has clearly now joined the ideas of Muhammad Abduh, Rashid Rida and Maududi in shaping Islamic thought and conviction in Indonesia. The essentialist argument that 'Indonesian Islam is different' no longer represents a tenable response to concerns about the reach of Islamist extremism into the Malay world. Moreover, the hopeful refrain that political Islamism is unrelated to Jihadi Islamism must give way to an acknowledgment that, whatever their differences, shared ideas must necessarily produce some common sympathies. This is not to say that the radical political Islamists are not being sincere when they speak of rejecting the methods of terrorism, but rather that for all their differences political and Jihadi Islamism at times relate to each other synergistically.

The central passion driving radical Islamism, both political Islamism and Jihadi Islamism, is the need for God to reign supreme. Ironically it is all about religion and yet, take away the religious language, and it is clearly recognisable as another manifestation of that great 20th century creation: utopian totalitarianism.

The struggle against radical Islamism needs to be waged on a number of levels, but the first of these is the level of ideas. Only when progressive Islamic writers make clear – with the same passion and eloquence as demonstrated by the radical Islamists – the profound ways in which the essential message of Islam is congruent with liberal, democratic values, can the powerful attraction of radical Islamist thought be countered in the marketplace of ideas.

The pattern of history points to the fact that, even if it only directly affects only a minute fraction of Indonesian society, the advent of Jemaah Islamiyah/al-Qaeda style Jihadi Islamism in the Indonesian archipelago marks a sea-change in Indonesian Islam. The 19th-century Padri movement in West Sumatra and the Darul Islam rebellion in 1950s both contained significant elements of Jihadi Islamism, but were each very local in their concerns. The Jihadi Islamism that Indonesia is experiencing today is global in orientation; it very much subscribes to 'acting locally but thinking globally'. This modern form of globalised and globalising Jihadi Islamism had its genesis in the mujahideen struggle in Afghanistan and in the related training camps and *madrasa*s of Pakistan.

The key to understanding Indonesia's Jihadi Islamist networks is first to understand the networks formed by the 'Afghan alumni', and the ways in which this network has been reinforced through marriage and through the associated network of Jihadi *madrasa*s and *pesantren*. Of no less importance is the need to learn the lesson of the Afghanistan experience and be alert and responsive to the possibility that the radicalising experience of the mujahideen in Afghanistan and Pakistan might now be repeated with a new generation of Jihadi Islamists in formation in Maluku, Sulawesi and Mindanao. Finally, at this difficult point in its transition to democracy Indonesian society is fragile and vulnerable. In this sense, the experience of Pakistan offers valuable lessons. It may be unpopular to talk of radical Islamism incrementally and strategically ratcheting up its influence over politics, society and culture, but the reality is that a great deal is now at stake: to deny the contest is to risk losing it.

ACKNOWLEDGMENTS: I am grateful for the generous advice and encouragement of Achmad Suaedy, Vedi Hadiz, Jaap Timmer, Bill Shepard, Judith Fergin, David May, Andy Trigg, Sidney Jones, Robert Hefner, Dharmawan Ronodipuro and other friends and colleagues in developing this chapter.

NOTES

1   Indonesia has around 14 000 *pesantren*, some with only a couple of hundred students and others with several thousand. The word *pesantren* is Javanese in origin and describes the sort of religious boarding school that elsewhere in the Muslim world would be known as *madrasa*. Confusingly, the term *madrasa* is also used for thousands of religious schools in Indonesia, although generally in Indonesia *madrasa*s are day schools only and have a largely secular curriculum. Most *pesantren* also house *madrasa*s within their complexes. *Pesantren* tend to be associated with NU and non-*pesantren*-linked *madrasa*s with Muhammadiyah, but many *pesantren* are independent of both organisations.

2   Most scholars agree that fundamentalism represents a reaction to modernity. In this sense fundamentalists – be they Christian, Jewish, Muslim or Hindu – despite their own sense of themselves are products of the modern era and mostly have their origins in the late 19th and early 20th centuries. The Amish do not fit this time-frame, but there is a sense in which their hyperconservativism, with its time-capsule preservation of 18th-century life, represents an early reaction to modernity.

3   This reality is, many Islamic scholars would argue, completely opposed to the spirit of Islam and the Shari'a. However, socioeconomic and political dynamics in countries such as Saudi Arabia, Iran, Egypt and Pakistan mean that like the rulings of the church in medieval Europe, the Shari'a – although potentially a powerful instrument of justice – is interpreted and applied to the advantage of the wealthy and powerful men. Many Islamic scholars argue that in the modern age the principles and values of the Shari'a are best realised through democratically accountable government and the true rule of law. Progressive Islamic scholars hold that modern 'Western' law, properly applied, reflects the core values of the Shari'a.

4   Refer to Ahmed Rashid, *Jihad: the Rise of Militant Islam in Central Asia* (New York: Penguin, 2002), pp. 45, 118, 138, 215, 223–24; Gilles Kepel, *Jihad: the Trail of Political Islam* (Cambridge, Mass: Harvard University Press, 2002), pp. 69–73.

5   Martin van Bruinessen argues that: 'Most of the student groups were quietist and apolitical; they were primarily concerned with individual moral self-improvement and with the *Usroh* as a moral haven in an immoral world. But there were also Usroh groups affiliated with such NII/TII leaders as Abu Bakar Bashir, which believed in the necessity of establishing an Islamic state and imposing the *shari'a* on fellow Muslims. No firm boundaries between these various groups existed.' See Martin van Bruinessen, 'Genealogies of Islamic radicalism post-Suharto Indonesia', *South East Asia Research*, Vol. 10, No. 2 (2002), pp. 117–24. I believe that this represents an acute and critically important observation, but van Bruinessen, like most other expert observers, also underestimated the extent of the threat represented by JI's subterranean Jihadi Islamism in this piece.

6   ICG Asia Briefing, *Al-Qaeda in Southeast Asia: the case of the 'Ngruki network' in Indonesia* (8 August 2002), authored by ICG Indonesia Director Sidney Jones with assistance from ICG Jakarta researchers. Refer also to ICG Asia Briefing, *Indonesia: Violence and Radical Muslims* (10 October 2001). Both documents can be found at the International Crisis Group website: <http://www.crisisweb.org/projects/reports.

cfm>. In April 2002 the Terrorism Project at the Washington DC–based Center for Defense Information (CDI) published a very brief report by analyst Reyko Huang entitled 'In the spotlight: Jemaah Islamiah', available on-line at <http://www.cdi.org/terrorism/Ji-pr.cfm>, two months after it had published a slightly longer report by the same analyst entitled 'Al-Qaeda in Southeast Asia: evidence and response', available on-line at <http://www.cdi.org/terrorism/sea.pr.cfm>.

7   Within two weeks of the Bali bombing, the ICG released a brief initial report: ICG *Indonesia Briefing: Impact of the Bali Bombing* (24 October 2002). After extensive research, including interviews with many either with people involved directly with Jemaah Islamiyah or through monitoring, this was followed by: ICG *Indonesia Backgrounder: How the Jemaah Islamiyah Terrorist Network Operates* (11 December 2002), available on-line at <http://www.crisisweb.org/projects/reports.cfm>.

8   One earlier work that speculated about al-Qaeda connections in Indonesia is Rohan Gunaratna, *Inside al-Qaeda: Global Network of Terror* (London: C Hurst & Co, 2002). Gunaratna devotes one chapter out of five to dealing with al-Qaeda in Asia, almost half of which is concerned with South-East Asia. Much of what Gunaratna has to say about Indonesia, however, is very general in nature and that which is more specific has been superceded by the ICG reports. Another stimulating study is Zachary Abuza, *Militant Islam in Southeast Asia: Crucible of Terror* (Boulder, Col: Lynne Reiner, 2003), which devotes one of its six chapters to tracing the development of Jemaah Islamiyah.

9   Robert Hefner, 'Civic pluralism denied? The new media and Jihadi violence in Indonesia', in Dale F Eickelman and Jon W Anderson (eds), *New Media in the Muslim World: the Emerging Public Sphere*, 2nd edn (Bloomington: Indiana University Press, 2003); Martin van Bruinessen 'Genealogies of Islamic radicalism in post-Suharto Indonesia', *South East Asia Research*, Vol. 10, No. 2 (2002), pp. 117–24.

10 ICG, *Jemaah Islamiyah in Southeast Asia: Damaged but Still Dangerous*, ICG Asia Report No. 63 (26 August 2003).

11 BAKIN (Badan Koordinasia Intelijen Negara – State Intelligence Coordinating Agency) was established by Soeharto in the 1980s as Indonesia's central intelligence-gathering agency and reported directly to the president. In October 2000, President Abdurrahman Wahid replaced BAKIN with BIN (Badan Intelijens Nasiona – National Intelligence Body) eliminating the agency's coordinating role. The agency was reinstated two years later by President Megawati Sukarnoputri.

12 Van Bruinessen, 'Genealogies of Islamic Radicalism', p. 17.

13 ———, 'Genealogies of Islamic Radicalism', p. 17.

14 ICG, *Jemaah Islamiyah in Southeast Asia*, p. i.

15 ———, *Jemaah Islamiyah in Southeast Asia*, p. 6.

16 ———, *Jemaah Islamiyah in Southeast Asia*, pp. 26–27.

17 ———, *Jemaah Islamiyah in Southeast Asia*, pp. 27–28.

18 The Transparency International *Corruption Perception Index 2002* on the 102 nations for which reliable data is available places Indonesia near the very bottom of the table (with Kenya, 96th out of 102), just above Bangladesh (102nd), Nigeria (101st) and Paraguay, Madagascar and Angola (all 98th), and well below the Philippines (78th), Pakistan (77th), Russia (74th), India (73rd) and Thailand (64th). The report is available online at <http://www.transparency.org/cpi/2002/bpi2002.en.html>. For an incisive examination of the state of Indonesia's legal system, refer to: Tim Lindsey (ed.), *Indonesia: the Commercial Court and Law Reform in Indonesia* (Sydney: Desert Pea Press, 2000).

9

AUSTRALIAN ISLAM, THE NEW GLOBAL TERRORISM AND THE LIMITS OF CITIZENSHIP

MICHAEL HUMPHREY

The US 'war on terror' declared in response to the terrorist attacks of September 11 divides the world into friends and enemies. Yet this division cannot correspond to any geographical and cultural reality in our globalising world. National security is not available through the fantasy of geographical or cultural separation, including 'ethnic cleansing'. International immigration into the cities of Western Europe, North America and Australia has made them irreversibly transnational and multicultural places. Thus while the war on terrorism rhetorically divides the world, it at the same time declares war everywhere. In the West the war on terrorism amounts to an undeclared state of emergency about which we are reminded almost daily by general terrorist alerts and 'official' travel warnings.[1] Moreover the war on terrorism is, like Huntington's 'clash of civilisations', code for conflict between Islam and the West; and, despite the denials of presidents and prime ministers, the primary targets of the war on terrorism are Muslim individuals, families, communities and societies internationally marked by the September 11 attacks as potentially hostile, a risk.

In Western societies, the fearful division of the world into 'them' and 'us' through the war on terrorism is premised on the facts of globalisation; that our world has become increasingly interconnected through mass migration from the South to the North. Islam and Muslims, the primary focus of the war on terrorism, have already been in the West for at least two generations. In Australia, Muslim immigrants began arriving in significant numbers in the 1970s during the era of multiculturalism, the liberal response to manage cultural diversity produced through immigration. The undeclared state of emergency produced by the war on terrorism has changed the terms of membership in Australian multicultural society. The Australian Government's legislative initiatives and political rhetoric to enhance national security and public safety have had the effect of intensifying surveillance of our own society, thereby producing new social categories of suspicion and undermining the equality of citizenship.

The Australian Government has shifted from a perspective of reconciliation to one of risk, from a future premised on social inclusion of diversity to one premised on social exclusion, based on suspicion of the dangerous 'Other'. Reconciliation refers to the period in Australian history when both immigrants and indigenous Australians won political recognition of cultural difference and rights. For immigrants, this was reflected in the policy of multiculturalism while for Aboriginal Australians it was the recognition of land rights and cultural heritage. Reconciliation, in the broad sense used here, refers to reconciling difference in order to imagine a shared future, a process that is mutually identity-altering. Hence the politics of multiculturalism (around immigration-induced cultural diversity) and national reconciliation (acknowledgment of Aboriginal suffering, loss and prior rights to land) carried with it the potential transformation of the national narrative and identity – for example, the 2001 referendum on constitutional reform to recognise the place of Aboriginal people and immigrants.

Risk engenders a perspective in which the future shapes the present. Risk not only refers to security but has also become an organising principle of a globalising world. In sociology, 'risk society' describes the social precariousness of institutionalised patterns of existence. In risk society the concept of risk has reversed the relationship of past, present and future. The past loses its power to determine the present and instead future possibilities increasingly determine decision making. The concept of risk becomes 'a peculiar intermediate state between security and destruction, where the perception of threatening risks determines thought and action'.[2] Risk society is 'an epoch in which the dark sides of progress increasingly come to dominate social debate'.[3]

While the threat of international terrorism to national security made the shift to risk explicit, the change was already under way and evident in the Australian Government's changing policies towards refugees and asylum seekers.[4] The changes were designed to restrict rights to asylum through remote detention and the creation of a migration exclusion zone (moving the goalposts!). Through the harmonisation of migration and asylum policies, the North has effectively erected what I have described as a 'transnational border'.[5] In Australia these policy changes have, coincidentally, been mainly directed at restricting the arrival of Muslim refugees primarily from Afghanistan, Iran and Iraq.[6]

This shift to a risk perspective has changed the terms of participation of Muslim immigrants in the West (especially in Western Europe and Australia). They had already been regarded as socially problematic and even culturally incompatible with multicultural values because of their social marginality and their conspicuous cultural identification through public Islamic rituals and symbolic dress.[7] The effect of the al-Qaeda terrorist attacks in the United States was to deepen racism towards Muslims in Western societies everywhere through the collective fear the attacks engendered.

The 'war on terror' has highlighted the fact that globalisation has made national security an issue that now reaches into the everyday life of all citizens. Because there is no clear culturally geographical place where the enemy can be found, the war on terrorism (not on terrorists) has no easily identifiable target and is globalised. The war on terrorism is the very antithesis of contemporary hi-tech war, which Paul Virilio argues is characterised by intensification of vision (once the searchlight metaphor, now the cruise missile video clip) and of destructive power (smart weapons) realised through remote visibility and speed.[8] By contrast, terrorism's 'individualisation' of war (the idea that you no longer need armies but individuals with powerful weapons and suicidal commitment) has only amplified the effect of cultural de-territorialisation. For Muslim immigrants, this undeclared state of emergency has revealed the contingency of social inclusion and belonging in the West, even if they are naturalised citizens or even born in the West.

My point about the war on terrorism as an undeclared state of emergency is that any discussion about Islam in the West must include an analysis of the relationship of the state to its people. The focus of our analysis cannot simply be an examination of Islamic responses or of Islam, since the very terms of Muslim immigrant social and political participation in the West have been changed by the war on terrorism. Thus, the critical issue underlying the current experience and predicament of Muslims in Australia is not just their particular connections to homeland politics or to global political Islam, but the Australian Government's shift from a discourse of full participation under multiculturalism to one about risk. The analysis must include the transformation of Islamic culture and politics, as well as the major shift in the national identity and the consequent conditionality of citizenship in the West.

While citizenship rights for first-generation immigrants to Australia have always been conditional, either legally (criminal convictions leading to loss of citizenship) or socially (racism and marginalisation), recent 'national security' legislation aimed at restricting rights of asylum and establishing emergency powers to fight the threat of global terrorism has expanded the conditionality of citizenship for all Australians.[9] The political effect of this legislation, loosely described as 'national security', has been to racialise immigration, asylum and nationality, thereby producing a differentiated citizenship and circumscribing the quality of democratic life.[10] The state focus on internal and external security risks has heightened perception of dangerous differences and a demand for techniques of bureaucratic control (profiling) to identify potential risk. This racialising technique turns broad categories of people into suspicious Others, even if they are members of families that have been in Australia for generations, long-term Australians.

This chapter explores the impact of September 11 and the 'war on terror' on Muslim communities and Islam in Australia. It does this firstly by sketching the formation of Muslim communities and Islamic institutions in the West through migration, and secondly by looking at the relationship between the Muslim diaspora, homeland politics and the new 'global Islam'. I will argue that the shift from reconciliation to risk marks an important change in Australian national identity and citizenship. It does not represent a mere return to the past national identity of White Australia. While it is racialising and exclusionary, it also reveals the way citizenship has become more than national as questions about identity, rights, security and culture become globalised.

ISLAM AS A RELIGION OF IMMIGRANTS

The construction of Muslim immigrants and Islam as the dangerous Other by the war on terrorism casts doubt on their integrity and loyalty as citizens. This experience of stigmatisation is not new for Muslims in the West. Many different international events have shaped how Western host societies have viewed their Muslim migrant communities, including the Iranian Revolution, the Rushdie Affair and the Gulf War in 1991. Moreover the impact of the social disadvantage of working class Muslim communities has also often led to their stigmatisation and marginalisation as being unwilling to fit into Western societies. Post–September 11, however, the West has intensified the surveillance of potential 'enemies within', implicitly Muslims. In time of war, the fear of the enemy within has always led to intensified state surveillance and even compulsory detention of the 'enemy alien' – for example, Italian and German Australians during the World War II. The 'war on terror', however, is not against a single nationality but against culturally diverse communities of many nationalities. Nevertheless, Muslim immigrants are viewed as if religious belief constituted them as a hostile political identity.

What is the character of immigrant Islam in Australia? Has immigrant Islam changed between the first and second generation? What is its relationship to homeland politics? What is its relationship to the emergence of a global (transnational) Islam?

Islam arrived in Australia through migration and today Muslims represent about 1.5 per cent of the Australian population.[11] Although Muslim immigrants first came in the mid-19th century, it was not until the 1970s that they began arriving in significant numbers. My own major ethnographic work on Lebanese Muslim communities in the late 70s and early 80s was during this period of rapid increase in Muslim immigrants, the first-generation Muslim communities.[12] The largest communities were the Turks and the Lebanese settling in Sydney and Melbourne. Today Lebanese-born Muslims (first generation) represent 10 per cent and Turks 8 per cent of Australian Muslims. In addition, of the Australian-born Muslims, now more than a third of all Australian Muslims, around 30 per cent claim Lebanese ancestry, while 18 per cent claim Turkish ancestry. Although Muslim immigrants come from more than 60 different countries, the image of Islam in Australia has been strongly shaped by these two communities, their size and their urban concentrations.

Lebanese and Turkish Muslim immigration resembles the pattern of Mediterranean migration and settlement in Australia – that of the Greeks, southern Italians and Yugoslavs – of the 1950s and 1960s, which was characteristically organised through chain migration based on kinship networks and obligations. The family and village community was used as the basis for recreating community and re-establishing religious life. The primary religious concerns of the first generation were with the organisation of Islamic life-cycle rituals (birth, marriage, death) in the context of local community life. Muslim village associations were the focal point of organisational life and served a prominent role in settlement.[13] Community meeting halls often evolved into temporary prayer halls and then became official mosques. This organic social and cultural development of Muslim institutions by local ethnic communities was at times experienced as cultural shock by the suburban communities in which they settled, giving them a sense that 'Australian' suburbs were being invaded by a hostile religion. When residents of Annangrove in suburban Sydney appealed in July 2003 to the Land and Environment Court against the local development of a prayer centre (*mehfil*) for the small local Indian Shi'ite community, they argued 'that "holy war" had been declared against the residents of Annangrove who opposed the centre'.[14]

The local community origin of many mosques is reflected in the strong ethnic character many still retain. This autonomous development of mosques has mostly been independent, although the larger mosques have received external national funding or international Muslim charitable funding. The 2003 Land and Environment Court decision to permit the development of the Annangrove prayer centre reflects this local community development,[15] since it had been promoted and funded by a prominent and successful member of the Indian Shi'ite community. The fact that the case was successfully appealed by the local association and not by one of the state or federal Islamic bodies also emphasises the local autonomy and self-reliance of these small communities.

The autonomous and local community character of religious life, however, is more than an expression of the ethnic diversity of Muslim immigrants. It also reflects the lack of an Islamic centre in the contemporary world, including in the West. In Australia, the Australian Federation of Islamic Councils was established as a consultative national Islamic body and has never been seen as a source of religious authority. The lack of a centre is only accentuated by the impact of homeland politics on Muslim communities and the competition amongst Islamic states for religious and political influence in the Muslim diaspora. In Australia this competition has focused on mosque building and the establishment of primary and secondary schools. In the 1980s and 1990s the main struggle for world leadership of Islam was waged between Saudi Arabia and the Islamic Republic of Iran. This had an impact on the large Muslim diaspora in Europe, but not in Australia.

The first generation of Muslim immigrants to the secular West confronted the threat of losing their culture and religion. Salman Rushdie's *Satanic Verses* was all about the experience of the disturbing and alienating loss of culture among Muslim immigrants in Britain. At the same time as being threatening, the act of travel can also bring a 'heightened sense of being Muslim'.[16] In Islamic practice travel, whether in the form of inner spiritual journeys or pilgrimages, is directed towards achieving greater religious consciousness. Far from being culturally assimilating, the experience of migration and settlement in the multicultural industrial cities of the West made Muslims more aware of their ethnic and religious differences. Moreover, for most, their social marginality as unskilled workers made them particularly vulnerable to unemployment, welfare dependence and racism as other sources of differentiation.[17] Even those who had professional qualifications often became working class because their qualifications were not recognised.

There is a commonality in the Muslim first-generation migration experience to the West. Overwhelmingly Muslim migrants have been from rural and urban poor backgrounds and have settled in major industrial cities, often during periods of de-industrialisation. This is true of the Lebanese and Turkish immigrants in Australia, the Maghrebi immigrants in France, the Pakistani, Indian and Bangladeshi immigrants in Britain and the Turkish labour migrants to Germany. An important contrast with Australia has been the restriction on their acquisition of citizenship in many European countries. As legal and illegal foreign workers in Europe, many were treated as temporary residents, whereas they came to Australia under migration and settlement programs.

This process of urban ethnic differentiation has affected Muslim immigrants differently. In the case of Lebanese Muslim immigrants, homeland political conflict served to reinforce sectarian identity alongside religious consciousness. Also, the Australian urban multicultural environment allowed a new equality between the Lebanese sects, which was not possible under Lebanese confessionalism. Some Turkish first-generation migrants put greater emphasis on their ethnic consciousness than on their religious one. Travel in their case permitted greater political and religious freedom than had existed in Turkey. Through the establishment of separate community associations, Kurdish language publications and Kurdish community radio, the Kurds differentiated themselves ethnically from Turks and small sects such as the Alevi to consolidate their separate sectarian consciousness and identity. Their associations reflected this consciousness. Turkish government control over religion continued in Australia through the mosque-building program and the appointment of imams from Turkey and this also served to reinforce internal ethnic and religious differentiation amongst Turkish immigrants.

Ruth Mandel describes a similar process of ethnic differentiation and religious consciousness among first-generation Turkish migrants in Germany. She notes that 'the foreign German context ... provides the initial catalyst for active involvement in religious organizations and worship'.[18] Whereas there were restrictions in Turkey, the German environment provided greater freedom to express their ethnic and religious identities. This was reinforced by their consciousness of the 'moral contamination' that threatened them and led to their revival of Islamic religious and ritual practices. Labour migrants returning to Turkey commented that it was in Germany that they started attending the mosque and practising their religion. Nevertheless, their revival of religious consciousness through ritual practice did not necessarily give the returnees a feeling of belonging. Mandel notes that 'the annual *izin* trip home neither provides an opportunity for collective solidarity with compatriots, nor offers an infusion of the stuff that reinforces identity. Rather it furthers the alienation resulting from the absence of a centre in the lives of the *Gastarbeiter*'.[19]

As well as emphasising their cultural difference, the urban multicultural experience allowed Muslims in the diaspora to institutionalise their collective religious identity through the normalisation of their social and ritual needs within the bureaucratic and legal system. Common concerns about ritual observance, such as marriage and burial, became important points of interaction and negotiation with Australian institutions and led to the development of umbrella organisations to represent the interests of all Australian Muslims, such as the Australian Federation of Islamic Councils and its state bodies. They also benefited from the official organisational and legal expressions of multiculturalism, such as the development of legislation on discrimination and racism, the establishment of ethnic representative bodies (Federation of Ethnic Communities' Councils of Australia – FECCA) and the Anti-Discrimination Board, as well as from general cultural policies such as the provision of a government-supported multicultural television station (SBS).

However, the extent to which multiculturalism, or 'reconciliation', engendered a new, inclusive national imaginary was always limited. In general, the opposition to building new ethnic places of worship (churches, temples and mosques) in the suburbs is an indication of the limits of multiculturalism. The tendency towards 'Othering' and separation creates an inherent ambiguity in recognising cultural difference within the multicultural national identity.[20] In the area of multiculturalism and justice, for example, the recognition of 'tradition' de-individualises and collectivises culture. Individuals come to be seen as bearers and products of different cultures and not individuals to be judged according to their personal subjectivities and motivations. Hence, the use of 'cultural defence' in criminal proceedings can actually produce more discriminatory outcomes instead of promoting justice. In the dramatic case of honour killings, 'cultural defence' is used only when men murder women, thereby transferring culturally gendered inequality into the Australian legal process.[21]

Multiculturalism in Australia never achieved the next step after the recognition of difference: it never reconciled difference and developed a multicultural citizenship or a new Australian identity that changed its perspective on the world. During the 1990s, the Labor government's push to reorient Australia's political, trade and cultural ties to Asia and the national movement for reconciliation with Aboriginal Australians were at first downgraded and then abandoned by the Liberal government after 1996.

FIRST-GENERATION IMMIGRANTS AND HOMELAND POLITICS

Another aspect of the cultural 'Othering' of multiculturalism has been the idea that migrants bring unwanted aspects of their past with them, especially internal political conflicts. In Europe, first-generation Muslim immigrants were characteristically dominated by political issues linked to countries of origin, particularly during the 1970s and 1980s.[22] This was hardly surprising, given that one reason for their migration was the political upheaval in the Middle East during that period: the October 1973 war between Israel and the neighbouring Arab states and the subsequent oil crisis, the Lebanese Civil War, the Iranian Revolution, the Soviet invasion of Afghanistan, the Iran–Iraq War, the first Palestinian Intifada, the Gulf War and the military coup in Algeria in 1992, to mention only the major events.

However, identification with homeland politics among first-generation Muslim immigrants in Australia is not a good measure of whether communities consist of political exiles waiting to return home[23] or whether they have imported homeland politics into the diaspora. The case of religious identification among Lebanese Muslim immigrants in Australia during the Lebanese Civil War demonstrates the strength of the issues of homeland politics in the immigrant context, even if they have formed the backdrop to local struggles.

Lebanese Muslim immigrant identity has always been juxtaposed to Christian Lebanese identity in Lebanon and the diaspora. In Australia, the Muslim immigrants arrived into an established majority Lebanese Christian diaspora that had a long history of involvement in Lebanese nationalist politics from the Ottoman period. In fact, Lebanon's very existence as a nation-state had historically depended on the efforts of the Lebanese Christian diaspora, particularly in the Americas. However, despite the continuing connections with Lebanon, the contemporary Lebanese diaspora has largely been involved in what Benedict Anderson calls 'long-distance nationalism'. They are not usually 'true exiles' waiting for victory to return home but 'emigrés who have no serious intention of going back home, which, as time passes, more and more serves as a phantom bedrock for an embattled metropolitan ethnic identity'.[24] In other words, according to Anderson, Lebanese immigrant politics and communal identification during the war can best be understood as an expression of the immigrant metropolitan experience of exclusion or marginalisation than the direct influence and interest of Lebanese politics.

The present sectarian consciousness and identification in the Australian Lebanese diaspora was brought about by displacement from the Lebanese civil war. War refugee communities encountered the older Australian Lebanese communities whose diasporic identity was a nostalgic sense of exile and a story of successful Lebanese integration into Australian society. The intense rivalry between Lebanese immigrant community associations that emerged during the Lebanese war was a measure of the intensification of communal identification, especially in Sydney. The new political environment of multiculturalism permitted communal discourse as a legitimate immigrant identity.[25] The government's most important decision in expanding the significance of Lebanese sectarian identity was the policy to accept humanitarian migration through approved lists of relatives based on equal treatment of all sects in Australia. Lebanese community leaders from all sects successfully lobbied for representation on the basis of sect and were sent to Lebanon 'to arrange for group movements of those accepted'.[26] The Australian Government's response to the proliferation of community associations and competition for sectarian influence was to establish the Lebanese Settlement Committee and subsequently the Lebanese Community Council as representative umbrella organisations.

At the end of the Lebanese Civil War in 1990, the transnational nationalist issues and communal identification informed by the emotions of the distress of the war gradually receded from Lebanese community politics. The Lebanese immigrant community did not remain focused on the Lebanese national project during the post-war reconstruction and reconciliation period. Community identification with sect declined as the problems that developed around making a life in Australia dominated. Nevertheless, the legacy of the war in the form of broken lives and poverty continued to have an impact on Lebanese image and reputation in the urban multicultural hierarchy. The problems now faced by the second generation included adolescent unemployment in industrially depressed western Sydney and involvement in crime.[27] Lebanese sectarian identity was once again primarily shaped internally by ethnic differentiation measured by distance from assimilation. The community had little control over its ethnic devaluation, especially when it became connected to domestic and international politics in the Australian popular consciousness, the arrival of unwanted Middle Eastern refugees (boat people) and international Islamic terrorism.

Another dimension of the 1990s was the way external political events like the Gulf War, and to some extent the Israeli-Palestinian conflict, articulated broader Arab and Muslim identification in the Lebanese diaspora. However, this did not usually take the form of an organised transnational Arab or Muslim political community but one shaped by public response to media vilification and discrimination through collective stereotyping of Arabs and/or Muslims. Often the distinction between Arab and Muslim in the media was very blurred and politically undirected, except negatively. Such media reporting essentially used local Arab/Muslim immigrant communities as a context to tell a story often directed at the potential enemy within. Consequently external events introduced via the media have provided an ongoing impetus for scrutinising the 'internal' racialised borders (which citizens are really to be trusted?) as a means of keeping open the question of entitlement and citizenship of Arab and Muslim immigrants. Lebanese engagement with the media has become a means of including or excluding individuals from the mediated categories for complex reasons.

Muslim immigrant response to media representations reveals their political inequality through the inability to define their own cultural identity. In multicultural societies the value of cultural difference is not stable. The Lebanese, or different sections of the community, cannot fix the co-ordinates of their identity. Neither can they easily opt out of the labelling process 'to become the invisible against which others' visibility is measured'.[28] The media itself becomes their source of identity, often with the reciprocal effect of stereotyping both their own Islamic culture and Australian culture; for example, Islam is seen as as unitary and unchanging, and the West as bad and threatening their values.[29]

The example of Lebanese Muslim immigrants suggests there is no simple reading of the significance of homeland politics in immigrant communities. Certainly the radicalisation of Lebanese Muslim communities and the emergence of political Islam after the Israeli invasion of Lebanon in 1982 were reflected in religious politics among both the Lebanese Sunni and Shi'ite immigrant communities. There were direct links through clerical appointments in Sydney mosques with both the pro-Khomeinist Sunni Harakat al-Tawhid al-Islami (Movement for Unity in Islam) in Tripoli and the Shi'ite political movements (and now Lebanese political parties with elected parliamentary deputies) of Amal and Hizbollah.[30] In the mid-1980s *Hizbollah* became closely identified with Iranian politics overseas, taking Western hostages in Lebanon and undertaking terrorist actions in Paris in 1985 and 1986 on behalf of Iranian Islamic revolutionaries.[31] In Australia, Lebanese Shi'ite immigrant solidarity with Hizbollah was more nationalist than religious. The Lebanese Shi'ite community in Sydney, most of whom had emigrated from a small number of border villages in southern Lebanon, viewed Hizbollah as the 'liberators' of Israeli-occupied southern Lebanon.

Political activism and recruitment into homeland politics was quite limited in Australia in contrast with what occurred in Europe, where Islamic political currents from all over the Muslim world competed for influence among Europe's six million Muslims. After the French experience in the late 1970s of hosting Ayatollah Khomeini's religious revolution which led to the fall of the Shah in Iran, European governments (French, German and Belgian) curtailed radicalism by assigning the management of Islam to foreign governments. Thus from 1982 the Algerian Government ran the Grand Mosque in Paris to counter the influence of radical Algerian clerics in France. In Germany, the Turkish Department of Religious Affairs sent its own preachers and teachers to counter the influence of Turkish brotherhoods and Islamic movements among the Turkish labour migrants.[32] Kepel argues that, before 1989, to avoid conflict with European authorities Islamic movements treated European countries as sanctuaries for political exiles who were concerned only with homeland politics: 'they were places where militants and sympathizers could be recruited, who would then go home to their native countries to carry on the only fight that was worth the candle, against the regimes of the ungodly'.[33] In Norway, when visiting Muslim clerics recommended to Somali and Sudanese Muslim refugees that to live a good Muslim life they should leave *dar al-harb* (the land of war, the non-Muslim world) and return to *dar al-Islam* (land of Islam and peace, the Muslim world), their recommendations were met with scepticism. From the perspective of the refugees, the war-torn Muslim societies they had fled were not examples of *dar al-Islam*.[34]

The Australian Government, on the other hand, never gave the home governments of Muslim immigrants a management role, with the exception of the Turkish Government, which on its own initiative is the only government directly involved in organising and managing the religious affairs of its immigrant community in Australia. Other Middle Eastern governments have sought to intervene indirectly in Muslim religious affairs in Australia, such as the 1980s campaign to have Imam Taj ad-din al-Hillali deported. As the leader of the Imam Ali (Lakemba) Mosque, the largest mosque congregation in Sydney with a majority of north Lebanese Sunni background, Imam Hillali was seen as both radical and also very conservative.[35] At different times representatives from the Lebanese, Egyptian and Saudi governments as well as Australian Jewish organisations all lobbied the Australian Government not to extend his visa to stay in Australia as imam of the Imam Ali Mosque. The Australian Federation of Islamic Councils also became involved, supporting him by elevating his status to mufti.[36] Foreign governments have also often played an important role in Australia as benefactors for religious building (mosques) and education. Many Muslim states have made substantial donations for mosque building, including Libya, Saudi Arabia, Iraq, Iran and the United Arab Emirates, to name a few.

SECOND-GENERATION IMMIGRANTS

Gilles Kepel argues that in Europe the second generation shifted its political focus to their homeland, Europe. It was not the 'home' (of their parents) that was *dar al-Islam*; now Europe itself was included in that domain, a place where they could live an Islamic life in accordance with the Shari'a. Thus, in France for example, the 'militants felt that Muslim schoolchildren should be authorised to respect the prescriptions of the Shari'a, as interpreted by the disciples of Qutb and Maududi, and that women and girls should wear the veil'.[37] The appeal of Islamic politics and identity to this second generation, Kepel argues, was their experience of racism and social marginality. These religious rights, however, are being claimed on the basis of their rights as European citizens, not as members of another religion and nationality.

In Australia Muslim immigrants set out to establish their rights in a multicultural society from the first generation. In other words, multicultural Australia was from the outset looked at as *dar al-Islam*, a place to live a good Muslim life. Very early on in my own ethnographic work I was told by a Sunni Imam that Australia was almost an Islamic society already because it shared very similar values such a individual freedom, welfare and democracy! Another measure of Muslim immigrant identification with Australia is the very high levels of naturalisation. The take-up of citizenship by the Middle East–born population is 74 per cent, while that of the Lebanese-born population is 91.6 per cent.[38]

The second generation experience varies across different Muslim ethnicities in Australia. Nevertheless the largest communities, the Lebanese and Turkish Australian Muslims, have faced similar problems of racism and marginality to those encountered by the Maghrebis in France, the Turks in Germany and Pakistanis in Britain. For them Islam is a source of authentic identity, something in which they take pride. In Europe the second generation are participating in what Lars Pedersen refers to as the 'newer Islamic movements ... [which] are developing a region of consciousness and culture in which the social norms of the majority society do not count'.[39] These movements represent a defence of their devalued and dissolving Muslim life .

In Australia, new non-ethnic Islamic *da'wah* (call to Islam) movements similar to those in Europe have emerged. These include the Islamic Youth Movement,[40] as well as older movements such as the Jamaat Daawah Islamiah and the Tablighi Jamaat, an ascetic non-political movement focused on personal intensification of faith through occasional withdrawal from normal daily routines of work and family life.[41] While social marginality may have led many to revive their faith, it has also led to social alienation and dysfunctional family crisis. The media headlines about Lebanese and Muslim youth gangs involved in crime and sexual assault in Sydney between 1999 and 2002 represented a crisis in parental and moral authority of families and community. Despite the fact that this criminality itself was a sign of the loss of Islamic religious values and belief among some second-generation youth, these incidents inflamed racist sentiment towards Islam, Muslims, Lebanese, and Arabs, all readily conflated identities in the popular media. Yet these very processes of misrecognition of Islam and racialising the criminal or immoral Other only reinforce the devaluation of Islam and its revaluation by Muslims feeling unjustly stigmatised.

The gradual de-ethnicising of Islam in the second generation and the emergence of *da'wah* movements do not mean there is a re-centring of Islam in Australia or globally, despite the polarising impact of the September 11 attacks and the war on terrorism. What is emerging is a networked Islam in the sense of Castells' 'networked society'.[42] Through the communications revolution, the world becomes de-territorialised and connected through interlocking ties. In other words, globalisation is reconstitutive of all cultures, not just the dominant Western global consumer culture. At a regional level in Europe, this is leading innovative Islamic institutions such as the European Council for Fatwa and Research to provide religious advice (fatwa) on how Muslims can fulfill religious obligations as a minority. There are also websites now offering online fatwa services for Muslims in Europe.[43] While at one level globalisation is creating a 'one religion, one culture' – religion as a complete way of life – discourse, it is also revealing to Muslims how culturally and socially diverse the *umma* is becoming.[44]

But 'networked' Islam is being articulated in the context of networked global society and in the global political context in which power is dispersed but nothing can be outside.[45] The Internet is a mode of resistance and personal communication available to all who can be networked. There are limits, however, to the focus of expression of visible power which can be only momentarily demonstrated through opportunities for mass perception, the creation of global audiences. One illusion created by the networked society is what Virilio calls the efficacy of the totalising tendency, in which it is possible to engender mass perception but not mass apprehension. Power is momentarily revealed through the production/appropriation of mass events via mass communications. Now, both terrorism and war draw on networked power to achieve a totalising moment of power. This is the politics of mass perception and emotions focused on the use of apocalyptic violence, which is permitting a fantastic reordering of the world by dramatically essentialising as 'a risk' whole cultures and peoples, thereby setting them apart.

CONCLUSION

The risk model that informs the war on terrorism and the undeclared state of emergency in Australia offers no social future except cultural separation. It is a contagion model of society in which those potentially dangerous parts – Muslim individuals and communities – must be either assimilated or kept under surveillance and controlled. This is the antithesis of the reconciliation model, which offers the potential for new and transformed identities and shared social futures.

The risk model is a political fantasy in a globalising world. In our increasingly interdependent world, we cannot conceive of the world as if it were made up of separate cultural geographies. There is no cultural geography corresponding to the 'clash of civilisations'. The networks of transnational multiculturalism will ensure that interconnection persists. The risk perspective of the war on terrorism is a recipe for alienation and division. It also ignores the sociological and political trends of continued de-centring of Islam in networked worlds, in the diaspora in the West.

The contemporary sociological and political analysis of Muslims in the West suggests that they are not being homogenised either through assimilation into secularism or through the new Muslim consciousness engendered by the immigration experience. Islam is becoming networked within the global structures of power and communication and is trying to work out the terms of participation. Moreover, the competing political centres of Islamism are not surviving well into the second generation. Kepel argues that in Iran and Algeria the youth are rejecting religious authoritarianism as irrelevant to their lives. He comments:

> When we consider the Muslim world as a whole, the opposition Islamist movements still face an unprecedented moral crisis. Their political project – which was always vague in its promises of a radiant Islamic state applying the Shari'a – now has a track record showing that it banks on the future but is mired in the past.[46]

The story of Muslim first and second immigrants reveals that Islam is here and working out its relationship with the West. Muslim immigrants have always approached Australia as a society in which they wanted to live good Muslim lives, a space of *dar al-Islam,* unlike Muslim immigrants in Europe who have mainly come to that position in the second generation.

Working out our relationship to cultural difference through reconciliation is a project that cannot be replaced by risk, by a social imagination driven by isolating fear. Our challenge is to be able to address national security in the age of 'international terrorism' without dissolving the collective values and morality that sustains our social world in our cities, nations and transnational relationships.

NOTES

1   The US terrorist alert in August 2003 of possible al-Qaeda actions initiated through Australian airports highlights the global nature of this state of emergency. As it turned out, US and Australian intelligence agencies disagreed about the threat and the US Homeland Security agency withdrew the warning.
2   Barbara Adam, Ulrich Beck and Joost van Loon (eds), *The Risk Society and Beyond: Critical Issues in Social Theory* (London: Sage Publications, 2002), p. 213.
3   Ulrich Beck, *Ecological Politics in an Age of Risk* (Cambridge: Polity Press, 1995), p. 2.
4   Michael Humphrey, 'Humanitarianism, terrorism and the transnational border', *Social Analysis,* Vol. 6, No. 1 (2002), pp. 117–22.
5   ——,'Humanitarianism, terrorism and the transnational border'.
6   During the period of boat arrivals (1999–2002) the overwhelming majority came from Afghanistan and Iraq. Up until the 'regime change' in Afghanistan in 2001 brought about by the United States–led military invasion, the great majority of asylum seekers from these countries were granted temporary protection visas.
7   Michael Humphrey, 'Islam: a test for multiculturalism', *Asian Migrant,* Vol. 2, No. 2 (1989), pp. 48–56.
8   Paul Virilio, *War & Cinema: the Logistics of Perception* (London: Verso, 1989).
9   Another example of the erosion of Australian citizenship rights is the predicament of Australian citizens David Hicks and Mamdouh Habib. Having been detained in Afghanistan at the end of the US war against al-Qaeda and the Taliban government, they are being held without charge in Guantanamo Bay without access to their own legal representation and now face the prospect of being tried by a US military tribunal with the power of capital punishment and with the acquiescence

of the Australian Government. See Aaron Partick, Penelope Debelle and Louise Dobson, 'No return for David Hicks', *The Age,* 20 July 2003.

10 Julia Paley, 'Toward anthropology of democracy', *Annual Review of Anthropology,* Vol. 31 (2002), pp. 469–96.

11 Australian Bureau of Statistics, Census 2001, cited in Human Rights and Equal Opportunities Commission, *Fact Sheets: Australian Muslims* (March 3003), available online at <>.

12 Michael Humphrey, 'Islam: a test for multiculturalism'.

13 Gary Bouma, *Mosques and Muslim Settlement in Australia* (Canberra: Bureau of Immigration and Population Research, 1994).

14 Jim O'Rourke, 'Judge gives Muslim centre a green light', *Sydney Morning Herald,* 31 July 2003.

15 ——, 'Judge gives Muslim centre a green light'.

16 Dale F Eickelman and James Piscatori, 'Social theory', in Dale F Eickelman and James Piscatori (eds), *Muslim Travelers: Pilgrimage, Migration, and the Religious Imagination* (Berkeley: University of California Press, 1990), p. 16.

17 Michael Humphrey, 'Racism and unemployment amongst Lebanese' in Seminar Proceedings of *The Arabic Community: Realities and Challenges* (Sydney: The Arabic Welfare Inter-Agency, 1986), pp. 29–41.

18 Ruth Mandel, 'Shifting centres and emergent identities: Turkey and Germany in the lives of Turkish *Gastarbeiter*', in Dale F Eickelman and James Piscatori (eds), *Muslim Travelers: Pilgrimage, Migration, and the Religious Imagination,* p. 163.

19 ——, 'Shifting centres and emergent identities', p. 168.

20 Michael Humphrey, 'Globalization and Arab diasporic identities: the Australian Arab Case', *Bulletin of the Royal Institute for Inter-Faith Studies,* Vol. 2 (2002), pp. 141–58.

21 ——, 'Globalization and Arab diasporic identities'.

22 Gilles Kepel, *Jihad: the Trail of Political Islam* (Cambridge, Mass.: Harvard University Press, 2002).

23 Benedict Anderson, 'Long-distance nationalism: world capitalism and the rise of identity politics', *Wertheim Lecture* (CASA: University of Amsterdam, 1992).

24 ——, 'Long-distance nationalism: world capitalism and the rise of identity politics', p. 12.

25 Michael Humphrey, 'Sectarianism and the politics of identity: the Lebanese in Sydney', in Albert Hourani and Nadim Shehadi (eds), *Lebanese in the World: a Century of Lebanese Migration* (London: IB Tauris, 1993).

26 Minister for Immigration and Ethnic Affairs, the Hon. JR Mackellar, 'New initiatives to help Lebanese', news release 45/76 (9 September 1976).

27 Michael Humphrey, *Family, Work and Unemployment: a Study of Lebanese Settlement in Sydney* (Canberra: Australian Government Publishing Service, 1984), p. 151.

28 Brackette Williams, 'A class act: anthropology and the race to nation across ethnic terrain', *Annual Review of Anthropology,* Vol. 18 (1989), p. 420.

29 Michael Humphrey, 'An Australian Islam? Religion in the multicultural city', in Abdullah Saeed and Shahram Akbarzadeh (eds), *Muslim Communities in Australia* (Sydney: UNSW Press, 2001), pp. 33–52.

30 ——, 'Harakat al-Tawhid al-Islami', in John Esposito (ed.), *Encyclopaedia of the Modern Islamic World* (New York/Oxford: Oxford University Press, 1994).

31 Gilles Kepel, *Jihad: the Trail of Political Islam.*

32 ——, *Jihad: the Trail of Political Islam,* pp. 184–203.

33 ——, *Jihad: the Trail of Political Islam*, p. 196.

34 Munzoul Assal, *Beyond Labelling: Somalis and Sudanese in Norway and the Challenge of Homemaking*, unpublished PhD thesis, Department of Anthropology, University of Bergen, Norway, 2003.

35 Michael Humphrey, 'Community, mosque and ethnic politics', *ANZ Journal of Sociology*, Vol. 23, No. 2 (1987), pp. 233–45.

36 Abdullah Saeed, *Islam in Australia* (Sydney: Allen and Unwin, 2003).

37 Gilles Kepel, *Jihad: the Trail of Political Islam*, p. 199.

38 While naturalisation is not necessarily a good measure of commitment to Australia as a place to live 'a good Muslim life', since dual nationality means a choice does not have to be made, only lived, it is at least indicative of aspirations.

39 Lars Pedersen, *Newer Islamic Movements in Western Europe* (London: Ashgate, 1999), p. 3.

40 Gary Bouma, *Mosques and Muslim Settlement in Australia;* Abdullah Saeed and Shahram Akbarzadeh, 'Searching for identity: Muslims in Australia', in Abdullah Saeed and Shahram Akbarzadeh (eds), *Muslim Communities in Australia*, pp. 1–11.

41 Jan Ali, 'Islamic revivalism: the case of the *Tablighi Jamaat*', *Journal of Muslim Affairs*, Vol. 23, No. 1 (2003), pp. 173–81.

42 Manuel Castells, *End of Millennium* (Malden, Mass.: Blackwell Publishers, 1998).

43 Martin van Bruinessen, 'The production of Islamic knowledge in Western Europe', *International Institute for the Study of Islam in the Modern World Newsletter*, Vol. 12, No. 6 (2003).

44 Riaz Hassan, 'Globalisation's challenge to the Islamic *Ummah*', presented at the Conference on Risk, Complex Crises and Social Futures, Royal Institute for Inter-Faith Studies, Jordan, 2000.

45 Michael Hardt and Antonio Negri, *Empire* (Cambridge, Mass. Harvard University Press, 2000).

46 Gilles Kepel, *Jihad: the Trail of Political Islam*, p. 371.

10

CITIZENSHIP, IDENTITY AND BELONGING IN CONTEMPORARY AUSTRALIA

FETHI MANSOURI

Within the ongoing debates about identity, nationalism and citizenship, the history of Arab and Muslim settlement in Australia has been the subject of scant research and analysis. While major studies have examined the racialised representations of Chinese and Pacific Islander migrants in literary and media genres,[1] no significant study has conducted an equivalent analysis of the media representation and discriminatory migration policies towards Arab/Muslim workers in pre-Federation Australia. It is still little known, for example, that many European explorations across the Australian outback were aided considerably by Afghan Muslim camel drivers, of whom there were between 2000 and 4000 in the late 19th century.[2] After Federation and the adoption of the White Australia policy in 1901, Afghans found it increasingly difficult to find employment and live comfortably in Australian society. The Lebanese immigration to Australia, on the other hand, began in the 1870s and 1880s, although these early Lebanese immigrants identified themselves as Syrians.[3] They were classified as Asians under the Immigration Restriction Act of 1901, and while passing the test that assessed eligibility for immigration, they were often excluded from being able to apply for Australian citizenship.

As a preview to what was to occur more than a century later, racial vilification and open discrimination were practised and justified against both the Afghan and Lebanese communities in the name of cultural homogeneity and national interest. The Afghan camel drivers were the first victims of 'Orientalism'.[4] Edward Said defines Orientalism as 'a Western style [of discourse] for dominating, restructuring, and having authority over the Orient'.[5] Orientalism, therefore, provides a conceptual framework for the West to construct knowledge about the Orient from a position of cultural superiority and political power. Such a tradition, which has its roots in age-old ideas about Muslims and Orientals, has surprisingly survived centuries of dominant discourses in contemporary Western societies like Australia.

As early as the latter parts of the 19th century, Afghan Muslim camel drivers were subjected to a major campaign of racial vilification because of tensions with Anglo-Australian bullock drivers in western Queensland.[6] At the same time, other campaigns against Syrian hawkers in the capital cities of the eastern seaboard resonated with wider colonial campaigns against the Chinese community. In Melbourne, the *Leader* in particular ran a major public campaign against Indian Muslim and Syrian hawkers in 1898, involving allegations of criminality, disease and bullying housewives. As if to confirm these popular myths, post-Federation immigration and citizenship legislation introduced restrictions that reduced the Muslim population of Australia to insignificant numbers. The racial vilification and internment of enemy migrants during World War I saw Lebanese and Syrians categorised as 'Turkish subjects' and, thus, singled out as disloyal and a potential risk to Australian society.

The numbers of Muslim immigrants did not recover until after World War II when, initially, the largest group of Muslims to migrate were Turkish Muslims. However, in more recent times, since the adoption of a multicultural policy and owing to overseas conflict, Arab immigration has increased.[7] Amid this recent Arab immigration, there have been a diversity of religious beliefs that, sadly, have not been reflected in public and media reductionist discourse in relation to Middle Eastern migrant communities.

MULTICULTURALISM, CULTURAL DIVERSITY AND NATIONAL IDENTITY

'Cultural diversity' and 'multiculturalism' are widely used terms whose meanings are often contested, particularly in academic circles, but whose assumptions are rarely debated in public discourse. Thus, social processes in Australia that may appear contradictory are more cognisable if we examine the dominant practice and discourse of multiculturalism and its place in Australia's history. For example, it may appear contradictory that many Australians appear to take pride in the culturally diverse nature of the population's makeup while supporting a government that has taken a particularly harsh stance towards Middle Eastern asylum seekers who have arrived in Australia in recent years. However, as this chapter shows, the ambiguous and sometimes problematic intersection of such fluid notions as identity, nationalism, citizenship and multiculturalism can create particular instances of exclusionary discourse and practice. This is, in fact, not totally unexpected since:

one of the most difficult things to comprehend nowadays about this society ... [is] the absolute coincidence of multiculturalism and racism. Far from being the opposite ends of a pole so that one can trade the rise of one against the decline of the other, it seems to be absolutely dead central to society that both multiculturalism and racism are increasing at one and the same time.[8]

Rarely does differential treatment for minority groups, characteristic of democratic multiculturalism, garner support from a majority of the Australian public. This is seen, for example, in the vociferous debates about indigenous land rights or economic support directed at particular minority groups.[9] Yet a liberal discourse of equality and equal opportunity (i.e, a 'difference-blind' model of multiculturalism) is commonly supported and openly preferred by policy makers, many groups within civil society, and the general public. The Labor Government under Whitlam officially enacted multiculturalism in Australia in 1973. Yet, in 2003 Prime Minister John Howard dismissed the very term 'multiculturalism', favouring 'cultural diversity' instead: 'It's [multiculturalism] not a word I use a lot, but there is no other word. I mean I tend to talk about cultural diversity. I tend to talk about people's different heritage.'[10]

The official government rhetoric on multiculturalism and ethnic communities is a crucial factor shaping public opinion towards migrant communities. This is because official government discourse and policies are inherently accorded a high degree of legitimacy and certainty in times of insecurity. Yet the concept of public opinion is 'an exceptionally ambiguous and volatile term and idea ... [because it is] a construction of governments, the media, and of everyday conversation influenced by the government and the media'.[11] In this context, the policies of the current Australian Government and the largely supportive media coverage have, indeed, shaped public attitudes and views towards Muslim and other migrant communities. This task was made easier by the fact that the current Australian Government promotes a version of Australian multiculturalism which, while acknowledging the reality of cultural diversity, asserts the dominance and power of an Anglo-Celtic Australian core at the heart of the nation, its institutions of power and the Australian identity.[12] Prime Minister Howard appears willing to use the term 'cultural diversity' only descriptively, rather than prescriptively, with little commitment to an active development of a polity that engages in a meaningful cross-cultural discourse. Moreover, Prime Minister Howard's particular use of the term 'cultural diversity' and reference to 'cultural heritage' appears to denote a relegation of cultural difference to the past, as something that must be largely abandoned away from the migrant's homeland or practised only privately and minimally if minority cultural groups are to be part of an Australian nation. By contrast, however, Howard's Australia has an Anglo-Celtic past that needs to be maintained in the present:

> [W]hatever we say about our diverse background, the Anglo-Celtic cul-
> tural influence is still the most dominant because we speak English and
> our institutions are, and they were the institutions that attracted a lot of
> people to this country. We've reached a very comfortable compromise, in
> a way that I don't think people think our historical antecedents are threat-
> ened in any way by this, whereas I do think a generation ago some peo-
> ple felt that. Some people felt that multiculturalism meant that we had to
> in some way disown our past ... [I]t did sort of sound ... like that.[13]

Current policies and rhetoric, therefore, appear to diminish the importance of cultural identity for people in the present and in their imagin-
ings for the future. The negative, minimal form of tolerance and
recognition of cultural difference that Howard embodies does not
accord cultural identity the importance that it requires:

> [J]ust 'being tolerated' would not endow the identity they claim with the
> comforting and healing faculties for which it has been desired. The cog-
> nitive frame in which tolerance is granted is totally out of tune with the
> frame in which it is sought and received ... The act of tolerance dimin-
> ishes, instead of magnifying, the identity's importance.[14]

The government's rhetoric leaves minority group members in a difficult position: it does not acknowledge the importance of cultural identity in providing, amongst other affective and substantive aspects, a
sense of belonging. It is very difficult for the non–Anglo-Celtic
Australian to truly feel a sense of belonging in Howard's Australia.

At this point, it is worth examining the intersection of notions of
identity, nationalism and citizenship in the discourse of dominant political elites. The current political leadership appears to have tapped into
feelings of uncertainty, loss and threat in substantial sections of the
Australian public, which manifested themselves spectacularly during
the sudden rise of right-wing Hansonism. This has resulted in conservative governments putting the breaks on the practice of a pluralist,
inclusive multiculturalism, which appears to be felt as a threat to a
cohesive, Anglo-Australian national identity. This conservative backlash
against multiculturalism is a trend found in many Western nations:

> A second level [of the crisis of modernity] relates to the supposed threat
> to national culture through imported ethnic cultures. By maintaining
> their languages, folklore, cultural practices and religions, immigrants are
> seen as undermining national culture. Racists who attack women in
> Islamic dress claim to be defending the nation, or even European culture
> – a stereotype which links up with older racist notions on the threat of
> the Other to Christianity or civilization.[15]

A shifting and more amorphous sense of national identity that extends
citizenship and a sense of belonging to the nation to different peoples
seems to have created a sense of confusion and insecurity for those

Australians who may once have felt confident that they themselves embodied concrete values and characteristics that could be termed 'Australian'. They may have felt a greater sense that they belonged to a nation, or an 'imagined community' to use Benedict Anderson's phrase, when they believed in a common history, common myths and a common culture. Multiculturalism, however, asks them to imagine that they and non–Anglo-Australians are all different, with different histories, values, cultures, languages and group associations, but that they still 'belong' to a common community – the nation. Our sense of national identity as multicultural citizens is differentiated, yet shared in its acknowledgment of the diversity of citizens. Multiculturalism asks us to imagine a nation of citizens who do not necessarily share a common culture, but all of whom are still citizens in the sense of having common rights and duties and who have the right to participate in the life and workings of a political community. Citizenship, as a bond between citizens, is more challenging in a multicultural setting for some, who may see only difference in the Other and not anything shared with which to establish a bond.

Notions of nation and citizenship also involve the political community deciding who is part of the nation and who can be a citizen; thus both terms have exclusionary implications. Both 'nation' and 'citizenship' involve definitions in relation to otherness.[16] The conservative brand of multiculturalism supported by many political elites in Australia actively preserves the power of a dominant ethnicity to define the parameters of difference and safeguard the myths of Australian national identity that it has created in its own image. To protect this powerful position, the rights of citizenship for minorities in Australia do not appear to be progressively expanding – in fact they are severely constrained. Social and cultural rights are rarely promoted as a means of ensuring access to democratic process and distributive justice. Recent onshore asylum seekers, predominantly Middle Eastern and Muslim, are practically prevented from ever attempting to claim the rights of a permanent citizen.[17] As Howard has said, the exclusionary and punitive policies are warranted because 'we [not 'they'] will decide who comes into this country and the manner in which they come'.

MUSLIM ASYLUM SEEKERS AND THE POLITICS OF NATIONAL SECURITY

The challenges facing Australians of Muslim background to be fully integrated into Australian society were made even more difficult following a series of national and international events that resulted in a new wave of race politics. Australian Muslims were viewed in the light of global politics and its implications for national security. In this regard, Murray Edelman notes that 'national security [is] a symbol that generates fears that other nations might act in a hostile way'.[18]

Edelman further argues that 'because such anxieties are easily aroused and because they can easily be directed against any domestic or foreign group that is labeled a threat, worries about national security are constantly evoked'.[19] National security can, therefore, be used to legitimate racial and religious misrepresentations against minority groups with impunity. The national paranoia that followed national security issues such as the 'war on terror' and 'border protection' resulted in a discourse of demonisation, misrepresentation, mistrust and exclusion aimed at Australians of Muslim and Arabic backgrounds. This discussion focuses on the representation of asylum seekers post–September 11 and the emergent politicised discourse of identity and the Muslim cultural Other.

The Australian Government's negative representations of asylum seekers from Middle Eastern countries appeared to reach a climax during the so-called '*Tampa*' and 'children overboard' incidents, both of which occurred shortly before the 2001 election. Both appeared to be important in securing the Coalition's re-election. In the *Tampa* incident,[20] the Norwegian freighter *Tampa* rescued 433 asylum seekers whom the Norwegians had found in a sinking Indonesian ferry. The *Tampa* crew, in response to the wishes of the asylum seekers and in line with maritime conventions, attempted to take them to Australian waters. However, on 27 August 2001 the Australian Government refused the *Tampa* entry to Australian waters. Despite this refusal, the *Tampa* reached Australian waters on 29 August but was prevented from proceeding any further by the Australian Navy. The government, vowing that the asylum seekers would 'never set foot on Australian soil', did not allow them to move from this sea-bound position until New Zealand, Nauru and Papua New Guinea agreed to process them.[21] Following this incident, the government made substantial legislative changes to the migration zone of Australia to make it more difficult for future asylum seekers to reach Australian waters. It has also cemented its processing arrangements with Pacific island nations, resulting in what has become known as the 'Pacific solution'.

In the 'children overboard' affair, on 7 October 2001, one month before the federal election, Minister for Immigration Philip Ruddock claimed on national television that asylum seekers had 'thrown their children into the water, with the intention of putting us under duress'.[22] The government released photographic and video evidence that they claimed proved that this incident had taken place. A Senate inquiry found that the government had in fact been informed that no such incident took place and that the photographic and video evidence released was deliberately misleading.

These two incidents were used by the government as a 'central motif' of their 2001 election campaign.[23] Both involved the government as the representatives of the Australian nation clearly defining an

Australian national identity against an Other that was Muslim and primarily Middle Eastern. This Other was first clearly established in the *Tampa* incident, when Middle Eastern Muslim asylum seekers were shown as a threat to the Australian nation by the use of words such as 'floods' and 'waves' of onshore asylum seekers, when in reality the numbers of onshore asylum seekers were relatively small.[24]

The discourses of misrepresentation, exclusion and denigration were reinforced throughout 2001–02, when a systematic pattern of government misrepresentation sought to portray asylum seekers as serial child-abusers.[25] This was not limited to the 'children overboard' incident. Other episodes include the claim made by Liberal Senator George Brandis that 'a potential illegal immigrant [had] attempted to strangle a child'. A subsequent Senate inquiry found that Navy witness statements reportedly relating to this alleged episode did not exist.[26] In the case of the lip-sewing protests of Afghan hunger strikers, government responses also involved unfounded accusations of child abuse.[27] It was alleged that adult detainees had forcibly sewed the lips of children. Separate investigations by the South Australian Government and the Human Rights and Equal Opportunity Commission, with the co-operation of Australian Correctional Management, found no evidence of parents encouraging children to engage in acts of self-harm. This too was found to be an unsubstantiated allegation, but a pattern or regime of misrepresentation was now apparent. Under pressure, or to gain electoral mileage out of its tough stance, the government appeared quite willing to portray asylum seekers as an irresponsible and aberrant group, hostile to Australian standards of decency and parental responsibility, with little regard for their children's well-being or safety.

As Sharon Pickering argues, media stereotypes portraying asylum seekers as a threat to the nation seek to validate a host of increasingly repressive state responses.[28] Recently, the systematic attempt to depict unauthorised arrivals as 'undeserving' has been paralleled by new temporary protection visa (TPV) regulations in Australia. Under the TPV policy, some of the most vulnerable people in the Australian community, most of whom are incidentally of Muslim background, live with the ongoing fear of being refused a visa extension after three years, and are deemed ineligible for English classes, housing assistance and a range of settlement assistance measures available to refugees on permanent protection visas. Of particular concern, is the fact that TPV holders are permanently isolated from their spouses and children. This policy of blatant discrimination against TPV holders has resulted in considerable levels of anguish and hardship for already traumatised asylum seekers. Australia remains the only country in the world to provide 'temporary' sanctuary to those who have been recognised as genuine refugees under the 1951 United Nations Refugee Convention.[29]

These (Muslim) asylum seekers have been further stigmatised by Ruddock's 'verbal master stroke' in coining the 'unlawful' tag.[30] This view of 'illegal intruders' committing premeditated acts of self-harm[31] or harm to their own children has been systematically reinforced by politicians, with little serious media scrutiny or debate. The deliberate manipulation of language to exclude asylum seekers from any category of people with whom one might feel human solidarity demonstrates the power of language to demonise and dehumanise the most vulnerable of human beings: those in desperate need of protection and care. The majority support for the government's harsh treatment of asylum seekers has been built on the twin themes of 'war on terror' and national security. In this context, Muslim asylum seekers were portrayed as a potential risk to Australian society and, therefore, needed to be treated with the utmost caution and alertness.

This is reminiscent of the pre-Federation fear and anxiety about the 'yellow peril', as captured powerfully in David Walker's 'Anxious Nation'.[32] In the present situation, the government constructed and exaggerated particular representations of cultural difference as 'foreign' and threatening to the Australian nation.[33] For example, in referring to the parents who supposedly threw their children into the sea from the boat, Howard was quoted as saying 'I certainly don't want people like that coming to Australia'.[34] The government constructed an image of abhorrent parental behaviour framed by cultural practice and inimical to Australian values of parental responsibility: 'The "children overboard" affair again presented Islam as an alien culture in which parents were so barbaric, so subhuman that they would endanger their children by throwing them into the sea to stop the Australian navy from doing its "duty".' [35] The government appeared to be deliberately blurring the distinctions between Middle Eastern, Muslim and terrorist. In the fearful environment of post–September 11, government ministers declared that one could not rule out that some asylum seekers may be linked to global terror networks.[36] In excluding Muslim and Middle Eastern asylum seekers from the Australian nation, the government established, or built upon, a discourse of Australian nationalism that largely excludes Muslim- and Arab-Australians. In fact, 'the facile associative logic of racism being what it is, the dehumanising and demeaning claims about the asylum seekers ended up attaching themselves to Muslim and Arab-Australian in general'.[37] This cemented a hostility and distrust within the Australian nation of those associated with Islam, whether they are Muslim Australians, or mistakenly identified with Islam because they are of a certain ethnicity, particularly Arab. These images were reinforced by shallow media coverage, as a survey of refugee and asylum seeker issues in the *Sydney Morning Herald* and *Brisbane Courier Mail* from the start of 1997 to the end of 1999 illustrates:

Press coverage has focused on the deviant problem that asylum seekers and refugees represent to the robust Australian nation and the need for a strong state to keep out and control the menace. With few exceptions, reports on asylum seekers and refugees have not been interested in listening to the voices of asylum seekers, nor of home country conditions or conditions of flight. When alternative views are offered, they are usually presented as 'human interest' stories rather than 'hard' news.[38]

While Pauline Hansen was scorned for ignorance and racism when she suggested in 1996 that 'boat people' should be turned around and refugees sent home when their countries 'get better', both Liberal and Labor have now been complicit in instituting punitive inhumane measures in Australian law. For Chris Sidoti, former human rights and equal opportunity commissioner, such changes signify that 'our leaders, from both major political groupings, are turning us into a nation of thugs'.[39] The question, then, is why have these political leaders acted in such 'thuggish' ways and why do opinion polls suggest that they are acting in ways that are widely supported by the Australian people? One of the reasons why Australians have acted so adversely to the arrival of asylum seekers is that they have a deep-seated fear of invasion and that this has been present since the arrival of the British in 1788.[40] Having seized the first bit of Australia so easily, it was initially the Dutch and the French who were seen as the enemy, and then later the Japanese, Germans, Indonesians, Vietnamese and Chinese each took their turn in providing the potential threat of invasion. Ironically there has never been any real threat of invasion, with the Japanese in 1942 specifically rejecting the idea on the basis that it would require too many personnel and that the 'national character' of Australians would mean they would 'resist to the end'.[41] Despite this, there remains in the Australian psyche a fear of being overrun by foreign hordes, and the influx of asylum seekers is seen as yet another kind of foreign horde.

The language of demonisation and misinformation reached its zenith when Mr Howard introduced the 'them' and 'us' rhetoric into the debate, when he stated unequivocally: 'I express my anger at the behaviour of those people and I repeat it. I can't comprehend how genuine refugees would throw their children overboard ... I certainly don't want people of that type in Australia, I really don't'.[42] This statement critical of asylum seekers and casting doubts over their integrity and ethics has become the dominant theme in other statements made by senior government ministers including the then Defence Minister Peter Reith, who argued that immigration control had become an important security issue and that '[illegal immigration] can be a pipeline for terrorists to come in and use your country as a staging post for terrorist activities'.[43] The danger in using such language in media statements and other press coverage of the asylum seekers crisis is that its divisive rhetoric tends to evoke prejudices and emotions that exceed rational interpretations. The deliberate link between national security, global terrorism and the boat people in the above excerpts has constructed strong prejudices against asylum seekers, who are increasingly portrayed as different and manipulative Others capable of irrational and despicable behaviour such as risking the lives of their children for migration outcomes. The neat distinctions between the uncivilised, unlawful and dangerous intruders as represented by asylum seekers on the one hand and a civilised, ethical and democratic Australia on the other succeeded in generating fears and hostility towards this imagined enemy.

THE PROBLEMATIC STATUS OF ISLAM IN THE WEST

To understand the current images and representations of Muslim- and Arab-Australians, it is important to look for historical parallels as a way of unlocking the anomalies of the present. In fact, like anti-Semitism, Islamophobia in Western societies has been fuelled by a history of religious competition and antagonism. As Edward Said has pointed out, 'Orientalism carries within it the stamp of a problematic attitude towards Islam'.[44] He further explains that:

> Islam was a real provocation in many ways. It lay uneasily close to Christianity, it could boast of unrivalled military and political successes. Nor was this all. The Islamic lands sit adjacent to and even on top of the Biblical lands; moreover, the heart of the Islamic domain has always been the region close to Europe, what has been called the Near Orient or Near East. Arabic and Hebrew are Semitic languages, and together they dispose and redispose of material that is urgently important to Christianity. From the end of the seventh century until the battle of Lepanto in 1571, Islam in either its Arab, Ottoman, or North African and Spanish form dominated or effectively threatened European Christianity. That Islam outstripped and outshone Rome cannot have been absent from the mind of any European past or present.[45]

Similarly, 'while these stereotypes are born in Europe and increasingly in the United States, the media and Hollywood have provided an important means of spreading such images in already fertile and well-disposed environments such as Australia'.[46] Research has shown how these images are present in the Australian press and in school textbooks. The report of the National Inquiry into Racist Violence in Australia noted that:

> Anti-Arab and Muslim feelings are largely based on stereotypes about Arabs and Muslims: a generalized identification of Arabs and Muslims with violence (such as terrorism and the taking of hostages), stereotyped identification of Arabs and Muslims with 'un-Australian values' (for example, religious fundamentalism, conservative views about women and moral issues, dietary restrictions, conservative and conspicuous clothing ...).[47]

Many commentators make direct links between recent world and local events and defamatory attacks against Muslim- and Arab-Australians. It is worth exploring further how these 'new' Australians have come to be seen by some to be implicated in events that, in reality, are often far beyond their control. This might be understood through the conflation of Muslim and Arab, the lack of understanding of Islam in Western cultures and the presentation of Islam as a homogeneous entity that is now associated with terrorism. It might also be regarded as part of a conservative backlash against multiculturalism, or at least a conservative hardening of the notion of multiculturalism, involving a fear and a deep suspicion of any Australian with multiple cultural and national allegiances, and a fear of visible communities who do not assimilate to Anglo norms. Ironically, the isolation that has been almost forced upon some members of Muslim- and Arab-Australian communities has been interpreted as a rejection of and dissociation with 'Australian-ness', and as evidence of loyalty to a religious or political order that is thought to be an enemy of the West.

Muslim and Arab-Australians have not been immune to harassment, prejudice and exclusion from a wider Australian society up to this point. The violent and abusive experiences suffered by many Muslim- and Arab-Australians appear to have exceeded the voracity of negative experiences around the time of the Gulf War. However, Muslim- and Arab-Australians faced serious levels of discrimination and xenophobia at that earlier point in history, and many relate stories of their continued experiences of harassment and xenophobia throughout the turbulent 1990s. How, then, are we to understand the existence of this xenophobia before September 11?

Western discourse on world events from the 1970s onwards has led to a historical association of Islam with 'extremism, intolerance and violence'.[48] Such events include the Iranian revolution of 1979, the Arab–Israeli conflict, the Gulf War of 1990–91, and terrorist activities undertaken around the world committed in the name of Islam, for example in the Middle East, Philippines and Indonesia. Such a relationship between Islam, Arabs, violence and oppression has not been constructed simply following September 11. Indeed,

> [a]nti-Arab racism in the West has a long genealogy. One of the most important aspects of its formation is that it is intricately related to the genealogy of anti-Muslim sentiments. In both the academic orientalist tradition analysed by Edward Said, and the dominant popular Western racist imaginary the boundaries between being an Arab and being a Muslim is greatly blurred.[49]

Certainly such a negative, essentialist and misguided discourse has been heightened in the aftermath of the events in New York and Washington, but it must be remembered that it is simply a new point on the continuum of a Western discourse. Writing in 1997, several years before September 11, postcolonial theorist Edward Said worriedly commented that 'malicious generalizations about Islam have become the last acceptable form of denigration of foreign culture in the West'.[50] Said challenges the 'clash of civilisations' thesis epitomised by Western scholar Samuel P Huntington, in which Islam is portrayed as a 'single, coherent entity' that is forever inevitably on a path towards violent conflict with 'the West'.[51] Huntington writes:

> So long as Islam remains Islam (which it will) and the West remains the West (which is more dubious), this fundamental conflict between two great civilizations and ways of life will continue to define their relations to the future even as it has defined them for the past fourteen centuries.[52]

Said's challenge to this thesis is that sweeping and hostile generalisations about Islam are made by Orientalist scholars, the Western mass media and Western policy makers. Through these commentators, Islam is denied any diversity in character, practices and beliefs, and all Muslims and Arabs are presented as having intrinsic natures that are mostly discussed pejoratively.[53] Said writes that this has dangerous consequences for inciting hatred and distrust towards Muslims and those associated in the West with Islam:

> The deliberately created associations between Islam and fundamentalism ensure that the average reader comes to see Islam and fundamentalism as essentially the same thing. Given the tendency to reduce Islam to a handful of rules, stereotypes, and generalizations about the faith, its founder, and all of its people, then the reinforcement of every negative fact associated with Islam – its violence, primitiveness, atavism, threatening qualities – is perpetuated.[54]

Thus well before September 11, there existed in the Western imagination an acceptance of an Islamic totality and its association with violence, oppression and terror. Impacts of recent events on Muslim- and Arab-Australians must, therefore, be understood as being fed by a history of hostility, antagonism and misunderstanding towards Islam and Arabs by many sections of Western society.

CONCLUSION

The above discussion of recent events shows that Australian Muslims have been reduced to the same monolith of pejorative stereotypical images of Islam that Said describes. Australian Muslims have been denied their individuality, their cultural diversity as well as their humanity:

> What is constantly ignored by 'Muslim watchers' in Australia is the enormous diversity among Australian Muslims, for everyone is not cut from the one cloth: differences in education, socioeconomic background, ethnicity, customs and religious outlook play their part ... Stereotypes now

define people as less than human and what a litany there is to choose from: veiled women, fierce bearded men, barbaric parents, rapists and suicide bombers – these are the images taken to represent Islam. But where is the human face that I know? Where are my parents, my brothers and my sister. Where are my friends?[55]

While global political events involving Muslims have undoubtedly contributed to much of the anti-Arab and anti-Muslim sentiment in Australia, it would be unhelpful to disregard the effect of historical and local factors. Negative attitudes towards Muslim- and Arab-Australians need, therefore, to be viewed in the light of interrelated factors, including media representations, social policies (in the form of a folkloric version of multiculturalism), as well as the deep, if unconscious, influence of 'Orientalist' discourse on perceptions of Islam and the East. In Australia, such a situation is further compounded by the current political debate about national security and the almost daily 'terror alerts' issued by government ministers, self-declared experts and media reporters. As Said proposes, the mere use of the term 'Islam' to either explain or indiscriminately condemn the diverse Islamic world is an irresponsible overgeneralisation that is problematic, counterproductive and would be unacceptable if applied to any other cultural or demographic group.

This should be all the more unacceptable in the context of a culturally diverse society such as Australia. Instead we are witnessing a Hansonite-type of nationalism, reminiscent of pre-Federation arguments for cultural unity. Such cultural unity required for a stable and unified population is perceived by conservatives to be undermined by multiculturalism and threatened by different cultural groups, in particular Muslims and Asians. Within the conservative political thinking about multiculturalism and immigration 'the existence of difference within a community is strongly coded as disunity, as a pathogen or weakness'.[56] It is in this political and social climate that immigrant Muslims in Australia, because of their cultural difference and pronounced visibility in a predominantly secular society, have been constructed both as a threat to social homogeneity and increasingly as a potential risk to national security in the age of the 'war on terror'. Social, political and academic debate on identity in Australia continues, with a range of responses evident. Some prefer to assert the primacy of the Anglo-Celtic cultural core, some perceive multiculturalism as the irreversible cultural reality, while others advocate an approach based on the notion of civic identity underpinned by citizenship rights. The ongoing discourse on the Australian identity is of course important and relevant to Muslim- and Arab-Australians. Like other ethnic groups, Muslims would be reassured to see the re-emergence of a more inclusive society that ensures fairness, dignity and honourability for all – irrespective of race, religion or culture.

ACKNOWLEDGMENTS: I would like to thank Anna Trembath for the excellent research assistance she provided for this chapter, and Michael Leach and Caroline Anderson for their helpful comments on the final draft. The helpful comments and suggestions of the anonymous reviewer are also much appreciated.

NOTES

1   See David Walker, *Anxious Nation: Australia and the Rise of Asia 1850–1939* (Brisbane: University of Queensland Press, 1999).

2   Michael J Cigler, *The Afghans in Australia* (Melbourne: AE Press, 1986); Christine Stevens, *Tin Mosques and Ghantowns: a History of Afghan Camel Drivers in Australia* (Melbourne: Oxford University Press, 1989).

3   See Trevor Batrouney, 'From "White Australia" to multiculturalism: citizenship and identity', and Anne Monsour, 'Whitewashed: the Lebanese in Queensland, 1880–1947', in Ghassan Hage (ed.), *Arab-Australians Today: Citizenship and Belonging* (Melbourne: Melbourne University Press, 2002).

4   Michael Cigler, *The Afghans in Australia*; Christine Stevens, *Tin Mosques and Ghantowns: a History of Afghan Camel Drivers in Australia*.

5   Edward Said, *'Orientalism': Western Conceptions of the Orient* (London: Penguin Books, 1978), p. 3.

6   Christine Stevens, *Tin Mosques and Ghantowns: a History of Afghan Camel Drivers in Australia*.

7   See Bilal Cleland, 'The history of Muslims in Australia', in Abdullah Saeed and Shahram Akbarzadeh (eds), *Muslim Communities in Australia* (Sydney: UNSW Press, 2001), pp. 12–32.

8   Stuart Hall and Sarat Maharaj, *Annotations: Modernity and Difference* (London: Iniva Publication, 2001), pp. 48–49.

9   See for example Barry Hindess, 'Multiculturalism and citizenship', in Chandran Kukathas (ed.), *Multicultural Citizens: the Philosophy and Politics of Identity* (Sydney: The Centre for Independent Studies Limited, 1993), p. 34.

10 George Megalogenis, 'Multicultural Australia examined: the full-text of the John Howard interview', *The Australian*, 6 February 2002. See also David Hollinsworth, *Race and Racism in Australia* (Sydney: Social Science Press, 1998), pp. 269–76.

11 Murray Edelman, *The Politics of Disinformation* (Cambridge: Cambridge University Press, 2001), p. 53.

12 See David Hollinsworth, *Race and Racism in Australia*, p. 274; Ghassan Hage, quoted in David Hollinsworth, *Race and Racism in Australia*, p. 274.

13 John Howard, quoted in George Megalogenis, 'Multicultural Australia examined: the full-text of the John Howard interview'.

14 Zygmunt Bauman, 'The great war of recognition', *Theory, Culture & Society*, Vol. 18, Nos. 2–3 (2001), p. 144.

15 Stephen Castles, 'The racisms of globalisation', in Ellie Vasta and Stephen Castles (eds), *The Teeth are Smiling: the Persistence of Racism in Multicultural Australia* (Sydney: Allen & Unwin, 1996), p. 40.

16 Barry Hindess, 'Multiculturalism and citizenship', in Chandran Kukathas (ed.), *Multicultural Citizens: the Philosophy and Politics of Identity* (Sydney: The Centre for Independent Studies Limited, 1993), pp. 33–45.

17 Fethi Mansouri and Melek Bagdas, *Politics of Social Exclusion: Refugees on*

Temporary Protection Visas in Victoria (Melbourne: Centre for Citizenship and Human Rights, Deakin University, 2002).

18 Murray Edelman, *The Politics of Disinformation*, p. 7.

19 ——, *The Politics of Disinformation*, p. 7.

20 For a comprehensive discussion, see David Marr and Marian Wilkinson, *Dark Victory* (Sydney: Allen & Unwin, 2003).

21 Prime Minister John Howard, quoted in Michael Leach, ' "Disturbing practices": dehumanizing asylum seekers in the refugee "crisis" in Australia, 2001–2002', *Refuge*, Vol. 21, No. 3 (2003), p. 26.

22 Philip Ruddock, quoted in Michael Leach, ' "Disturbing practices": dehumanizing asylum seekers', p. 26.

23 ——, quoted in Michael Leach, " "Disturbing practices": dehumanizing asylum seekers', p. 25.

24 ——, quoted in Michael Leach, ' "Disturbing practices": dehumanizing asylum seekers', p. 27.

25 See Michael Leach, ' "Disturbing practices": dehumanizing asylum seekers', pp. 25–33.

26 Matt Price, 'Strangling claims unsupported', *The Australian,* 6 April 2002.

27 See, for example, 'Woomera hunger strike continues as talks fail', *ABC Online News,* 25 January 2002, available at <http://www.abc.net/news/2002/01/item20020125080108_1.htm>.

28 Sharon Pickering, 'The hard press of asylum', *Forced Migration Review*, No. 8 (2000), p. 173.

29 Fethi Mansouri and Michael Leach, 'Temporary protection of refugees: Australian policy and international comparisons', in Michael Leach and Fethi Mansouri (eds), *Critical Perspectives* (Melbourne: Deakin University Press, 2003), pp. 103–22.

30 Mungo MacCallum, 'Girt by sea', *Quarterly Essay*, Vol. 5 (2002).

31 Michael Clyne, 'When the discourse of hatred becomes respectable: does the linguist have a responsibility?', *Australian Review of Applied Linguistics*, Vol. 26, No. 1 (2003), p. 4.

32 See David Walker, *Anxious Nation: Australia and the Rise of Asia 1850–1939* (Brisbane: University of Queensland Press, 1999).

33 See Michael Clyne, 'When the discourse of hatred becomes respectable', p. 4.

34 See John Howard, quoted in Hanifa Deen, *Caravanserai: Journey among Australian Muslims* (Fremantle: Fremantle Arts Centre Press, 2003), p. 286.

35 Hanifa Deen, *Caravanserai: Journey among Australian Muslims,* p. 285.

36 See Michael Leach, "Disturbing practices": dehumanising asylum seekers', p. 29.

37 Ghassan Hage, 'The differential intensities of social reality: migration, participation and guilt', in Ghassan Hage (ed.), *Arab-Australians Today: Citizenship and Belonging*, p. 241.

38 Sharon Pickering, 'The hard press of asylum', p. 173.

39 Chris Sidoti, quoted in *Sydney Morning Herald,* 28 September 2001.

40 Keith Suter, 'Australia and asylum seekers', *Contemporary Review,* Vol. 279, No. 630 (2001), pp. 278–84.

41 ——, 'Australia and asylum seekers'.

42 John Howard, media conference, 6 December 2001. Transcript available online at <http://afr.com/election2001/transcripts/2001/12/06/FFXDZHPOMSC.html>.

43 Editorial, 'Refugees threaten to jump', *Hobart Mercury,* 14 September 2001.

44 Edward Said, *'Orientalism': Western Conceptions of the Orient,* p. 74.

45 ——, *'Orientalism': Western Conceptions of the Orient,* p. 74.

46 Refer to Abe W Ata, 'Moslem Arab portrayal in the Australian press and in school textbooks', *Australian Journal of Social Issues,* Vol. 19, No. 3 (1984); Kevin M Dunn, 'Racism in Australia: findings of a survey on racist attitudes and experiences of racism', The National Europe Centre Conference – the Challenges of Immigration and Integration in the European Union and Australia, Paper No. 77 (Sydney: University of Sydney, 18–20 February 2003), available online at <>.

47 Ghassan Hage, *Arab-Australians Today: Citizenship and Belonging,* p. 175.

48 ——, *Arab-Australians Today: Citizenship and Belonging,* p. 184.

49 Ray Jureidini and Ghassan Hage, 'The Australian Arabic Council: anti-racist activism', in Ghassan Hage (ed.), *Arab-Australians Today: Citizenship and Belonging,* p. 173.

50 Edward Said, *Covering Islam: How the Media and the Experts Determine How We See the Rest of the World* (London: Vintage Books, 1997), p. xii.

51 ——, *Covering Islam,* in particular see p. xvi.

52 Samuel P Huntington, *The Clash of Civilizations and the Remaking of the World Order* (London: Simon & Schuster, 2002), p. 212.

53 Edward Said, *Covering Islam,* see in particular pp. xi–xxii.

54 ——, *Covering Islam,* p. xvi.

55 Hanifa Deen, *Caravanserai: Journey among Australian Muslims,* p. 285.

56 Michael Leach, 'Hansonism, political discourse and Australian identity', in Michael Leach, Geoffrey Stokes and Ian Ward (eds), *The Rise and Fall of One Nation* (St Lucia, Qld: University of Queensland Press, 2000), p. 51.

11

ISLAM AND THE WEST: SOME REFLECTIONS

SAMINA YASMEEN

Transnational religious links have attracted attention in the post–Cold War era. In contrast to the past, when religion and culture received scant attention in studies of world politics, the more recent literature accepts and highlights the significance of subjective factors and feelings in understanding global trends.[1] Of all the religions, however, Islam retains the dubious honour of being identified in most of the literature as distinct from 'the West'.[2] Such a categorisation seems to imply that Islam and the Western world constitute two separate identities, and that those belonging to one community are *ipso facto* excluded from membership of the other. Each of the communities, or the civilisations, as argued by Huntington, is assumed to have values and symbols that are distinct from those of the other, as well as boundaries that separate them more so than is the case with other religious traditions. The distinction is essentially limiting and contrary to the reality of a globalised world: it ignores the fact that Islam is not merely a religion of the developing world – some from the Anglo-Celtic tradition have also opted for it. Their conversion to Islam does not automatically deny them the right to claim their Western heritage. The false dichotomy also fails to take into account the process of migration, which has resulted in a number of Muslims living in what is identified as the West. A Muslim citizen does not remain outside the imaginary boundary of the West while living in a Western society. The problem is further compounded by the fact that neither of the two communities is devoid of plurality and multiplicity of ideas and traditions.

Despite the problems inherent in such categorisations, however, the discussion on Islam and the West persists. At one level, there is the implied recognition that division of opinion within a specific community does not negate its existence, as long as its members continue to assume that their understanding of the symbols and values gives them a distinct identity, and a right to remain members of the community thus created. At another level, however, the categorisation has been encouraged and justified by international events, particularly since the September 11 terrorist attacks on the United States in 2001. Huntington's idea of the 'clash of civilisations', while criticised soon after being published, has emerged at centre stage of any discussion of Islam's relations with Western societies. The relationship between the two communities/civilisations is now assumed to be more conflictive than co-operative in nature. These assumptions and ideas gain credence with the frequent reporting of tensions, misunderstandings and policies of the one against the other: but *is* the relationship between Islam and the West essentially antagonistic? Other related questions also require attention: does a conflictive relationship need to continue or can the two communities explore ways of relieving the tension and mutual antagonism? What role can states play in improving the nature of this relationship? What are the responsibilities of moderate/liberal Muslims in building confidence between the two communities/civilisations?

LOCAL AND GLOBAL ISLAMS

The answers to these questions require an understanding of the relationship between local and global manifestations of political Islam. This, in turn, is closely related to diversity and plurality in the Muslim world. At the heart of the diversity lies a difference in the reading of the relationship between the 'text' and the 'context'.[3] At one end of the spectrum are Muslims who consider the relationship to be relatively fixed: the early Islamic period is treated as the manifestation of the ideal. Interpretations of the Qur'an and Prophetic practices are considered immutable: what was practised in the 7th century is regarded as the standard that all Muslims must strive to meet. Muslims at the other end of the spectrum subscribe to a more flexible view of the relationship between the text and the context. For them, the essence of Islam can be preserved only by relating the text to a continuously altering context. While relying on the Qur'an and Sunna (Prophetic traditions), these Muslims emphasise the need for reinterpretation. The notion of *ijtihad* (interpretation), however, is not restricted to a class of *ulama* (Islamic scholars). Those with knowledge can provide their own insights as well. Such a view of the text and the context places the 'reader' of the 'documents' in a special position: who a person is cannot be divorced from how that person reads the texts.

This diversity of views is seen in the different practices and cultural manifestations of Islam around the globe. It also finds expression in differing views about the nature of an Islamic state.[4] Those with a fixed notion of the relationship between the text and the context favour returning to the ideals of the Medina state of the 7th century. They are often identified as fundamentalists, but the categorisation ignores the variety of opinion within this group as well: their views can range from being simply fundamentalist to radical, with an emphasis on militancy in the name of fulfilling the standards set by Muslims of the early Islamic era. Liberal and/or moderate Muslims, on the other hand, are prepared to accept that divine will could simply be the context in which an Islamic community determines the nature of the state. For them, notions of democracy are not merely introduced concepts but are seen to be the essence of Islam. Those who selectively opt for a fixed or a flexible relationship between the text and the context occupy the ground between the two extremes. These choices, it is important to emphasise, can be influenced by the economic, social, educational and geographical context in which Muslims find themselves. For instance, the poor living in the distant regions of Baluchistan (Pakistan) with limited access to education may find themselves accepting the ideas of Islam conveyed to them by a religious leader who himself has limited knowledge of Islam. Without any choice, they may be adopting fundamentalist views as 'the only true meaning of Islam'. In contrast, those from the elite with access to overseas education may favour a more moderate reading of the texts.

The diversity of views among Muslims about state and society, however, is not solely determined by domestic factors. Local versions of Islam are influenced by global versions of Islam. To put it differently, ideas about the ideal types of Islamic societies travel around the globe, and are taken up, adopted and modified by Muslims in different localities. The process is not new. Historically, a number of Islamic thinkers and philosophers moved across national boundaries and disseminated their ideas about Islamic states and appropriate religious practices.[5] Transnational Islam, in other words, played a role in shaping the discourse on Muslim beliefs and practices in a number of societies. Technological developments assisted the process: tape recorders, for instance, were used to spread Ayatollah Khomeini's ideas during the Shah of Iran's reign before 1979. The speed with which these ideas are disseminated, however, has increased with the advent of information technology and the introduction of satellite television networks. The Internet is increasingly emerging as a major source of ideas about Islam, which those familiar or unfamiliar with the religion can tap into.[6] Websites have been established by different groups propagating their views on Islam, Muslim practices and the value-laden distinctions between 'good' and 'bad' Muslims. Satellite television networks also play a significant role in the process: programs on learning about Islam, for instance, provide a forum for fundamentalist and liberal Muslims alike. The audience is encouraged to participate by using Internet or telephone links to ask questions on these programs. The knowledge about Islam thus developed becomes part of the global Islam that Muslims residing in different societies can access. The diversity of ideas available at the global level becomes an added dimension in discussion about local manifestations of Islam.[7] Those subscribing to fundamental ideas, for instance, can be seen citing the opinions of other Muslims to validate their own views. Moderate and liberal Muslims engage in a similar process. The link between the global and local versions of Islam, in other words, becomes one of the variables that determines the domestic situation in a given state.

The global–local link , it must be noted, does not follow one direction only, namely from the global to the local. In fact, as discussed in previous chapters, local versions of Islam also contribute ideas to global versions of Islam. Tablighi Jamaat, Hizb al-Tahrir and al-Muhajiroun are examples of this phenomenon, whereby ideas from one society are exported and introduced into other societies. Muslim societies become both consumers and producers of ideas about Islam.

The process also has relevance for the foreign policies of Muslim states. As ideas develop about the Islamic state and societies at the local and global levels, those developing them also engage in a process of developing their view(s) of the world. These ideas centre on their identification of the main actors in the international system, their relative power status, the relationships between these actors and the forces governing those relationships. The ideas also deal with Islam's place in the global context. The diversity of views about the construction of an Islamic state also manifests itself in different world views among Muslims. For some, the world is constructed along the realist paradigm, where national interest remains paramount. Religion is viewed as the context in which national interest is pursued and maximised, but is not necessarily a major determinant of the state's relationship with the outside world. The choice of allies and enemies, and of policies relating to these two categories, is therefore made with a view to sustaining the state as a secular entity. For others, the ideas circulating in the global and local arenas construct a world view that is predominantly determined by religious identities. Islam is placed at centre stage and the relationship with other communities is judged in terms of *their* approach towards Muslims. Adopting the neo-Marxists' language, those subscribing to such a view of the world talk in terms of exploitation and oppression: Islam is seen as being oppressed and exploited by those at the core of the system. Local elites are judged in terms of collaboration or opposition to the dominant oppressive forces operating at the global level. The suggested response to the links between the local and global forces varies: while some promote the idea of Jihad as the only solution, others encourage introspection with the aim of helping Islam realise its true destiny as a global power.

INHERENT ANTAGONISM?

It is within the context discussed above that the relationship between Islam and the West can be addressed in today's world. Against the background of the colonial experiences of most Muslims, the emergence of the United States as the sole superpower in the post–Cold War era, and the failure to resolve the Palestinian–Israeli dispute, two broad schools of thought have emerged in the Muslim world at opposite ends of a spectrum.

The first group accepts the reality of the post–Cold War order and American primacy in the new structure. Motivated by a mixture of political, economic and regional factors, those belonging to this group favour accommodation with the West in general and with the United States in particular. For them, the relationship between Islam and the West is not inherently hostile and can even be mutually beneficial. This does not exclude the possibility of differences of opinion on a range of issues, but the differences are not considered to be so fundamental that they cannot be overcome.

The second group divides the world into Muslim and non-Muslim sections. The West, led by the United States, is perceived as posing a threat to the core values of Islamic culture, community and civilisation. The Muslim community, therefore, is expected and encouraged to combat the Western threat by engaging in Jihad. So strong is this commitment that some in this group elevate Jihad to the status of the sixth pillar of Islam. Those Muslims unwilling to accept this understanding of the world are excluded from the fold of Islam.

The views on Islam's relationship with the West, it is important to note, are not purely a function of the dynamics *within* the Islamic community: they are shaped by events at the local, regional and international levels. The policies of the main hegemon, the United States, play a major role in the process. Analyses of these events and US policies are produced in various parts of the world and are then disseminated to influence those who belong to one or the other end of the spectrum. The media, Internet and satellite television become the vehicles for this dissemination of ideas. Effectively, a condition is created whereby local and global versions of Islam continuously interact and evolve *in response to the policies of the Western world*. These different kinds of Islam also become *agents* of change at the global level: the terrorist activities undertaken by militant Muslim groups, for instance, cause Western states to take stringent actions. These, in turn, are seen as evidence by the militants of the West's unconditional hostility towards Islam and further spurs them to action.

The developments in the relations between the West and the Muslim world since the terrorist attacks of September 11 demonstrate these multiple, multidirectional links between the two communities.

The attacks took place against the backdrop of growing disillusionment with US policies towards Muslims, particularly with reference to the Palestinian–Israeli issue and the stationing of US troops in Saudi Arabia. The attacks created a wave of sympathy for the United States among moderate sections of Muslim societies. They felt that it was imperative to join the United States in its war on terrorism. However, others viewed the same developments as evidence of American oppression of Muslims and Islam. These ideas were not restricted to the South-West Asian scene: they passed through cyberspace to reach South-East Asia, the Middle East and even some Muslim immigrants in liberal democratic societies. The US invasion of Iraq in March 2003 further reinforced these views. Significantly, the faulty logic used to justify going to war and the way the United States has conducted the occupation have also convinced some moderate Muslims of the Western hostility towards Islam. This was particularly apparent when the news broke of prisoner abuse in Abu Ghraib. Muslim societies have reacted negatively to the photographs and the reports of continuing humiliation, rape and torture of Iraqi prisoners. These have been interpreted as evidence of US double standards and interest in undermining Islam's cultural values.[8] Such a perception seems to have opened the way for the gruesome murder of Nick Berg and others in the name of revenge for the abuses committed against Iraqi prisoners.

BUILDING CONFIDENCE

How can this situation be changed? Given the emphasis placed by both radical and moderate Muslims on US policies, the answer resides primarily in the adoption by Washington of a different approach to issues related to Islam and Muslims. The US invasion of Iraq on the pretext of controlling the spread of weapons of mass destruction has already created doubts among Muslims – both moderate and radical – about the US agenda in the Middle East. The justification of the invasion in the name of regime change and ridding Iraq of Saddam Hussein has also started to lose its appeal to those who accuse the United States of adventurism. In the face of continuing resistance by Shi'ites, Sunnis and foreign insurgents, the United States has been unable to control the situation: the war has not come to an end. More seriously, the news of prisoner abuse has further galvanised those determined to view US policies in a negative light. US policy is strengthening the radical Muslims at the expense of the moderates. The United States needs to develop a better grasp of the situation in Muslim societies and the body of ideas circulating at local and global levels. Discounting them can only open up further opportunities for American mistakes and the empowerment of Islamic militancy.

A deeper understanding of the multiplicity of views and ideas in the

Muslim world requires renewed attention to the educational sector. Since the September 11 attacks, *madrasa*s (religious schools) have increasingly been identified as the source of the problem. As Abdullah Saeed points out, such an identification does not take into account that the majority of the *madrasa*s are *not* producing militants. While this does not remove the need to focus attention on the curricula taught in these educational institutions, it is important that they do not become the only target of reassessment. Curricula in educational institutions in the West require close attention as well. Either subconsciously or inadvertently, the ideas about Islam and Muslims communicated by these institutions tend generally to perpetuate negativity. The sense of 'us' versus 'them' that they create plays an indirect role in the conflict by denying to the decision makers the ability to appreciate and fully grasp the views prevalent among Muslims. The need for reassessment of the curricula has been amply demonstrated by prisoner abuse at Abu Ghraib. It is quite possible that in the absence of adequate knowledge of the rules embodied in the Geneva Convention, those charged with the responsibility of interrogation relied upon the images they developed of the 'Other' during their formative years. The willingness to dehumanise the 'Other' reflects as much a lack of understanding of the 'Other' as a failure in the chain of command.

The West also needs to engage the Muslims who live in their midst. The process has already started with the US Government paying greater attention to the needs of its Muslim population. Similar trends are apparent in other liberal democratic societies as well. The Australian Government, for instance, has taken steps to indicate that it has developed a nuanced view of Islamic communities: while the militants are being 'targeted', other Muslims are being engaged. The manner in which this engagement is taking place, however, reflects the limited knowledge of those interested in the process. With occasional exceptions, both the federal and state governments in Australia have chosen to engage with those Australian Muslims who adopt the traditional Islamic dress code. This choice fails to acknowledge that a large majority of Australia's Muslim population subscribes to moderate/liberal ideas. It also ignores that choosing those who 'look' Muslim not only reinforces stereotypes but also empowers orthodox groups in the country. Inadvertently, liberal democracies thus appear to be promoting Islamic orthodoxy.

Confidence cannot simply be built by the efforts of those categorised as the West, however. Muslim moderates, whether in Muslim majority areas or in liberal democracies, need to accept the responsibility of playing an active role at local and global levels. By remaining silent about the excesses of militants and condoning the unfair policies of the extremists on either side, they run the risk of empowering the minority at the expense of the majority. Muslim moderates around the world need to voice their opinions and not leave the arena only to the voices of the 'Other'. Some moderate Muslims have already initiated this process.[9] The contributors to this volume have attempted to do the same. It is to be hoped that others will also take up the challenge.

NOTES

1 For an excellent analysis of transnational religions, see Susanne Hoeber Rudolph and James Piscatori (eds), *Transnational Religions Fading States* (Boulder, Colo.: Westview Press, 1997).

2 See, for instance, Bernard Lewis, *Islam and the West* (Oxford: Oxford Press, 1994).

3 These differences are well documented in Mansoor Moaddel and Kamran Talattof (eds), *Modernist and Fundamentalist Debates in Islam: a Reader* (New York: Palgrave Macmillan, 2000).

4 Ishtiaq Ahmed, *The Concept of an Islamic State* (London: Frances Pinter, 1987).

5 For a good discussion of some of the personalities, see Ali Rahnema (ed.), *Pioneers of Islamic Revival* (London: Zed Books, 1994).

6 See, for example, Trudy Harris, 'Virtual camp for killers', *The Australian*, 13 May 2004, p. 15.

7 For instance, Geo TV, operating from United Arab Emirates, telecasts a program 'Aalim on Line' every Saturday, Tuesday and Thursday at <http://www.geo.tv>. Similarly ARY Digital telecasts regular programs on religious issues at <http://www.arydigital.tv/main.php3>.

8 See, for example, 'US to conduct transparent probe into abuse of Iraqi prisoners', Bernama, 11 May 2004, available online at <http://www.bernama.com.my/bernama/v3/news.php?id=66247>; 'Rumsfeld's late apology fails to calm Arab anger', *Khaleej Times*, 9 May 2004, available online at <http://www.khaleejtimes.com>; and Hasan Baswaid, 'Saudis voice DEEP skepticism, anger over Bush interview, *The Saudi Gazette Online*, 7 May 2004, at <http://www.saudigazette.com.sa/sgazette/Common/sGazette/print.asp?Artfile=2004/5>.

9 Feisal Abdul Rauf, *What is Right with Islam* (San Francisco: Harper, 2004).

SELECT BIBLIOGRAPHY

Abdul Rauf, Feisal, *What is Right with Islam* (San Francisco: Harper, 2004).

Abou el Fadl, Khaled, *The Place of Tolerance in Islam* (Boston: Beacon Press, 2002).

Abuza, Zachary, *Militant Islam in Southeast Asia* (Boulder, Col.: Lynne Rienner, 2003).

Adam, Barbara, Ulrich Beck and Joost Van Loon (eds), *The Risk Society and Beyond: Critical Issues in Social Theory* (London: Sage Publications, 2002).

Ahmad, Manzoor, *Islamic Education: Redefinitions of Aims and Methodology* (New Delhi: Genuine Publications, 2002).

Ahmed, Ishtiaq, *The Concept of an Islamic State* (London: Frances Pinter, 1987).

Akbarzadeh, Shahram, 'State legitimacy', in Shahram Akbarzadeh and Abdullah Saeed (eds), *Islam and Political Legitimacy* (London: RoutledgeCurzon, 2003).

Aksu, Eşref and Joseph Camilleri, *Democratizing Global Governance* (London: Palgrave, 2003).

Ali, Jan, 'Islamic revivalism: the case of the *Tablighi Jamaat*', *Journal of Muslim Affairs*, Vol. 23, No. 1 (2003), pp. 173–81.

Amayreh, Khalid, 'Settlement fears', *Middle East Journal*, No. 723 (16 April 2004), pp. 14–17.

Appleby, R Scott, 'History in the fundamentalist imagination', *Journal of American History*, Vol. 89, No. 2 (2002), pp. 498–514.

Ata, Abe W, 'Moslem Arab portrayal in the Australian press and in school textbooks', *Australian Journal of Social Issues*, Vol. 19, No. 3 (1984).

Azhar, Maulana Mohammad Masood, *Khutbat-e-Jihad [Lectures on Jihad] Vols 1 & 2* (Karachi: Maktaba Hassan, April 2001).

Barfield, Thomas J, *The Central Asian Arabs of Afghanistan* (Austin: University of Texas Press, 1981).

Barton, Greg, *Abdurrahman Wahid, Indonesian President, Muslim democrat: a view from the inside* (Sydney and Honolulu: UNSW Press and University of Hawaii Press, 2002).

Barton, Greg, 'Indonesia's Nurcholish Madjid and Abdurrahman Wahid as intellectual *ulama*: the meeting of Islamic traditionalism and Modernism in neo-Modernist thought', *Islam and Christian–Muslim Relations*, Vol. 8, No. 3 (1997), pp. 323–50.

Barton, Greg, 'Islam and politics in the new Indonesia', in Jason F Issacson and Colin Rubenstein (eds), *Islam in Asia: Changing Political Realities* (London: Transaction Press, 2002).

Barton, Greg, 'Islam, Pancasila and the middle path of *Tawassuth*: the thought of Achmad Siddiq', in Greg Barton and Greg Fealy (eds), *Nahdlatul Ulama, Traditional Islam and Modernity in Indonesia* (Clayton: Monash Asia Institute, 1996).

Barton, Greg, 'Islam, politics and regime change in Wahid's Indonesia', in Julian M Weiss (ed.), *Tiger's Roar: Asia's Recovery and Its Impact* (New Jersey: ME Sharpe, 2002).

Barton, Greg, 'The impact of Islamic neo-modernism on Indonesian Islamic thought: the emergence of a new pluralism', in David Bourchier and John Legge (eds), *Indonesian Democracy: 1950s and 1990s* (Clayton: Monash University, 1994).

Barton, Greg, 'The international context of the emergence of Islamic neo modernism in Indonesia', in Merle C Ricklefs (ed.), *Islam in the Indonesian Social Context* (Clayton: CSEAS, Monash University, 1991).

Barton, Greg, 'The liberal, progressive roots of Abdurrahman Wahid's thought', in Greg Barton and Greg Fealy (eds), *Nahdlatul Ulama, Traditional Islam and Modernity in Indonesia* (Clayton: Monash Asia Institute, 1996).

Barton, Greg, 'The origins of Islamic liberalism in Indonesia and its contribution to democratisation', in Michele Schmiegelow (ed.), *Democracy in Asia* (New York: St Martin's Press, 1997).

Barton, Greg, 'The prospects for Islam', in Grayson Lloyd and Shannon Smith (eds), *Indonesia Today: Challenges of History* (Singapore: Institute of Southeast Asian Studies, 2001).

Barton, Greg, 'The Wahid presidency in context: regime change, inflated expectations, Islam and the promise of democracy', in Thang D Nguyen and Frank-Jürgen Richter (eds), *Indonesia Matters: Unity, Diversity and Stability in Fragile Times* (Singapore: Times Editions, 2003).

Batrouney, Trevor, 'From "White Australia" to multiculturalism: citizenship and identity', in Ghassan Hage (ed.), *Arab-Australians Today: Citizenship and Belonging* (Melbourne: Melbourne University Press, 2002).

Bauman, Zygmunt, 'The great war of recognition', *Theory, Culture & Society*, Vol. 18, Nos. 2–3 (2001), pp. 137–50.

Beck, Ulrich, *Ecological Politics in an Age of Risk* (Cambridge: Polity Press, 1995).

Bergen, Peter L, *Holy War, Inc.: Inside the Secret World of Osama bin Laden* (New York: The Free Press, 2001).

Berman, Paul, *Terror and Liberalism* (New York: WW Norton & Company, 2002).

Binder, Leonard, *Islamic Liberalism: a Critique of Development Ideologies* (Chicago: University of Chicago Press, 1988).

Boland, BJ, *The Struggle of Islam in Modern Indonesia* (The Hague: Martinus Nijhoff, 1971).

Bouma, Gary M, *Mosques and Muslim Settlement in Australia* (Canberra: Australian Bureau of Immigration and Population Research, 1994).

Brecher, FW, 'French policy toward the Levant 1914–1918', *Middle Eastern Studies*, Vol. 29, No. 4 (1993), pp. 641–64.

Bunt, Gary, 'Islam@Britain.net: British Muslim identities in cyberspace', *Islam and*

Christian Muslims Relations, Vol. 10, No. 3 (1999), pp. 353–63.

Castells, Manuel, *End of Millennium* (Malden, Mass.: Blackwell Publishers, 1998).

Cigler, Michael J, *The Afghans in Australia* (Melbourne: AE Press, 1986).

Cirincione, Joseph, Jessica T Mathews and George Perkovich, *WMD in Iraq: Evidence and Implications* (Washington DC: Carnegie Endowment for International Peace, 2004).

Clarke, Richard A, *Against All Enemies: inside America's War on Terror* (New York: Free Press, 2004).

Cleland, Bilal, 'The history of Muslims in Australia', in Abdullah Saeed and Shahram Akbarzadeh (eds), *Muslim Communities in Australia* (Sydney: UNSW Press, 2001), pp. 12–32.

Clyne, Michael, 'When the discourse of hatred becomes respectable: does the linguist have a responsibility?', *Australian Review of Applied Linguistics,* Vol. 26, No. 1 (2003), pp. 1–5.

Cole, Juan, 'The United States and Shi'ite religious factions in post-Ba'thist Iraq', *The Middle East Journal,* Vol. 57, No. 4 (Autumn 2003), pp. 543–66.

Dann, Uriel, 'The Hashmite monarch 1948–88: the constant and the changing – an integration', in Joseph Nevo and Ilan Pappe (eds), *Jordan in the Middle East. The Making of a Pivotal State 1948–88* (Essex: Frank Cass, 1994).

Deen, Hanifa, *Caravanserai: Journey among Australian Muslims* (Fremantle: Fremantle Arts Centre Press, 2003).

Dixson, Miriam, *The Imaginary Australian: Anglo-Celts and Identity – 1788 to the present* (Sydney: UNSW Press, 1999).

Doran, Michael, 'The pragmatic fanaticism of al-Qaeda: an anatomy of extremism in Middle Eastern politics', *Political Science Quarterly,* Vol. 117, No. 2 (2002), pp. 177–91.

Edelman, Murray, *The Politics of Disinformation* (Cambridge: Cambridge University Press, 2001).

Edwards, David B, *Before Taliban: Genealogies of the Afghan Jihad* (Berkeley and Los Angeles: University of California Press, 2002).

Edwards, David B, 'Summoning Muslims: print, politics, and religious ideology in Afghanistan', *Journal of Asian Studies,* Vol. 52, No. 3 (1993), pp. 609–28.

Edwards, David B, 'The evolution of Shi'i political dissent in Afghanistan', in Juan RI Cole and Nikki R Keddie (eds), *Shi'ism and Social Protest* (New Haven: Yale University Press, 1986).

Eickelman, Dale, and James Piscatori, 'Social theory', in Dale F Eickelman and James Piscatori (eds), *Muslim travelers: Pilgrimage, Migration, and the Religious Imagination* (Berkeley: University of California Press, 1990).

Eliraz, Giora, *Islam in Indonesia: the Local Context and the Middle Eastern Perspective* (Singapore: ISEAS, 2004).

Emadi, Hafizullah, 'Exporting Iran's revolution: the radicalization of the Shiite movement in Afghanistan', *Middle Eastern Studies,* Vol. 31, No. 1 (1995), pp. 1–12.

Emadi, Hafizullah, 'The Hazaras and their role in the process of political transformation in Afghanistan', *Central Asian Survey,* Vol. 16, No. 3 (1997), pp. 363–87.

Esposito, John L, 'Introduction', in John L Esposito (ed.), *Political Islam: Revolution, Radicalism, or Reform?* (Boulder, Col. Lynne Rienner, 1997).

Esposito, John L, *Unholy War: Terror in the Name of Islam* (New York: Oxford University Press, 2002).

Euben, Roxanne, 'Premodern, antimodern, or postmodern? Islamic and Western critiques of modernity', *The Review of Politics*, Vol. 59, No. 3 (1997), pp. 429–60.

Fealy, Greg, 'Islamic politics: a rising or declining force?', in Damien Kingsbury and Arief Budiman (eds), *Indonesia: the Uncertain Transition* (Bathurst: Crawford House Publishing, 2001).

Fealy, Greg, 'Rowing in a typhoon: Nahdlatul Ulama and the decline of constitutional democracy', in David Bourchier and John Legge (eds), *Indonesian Democracy: 1950s and 1990s* (Clayton: Monash University, 1994).

Fealy, Greg, 'The 1994 NU Congress and aftermath: Abdurrahman Wahid, Suksesi and the battle for control of NU', in Greg Barton and Greg Fealy (eds), *Nahdlatul ulama, traditional islam and modernity in Indonesia* (Clayton: Monash Asia Institute, 1996).

Freitag, Ulrike, 'In search of "historical correctness": the Ba'th party in Syria', *Middle Eastern Studies*, Vol. 35, No. 1 (1999), pp. 1–16.

Fuller, Graham E, *Islamic Fundamentalism in Afghanistan: Its Character and Prospects* (Santa Monica: RAND R-3970-USDP, 1991).

Fuller, Graham E, *The Future of Political Islam* (New York: Palgrave Macmillan, 2003).

Geertz, Clifford, *The Religion of Java* (New York: Free Press, 1960).

Ghani, Ashraf, 'Islam and state-building in a tribal society: Afghanistan 1880–1901', *Modern Asian Studies*, Vol. 12, No. 2 (1978), pp. 269–84.

Gray, John, *Al Qaeda and What it Means to be Modern* (London: Faber & Faber, 2003).

Gunaratna, Rohan, *Inside al-Qaeda: Global Network of Terror* (New York: Columbia University Press, 2002).

Hage, Ghassan, 'Postscript: Arab-Australian belonging after "September 11" ', in Ghassan Hage (ed.), *Arab-Australians Today: Citizenship and Belonging* (Melbourne: Melbourne University Press, 2002).

Hage, Ghassan, 'The differential intensities of social reality: migration, participation and guilt', in Ghassan Hage (ed.), *Arab-Australians Today: Citizenship and Belonging* (Melbourne: Melbourne University Press, 2002).

Hall, Stuart and Sarat Maharaj, *Annotations: Modernity and Difference* (London: Iniva Publication, 2001).

Halliday, Fred, 'Transnational paranoia and international relations: the case of the "West versus Islam" ', in Stephanie Lawson, *The New Agenda for International Relations: from Polarization to Globalization in World Politics?* (London: Polity, 2002).

Hammad, Umm, *Hum Maein Lashkar-e-Toiba Ki [We the Mothers of Lashkar-e-Toiba]*, Vol. 2 (Lahore: Darul-Andulus, October 2003).

Haqqani, Hussain, 'The American Mongols', *Foreign Policy*, No. 136 (2003), pp. 70–71.

Hardt, Michael and Antonio Negri, *Empire* (Cambridge, Mass.: Harvard University Press, 2000).

Harpviken, Kristian Berg, *Political Mobilization among the Hazaras of Afghanistan: 1978–1992* (Oslo: Report No. 9, Department of Sociology, University of Oslo, 1996).

Hefner, Robert W, 'Civic pluralism denied? The new media and Jihadi violence in Indonesia', in Dale F Eickelman and Jon W Anderson (eds), *New Media in the Muslim World: the Emerging Public Sphere,* 2nd edn (Bloomington: Indiana University Press, 2003).

Hefner, Robert W, *Civil Islam: Muslims and Democratization in Indonesia* (Princeton: Princeton University Press, 2000).

Hefner, Robert W, 'Introduction: Islam in an era of nation states: politics and religious renewal in Muslim Southeast Asia', in Robert W Hefner and Patricia Horvatich (eds), *Islam in an Era of Nation States: Politics and Religious Revival in Muslim Southeast Asia* (Honolulu: University of Hawaii Press, 1997).

Hefner, Robert W, 'Islamization and democratization in Indonesia', in Robert W Hefner and Patricia Horvatich (eds), *Islam in an Era of Nation States: Politics and Religious Revival in Muslim Southeast Asia* (Honolulu: University of Hawaii Press, 1997).

Herold, Marc, *Blown Away: the Myth and Reality of Precision Bombing in Afghanistan* (Monroe, Maine: Common Courage Press, 2004).

Hindess, Barry, 'Multiculturalism and citizenship', in Chandran Kukathas (ed.), *Multicultural Citizens: the Philosophy and Politics of Identity* (Sydney: The Centre for Independent Studies Limited, 1993).

Hiro, Dilip, *Holy Wars: the Rise of Islamic Fundamentalism* (London: Routledge, 1989).

Human Rights Watch, *'Killing You Is a Very Easy Thing for Us': Human Rights Abuses in Southeast Afghanistan* (New York: Human Rights Watch, 2003).

Humphrey, Michael, 'An Australian Islam? Religion in the multicultural city', in Abdullah Saeed and Shahram Akbarzadeh (eds), *Muslim Communities in Australia* (Sydney: UNSW Press, 2002).

Humphrey, Michael, 'Community, mosque and ethnic politics', *ANZ Journal of Sociology*, Vol. 23, No. 2 (1987), pp. 233–245.

Humphrey, Michael, *Family, Work and Unemployment: a Study of Lebanese Settlement in Sydney* (Canberra: Australian Government Publishing Service, 1984).

Humphrey, Michael, 'Globalization and Arab diasporic identities: the Australian Arab case', *Bulletin of the Royal Institute for Inter-Faith Studies*, Vol. 2 (2002), pp. 141–58.

Humphrey, Michael, 'Harakat al-Tawhid al-Islami', in John Esposito (ed.), *Encyclopaedia of the Modern Islamic World* (Oxford: Oxford University Press, 1994).

Humphrey, Michael, 'Humanitarianism, terrorism and the transnational border', *Social Analysis*, Vol. 46, No.1 (2002), pp. 117–122.

Humphrey, Michael, 'Injuries and identities: authorising Arab diasporic difference in crisis', in Ghassan Hage (ed.), *Arab-Australians Today: Citizenship and Belonging* (Melbourne: Melbourne University Press, 2002).

Humphrey, Michael, 'Islam: a test for multiculturalism', *Asian Migrant*, Vol. 2, No. 2 (1989), pp. 48–56.

Humphrey, Michael, *Islam, Multiculturalism and Transnationlism: from the Lebanese Diaspora* (London: Centre for Lebanese Studies with IB Tauris, 1998).

Humphrey, Michael, 'Racism and unemployment amongst Lebanese', in seminar proceedings, *The Arabic Community: Realities and Challenges* (Sydney: The Arabic Welfare Inter-Agency, 1986).

Humphrey, Michael, 'Sectarianism and the politics of identity: the Lebanese in Sydney', in Albert Hourani and Nadim Shehadi (eds), *Lebanese in the World: a Century of Lebanese Migration* (London: IB Tauris, 1993).

Huntington, Samuel, 'The clash of civilizations?', *Foreign Affairs*, Vol. 72, No. 3 (1993), pp. 22–49.

Huntington, Samuel P, *The Clash of Civilizations and the Remaking of the World Order* (London: Simon & Schuster, 2002).

Hyman, Anthony, 'Arab involvement in the Afghan War', *The Beirut Review*, No. 7 (1994), pp. 73–89.

Jalalzai, Musa Khan, *Sectarianism and Ethnic Violence in Pakistan* (Lahore: Izharsons,

1996).

Judah, Tim, 'The Taliban papers', *Survival*, Vol. 44, No.1 (2002), pp. 68–80.

Jureidini, Ray and Ghassan Hage, 'The Australian Arabic Council: anti-racist activism', in Ghassan Hage (ed.), *Arab-Australians Today: Citizenship and Belonging* (Melbourne: Melbourne University Press, 2002).

Kedourie, Elie, *Afghani and Abduh: an Essay on Religious Unbelief and Political Activism in Modern Islam* (London: Frank Cass, 1966).

Kepel, Gilles, 'Islamism reconsidered', *Harvard International Review*, Vol. 22, No. 2 (2000), pp. 22–28.

Kepel, Gilles, *Jihad: the Trail of Political Islam* (Cambridge, Mass.: Harvard University Press, 2002).

Khadduri, Majid, *The Islamic Conception of Justice* (Baltimore: Johns Hopkins University Press, 1984).

Khan, Muhammad Sharif, *Education, Religion and the Modern Age* (New Delhi: Asish Publishing House, 1999).

Kimball, Charles, *When Religion Becomes Evil* (New York: HarperCollins, 2002).

Kingsbury, Damien and Arief Budiman (eds), *Indonesia: the uncertain transition* (Bathurst: Crawford House Publishing, 2001).

Kurzman, Charles, *Liberal Islam* (Oxford: Oxford University Press, 1998).

Leach, Michael, 'Disturbing Practices: dehumanizing asylum seekers in the refugee 'crisis' in Australia, 2001–2002', *Refuge*, Vol. 21, No. 3 (2003), pp. 25–33.

Leach, Michael, 'Hansonism, political discourse and Australian identity', in Michael Leach, Geoffrey Stokes and Ian Ward, *The Rise and Fall of One Nation* (St Lucia, Qld: Queensland University Press, 2000).

Leach, Michael and Fethi Mansouri, *Critical Perspectives on Refugee Policy in Australia* (Melbourne: Deakin University, 2003).

Leach, Michael and Fethi Mansouri, 'Strange words: refugee perspectives on government and media stereotypes', *Overland*, No. 171 (2003), pp. 19–26.

Leach, Michael, Geoffrey Stokes and Ian Ward. *The Rise and Fall of One Nation* (Queensland: Queensland University Press, 2000).

Lewis, Bernard, *Islam and the West* (Oxford: Oxford Press, 1994).

Lewis, Bernard, *The Crisis of Islam, Holy War and Unholy Terror* (London: Weidenfeld & Nicolson, 2003).

Lindsey, Tim (ed.), *Indonesia: the Commercial Court and Law Reform in Indonesia* (Sydney: Desert Pea Press, 2000).

Mahathir, Mohammed, *Terrorism and the Real Issues* (Subang Jaya: Pelanduk Publications, 2003).

Maley, William, 'Confronting creeping invasions: Afghanistan, the UN and the world community', in K Warikoo (ed.), *The Afghanistan Crisis: Issues and Perspectives* (New Delhi: Bhavana Books, 2002).

Maley, William, 'Institutional design and the rebuilding of trust', in William Maley, Charles Sampford and Ramesh Thakur (eds), *From Civil Strife to Civil Society: Civil and Military Responsibilities in Disrupted States* (New York and Tokyo: United Nations University Press, 2003).

Maley, William, 'Introduction: interpreting the Taliban', in William Maley (ed.), *Fundamentalism Reborn? Afghanistan and the Taliban* (London: Hurst & Co., 1998).

Maley, William, 'Security and stability in Southwest Asia', in David W Lovell (ed.), *Asia-Pacific Security: Policy Challenges* (Singapore: ISEAS, 2003).

Maley, William, 'Talibanisation and Pakistan', in Denise Groves (ed.), *Talibanisation:*

Extremism and Regional Instability in South and Central Asia (Berlin: Conflict Prevention Network: Stiftung Wissenschaft und Politik, 2001).

Maley, William, *The Afghanistan Wars* (London: Palgrave Macmillan, 2002).

Maley, William, *The Foreign Policy of the Taliban* (New York: Council on Foreign Relations, 2000).

Maley, William, 'The future of Islamic Afghanistan', *Security Dialogue*, Vol. 24, No. 4 (1993), pp. 383–96.

Mandel, Ruth, 'Shifting centres and emergent identities: Turkey and Germany in the lives of Turkish *Gastarbeiter*', in Dale F Eickelman and James Piscatori (eds), *Muslim travellers: Pilgrimage, Migration, and the Religious Imagination* (Berkeley: University of California Press, 1990).

Mansour, Anne, 'Whitewashed: the Lebanese in Queensland 1880–1947', in Ghassan Hage (ed.), *Arab-Australians Today: Citizenship and Belonging* (Melbourne: Melbourne University Press, 2002).

Mansouri, Fethi and Melek Bagdas, *Politics of Social Exclusion* (Melbourne: Centre for Citizenship and Human Rights, 2002).

Marr, David and Marian Wilkinson, *Dark Victory* (Sydney: Allen & Unwin, 2003).

McHugo, John, 'Resolution 242: a legal reappraisal of the right-wing Israeli interpretation of the withdrawal phase with reference to the conflict between Israel and the Palestinians', *International and Comparative Law Quarterly*, Vol. 51 (October 2002), pp. 851–82.

Metcalf, Barbara D, *Islamic Revival in British India: Deoband, 1860:1900* (Princeton: Princeton University Press, 1982).

Moaddel, Mansoor and Kamran Talattof (eds), *Modernist and Fundamentalist Debates in Islam: a Reader* (New York: Palgrave Macmillan, 2000).

Mousavi, Sayed Askar, *The Hazaras of Afghanistan: an Historical, Cultural, Economic and Political Study* (New York: St Martin's Press 1997).

Murden, Simon, *Islam, the Middle East and the New Global Order* (Boulder, Col. & London: Lynne Rienner, 2002).

Naby, Eden, 'Islam within the Afghan resistance', *Third World Quarterly*, Vol.10, No. 2 (1988), pp. 787–805.

Naby, Eden, 'The changing role of Islam as a unifying force in Afghanistan', in Ali Banuazizi and Myron Weiner (eds), *The State, Religion, and Ethnic Politics: Afghanistan, Iran, and Pakistan* (Syracuse: Syracuse University Press, 1986).

Naby, Eden, 'The concept of Jihad in opposition to communist rule: Turkestan and Afghanistan', *Studies in Comparative Communism*, Vol. 19, Nos. 3–4 (1986), pp. 287–300.

Nakamura, Mitsuo, *The Crescent Arises over the Banyan Tree: a Study of the Muhammadiyah Movement in a Central Javanese Town* (Yogyakarta: Gadjah Mada University Press, 1983).

Nawid, Senzil K, *Religious Response to Social Change in Afghanistan 1919–1929: King Aman-Allah and the Afghan Ulama* (Costa Mesa: Mazda Publishers, 1999).

Noelle, Christine, 'The anti-Wahhabi reaction in nineteenth-century Afghanistan', *The Muslim World*, Vol. 85, Nos. 1–2 (1995), pp. 23–48.

Nojumi, Neamatollah, *The Rise of the Taliban in Afghanistan: Civil War, Mass Mobilization, and the Future of the Region* (New York: Palgrave Macmillan, 2002).

Nozick, Robert, *Anarchy, State and Utopia* (Oxford: Basil Blackwell, 1974).

Olesen, Asta, *Islam and Politics in Afghanistan* (Richmond: Curzon Press, 1995).

Omar, Saleh, 'Philosophical origins of the Arab Ba'th Party: the work of Zaki Al-

Arsuzi', *Arab Studies Quarterly*, Vol. 18, No. 2 (1996), pp. 23–38.

Paley, Julia, 'Toward anthropology of democracy', *Annual Review of Anthropology*, Vol. 31 (2002), pp. 469–96.

Pedersen, Lars, *Newer Islamic Movements in Western Europe* (London: Ashgate, 1999).

Pipes, Daniel, 'There are no moderates: dealing with fundamentalist Islam', *The National Interest*, No. 41 (1995), pp. 48–57.

Poullada, Leon B, *Reform and Rebellion in Afghanistan, 1919–1929: King Amanullah's Failure to Modernize a Tribal Society* (Ithaca: Cornell University Press, 1973).

Raana, Mohammad Aamir, *Jihad Aur Jihadi: Pakistan Aur Kashmir key Aham Jihadi Rahnamaoon ka Ta'arif [Jihad and Jihadis: Introduction to Significant Jihadi Leaders of Pakistan and Kashmir]* (Lahore: Mashal, 2003).

Raana, Mohammad Aamir, *Jihad-e-Kashmir Au Afghanistan [Jihad in Kashmir and Afghanistan]* (Lahore: Mashal, 2002).

Rahman, Fazlur, *Islam and Modernity: Transformation of an Intellectual Tradition* (Chicago: University of Chicago Press, 1982).

Rahman, Fazlur, *Islam: Challenges and Opportunities* (Edinburgh: Edinburgh University Press, 1979).

Rahnema, Ali (ed.), *Pioneers of Islamic Revival* (London: Zed Books, 1994).

Ramage, Douglas E, *Politics in Indonesia: Democracy, Islam and the Ideology of Tolerance* (London: Routledge, 1995).

Rashid, Ahmed, *Taliban: Militant Islam, Oil and Fundamentalism in Central Asia* (New Haven: Yale University Press, 2000).

Robinson, Francis (ed.), *Cambridge Illustrated History: Islamic World* (Cambridge: Cambridge University Press, 1998).

Roy, Olivier, *Islam and Resistance in Afghanistan* (Cambridge: Cambridge University Press, 1990).

Roy, Oliver, *The Failure of Political Islam* (Cambridge, MA: Harvard University Press, 1994).

Rubin, Barnett R, 'Arab Islamists in Afghanistan', in John L Esposito (ed.), *Political Islam: Revolution, Radicalism, or Reform?* (Boulder, Col.: Lynne Rienner, 1997).

Rubin, Barnett R, *The Fragmentation of Afghanistan: State Formation and Collapse in the International System* (New Haven: Yale University Press, 2002).

Rubin, Barnett R, Ashraf Ghani, William Maley, Ahmed Rashid and Olivier Roy, *Afghanistan: Reconstruction and Peacebuilding in a Regional Framework* (Bern: KOFF Peacebuilding Reports 1/2001, Swiss Peace Foundation, 2001).

Rudolph, Susanne Hoeber and James Piscatori (eds), *Transnational Religions Fading States* (Boulder, Col: Westview Press, 1997).

Ruthven, Malise, *Islam in the World*, 2nd edn (New York: Oxford University Press, 2000).

Saeed, Abdullah, *Islam in Australia* (Sydney: Allen & Unwin, 2003).

Saeed, Abdullah, 'The official ulema and the religious legitimacy of modern nation state', in Shahram Akbarzadeh and Abdullah Saeed (eds), *Islam and Political Legitimacy* (London: RoutledgeCurzon, 2003).

Saeed, Abdullah, 'Towards religious tolerance through reform in Islamic education: the case of the State Institute of Islamic Studies of Indonesia', *Indonesia and the Malay World*, Vol. 27, No. 79 (1999), pp. 177–91.

Saeed, Abdullah and Shahram Akbarzadeh, 'Searching for identity: Muslims in Australia', in Abdullah Saeed and Shahram Akbarzadeh (eds), *Muslim Communities in Australia* (Sydney: UNSW Press, 2001).

Said, Edward W, *Covering Islam: How the Media and the Experts Determine How We*

See the Rest of the World (London: Vintage Books, 1997).

Said, Edward W, *'Orientalism': Western Conceptions of the Orient* (London: Penguin Books, 1978).

Saikal, Amin, *Islam and the West, Conflict or Cooperation?* (New York: Palgrave Macmillan, 2003).

Saikal, Amin, 'Islam and the West?', in Greg Fry and Jacinta O'Hagan (eds), *Contending Images of World Politics* (Basingstoke and New York: Macmillan & St Martin's Press, 2000).

Saikal, Amin, 'The Rabbani Government, 1992–1996', in William Maley (ed.), *Fundamentalism Reborn? Afghanistan and the Taliban* (London: Hurst & Co., 1998).

Saikal, Amin, 'The United Nations and the Middle East', in Amin Saikal and Albrecht Schnabel (eds), *Democratization in the Middle East, Experiences, Struggles, Challenges* (Tokyo: United Nations University Press, 2003).

Schetter, Conrad, *Ethnizität und ethnische Konflikte in Afghanistan [Ethnicity and Ethnic Conflict in Afghanistan]* (Berlin: Dietrich Reimer Verlag, 2003).

Schwartz, Stephen, *The Two Faces of Islam: the House of Sa'ud from Tradition to Terror* (New York: Doubleday, 2002).

Sivan, Emmanuel, *Radical Islam: Medieval Theology and Modern Politics* (New Haven: Yale University Press, 1990).

Snyder, Jack, *From Voting to Violence: Democratization and Nationalist Conflict* (New York: WW Norton, 2000).

Staloff, Robert, *From Abdullah to Hussein: Jordan in Transition* (Oxford University Press: London, 1994).

Stenberg, Leif, *The Islamization of Science: Four Muslim Positions, Developing an Islamic Modernity* (Lund: Almqvist & Wiksell International, 1996).

Stevens, Christine, *Tin Mosques and Ghantowns: a History of Afghan Camel Drivers in Australia* (Melbourne: Oxford University Press, 1989).

Stokes, Geoffrey, *The Politics of Identity in Australia* (Melbourne: Cambridge University Press, 1997).

Suter, Keith, 'Australia and asylum seekers', *Contemporary Review*, Vol. 279, No. 630 (2001), pp. 278–84.

Taji-Farouki, Suha, *A Fundamental Quest. Hizb al-Tahrir and the Search for the Islamic Caliphate* (Grey Seal: London, 1996).

Tibawi, AL, *Islamic Education: Its Traditions and Modernization into the Arab National Systems* (London: Luzac & Company Ltd, 1979).

Van Bruinessen, Martin, 'Genealogies of Islamic radicalism in post-Suharto Indonesia', *South East Asia Research*, Vol. 10, No. 2 (2002), pp. 117–24.

Van Bruinessen, Martin, 'The production of Islamic knowledge in Western Europe', *International Institute for the Study of Islam in the Modern World Newsletter*, Vol. 12, No. 6 (2003).

Van Bruinessen, Martin, 'Traditions for the future: the reconstruction of traditionalist discourse within NU', in Greg Barton and Greg Fealy (eds), *Nahdlatul Ulama, Traditional Islam and Modernity in Indonesia* (Clayton: Monash Asia Institute, 1996).

Virilio, Paul, *War & Cinema: the Logistics of Perception* (London: Verso, 1989).

Vogelsang, Willem, *The Afghans* (Oxford: Blackwell, 2002).

Walker, David, *Anxious Nation: Australia and the Rise of Asia 1850–1939* (Brisbane: University of Queensland Press, 1999).

White, Jenny B, *Islamist Mobilization in Turkey: a Study in Vernacular Politics* (Seattle:

University of Washington Press, 2002).

Wiktorowicz, Quintan, 'Islamists, the state and cooperation in Jordan', *Arab Studies Quarterly*, Vol. 21, No. 4 (1999), pp. 1–17.

Williams, Brackette, 'A class act: anthropology and the race to nation across ethnic terrain', *Annual Review of Anthropology*, Vol. 18 (1989), pp. 410–44.

Woltering, Robert, 'The roots of Islamist popularity', *Third World Quarterly*, Vol. 23, No. 6 (2002), pp. 1133–43.

Yasmeen, Samina, 'Pakistan and the struggle for "real" Islam', in Shahram Akbarzadeh and Abdullah Saeed (eds), *Islam and Political Legitimacy* (New York: Routledge, 2003), pp. 70–87.

Zaman, Muhammad Qasim, *The Ulama in Contemporary Islam: Custodians of Change* (Princeton: Princeton University Press, 2002).

INDEX

Abduh, Muhammad 67, 79, 128
Abdul Rahman, Sheik Umar 123
Abu Jibril 124
Abu Sayyaf 94, 95, 96
Afghan Muslim Youth Organisation 82
Afghani, Sayyid Jamaluddin 79
Afghanistan 4, 24, 41, 48, 49, 56, 58,
  77–89, 98–9, 102, 106, 107, 125, 129
  communist coup 82
  and Islam 78–84
  Islamic forces in contemporary 84–8
  Islamic Society 82
  mujahideen 50, 82, 83, 129
  Party of Islam 82
  politicisation of Islam 80–8
  Soviet invasion 48, 49, 80, 82, 102–3
  Taliban 18, 19, 56, 58, 81, 84, 85,
    86, 87, 96, 98, 100
Afghans in Australia 149–50
Al-Aqsa Intifida 36
Akbari, Muhammad 83
al-Banna, Hassan 79, 123
al-Ghazali, Abu Hamid 65
al-Ghozi, Fathur Rahman 124, 125
al-Hillali, Taj ad-Din 143
Al-Mahdal-Aala-ud-Dawa-wal-Irshad 49
al-Muhajiroun 4–5, 27, 31–5, 36–7,
  38–41, 168
al-Nabhani, Taqi al-Din 28–9

al-Qaeda 3, 14, 15, 16, 17, 18, 19, 22,
  24, 84, 89, 93, 95, 98, 100, 121–6
al-Rasoul Sayyaf, Abdul Rab 82, 86–7
Amin, Hafizullah 86
Ansari, Bayezid 80
Arafat, Yasser 16
Ataturk, Mustafa Kemal 79
Australia
  Afghan camel drivers 149–50
  cultural diversity 150–3
  first-generation Muslim immigrants
    and homeland politics 139–43
  immigration 132–3, 145–6
  Lebanese immigration 136, 137–8,
    140–2, 144
  multiculturalism 132–4, 138–9, 143,
    150–3
  Muslim asylum seekers 153–8
  Muslim immigrants 135–45, 149–50,
    160–1
  national identity 150–3
  national security 153–8
  second-generation Muslim immigrants
    139–43
  and threat of terrorism 132–4
  Turkish immigration 136, 137, 138,
    144
Australian Federation of Islamic Councils
  137, 138, 143

Ayatollah Khomeini 8, 18, 22, 27, 142, 167
Ayatullah Beheshti 83
Azad Kashmir 50, 51, 54–5
Azhar, Masood 50, 52, 53, 56, 58

Badawi, Abdullah 107, 108–10
Bakri, Omar Muhammad 31–4, 35, 37
Bali 93, 94, 114, 121, 127
Bangladesh 54
Baraja, Abdul Qadir 124
Barelvi, Sayed Ahmad 80
Bashir, Abu Bakar 73, 120, 122, 123, 124
Belfour Declaration 36
Berlusconi, Silvio 14
Bhutto, Benazir 48
Bhutto, Zulfiqar Ali 47
bin Laden, Osama 3, 16, 18, 32, 50, 52, 83, 84
Blair, Tony 13, 38–9
Bosnian Muslims 6
Bruinessen, Martin van 122
Bush, George 14, 16, 18, 95, 98–9
Bush Administration 20, 22–3, 93, 95, 99, 101

Caliphate 4, 26–42, 124
Central Asia 2
Choudry, Anjem 35, 37
Cold War 45

Daoud, Muhammad 82
dar al-harb 4, 6, 31
dar al-Islam 4, 6, 9, 31, 143, 146
Darul Islam 122, 123
Deoband ulama 79, 82
Dwikarna, Agus 124

Eshaq, Muhammad 82

Fahim, Muhammad Qasim 85
Failure of Political Islam, The 27
Falwell, Jerry 14
Finsbury Park mosque 37
Fuller, Graham 80

Gahez, Minhajuddin 81
Gama Islami 123
Gaza 16

Gulf War 45
Hadith 26, 63–4, 78
HAMAS 16, 18, 36, 38
Hambali (Riduan Isamuddin) 124
Hanif, Asif Muhammad 37
Haq, Zia ul- 48
Harakat-e Islami 82, 83
Harkatul Mujahideen 50
Harkatul-Ansar (HA) 50
Harkatul-Jihad-ul-Islami (HJI) 50
Haz, Hamazah 119
Hazara 78, 87
Hefner, Robert 122
Hekmatyar, Gulbuddin 82, 83, 84, 86, 87
Heritage Foundation 28
Hizb al-Tahrir 4–5, 8, 27, 28–31, 32, 36, 38, 83, 168
Hizb-e Islami 82, 84
Hizb-e Wahdat 83
Howard, John 151–2, 156, 157
Huntington, Samuel 45, 95, 132, 160, 165, 166
Hussain, Abida 48
Hussein, Saddam 8, 19–20, 21, 22, 40, 59, 96

Ibrahim, Anwar 101–5, 107–8, 109–10
India 49, 53, 54, 67, 71
Indonesia 69, 71, 114–30
    al-Qaeda and South-East Asia 121–6
    Crescent Moon and Star Party 120
    Islam and Islamism 117–21
    Justice and Welfare Party (PKS) 120
    radical Islam 115–16, 118, 119, 120, 121–2, 127–8, 129
    reading Islam 116–17
    regime change and reform 126–7
    United Development Party (PPP) 119, 120
Institut Agama Islam Negeri (IAIN) 69–70
institutions of higher learning 68–70
International Crisis Group (ICG) 121, 122, 124–5
International Monetary Fund 5
Iran 2, 31, 45, 47
Iraq 4, 7, 10, 19–24, 38–41, 59, 96, 98, 100, 170
Islam

in Afghanistan 78–84, 102
and Islamism 117–21
local and global 166–8
moderate 17
Orthodox 47–9
political 26, 45–6, 80–8, 119
radical 17–18, 26, 115–16, 118, 119, 120, 121–2, 127–8, 129
and society 46–8, 85, 158
and the West 165–71
Islamic law and theology 71
Islamic liberalism 17
Islamic religious education 63–75
early Islamic period 63–6
from individuals to institutions 65–6
institutions of higher learning 68–70
mystical orders 64
public schools 70–1
reform debate in the modern period 67–72
reform debate post-September 11 72–5
seminaries 71–4
Islamic Youth Movement 144
Israel–Palestine conflict 6, 8–9, 10, 16, 18, 23, 35, 36–7, 41, 42, 103, 104, 141, 159
Ittehad-e Islami 82

Jaish Muhammad 46, 49–53
Jamaat Daawah Islamiah 144
Jamaat-i-Islami 48
Jamaat-ud-Dawa 56, 59
Jemaah Islamiyah (JI) 73, 94–5, 114, 122, 123, 124–6
Jihad 36, 37, 41, 51–3, 74, 99, 120–1, 129
Jihadi Islamism 120–1, 126, 128–9
Jones, Sidney 121
Jordan 29

Kalimantan 53
Kartosuwirjo, Sekarmadji Maridjan 122
Karzai, Hamed 85, 87
Kashmir 49–50, 53, 54–6 (see also Azad Kashmir)
Kepel, Gilles 143
Khalis, Younos 82
Khan, Amir Abdul Rahman 80
Khan, Sayyid Ahmad 67
Kimball, Charles 81

Lantos, Tom 14
Lashkar-e-Toiba 46, 49–53

Mahaz-e Milli-I Islami Afghanistan 82
Maidin, Ibrahim 94
Majelis Mujahidin Indonesia (MMI) 123, 124
Malaysia 69, 93–110
and Anwar Ibrahim 101–5, 107–8, 109
democracy and terrorism 108–10
impact of September 11 96–7
Islamic militancy 105–8, 109
politics and September 11 105–8
and war on terror 97–101
Mandel, Ruth 138
Markaz-ud-Dawa-wal-Irshad 49
Massoud, Ahmad Shah 81, 82, 83, 89
Maududi, Maulana 79, 123
Mazari, Abdul Ali 83
Mojadiddi, Sebghatullah 82, 83, 85
Moussaoui, Zacharias 37
Muhammad 63
Muhammad, Mahathir 1, 93, 95, 97, 98–9, 103, 105, 106–7
Muhammadiyah 115
Musharraf, General Pervez 2, 53, 57, 58
Muslim Brotherhood 29, 30, 31, 38, 79, 86, 121, 123
Muslims
attitudes 16–18
communities 75, 78
and conflict with West 3–11, 12, 18, 132, 158–60, 169–70
immigrants 135–45
Mutahhari, Murtaza 123
Muzaffar, Chandra 108

Nabi Muhammadi, Mawlawi Muhammad 82
Nahdlatul Ulama (NU) 115
neo-fundamentalists 18–19
Niazi, Ghulam Muhammad 81
Noor, Fadzil 97, 99
Nozick, Robert 81

Omar, Muhammad 84
Organisation of Islamic Conference (OIC) 6–7, 8

Pakistan 2, 24, 46–60, 125, 129
  foreign policy 54–60
  and Islam 81
  militancy 46, 59–60
  and Orthodox Islam 47–9
  role of Islamic groups 46
  seminaries 71, 74
Palestine 6, 8–9, 18, 30
Palestinians 36–8, 42
  Israel–Palestine conflict 6, 8–9, 10,
    16, 18, 23, 35, 36–7, 41, 42, 103,
    104, 141, 159
Philippines 94, 95, 97
Pickering, Sharon 155
Pipes, Daniel 81
Pir Sayid Ahmad Gailani 82
Pondok Ngruki 122, 123, 124
Powel, Colin 14, 94
public schools 70–1

Qizilbash 78
Qur'an 26, 35, 52, 63–4, 70, 78, 88, 166
Qutb, Sayyid 29, 32, 79, 86, 121, 123,
  128

Rabbani, Burhanuddin 81, 82, 86-7
Reid, Richard 37
Robertson, Pat 14
Roy, Olivier 27, 80, 81, 85
Ruddock, Philip 154, 156
Rumsfeld, Donald 20
Rushdi, Usama 123

Saeed, Abdullah 171
Saeed, Hafiz Mohammad 49, 56
Said, Edward 158–60
Saikal, Amin 8
Samudra, Imam 125
Saudi Arabia 5, 14, 32, 68, 70, 72
Saudi dynasty 2–3, 4
Sazman-e Nasr 83
seminaries 71–2
Sepah-i Pasdaran 83
September 11 1, 17, 18, 19, 34, 46,
  56–60, 72–5, 93, 95, 96–7, 101–10,
  132, 160
Shari'a (Islamic law) 17, 29
Shariati, Ali 123
Sharif, Nawaz 48
Sharif, Omar Khan 37

Sharon, Ariel 16, 23, 42
Sheikh Abu Ivad 40
Sheikh Mohseni 83
Shi'ites 21, 78, 83, 86, 87, 142
Shura-i Ettefaq 83
Singapore 94
societal Islam 19
Soeharto 115, 124, 126
South-East Asia 93–5, 96, 121–6
Soviet Union 48, 49, 80, 82
Sufaat, Yazid 95
Sungkar, Abdullah 123, 124, 125
Sunni Islam 65, 66, 78, 82, 86, 142
Sykes-Picot Agreement 36

Tablighi Jamaat 144, 168
Taliban 18, 19, 56, 58, 81, 84, 85, 86,
  87, 96, 98, 100
Tampa incident 154–5
Tarzi, Mahmoud 79
Tawana, Sayed Musa 81
Tel Aviv 36–7
terrorism 13–14, 15–16, 17, 34, 37, 38–9,
  41, 46, 56, 59, 93–5, 97–105, 132–4
Turkey 2

United Kingdom 5, 32, 33–4, 35, 37
United Nations 4, 8–10, 24
United States 2, 4, 5, 9, 10–11, 14–15,
  18, 20–4, 34, 35, 38, 39, 40–1, 46,
  51, 53, 93–5, 96, 98–100, 170–1
Uzbekistan 31, 53

Virilio, Paul 134

Wahhab, Abdul 80
Wahhabi Islam 120–1, 122, 128
Wahid, Abdurrahman 2, 115, 123
West
  and conflict with Muslims 3–11, 13,
    18, 132, 158–60, 169–70
  and Islam 165–71
West Bank 16, 23, 42
Western political theory 80
Western society 158–60, 165
World Bank 5

Yahya, General 47

Zahir Shah 82

Also published by UNSW Press

ABDURRAHMAN WAHID
Muslim Democrat, Indonesian President

by Greg Barton

In this authorised biography, much of it based on unique first-hand observation, Greg Barton introduces us to both the man and his world and attempts to make sense of his controversial public career and presidency. Barton has known Wahid since 1998, when he started researching the influence of Islamic liberalism in Indonesia, and has subsequently spent many months with his subject, including seven months during Wahid's 21-month presidency, both in Indonesia and travelling with him abroad.

Anyone who is at all interested in the drama of modern Indonesia will find this view from the inside an essential read.

GREG BARTON is a senior lecturer in the Faculty of Arts at Deakin University, Geelong, Victoria. Since the late 1980s he has researched the influence of Islamic liberalism in Indonesia and its contribution to the development of civil society and democracy. One of the central figures in his research has been Abdurrahman Wahid, whom Barton has come to know better than perhaps any other researcher.

ISBN 0 86840 405 5

Also published by UNSW Press

BRIEFINGS SERIES

INDONESIA'S STRUGGLE: JEMAAH ISLAMIYAH AND THE SOUL OF ISLAM

by Greg Barton

The Bali bombings shocked and challenged our understanding of Indonesian Islam. Enacted by only a select few of the 200 million Muslims living in Indonesia, the actions of these extremists – linked to Jemaah Islamiyah – branded the global ramifications of Islamic extremism onto our minds indelibly.

In this new Briefings title, Greg Barton traces the religious, cultural and political development of JI, and argues that it has many important features in common with other organisations linked to al-Qaeda. Based on extensive research in Indonesia, he assesses the level of support for JI and the Indonesian government's success in dealing with the threat it poses to stability. Barton argues that, while the Indonesian authorities reacted quickly to the events in Bali, their response has not been as effective and timely as is commonly assumed in Australia.

GREG BARTON is a well-known writer and commentator on Indonesian religious and political affairs. He was an adviser to former Indonesian President, Abdurrahman Wahid (Gus Dur) and wrote the authorised biography *Abdurrahman Wahid: Muslim Democrat, Indonesian President* (UNSW Press and University of Hawaii Press, 2002).

ISBN 86840 759 3

Also published by UNSW Press

MUSLIM COMMUNITIES IN AUSTRALIA

Edited by
Abdullah Saeed & Shahram Akbarzadeh

Urged by the Prophet Muhammed to venture even as far as China in the pursuit of knowledge, increasing numbers of Muslims over the past hundred years have reached the shores of Australia in pursuit of life and livelihood, becoming part of the Australian community and nation. In history and background a precociously global people, Muslims from many countries have brought with them their own multicultural diversity, which they have in turn pieced into Australia's rich ethnic and cultural mosaic.

Muslim Communities in Australia highlights the complex human diversity presented by Australia's Muslims, as well as their distinctive contribution and the challenges they pose to a still-evolving Australian multiculturalism. Emphasising the diversity of the Islamic experience in Australia, it presents a useful antidote to the stereotypical image that still colours mainstream perspectives of Islam.

> 'A well-researched and highly engaging book that fills a gap in our understanding of contemporary Australia. Written with insight and clarity, the rich collection of essays sheds new light on the faith and practice of Australia's Islamic communities. A must for teachers and students of religion and society, and for anyone interested in the future of Australian multiculturalism.'
>
> PROFESSOR JOSEPH A CAMILLERI, LA TROBE UNIVERSITY

ISBN 0 86840 580 9

Also published by UNSW Press

THE INDONESIAN LANGUAGE: ITS HISTORY AND ROLE IN MODERN SOCIETY

by James Sneddon

Indonesia is the fourth most populous nation in the world, and one of the most linguistically complex. Its ethnic groups speak more than 500 languages and of these Malay, renamed Indonesian, was chosen to be the sole national and official language. Indonesian's development into a modern world language has been described by one socio-linguist as 'miraculous'. The language has been a key factor in the shaping and unification of modern Indonesia.

This important book traces the origins and pre-colonial development of the language, the emergence of Classical Malay from the fourteenth century, the choice by the nationalist movement of Malay as the national language prior to Independence, the planning associated with the adoption and implementation of the language, its borrowings from other languages, its use in contemporary Indonesia and its future. The book challenges many assumptions about Indonesian, particularly countering the myth that Indonesian is a simple language.

JAMES SNEDDON is Head of the School of Languages and Linguistics at Griffith University in Brisbane. A university-level teacher and researcher of linguistics and Indonesian language for over 20 years, he is the author of *Indonesian Reference Grammar* (1996) and *Understanding Indonesian Grammar* (2000).

ISBN 086840 598 1